the mocking program

ALSO BY ALAN DEAN FOSTER

Kingdoms of Light

The Dig

The Journeys of the Catechist series:
Carnivores of Light and Darkness
Into the Thinking Kingdoms
A Triumph of Souls

AVAILABLE FROM WARNER ASPECT

DEATH TRAP

Whirling, Inspector Cardenas broke into a desperate sprint. He shouted as he burst out of the hallway, racing for the front door, his lungs pounding. Observing the expression on his partner's face, the sergeant erupted from the couch where he had been relaxing, scattering hardzine and peanuts in several directions. Cardenas's hand reached for the door handle.

There was no door handle. He had not looked to see if one was present when they had entered the house. It was, after all, a not unnatural assumption that there would be a matching handle on the inside of the door. But there was nothing, only smooth, wood-grained composite. Nor did the barrier before him respond to verbal command, or the anxious press of hands. From behind them, from somewhere within the distant bedroom, a feminine voice chillingly declared, "Almost ready. I hope you're not getting too bored waiting for me."

Then the house blew up.

ACCLAIM FOR ALAN DEAN FOSTER
AND *THE MOCKING PROGRAM*

"A tremendous futuristic police procedural that grips the audience from the beginning until the very final twist…a triumph that speculative fiction and mystery fans will fully appreciate….Foster is the modern day Renaissance writer, as his abilities seem to have no genre boundaries."

—*Midwest Book Review*

more…

ALAN DEAN FOSTER

the mocking program

ASPECT®

WARNER BOOKS

An AOL Time Warner Company

WARNER BOOKS EDITION

Copyright © 2002 by Thranx, Inc.
All rights reserved. No part of this book may be reproduced in any form or by any electronic or mechanical means, including information storage and retrieval systems, without permission in writing from the publisher, except by a reviewer who may quote brief passages in a review.

Cover design by Don Puckey
Cover illustration by John Blackford

Aspect® is a registered trademark of Warner Books, Inc.

Warner Books, Inc..
1271 Avenue of the Americas
New York, NY 10020

Visit our Web site at www.twbookmark.com

W An AOL Time Warner Company

Printed in the United States of America

Originally published in hardcover by Warner Books
First Paperback Printing: August 2003

10 9 8 7 6 5 4 3 2 1

the mocking program

ONE

First they took his talk. Then his cards. Then somebody boosted his *bosillos* thorough. After that, they vacuumed his clothes. Then some buitrees did a *muy rapido* scope-and-scoop, canyoning him from neck to crotch. His kidneys, liver, lungs, testes, and eyes were gone missing. They'd left the heart. Not much of a demand for hearts these days. Not with good, cheap artificial models flooding the market. Titanium or pig—take your choice. After that, he'd been drac'd and boneyed for his recyclable blood and marrow. The pitiful shattered remnants of who-ever the hell the poor unfortunate had been lay limp as an oily rag in the steadily drumming-down rain, denied even the dignity of staining the pavement with blood.

Amid flashing lights, assembled vehicles, and grum-bling federales, Angel Cardenas stood gazing down at the carcass, imaging in his mind a celestial vision of steaming hot coffee and the old-shoe comfortable booths of a certain café and wondering why the devil he didn't do as Chief Pangborn kept repeatedly suggesting and take early retire-ment. Fredoso Hyaki, Cardenas's assistant, rose from his crouch, having finished making a recording of the grue-some tableau. Hyaki was half Japanese, half Peruvian, and all huge. A friendly, expansive, baby-faced massif of a man in his mid-thirties, he very much resembled an Incan Buddha. Despite the cosmic arc of his abdomen, he was rock-solid as cured concrete. Grunting softly as he straightened up, he stuffed the recorder into a pocket and summed up the crime scene with a single terse observation.

"Just about enough left for relatives to lay a claim, Angel. Angel?"

Cardenas raised his voice so he could be heard above the Southwest monsoon shower. In the harsh nocturnal glow from the nearby commercial complex, glistening droplets trickled from the ends of his hangdog mustache. The sweet, invigorating rain was the only thing on the street that was uncontaminated. Though if the chemical analyses carried out by the more fanatical Green Verdes and their ilk were to be believed, the summer downpour failed that test also.

Would he ever get used to seeing dead bodies on the street? Even after thirty years in the Department, the inventiveness demonstrated by people in slaughtering their fellow citizens never ceased to astonish him.

Why, he wondered amid the lights and night, *could I not have been born a dog, like Charliebo?*

"I think it must have been easier to be a cop in the old days, when all they boosted from a citizen was his money." He glanced at his companion. "Why are you all wet?" Unlike the other slickered cops milling around the corpse, Hyaki was soaked from head to toe. Rain poured off his round face like sweat.

His partner looked abashed. "Forgot to charge my jacket." Devoid of power, the electrostatic charge that kept water from making contact with a cop's rain slicker was nothing more than a failed promise. Hyaki stood out as the only sopping-wet federale on the dark back street.

Not that the big man probably minded. The monsoon rains that faithfully drenched this part of the Namerican Southwest from July onward through late September made a welcome dent in the otherwise brutal temperature. Cardenas enjoyed feeling the rain on his face. Thanks to the patented efforts of his softly humming slicker, the rest of him stayed perfectly dry.

An advert appeared from nowhere, materializing out of the nighttime to buzz around him like an insistent bee in search of pollen, all the while loudly declaiming the virtues of Newer! Fresher! Better-Tasting! Lime-and-Salsa Posteeto Chips! via a frantic directional audio. He waved irritably at it and it flew off to pester Gergovitch from Forensics. Such mobile attack ads were technically illegal, but like the omnipresent wall posters of yore, whenever they were eradicated from one part of the Strip they quickly put in an appearance somewhere else, endlessly repeating their annoying spiels, vomiting forth discount coupons, and trying to wheedle addresses out of exasperated pedestrians.

Gergovitch stood up in the rain. "Sudden neural interrupt," he was muttering to no one in particular. "Trying to make it look like cardiac arrhythmia." The medoggles that were his principal tool were alive with the readouts that flitted like fireflies behind the lenses. Flickering pastel rainbows danced across his partially shadowed face. Only when he switched off the internal telltales could Cardenas see the man's eyes through the gleaming, sensormaxed transparencies. "At least it was quick." He took a half-hearted swipe at the motile ad, missed.

Stretching from Sanjuana to Masmatamoros, the evolved maquiladora manufacturing facilities and assembly plants of the Montezuma Strip constituted the western hemisphere's largest concentration of industry, commerce,

assemblage, cutting-edge technology, and trouble. Poor im-
migrants from the south collided with development money
from the north and infolktech from everywhere. The result
was a modest population of very rich people living alongside and lording it over very hopeful, but often very poor
people. If you couldn't make it on the Strip, was the word
in the soulpools of Buenos Aires and Barreras and Lima,
you couldn't make it anywhere. Job security was not guaranteed. Those who failed turned despondent, then desperate, and finally feral. Under such circumstances, with so
much glistening, beckoning credit floating around, it was
all too easy for a despairing immigrant to slip over the
linea. If you couldn't manufacture it, then you stole it and
sold it.

That was what had happened to this poor monger's most
marketable organs. Someone always needed a real kidney,
someone else an unpolluted transfusion. Black-market
blood was an easily transportable commodity. So were eyes
and viable testes. Cardenas knew that better than most. His
own incongruously blue eyes were donations. Legal ones,
biosurged into his sockets after his own optics had been
bungoed by— But that was old news, ancient history, chip
spume. Right now, he had a dead guy to eyedee.

The presence of the federales and the Forensics team on
the damp back street drew no crowd. No one was out walking in the rain in the commercial zone of the Quetzal inurb.
That was fine with Cardenas and his colleagues. They disliked spectators. The silence left them to do their work un-
encumbered by yapping inanities. Even better, the media
had yet to turn up. Vit anchors, the senior police Inspector
knew, disliked the rain. It played havoc with their hair and
makeup.

Absent body parts notwithstanding, there was nothing

notable about the corpse. It was one of many that turned up on a regular basis, week to week, month to month, as if ejected from the roller-coaster of life by some capriciously snapped safety belt. Individuals who turned up smashed and broken like the unidentified man at his feet were the rule rather than the exception. In the frantic, feverish, frenetic depths of the Strip, nothing went to waste. The street scavengers and the algae wallowers saw to that.

Ellen Vatubua was crouched over the torso of the corpse. Having run a quick scan and found what she was looking for, she was patiently excavating in the vicinity of the exposed left forearm. Nestled there among the bruised muscle fibers and blued capillaries, just under the skin, was a miniscule fragment of insoluble imprinted plastic. Gently removing the head of her probe, she transferred the extraction tip to her specialty spinner and injected her tiny find. Moments later she was reading its contents aloud. Cardenas and Hyaki wandered over to listen.

For a dumpy, middle-aged Forensics spec, her voice was surprisingly sensuous. Alerted to and made aware of this quality, Lazzario in Personnel kept trying to get her to transfer to Dispatch. But Ellen liked being out in the field, and analysis, and preferred working with dead folk to live ones.

"George Anderson. Thirty-two, married, residence four-eight-two-two-three-six West Miñero Place, Olmec." She hesitated as the spinner worked. "He comes up bare as a baby's butt; no record. Not even a commuting violation. Blood type . . ." She glanced up at the everlastingly mournful Cardenas. "You want me to pop the rest of the bubble, Inspector?"

Cardenas shook his head. "I'll read it when the vetted report is posted. Anything of particular interest?"

The owlish spec glanced back down at her spinner's readout. "Records identifies him as a 'promoter,' but doesn't say a promoter of what, and doesn't list a place of business. Only a home address."

"So he works out of his home." Hyaki fidgeted. He was growing tired of the rain. "There's a novel conclusion."

Ellen smiled up at the beatific mass of humanity that loomed over both her and Cardenas. "Like your bowels backing up during stakeout?"

"Run a deep scan." Ignoring the both of them, Cardenas was staring at the body, forlorn and shriveled in the reflected light from the massive nearby structures.

She gaped at him in disbelief. "Why?" She gestured with the spinner that was reading the extracted implant. "This unlucky citizen's whole life is right here, where it belongs, available for casual perusal. In a *dry* place," she added for emphasis. When no comment was forthcoming, she proposed, "At least let's wait until we get it back to the lab."

The sideways twitch of the Inspector's head was barely perceptible. "Deep scan. Now."

The Forensics spec turned to shout at her superior. "Hey, Gergo! Inspector here wants a scan. Onsite, right now, even though we got the *muerto*'s ident pill."

Gergovitch looked out from behind his medoggles. "He's the intuit, not me. Run it, Ellen."

Making no secret of her displeasure, the woman slipped her spinner into a holder on her belt and removed another tool from a second holster. As she snapped it to life, she muttered, "I thought you freaks couldn't intuit a dead guy. No disrespect intended, *Inspector*."

Cardenas's tone did not change. "We can't. I don't sense or suspect anything unusual. I just want to leave here confident in the knowledge that nothing's been overlooked."

"Yeah, yeah; *sí, sí,* siryore." Taking a deep breath, she went to work. Cardenas looked away. Grabbing the body's detailed DNA scan and then running it past Records would take a few minutes.

Hyaki hovered close by; part mutt, part truck, all business. But wet. "Any reason why the scan, Angel?"

Why indeed? What made him worry about dead people as much as live ones? A desire to seek justice? Or was it nothing more than professional pride? Cardenas spoke without looking back, not wanting to distract the irritated spec from her work. He indicated the corpse. "Good hair— expensive transplant graft. Soft skin. Two regenerated bicuspids, maybe more. All nice work." Raising a hand, he gestured at their surroundings. "This is not a nice place. They don't match up." He looked back at his assistant. "Why vape the guy from the inside out, instead of the outside in?"

Hyaki considered. "One kidney's worth more than a truckload of clothes."

"I don't mean that." Cardenas squinted into the rain-swept darkness. "I mean, what's a citizen from a nice, genteel neighborhood like Olmec, an apparent cleanie, doing down in a muck urb like Quetzal on a nasty night like this? Why isn't he home with his wife, watching the rain come down, or the game between Arsenal and Chicago?"

Five minutes later, sensing movement behind him, he turned just in time to confront Ellen. No one commented on the perfect timing of his reaction, least of all the Forensics spec. If anyone could get used to the sometimes unsettling actions of intuits, it was other cops.

Her earlier resentment had given way to a grudging respect, tempered by just a hint of awe. "How did you know?" she murmured.

Cardenas took no joy in the small vindication. He had only been doing his job. "Know what?" he responded encouragingly, even though he already knew perfectly well what.

"That there was something not right about the *muerto*'s ident." Intelligent and perceptive, she was peering hard into the lined face that was half masked by darkness and rain.

"I didn't know. Like I said, I just wanted to be thorough."

"Yeah, *verdad*." Her attention dropped to the very expensive and very wet apparatus she was holding. "His embedded citizen's ident insists he's George Anderson of Olmec inurb. When I coupled that info with the results of the DNA scan and ran it through Archives, the readout suddenly looked like it had caught the measles. Angry little red pinpricks started popping up all over my nice, clean screen."

"So who is he?" Hyaki asked, vouchsafing new interest.

She held the screen up to them as she read. "Depends which you believe: local eyedee or national. Archives says he's really somebody named Wayne Brummel, of Greater Harlingen, Texas. And guess what? It also lists no place of business, only a home address. In Harlingen."

Cardenas blinked at the small screen. "Physical description is a match. At least, it matches what the wallowers left." He glanced past the handheld, at the uninformative and now somehow ominous body. "Same question applies: what's a cleanie like this doing here in Quetzal? And with two identities." He passed her his spinner.

She mated it to her own, waited the necessary couple of seconds for the two police devices to swap the requisite information, and then placed hers neatly back in its holster. "How should I know? You're the intuit." She glanced upward, shading her eyes from the rain. "Weather's starting to clear. Going to be very hot tomorrow." It being late summer in the Sonoran Desert, her comment was worse than super-fluous.

"What do you want to do, Angel?"

Cardenas considered. He ought to let Homicide handle it, he knew. Except—National didn't make mistakes. It insisted the body belonged to Wayne Brummel of Greater Harlingen. Subcutaneous idents were difficult to forge. The man's insisted he was George Anderson, of Olmec. Taken together they added up to a real *mierde* magnet.

He ought to leave it alone, he knew. Follow-up on something like this was not his responsibility. He and Hyaki just happened to have been in the neighborhood when the flash came in. He could leave that particular neighborhood at will. Instead, he opened his spinner and mumbled the phone number imprinted on the dead man's ident into the built-in vorec.

Observing this, Hyaki was not surprised. Disappointed, but not surprised. He'd seen it all before. The Inspector latched onto contradictions like a remora onto a shark. The older man would be unable to sleep until this one was resolved. Dragged along by his superior's persistence, the same would be true of Hyaki.

Still, he tried. "It's late, Angel. Maybe she has her phone turned off."

"Maybe she doesn't." The Inspector checked his bracelet while his spinner dialed the unlisted number. "Yeah, it's too late for socializing. No, it's not too late to learn that your husband's been found dead and boosted on a back street in a rotten part of town."

He turned slightly away from his partner as the call connected. A sleepy woman's voice emerged from the spinner.

The screen remained blank: she had her video pickup turned off.

"Yes? Who's this? George?"

The rain had almost stopped. By mid-morning tomorrow the amorphous puddles birthed by the fading clouds would have evaporated completely beneath the relentless desert sun. It would be as if the downpour had never been.

"Ms. Anderson?" Cardenas responded.

There was a pause at the other end. "Who is this? There's no Anderson at this number."

Hyaki made a face. Cardenas's expression did not change. "This is Inspector Angel Cardenas of the Namerican Federal Police. I am presently in the industrial-commercial district of Quetzal, where the body of a man identified as George Anderson, of four-eight-two-two-three-six West Miñero Place, is presently being prepped and bagged for a trip to the Nogales municipal morgue. His subcue identifies him as George Anderson and lists this number alongside that address. If this is not Ms. Anderson, with whom am I speaking, please?"

Another pause, then a guarded response. "How do I know you are who you say you are?"

Now Cardenas's expression did change. "Who else might I be? And for that matter, how do I know you're Ms. Anderson?"

"There is no Ms. Anderson." The voice broke. "How—how did he die?"

Cardenas covered the vorec with his hand and whispered to his companion. "She's panicking." Hyaki just nodded. He could detect nothing suggestive in the woman's voice, certainly not panic. But that was Cardenas. To a competent intuit a dropped vowel, a twisted consonant, spoke volumes. And Angel Cardenas was not merely competent: he was the faz, the very best. *Muy duroble.*

"We don't know. The wallowers and the scaves didn't leave much. When was the last time you saw him?"

"This—this morning, when he left for work. Are you sure you're a federale?"

"Extremely federale," Cardenas assured her. "So you're not Ms. Anderson. But you know the George Anderson who lived at this number and address?" Again he whispered an aside to the attentive sergeant. "She's crying."

Again Hyaki heard nothing in the voice emerging from the spinner. This time he said so. Cardenas shook his head brusquely.

"Inside. She's crying inside." To the vorec he said, "Please, ma'am. This is a necessary routine follow-up. Did you know the deceased?"

"Y-yes. I know—I knew him. You have no idea what happened to him?"

"No, ma'am. Did you also know a Wayne Brummel? And it would be helpful if you gave us a name, so I could stop calling you 'ma'am.' "

"I don't know anyone named Brummel. I'd like—I want to see him. George. Mr. Anderson."

"The bod— He's being taken to the police morgue, No-gales Division."

"All right—I understand. But I can't come now. I just can't. My daughter is here at the house, and I—I have to take care of some things first. Would—eleven o'clock to-morrow morning be all right?"

Hyaki's whisper ensured he would not be heard over the spinner. "He's not going anywhere."

Cardenas glanced disapprovingly in his assistant's direc-tion. "Eleven o'clock is fine, Ms. Anderson. I'm sure we could all do with some sleep. Have you ever been to the station?"

"N-no, but I have personal transportation. I'm sure my car can find it." She was stammering now. "This is just terrible, and I—I don't know what I'm going to do. What I should do."

"I'll see you there at eleven o'clock then, Ms. . . . ?" Cardenas lowered the spinner and looked up. "She cut off."

Hyaki shrugged. Beneath his disabled slicker, flesh rippled against the night. "Not surprising. You just told her that her husband, or boyfriend, or favorite gigolo, has been murdered. She needs for that to sink in, to do some serious bawling."

Cardenas nodded. "Hoh. That would be the normal thing to do. Except that this is looking less and less normal." Above the mustache, incongruously blue eyes that had once belonged to a beautiful nineteen-year-old French girl gazed up at the sergeant. "Why wouldn't she confirm her name? She must know we can pull it up from Records in a couple of minutes."

Hyaki considered. "You want to go out to the house now?"

The Inspector hesitated. "No, not now. It's late. Let's give her the benefit of the doubt."

"What doubt?" Hyaki was cozing his own spinner.

"Hell, I don't know. Think of something." Turning, Cardenas headed toward the waiting cruiser.

Hyaki found what he was looking for before the doors of the official vehicle slid silently aside to admit the two cops. "Funny thing. City records say there's a Surtsey Anderson living at the same address as our George Anderson. But she told us there was no Ms. Anderson. Ain't that odd? There's also a Katla Anderson, age twelve, listed as being in residence. Undoubtedly not the daughter of George and Surt-sey." He slipped the spinner back in his pocket. "Which leaves us with the question of where to find Wayne Brum-mel."

"On his way to the morgue, apparently, dwelling in silent symbiotic communion with George Anderson. A cleanie who doesn't have a wife named Surtsey or a daugh-ter named Katla." Muttering to himself, Cardenas slipped into the seat opposite Hyaki. Sensing clearance, the door automatically slid shut behind him. Hyaki put the un-marked vehicle in forward and the engine hummed on full charge.

"You want to follow the body?"

Cardenas shook his head. He knew where the body was going. It was not a place he was particularly fond of visit-ing, especially late on a cool night. He'd spent far too many nights there.

"Forensics needs time to do their work. Not that I think they're going to find anything else of significance. I'm tired, and confused. Let's go to Glacial."

Hyaki turned down the appropriate street. An advert tried to attach itself to the window, careful not to block the driver's field of view. Static charge flowing through the glass drove it away, squealing. The charge, like the advert, was technically illegal. But police work was tough enough without having to suffer an endless parade of flying neonic blandishments for snack foods, vit shows, technidrops, soche services, sporting events, and assorted gadgetry that was as unnecessary as it was remarkable.

The sergeant drove slowly, merging with the traffic. Even though the great mass of commuters used the climate-controlled induction tubes or company-supplied armored transport to travel to and from work, there was always independent traffic in the Strip. With forty million people, give or take ten million undocumenteds, spread out like people-butter from the Pacific to the Gulf of Mexico, it could not be otherwise. But now, approaching midnight, it was comparatively easy to get around. The evening maquiladora shift was still hard at work, laboring in the vast spread of manufacturing and assembly plants and their attendant facilities, and the bulk of the night shift wouldn't come online for another hour yet.

The unmarked police car slipped straightforwardly through the largely silent traffic. A renegade Ladavenz, tricked out to sound like it was running on an internal combustion engine instead of fuel cell and batteries, let out a primal growl as it accelerated among lanes. Though technically breaking the law against late-night noise pollution, the three kids inside were not seriously abusing the opportunity. Cardenas and Hyaki ignored them.

As soon as they skated out of Quetzal, passing the number eighty-five induction shuttle station with its opaque, solar-energy-absorbing walls and unseen commuters waiting patiently within, the looming shapes of the industrial-commercial district gave way to an architectural panoply of codo coplexes and enclosed shopping facilities. Coated in a wide range of solar energy–absorbing polymers, the pastel structures were a spirit-lifting shift in tone from the utilitarian gloom of Quetzal. The Glacial Café was situated at the end of one such pedestrian coplex, backed up against a garage and rapicharge station. Only two vehicles were parked at the latter, topping off their batteries for the night.

Hyaki dodged couples and families as he pulled into an empty parking space. There was a larger than usual number of pedestrians on the street, reveling in the rain-cooled night. Tomorrow, everyone would disappear indoors, when the sun reasserted its ancient dominance over this desiccated part of the world. One couple, feeling no pain, nearly ran into Hyaki as the two policemen approached the entrance to the café. Their eyes widened as they took in all of him. The sergeant hastened to reassure them with one of his wide, beatific smiles. Grateful, they staggered past, weaving more or less in the direction of the nearest mall entrance.

A blast of cooler air enveloped the two men as the door to the establishment scanned their faces. Failing to match them with any known or reputed antisocs, it granted them entrance.

Cardenas was fond of the Glacial. With its retro-2040s Alaskan décor, soft lights, and Brazilian-Namerican fusion menu, it reminded him of the good times of his youth. Married once, he had few dates these days. Relationships often began well, only to end in shock and wariness on the part of his partners when they found out he was an intuit. Explaining that he could not read minds, that he was only making use of highly specialized police training for which he had demonstrated a particular aptitude, did little to bolster a woman's confidence in her ability to feint and jab.

"You know what I'm thinking!" they would exclaim.

"No I don't," he would invariably protest. "Intuits aren't mind readers."

"But you can extrapolate from everything I do, everything I say. The way I look at you, the inflection of every syllable I mouth, how I hold my left hand, the way I . . ." At about that point they would break off the argument to declare, "You knew I was going to say all this, didn't you?"

Protests of innocence were of no use. Most women were convinced that dating an intuit was akin to trying to run through the starting defensive line of the Moscow Dynamo: a girl was simply outmatched before she could get started.

Not, Cardenas reflected as he and Hyaki settled into an empty booth, that the majority of single cops didn't lead lonely lives anyway.

Vitalizing before him, the menu politely inquired if he wanted to null the audio and read about the establishment's offerings in peace. Correctly taking Cardenas's lack of response as permission to continue, it proceeded to recite the late-night specials. Stuffed into the opposite side of the booth, Hyaki was mooting whether to order the tambaqui and chips or fejoada with barbecued capybara.

Not long after their respective orders were relayed to the kitchen, a waitress appeared with Cardenas's keoki coffee and the sergeant's double espresso milkshake. Hot and cold for slim and large, the Inspector reflected as he dosed down on his steaming mug. The confused identity of the corpse they had just encountered collided in his thoughts with the puzzling response of the man's wife-not-wife. One did not need to be an intuit to realize something more than the usual mug-and-drug was involved in the man's death. It was turning rapidly into a bona fide realimad, non compos mental, strain on the brain, jane. Cardenas didn't like that. He liked things direct and straightforward, in the manner of most cops. Neat and clean on the scene. Better if the scan on the dead cleanie had turned up no identity instead of two.

The ganglet of ninlocos arrived before his food did. They swaggered in past the protesting door, the lanky chieflado in the lead spizzing it with a spinner whose ident was torqued to reflect instead of inform. Behind the chingaroon ambulated a group of negs and poses, though which was who and who was witch was hard to say at first glance.

Hyaki looked over his shoulder, grunted a kata, and wished that their food would hurry up and emerge from hibernation in the kitchen.

Traying chow, the waitress delivered to another table. One of the nins, of inscrutable gender, tweeted at her and accompanied the whistle with an obscene vapowraith that oozed from the lipgrammable stimstick held in his/her mouth. The scented smoke sculpture wrapped itself around the unwilling waitress, wisps of pale suggestiveness clinging to her like glued air until with flailing hands she slapped the last of it away. Laughing at her fretful efforts to maintain her dignity, the nins took over a particularly well-situated table from a pair of uni students. Wholly intimidated, the young couple abandoned it without a word, pocketing their glowing vits and fleeing the restaurant with as much haste as they could manage.

One of the negs reached out to grab a rough handful of the girl's backside as she tried to hurry past. Hyaki started to get up. Cardenas motioned him back down. The neg held on to the terrified student for a few seconds before letting her go. The Inspector knew that he would. The antisoc had strutted a series of raw movements even a novice could have intuited.

When their food arrived, the two officers ate in silence. Like everyone else in the café, they ignored the loud and boorish antics of the ganglet. Collective rudeness was not yet a federal crime. But the ninloco cacophony did nothing to soothe Cardenas's already troubled thoughts, or improve his digestion.

Why wouldn't the woman give them a name she must know they could, and would, soon learn for themselves? Why wouldn't she admit to at least a live-in relationship with George Anderson? Or Wayne Brummel, the Inspector reminded himself.

"Yolaolla! *Sí*—you—you with the nasty 'stash. You sitting front-eyes with *el gordo,* there."

Ignoring the intrusion, Hyaki continued to nibble on the last of his fried fish. The yakk was directed at Cardenas anyway.

The Inspector looked up from his bison and eggs. Perpetually mournful eyes regarded the neg. The would-be chingaroon was not quite two decades, all sass and flash. How many kids had he dealt with like this one, busy burning their souls like matches? It was late, he was tired and hungry, and not in the mood to baby-sit. He could have let Hyaki deal with it, but there was always hope. Hope that a small lesson might spark a hint of maturity. Where feasible, words were always more efficacious than an arrest. In jail, kids tended not to talk to other kids about being kids.

"Don't do it." As always, his tone was quiet but firm. A little firmer now, perhaps, than when he had been delivering his supper order to the attentive menu.

It was not a response the ninloco had expected. It showed in the fleeting glance he gave his expectant colleagues. "Cay-yeh, homber—you don' ask me no questions. I'm the one hackin' the yakk here."

Picking up his knife and fork, Cardenas resumed eating. "Just don't do it."

Brows furrowing, the neg leaned toward him. "Didn' you hear me, homber? Just for the yell of it, what 'it' is it you don' want me to do?" He favored his companions with a knowing smirk, and they smiled appreciatively at their topboy's wit.

Sitting back, Cardenas dragged a cloth napkin across his lips, the slight charge in the fabric instantly disinfecting them. "Well, crazyboy, since you ask, first thing you need to turn off the knife in your calf scabbard. Don't you know that leaving something like that on is dangerous? The safety could slip, and you'd lose a leg." He looked up, past the leader of the ganglet. "The big kid behind you needs to forget about frogging my partner. Even with the slywire he's holding, Fredoso would break his arm. You young ladies," he continued, addressing the now wide-eyed and uncertain pair of poses, "want to leave your ordnance holstered. You don't want to see where mine is, because I don't flash it unless I intend to use it, and you don't want me digging yours out from where you have them supposedly perfectly concealed."

In full verbal if not physical retreat, the chieflado was glaring at the imperturbable Inspector. "Yola, homber, you spazzing, man! We don' got none of what you bubble. We just wanted to toss a little flak-chat, *sabe*? We only—"

One of the girls interrupted him. "*Mesmo,* Taypa—the homber's an intuit! He's comping your moves!" She and her companion were already backing away from the table.

Smiling while still chewing his fish, Hyaki raised his left arm. The sleeve slid back to reveal a blue bracelet alive with blinking LEDs. One vitalized a symbol morph that halted a few centimeters in front of topboy's face. The ninloco's eyes widened as he focused on it.

"We didn' mean nothing." Looking suddenly less imposing, the bigger boy had turned in the blink of an eye from predator to pound cake. He was backpedaling so fast he threatened to run over the two rapidly withdrawing poses. Eyeing the two soft-voiced men in the booth, the waitress gratefully resumed her rounds.

Full of fish, his bulging cheeks giving him the appearance of a gargantuan chipmunk, Hyaki shook his head sadly. "Kids! Things sure were better in the last century, when there was hardly any juvenile crime."

Cardenas nodded agreement as he shoved his cred into the table's receptacle. Tracking the cred's instructions, it would forward the cost to the departmental billing center in Nogales. He was careful, as always, to leave the tip in cash. That way the restaurant owner couldn't scam any cred off the top. Besides, a cash tip carried with it a certain cachet in the form of nostalgia value.

By the time the two men exited the café, with the door thanking them courteously for their patronage as it closed behind them, the only sign of the ganglet of fearless ninlocos was the faint and rapidly fading fragrance of the poses' perfume lingering on the still-damp night air.

TWO

THE SKY WAS UTTERLY DEVOID OF CLOUDS
the following morning. A sure sign, Cardenas knew as he
exited the induction shuttle and entered Nogales arcoplex's
NFP division headquarters, that it was likely to pour some-
time late this afternoon. Such was the predictable annual
pattern of the Southwest summer monsoon that he had
grown accustomed to since childhood. The July-August
rains came earlier and lasted longer these days, it was said,
because of global warming. That might be bad for Eskimos,
but it was fine with the residents of the Strip. Flash floods
notwithstanding, there was no such thing as too much rain
in the desert.

Working a late shift the previous night had allowed him
to sleep in this morning. It was funny, but the more he aged,
the harder he worked and the less sleep he seemed to need.

By the time I'm dead, I'll be ready to retire, he mused as
he arrived at the morgue. Somehow, knowing that his accu-
mulating pension would pay for a great funeral did little to
cheer him. It was a wonderful topic to be pondering as he
wended his way to the cold room where the unscavenged
remains of George-Wayne Anderson-Brummel were

housed in a cylinder of industrial formagas designed to preserve soft body parts while preventing decomposition.

Eleven o'clock came and went. Then twelve, after which the afternoon count began. No one named Anderson, or Surtsey, or Brummel appeared at the Nogales morgue to identify, inspect, caress, condemn, or otherwise make the acquaintance of the body of Anderson-Brummel. Running gag aside, the morgue was not a favorite place to kill time. Angel Cardenas grew impatient, then annoyed, and finally hungry.

At two-thirty he popped his spinner and hayoed the ident for Anderson-Brummel's self-proclaimed un-spouse. There was no response. That could be good, because it might mean she was in transit to the morgue. It could also be bad, because the house ought to automatically relay the call to whatever communications device she carried on her person. In the confusion and angst of the moment, it was possible she had taken off sans tech, he knew. Possible, but unlikely. Citizens simply no longer traveled without a means for continuously staying in touch with the rest of civilization.

However, all things were possible, he reminded himself. Especially in the Strip, where a cop's life was many things, but never boring. So he waited another half hour before intuition and stomach drove him out of the morgue and via peoplemover to Administration.

Entering NFP's Nogales command center entailed passing through somewhat stricter security than visiting the morgue—or, for that matter, the Glacial café. Elaborate precautions were necessitated by the uncomfortably large number of individuals and organizations who held grudges against the police. These good folk sporadically tried to give vent to their feelings by blowing up everything from parking meters to individual officers to entire city blocks.

Miniaturization having in the past hundred years affected the field of explosives as significantly as nearly every other component of modern civilization, it was incumbent upon those likely to be the target of such grievances to minimize the individual access of the congenitally disaffected.

So Cardenas was compelled to pass through a corridor that contained no fewer than five security stations, the first and last of which were administered by live humans, and the intervening three by machines. His ident bracelet was checked, his height and weight and body density were measured, his retinas were scanned, his cerebral cortex measured (and not found wanting), and in due course he was passed through to the inner sanctum of the Namerican Federal Police, Nogales Division.

Except for the chatter of officers and attendant civilian personnel moving from department to department, the spacious room was as quiet as Saguaro Park on a Tuesday morning. Each open office had its own husher. During working hours, every one of them was turned on. Within different cubicles, there might resound the chaos of a confrontation between quarreling police, the shouted curses of a suspect being interviewed, or the rants and ravings of barely manageable drunks and deviants. None of it escaped through the invisible walls of canceling sound that were far more effective than the thin plastiboard dividers that physically divided the duty room floor like so many cookie cutouts.

Cardenas wound his way through the maze, past busy techs and beat officers and bureaucrats, dodging self-propelled messenger carts and food trays, until he found himself outside the office he sought. Hyaki was visible within, conversing animatedly with Drosi Semagarya. Though their mouths moved, and Cardenas was not more than a couple of meters from them, he could hear nothing. Nevertheless, he was able to follow the gist of the conversation effortlessly. Almost as a by-product of their primary training, good intuits invariably made spectacularly adept lip-readers.

Glancing past Hyaki, Semagarya saw the Inspector waiting patiently outside. Reaching for his desk, he stroked a blue contact strip to mute the husher. When next he opened his mouth, Cardenas was able to hear his words.

"Come in, Inspector. We were just discussing the case."

Actually, Cardenas knew from reading their lip movements, they had been debating what team to bet on in the office pool for this week's big game between Chihuahua and St. Louis—but it would be undiplomatic of him to point it out. Instead, he replied casually, "Learn anything?"

"Uh, no sir," Semagarya murmured after a hesitant glance at Hyaki. "There's been no news."

The sergeant chipped in quickly. "How did the bereaved widow, or whatever the hell she is, hold up on viewing the body?"

"I wouldn't know." Cardenas folded himself into a sterile but comfortable Lantille chair. The pressurized cushions immediately molded themselves to his back and buttocks. "She never showed." Hyaki's eyebrows rose as the Inspector turned to the stat cruncher. "The ident she gave us is uncompromised. She's just not answering."

Relieved to have something to do that let him avoid the Inspector's gaze, Semagarya let his trained fingers dance over the inputs on his desk. A privacy shield promptly enveloped the cubicle in semi-darkness, much as the husher insulated the sound within from the walkway beyond. Although they could still see staff striding past outside, none of the passersby could see in. The wall on the other side of the desk darkened, became a tunnel that filled with data.

"Sequence is valid." When he was working, Semagarya's tone was as flat as that of any artificial membrane. "Dialing." Spark borders framed the dark tunnel, indicating that operation was continuing, but otherwise the screen void stayed blank. "No answer. Line-in is operational."

"Do a penetrate," Cardenas instructed him. At the spec's look of surprise, the Inspector reacted sharply. "No, I haven't got a warrant."

Semagarya nodded unenthusiastically. Whirligigging the query, he dumped it on Procedures. A pause of several minutes ensued, during which time no one said anything of significance while Bolivian Azul played Inca background over the wall speakers. Five minutes subsequent to initiation the warrant arrived, duly approved, witnessed, and recorded. As soon as it joined the Anderson-Brummel file, a small glowing sphere appeared near the bottom of the tunnel.

Semagarya could have operated his console verbally, but that could be disconcerting if anyone else tried to talk over him. Better to separate commands from conversation. Images danced within the energized, agitated tunnel that stretched out before the three men. After another ten minutes or so of hard crunching, the spec sat back and locked his fingers behind his head.

"Damn impressive security for a private residence. It is a private residence?"

"As far as we know." Cardenas was studying the screen. "Cogit a patch with Search and Rescue."

Semagarya sat up pronto. "I can't do that, Inspector! Those ports are reserved exclusively for emergency access."

"This *is* an emergency," Cardenas informed him dryly. "We're dealing with the dead here."

"That's *verdad*," Hyaki added. "A dead end."

"Go on." Cardenas exhorted the clerk gently. "I'll take full responsibility if a monitor snaks the patch."

"Easy for you to abla, homber. I'm the one sticking his pend into the grinder." But he leaned forward and danced the inputs.

The tunnel appeared reluctant to condone the break-in. Frowning, Semagarya threw a second police gram at the target, and then a rarely used third.

"Creepy—I've got a triple hammer pounding on the portal, and it's still resisting. Last gram is straight out of Vlad Targa Inc. and should be sharp enough to cut through a keiretsu's firewall." Curiosity won out over his initial trepidation as he looked up at Cardenas. "You bump up against this level of security at, say, city hall. You don't find it guarding some commonplace cleanie's codo."

"It's a house," the Inspector corrected him, "but I take your point. Keep trying."

"Oh, we'll get in. It's only a private box." Semagarya was quietly confident. "It'll just take a little time for the hooks to find the right corner. I just want you to know that somebody's spent some real money defending their privacy."

"What for?" Hyaki's gaze was fixed on the depths of the flickering tunnel. "Your average citizen doesn't need that kind of box wrapping." He glanced over at his partner. "What would a straight cleanie like George Anderson have to hide?"

Cardenas's attention was likewise focused on the tunnel. While box-probing in the background, it played back three-dimensional scenes of Semagarya's family on vacation.

"*Quien sabe*? Maybe Wayne Brummel." Unlike his companion, the intuit did not fidget in his chair. He was used to leaving machines alone to let them do their work.

It took twenty minutes for the screen to resolve. That was nineteen and a half minutes longer than a standard electronic penetration warrant should have taken to respond, Cardenas knew. With the domicile's communications system now under direct control of a police proxy, he found himself gazing intently at the interior of the residence at 482236 West Miñero Place, Olmec.

The view was touching in its banality. The phone's pickup showed a comfortable, deserted living room area. Visible furniture was of unexpectedly fine quality. There were framed art works discernible that, if originals, hinted at a higher income for the absent Andersons than the surrounding neighborhood would suggest. That was cause for interest but not necessarily suspicion, Cardenas believed. Citizens who could have afforded to live in larger houses in more exclusive surroundings often chose instead to apportion their income internally.

A Leeteg portrait glowed on the far wall, its accompanying audio muted. A bonded Swarovski crystal sculpture capered from one end of a free-form itapua-wood coffee table to the other, and then back again. There was no one present to admire them.

"Try the other rooms," the Inspector instructed the spec. Semagarya worked his control strips. A view of the backyard included a modest swimming pool, characteristic desert landscaping, and a rather more impressive glitter fountain, its kaleidoscopic particulates held in splendid colloidal suspension. Semagarya shifted back inside, first to a bathroom, then several comfortable if undistinguished bedrooms, and finally to a below-ground workshop or storeroom. Within the house at 482236 West Miñero, nothing moved but the art.

"That's *todos*." The monitor looked expectantly at Cardenas. "There are two more fixed terminals in the house, but they're not vited. Aural only. I can trace but not access the three mobiles."

Cardenas nodded accordingly. "Fine. Then just roto the audio."

Flashing a look that said he was convinced they were wasting their time, the spec complied with the order. The tunnel blanked. Nothing issued from the speakers. *"Casa nasa,"* he declared with finality. "Nobody's home."

"Maybe she's finally on her way over here," Hyaki suggested. "Might even be waiting for you down in the morgue."

Cardenas was doubtful. "Merriam would have flashed me if that was the case." He stared at the tunnel as if he could take a shovel to it and physically dig out some answers. "You're sure there's nothing moving?"

Semagarya rechecked his readouts. "Everything registered to that number and that name is in the house. If they're traveling, it's without personal communications or under a different ident." He waved at his board. "I show six registered terminals. Three fixed, three motile. Five static, one wiped."

Nodding, the Inspector rose. *"Verdad.* Anderson probably had number six on him when he was vaped. First thing the scummers would have done is wipe the registration on any personal electronics so they could be resold without being traced." Arching his back and stretching, he looked at the sergeant. "Warrant's open. Let's pay the house a visit. Merriam will let me know if the un–Ms. Anderson puts in an appearance at the morgue."

"Maybe she's out shopping for groceries." Hyaki had to turn sideways to fit through the entrance to the stat cruncher's cubicle.

"The morning after her husband gets extirpated?" Cardenas led the way down the hall. "Most people wouldn't have much of an appetite."

"She's got a kid." Hyaki sounded mildly defensive. "Besides, she said he wasn't her husband, and people do all kinds of weirds when pushed into crisis."

The Inspector turned thoughtful. "She didn't sound weirded. Wary, but not weirded. And we had an appointment. She picked the time."

"Like I said." The sergeant's conviction returned. "One woman is thrown into turmoil. She has a child to deal with. Crisis always lubricates logic."

"No police haiku." Cardenas turned down a corridor. "Not before lunch."

While the cruiser found its own way to Olmec, the two federales discussed possible scenarios. Though none were particularly plausible, neither was either officer more than usually concerned. They had a confused, possibly panicoed woman on their hands, and a demised citizen whose identity was curiously conflicted. The combination fell well short of a national emergency.

Their destination did not stand out among the neat, sun-baked homes that fronted a neighborhood green belt running along a dry wash—although in the Sonoran Desert, "green belt" meant something less than in other parts of the country. Nonetheless, the winding procession of landscaped nature, with its defiant cactus and struggling paloverde, was far more pleasant to look out upon than yet another row of tract homes, however appealing developers might try to make them. The front yard of the Anderson residence boasted mature, genetically engineered saguaro and ocotillo. A pair of topiaried pyracanthas posed invitingly. The outer wall's electronic security yielded uncomplainingly to Hyaki's police sesame, and the two men approached the house.

A residence of this class would be protected by two or three individual security sensors, Cardenas knew. Generale Electric or Thompson, maybe a Dynamo if they had the money. The units would be concealed among the decorative stone facing. He was not surprised when no one hailed them from within. Semagarya had said that the place was empty. So far the two officers had seen nothing to contradict that assessment. The door, and the garage, were locked. The Inspector stepped back to give his partner room.

"Open it."

There was, of course, no visible lock or door plate. Hyaki ran a tracer over the wood-grained composite until he located the upper and lower bolt. It took his tracer less than a minute to unravel the electronic combination, and only seconds to undo the first. As he was sliding the unit down the front of the door preparatory to snapping the second, the inner lock slid back. A voice greeted them from an artfully concealed speaker.

"Please excuse the delay. I was in the tub. Won't you come in?" Emitting a soft, disengaging click, the door popped inward a couple of centimeters. Hyaki pushed it aside.

Air-conditioning enveloped them in its comforting, artificial embrace as Cardenas shut the door behind them. "I'm in back," exclaimed the voice of Surtsey Anderson. "Getting dressed. Make yourselves at home. I'll be out in just a few minutes."

The two officers wandered out of the entryway and into

an open, circular den. Polarized light filtered down through the translucent material of the domed ceiling. Cardenas recognized their surroundings immediately: it was the first room Semagarya had remotely viewed. The Madrasink vit phone the spec had accessed was still in its charger.

Hyaki settled down on a curving couch that had been designed to resemble a pile of red sandstone. It was soft as silk. He patted the faux rock. "Designer furniture." Absently, he hunted for a label. "Whatever this poor dead homber promoted brought in some real green."

Cardenas was admiring the art on the walls and in the display cases. It was far more impressive in person than it had been when viewed via the phone's pickup. "Anyone can have money. Our friends the Andersons also have good taste." Raising his voice, he addressed himself to the rest of the house. "Take your time, Ms. Anderson. Did you forget about our appointment this morning?"

"Just another couple of minutes," came the response.

Cardenas paused before a pedestal on which a Seri mobile signed "Francisco" revolved in stately polished procession. At the same time, something he'd heard in Anderson's voice nagged at him. On the couch, Hyaki had spread out a hardzine and was manipulating the core projection with his fingertips, adjusting it so it could be viewed from different angles. Nothing in the woman's straightforward reply or tone had unsettled *him*. But then, he was not trained to detect, or suspect, miniscule variations in human voice patterns that were discernible only to perhaps one hundred-millionth of the population.

It was not that Anderson had failed to apologize for missing their rendezvous at the morgue, or even that she had declined to acknowledge it. No, it was something in the tone, in the timbre, of her response. Every person was different, of course. Everyone reacted differently to moments of personal crisis. The eccentric might respond with unaccountable cheerfulness, to the point where most folk would be repelled. Surtsey Anderson's response had been neither awash in sorrow, nor tinged with remorse, nor flickering with false jollity. What Cardenas had detected instead implied an entirely unnatural ordinariness.

Turning away from the gleaming, dark brown wooden carvings, ignoring their whispered plea for him to linger and admire, he headed for a back hallway that opened onto the den. Hyaki's brows rose, but the sergeant kept his seat and said nothing. No hallway sensors or interior security attempted to bar the Inspector's way.

He passed an open door that revealed a bedroom beyond. It was neat and tidy. There was no indication that it had been abandoned in haste, no sign that its occupant had fled in confusion. From the holos of metazon stars that blinkered on the walls to the clothing projector to the silent audibub generator that ejected floating sound bubbles, the room reeked visually of contented preadolescent female. One audibub drifted close. He burst it with a fingertip, releasing a five-second yowl of what passed these days for popular music.

As he approached a second bedroom, the voice they had heard earlier made him halt. "I'm just putting on some clothes. Please wait in the den." Surtsey Anderson again. Reassuring, polite, friendly—inviting, even. Cardenas's eyes widened ever so slightly. There was one important overtone missing from that voice.

Concern.

For all anyone could tell, today was a day like any other. A day for shopping, for work, for visiting her daughter at soche, for making a date at the beauty parlor, for having lunch with friends. Anything but a day for identifying a murdered maybe-husband. And still no apology for missing her meeting at the morgue. For that matter, she had not even asked her visitors to identify themselves. He and his partner might as well be two spizzers out for an afternoon's larking slice-and-dice.

"Ms. Anderson, it's me, Rocko Sanchez from the Nobodega Brothel. You're late for work."

"Just one more minute—I'm still putting on my face," replied the voice.

Whirling, the Inspector broke into a desperate sprint.

He shouted at the startled Hyaki as he burst out of the hallway, racing for the front door, his lungs pounding. Observing the expression on his partner's face, the sergeant erupted from the couch where he had been relaxing, scattering hardzine and peanuts in several directions. Cardenas's hand reached for the door handle.

There was no door handle.

He had not looked to see if one was present when they had entered the house. It was, after all, a not unnatural assumption that there would be a handle on the inside of the door. But there was nothing: only smooth, wood-grained composite. Nor did the barrier before him respond to verbal command, or the anxious press of hands. From behind them, from somewhere within the distant bedroom, a feminine voice chillingly declared, "Almost ready. I hope you're not getting too bored waiting for me."

Waiting for what? an increasingly frantic Cardenas wondered apprehensively as he scanned the sides of the doorway. Of one thing he was now confident: it would not be an appearance by Surtsey Anderson.

Stepping back, he pulled his gun and flipped up the projectile barrel. Hyaki turned his head away and closed his eyes as the Inspector fired. In the narrow enclosed space of the entrance hallway, the sound of the shell striking the door was ear-rattlingly loud. When the minced composite cleared, it revealed a hole in the material the size of a man's head. Unfortunately, behind the hole flashed the hard gleam of solid metal.

"Interesting door for a mid-income cleanie to have installed," he rumbled as he stepped aside to make room for Hyaki. Throwing himself against the barrier, the sergeant hit the obstruction with every kilo of his considerable mass. It shook but failed to give. With a second charge, he bent one hinge.

"Maybe together," he rasped tersely, his broad chest heaving.

On the third try, the two men succeeded in snapping the middle hinge and bending the door halfway outward, though Cardenas gave himself no credit for the accomplishment. Scrambling through the opening, he stumbled out onto the sun-drenched glassite walkway. A look back showed Hyaki struggling to fit through the gap they had made.

"Need a hand?"

The sergeant did not smile. "I'm not overweight—I'm just like the coffee I drink. Papua Robusta." Behind him a cheery, by-now familiar voice piped up clearly, "I'm ready—thanks for waiting for me!"

Then the house blew up.

The central dome that roofed the den vomited vertically, a half hemisphere of composite and wood and metal building materials erupting skyward. Shattered fragments of 482236 West Miñero rained down on desert landscaping, empty street, and stunned neighbors alike. The force of the blast blew the struggling Hyaki through the gap in the front door, and carried the damaged door along with him. It knocked Cardenas two meters backward and half out of his shoes. Shaking off the effects of the concussion, he climbed to his feet and staggered over to where his partner lay, shell-shocked and bleeding, on the decorative decomposed granite that in the Southwest often took the place of grass. Absently he noted that the back of the sergeant's jacket and most of his trousers had been blown away. Only the lightweight but virtually impenetrable forcewear he wore underneath had saved him from being torn to shreds by fragments of suburban house that had been unexpectedly transformed into lethal shrapnel.

"Get up." Reaching down, he got both hands under his partner's right arm and heaved. The mountain stirred. "*Vamos* your overpaid ass, Fredoso!"

With a tremendous effort of will, the wounded sergeant heaved himself to his knees. "I'm okay, Angel." Reaching up and around, he felt of the back of his neck. A callused palm came away syrupy with blood. "Maybe a little banged up."

"It's *verdad, compadre*? Shunt—now!" Leaning backward, Cardenas used his weight to drag his partner in the direction of the street. Behind them, neighbors were gathering outside the fencewall. They wore the vacant, bewildered expressions of lemmings who suddenly found themselves adrift in a sea of mayhem they could not comprehend. From somewhere within the collapsed, smoking center of the house, the voice of Surtsey Anderson cried out.

"Help me, please! I'm hurt! Can't somebody help me?"

Hyaki hesitated, rendering futile the effort of the worried Cardenas to keep moving his mountainous companion toward the street. "We've got to go back. The woman, she's—"

"Not there," Cardenas snapped at him. "It's a recording. Keep moving!" With one hand, he continued to tug on Hyaki's right arm, hoping the rest of the sergeant would follow. Using the other, he flipped open his spinner.

"I have a Red eight-two-four at four-eight-two-two-three-six West Miñero Place, Olmec inurb!" he barked at the vorec. "Officer down. Repeat, officer is down—requesting airmed!"

Still dazed, his head wobbling slightly, Hyaki was gazing back in the direction of the slumping structure. From damaged, hidden depths, a female voice continued to plead with any listeners. Hyaki frowned uncertainly.

"A recording? Angel, are you sur—?"

They had almost made it to the sidewalk when the house blew up all over again. This time there were multiple explosions. The gathering crowd of rubbernecking neighbors screamed. Those who were not knocked down, fled. Cardenas felt the heavy hand of the blast wave slam him to the hard ground. When the rain of debris finally ceased, he struggled to free himself from chunks of building material and shards of shattered window. Hyaki was unconscious and bleeding badly from the back of his skull. Shoving the insensible bulk of his partner to one side, the Inspector sat up, dug dust from his eyes, and stared.

The serpentine walkway that had previously led to the front door of the comfortable suburban home now led to a smoking hole in the ground. Overhead, the heavy hum of approaching chopters was beginning to mask the ongoing screams and shouts of stunned and injured onlookers.

He would not have expected so unassuming a residence to be equipped with so advanced a kamikaze security system. Instead of keeping trespassers out, the idea was to let them in, and then liquidate them. One also lost one's home and possessions in the process. As a security measure, the technique was devastatingly effective. Of course, it could be used only once. What had the recently deceased George Anderson-Brummel feared badly enough to induce him to turn his own home into the explosive equivalent of a low-grade munitions dump? Why had he gone to elaborate and expensive lengths to try to trap and kill?

Of more immediate interest, Cardenas wondered as he cradled the unconscious Hyaki's bruised, bleeding head in his lap and watched grim-faced airmeds drop from the descending lead chopter, where the hell were Surtsey and Katla Anderson?

THREE

ONLY WHEN HE WAS ASSURED THAT HIS PART-
ner was going to be okay and Hyaki had been choptered out
did he allow the airmeds to clean his own wounds and treat
the most seriously damaged areas with sprayskin. He declined to leave the scene, refusing a lift to hospital. As
might be expected, media teams were onsite almost as
quickly as the airmeds. When a team from Forensics finally
arrived, they had to run the usual gauntlet of vitwits who
peppered the new arrivals with questions they could not answer. Officers and a pair of department flashmen from
Comrel cordoned them off as two squads went to work on
the scene.

The nature of the destruction ruled out natural causes such
as a gas explosion even before the studious evaluators had a
chance to talk to Cardenas. Ignoring his wounds while trying
to keep visions of the battered, unconscious Hyaki from
flashing through his mind, the Inspector insisted on joining
them in their work.

"There was an initial detonation that was as much bait as
killing charge," he told the male and female officers who
confronted him, taking notes, "followed by the added lure of
an injured woman crying out for help. Then a whole series of

secondary explosions." Angrily, he kicked aside a twisted strip of metal wall cladding. "Whoever cojoned this *casa* wanted to make sure and kill anyone and everyone who was inside."

The female Forensics spec was kneeling, passing a scanner over a still-smoking cavity within the greater crater, applying the kind of high-class infosuck for which the department was well-known. "Pretty extreme way of dealing with burglars."

"Depends on what kind of insurance you have." Having dropped a select handful of dirt and debris into the mouth of a device that resembled a portable sonic oven, her partner waited patiently for it to produce intelligible results. "Some companies will pay full replacement if the homeowner can prove they expiated two or more intruders." He smiled thinly. "That's morally indefensible as well as highly illegal, of course. But try and get a conviction in court against the corporation making the payout. Plenty of cleanies own shady policies that carry evanescent forced-entry extermination riders." Frowning, he gave the oven a firm smack.

"Here we go," he muttered, staring at the readouts that promptly blinked to life. "Pretty stylish package of ingredients." He glanced meaningfully at the attentive Cardenas. "Where death-dealing is concerned, your suspects show some sophisticated taste. Hellex expanders, Tarifa bursters, and Jaffna jelly. All sequenced and set off with Taichug micros programmed to react in concert with your lady-in-distress reaper." He favored the intuit with a longer look. "I heard the preliminary. Your open spinner forwarded it downtown. How'd you know it was a recording, that there was nobody in the house?"

Cardenas was following the progress of the other specs.

"The anxiety in the voice rang false. She was a good actor; but it's still acting."

The specialist nodded, gesturing at the inurban devastation through which his colleagues were picking. "Whoever's behind this sure as hell didn't want anybody to get out."

"Or to find anything." Kneeling, Cardenas pulled something from the rubble. It was the upper half of a doll, the gelatinous simulated eyes still moist. Disconnected, it automatically gazed back up at him out of limpid synthesized oculars.

The spec blinked as he dumped the contents of the oven into a specimen bag. "Find what?"

The Inspector did not drop, but instead carefully placed, the piece of homunculus back on the ground. Something in the synthetic eyes made him use a foot to cover it with debris. "If I knew that, I wouldn't have to ask the question. What I do know is that no one turns their home into a bomb this sophisticated just to *muerto* a couple of skraggers."

Despite his injuries, he insisted on joining the assessors who were working the street, questioning stunned residents of the heretofore peaceful neighborhood. The two flashmen from the department were busy massaging the media, doing their best to persuade the skeets that the destruction could not have been prevented.

The few resident citizens on off-day who came stumbling out of their individually secured abodes wore the dazed expressions typical of cleanies for whom daily existence was a succession of relatively predictable concerns over bills, professional worries, and family. Ordinary, everyday problems that were not a matter of life and death as they were for the underfolk of the Strip.

Cardenas approached a wide-eyed older woman clad only in swimsuit and throwover. Evidently, she had been relaxing in a backyard pool when the Anderson home had tried its best to exterminate the two visiting federales. A few lingering beads of water still clung to her lower legs, fighting evaporation. She flinched slightly when the Inspector drew near.

"Nothing to be afraid of," he reassured her. "You don't need to run."

"I wasn't going to—well, maybe I was," she mumbled. No maybe about it, Cardenas knew. He did not explain to her that the subtle movements of her body and face revealed her intentions to him as clearly as if she had loudly declaimed them.

He flashed his ident, saw her relax slightly. "I won't involve you, I promise." He indicated the smoking ruins of the house in front of them, now smothered in flame suppressant from the hovering fire department chopter. "Did you know the occupants? A Mr. George Anderson and . . ."

"Surtsey," the woman stammered. "Her name is Surtsey. They had a daughter." Her eyes were pools of concern. Not for potentially extirpated neighbors, but for herself and her own kin. "What happened?"

"Too soon to tell." Cardenas felt no compunction about comforting her with a lie. "Maybe a gas line explosion. Maybe something volatile in the house." He did his best to make it sound as if nothing out of the ordinary had occurred. "Happens all the time."

"But *you're* here." She gestured past him. "There seem to be a lot of police."

"Routine," he confided casually. "Just depends on who happens to be in the area when the emergency happens. There was no one at home, so nobody got *muerto*ed. You knew the Andersons?"

"Very casually. A 'hello, good morning, how are you?' kind of knowing. People here in Olmec value their privacy."

And pay for it, she didn't have to add. "They seemed nice enough."

"Did Ms. Anderson have a job?"

Showing signs of relaxation, the woman turned thoughtful. "If she did, it was in-house. I didn't see her go out much. And she always seemed to be at home when her husband arrived. She drove the girl to soche, though. Every day. And brought her home. Not that I paid any attention, really."

Cardenas nodded, conveying the impression that she had provided valuable information. "Any idea which soche the daughter attended?"

The neighbor shook her head and tugged the throwover tighter around her bare, wrinkled shoulders. "No. My own children are grown." Glancing to her right, she pointed out a boy and girl standing in front of two younger citizens. All four were staring at the incomprehensible wreckage that had suddenly and explosively materialized in the middle of their quiet neighborhood. The parents said little, but their offspring were chattering away animatedly.

"You might ask the Martinez family. Their boy is about the same age as the Anderson child, and I seem to remember hearing that they went to the same soche."

So they did, the boy confirmed to Cardenas, although he was in a younger soche group than Katla Anderson. Thanking them, Cardenas turned to leave, only to find himself confronted by a pair of vitwits. He stalled the chattering skeets until Morgan from Comrel could intervene, pattering the pair away despite their persistent efforts to challenge the Inspector. By the time they succeeded in breaking free of the flashman, Cardenas was tucked into a cruiser and humming swiftly away from the site. *Have to mess the flashgal a gracias,* he told himself as the scene of suburban devastation receded behind him. He was not comfortable dealing with the media, especially those who recognized or knew him as an intuit.

The cruiser's spinner traced Hyaki's ambulance and the obedient car conveyed the Inspector to Nogales Central, the Department's hospital of choice for officers injured in the line of duty. The medico flashman who intercepted him in the fourteenth-floor hallway informed him that the sergeant was still in surgery. Cardenas did not press the earnest young man for details. His tone was sufficient to assure the Inspector that the big sergeant was going to be all right, because Cardenas could tell that the man was speaking the truth and not concocting a convenient professional lie. Nevertheless, he spent the rest of the afternoon there, staying on well into evening, until he was finally allowed a look into Recovery.

Eyes closed, facedown, Hyaki floated swathed in freshly adhering epispray. The pinkish, artificial epidermis was slowly blending with the sergeant's own skin, sealing and healing the horrific charring that covered most of his broad, naked back. It was impossible to tell how much of his own epidermis remained. As with any severe burn victim, he drifted in suspension above the bed, hovering in a magnetic field designed to keep his severely damaged skin from coming in contact with any solid surface. Even the finest, softest bedsheets could multiply the trauma of an acute burn victim. The diamagnetic properties of the human body that allowed it to oppose the magnetic field applied by the hospital Perkins projector had only been properly and practically realized in the last thirty years.

Tubes ran from the sergeant's nose and pelvis. Scanners focused on his torso monitored readings from nanosurges that had been inserted into his body at strategic points. Cardenas had spent enough time (too much time, he reflected calmly) in hospitals and seen enough apparatus in action to allow him to interpret many of the instrument readings. Overall, they were stable, if not cause for celebration.

A dark, quiet anger had been building in him ever since he had left the crime scene. The fact that the ordinary, unremarkable house in the inurbs had tried to kill him and his partner was reason enough for fury. That it had been indiscriminate in its murderous automaturgy only rendered the attempt that much more deserving of denunciation. That it had not been conceived to dissuade everyday crime such as burglary was self-evident. Not only was the system far too elaborate and expensive, it hardly succeeded in preserving the owner's household goods. It was designed to welcome intruders—and then slaughter them, to the extent that the owner of the system was prepared to sacrifice the entire dwelling in the effort.

If not thieves, and in all likelihood not visiting federales, then who? Rage was the rationale for most home security systems. Fear was the foundation of the much more sophisticated setup that had nearly killed him and his partner. Who, or what, did an apparently ordinary inurban family like the Andersons have to fear to the extent that they were willing to turn their own residence into as elaborate a booby-trap as Cardenas had ever encountered? Of one thing he was already certain: it was tied to the reason the deceased George Anderson needed two identities.

The floating body in IC Recovery stirred ever so slightly. Cardenas's expression did not change. He could not intuit the unconscious. He did not have to. The sight of his friend's hovering torso was enough. Endorphin drip or not, Hyaki had to be suffering. It would worsen when the sergeant awoke and was once more able to feel. There was nothing Cardenas could do about that.

But he could damn well do something else. For a start, he

very badly wanted to have a chat with the erstwhile Ms. George Anderson.

His fury at the indifferent instrumentation that had nearly robbed him of his friend and partner did not begin to ebb until that night, as he sat in his codo, overlooking the landscaped and artfully contoured channel of the Santa Rita River. Drip-watered vegetation softened the harsh terrain on either side of the waterway. A single nocturnal jogger, her shoes and cap suffused with glowing pale blue quantum dots, was all that moved beneath the half-moon. Her belt pulsed rhythmically, warning potential muggers that her outfit was fully charged and ready to stun any attacker foolish enough to make a grab for her.

Beyond the river stretched the lights of the Strip, running all the way to the Golfo California. The previous night's downpour had cleansed the air, revealing stars that were wholly indifferent to the insignificant alternations mankind had wrought on the ancient Sonoran terrain. The tranquil vista helped to ease his troubled thoughts. So did the chilled Dos Equis in his hand.

Downing the last of it, he set the empty bottle down alongside its three empty siblings. Evacuated of beer, the disposable induction coil that was woven into the glass promptly shut down. The glass began to warm immediately. Swiveling in the chair, Cardenas muttered at his vit. The wall unit blinked to life and offered up a selection of suggested inanities for casual viewing. Sprawled in a chair, clad only in his underwear, he stared at the slowly scrolling readout without seeing it.

The medical portents were fine, but as long as he was stuck in IC, Hyaki could not be regarded as being out of danger. If the big fat slotho died . . .

Ignoring the proffered offerings of laughter and docu-

mentary, he opted for a snooze soother. As he had done on in-
numerable other nights, he fell asleep in the chair.

Tucked into a quiet cul-de-sac, the Mary Anson Carter
Soche was a neat, self-contained complex designed to in-
struct children ages four to thirteen in all aspects of Real
Life. Pre-university academics, of course, had not been
taught in schools since the middle of the century. Those sub-
jects were far better mastered in the peace and privacy of a
child's residence, with the aid of home boxes and away from
the distractions of one's age peers. At fourteen, a child entered into two years of analytical studies and advanced
soche, and at sixteen, choices were made between higher education, vocational apprenticeship programs, public service,
and a plethora of less-defining adult options such as the military.

In soche, a child learned about the psychology of male-
female relationships, dating, the institution of marriage, sex,
how to open and manage a bank account, how to perform
simple household repairs, deal with credit, purchase a residence, handle lawyers, consult with doctors, plan a vacation,
shop for goods and services, buy and cook food—all the crit-
ical components of everyday life that bumbling previous
generations had somehow expected children to learn on their
own, usually by utterly inadequate variations of social osmo-
sis. In other words, all the really important things. Science
and math, geography and language, history and literature, art
and civics—all these were better studied at home, via a
household box.

From eight in the morning until noon, four days a week,
children gathered in their local soche to learn what the tribe
of mankind expected of them: how to be decent human beings and survive in a world that grew more complex not by

the year, but by the day. Into this bubbling preadolescent brew had been enrolled one twelve-year-old named Katla Anderson, whom Angel Cardenas badly wanted to interview. The elderly neighborhood resident he had spoken with outside the devastated Anderson dwelling had told him that the girl's mother always took her to soche and brought her home again. With that in mind, he found himself flashing his ident to the armed guard at the entrance.

"*Como se* happening?" he offered conversationally.

Automatic pistol protruding prominently from his hip holster, stun spray dangling from a chain attached to a vest pocket, the bored sentry strummed his beard and shrugged. "*Nada* much, homber. Who you here to arrest? Teacher or nin?" He perked up a little. "Hope it's a teacher. This is a quiet soche and I like most of the nins."

The Inspector stepped through the deactivated gate. As soon as he was through, the guard reactivated it. A soft, ominous hum indicated that a microwave barrier powerful enough to crisp an intruder had been reenergized in the visitor's wake.

"Neither *nada*," Cardenas explained. "I just need to talk to one of the students."

Swiveling in his seat, the guard scanned the security bib. "This ain't about the detonation of that ice cream truck last month, is it? That's been resolved. Our nins had nothing to do with it." He snorted disapprovingly. "Was a bunch of antisocs from Miranos urb."

"I just need to ask a few quick questions." Cardenas's tone was as patient as it was intentionally unenlightening.

The guard gave up trying to mine information from the visitor. "Identity of student?" he asked officiously.

"Anderson, Katla." Peering past the guard, the Inspector studied the security bib.

The sentry nodded to himself. "Yeah, I know the name. Got the attendance roster pretty well memorized. Don't recall actually talking to the girl, though." The brisk movements of his fingers on the keyboard belied his age. As a safety measure, the security bib was not designed to be operated by vorec.

More finger flicking. There were two hundred and sixty-three LEDs on the bib. Eighteen flashed red, the rest green. The guard tapped one of the red indicators. "She's not here today." He leaned back in his seat. "Out sick, maybe. But she's not here."

Cardenas was far less surprised by the news than the guard. "Could her monitor be defective? Or masked?"

The guard pushed out his lower lip. "Could have gone dead. Or if she's working in lab, the signal could be masked, although we try not to put the nins in a situation where that's possible. Sometimes happens en masse in cooking class, though. Radiation interference. It can get real bad when they're doing holiday poultry." He worked the board. "Go see Alicia Tavares; room eleven. She's Anderson's matriculator for the month." Swiveling in the chair, he pointed. "Down the entry hall, second door on your left, other side of the wildlife preserve. She's teaching Advanced Commuting right now."

The Inspector gave his thanks and strode off in the indicated direction, passing rooms in which children were learning the social skills necessary to survive in a society more multifarious than most. Exiting the main building, he found himself wandering through a miniature version of the celebrated New Mexican Jornada del Muerto, complete to desert landscaping, waterhole, and reproductions of historic artifacts—all replicated in the middle of the urban, industrialized Strip to show its youngest citizens what life once was, and in places still was, beyond the induction tubes and malls and playwhirls.

Entering a subsidiary structure, he found his way to room eleven. His ident bracelet ran through several thousand municipal code combinations before settling in a few seconds on one that operated the classroom door, granting him entrance.

Inside, he found two dozen pairs of eyes regarding him intently. The walls that were not windowed with shatterproof, polarized glass alloy were covered with drawings and motilites and artscapes depicting various modes of contemporary transportation. At the moment, the class was dissecting the interior of an intercontinental hypersonic transport, but not to study the aerodynamics of its design or the physics of its hydrogen-driven engines. For those who were interested, such technical details could be better analyzed at home. Instead, they were learning travel etiquette: how to order food, how to eat while onboard, how to use the bathroom, how to deal with troublesome other passengers—in brief, how to survive and get along in the world of modern air travel.

Their instructor was a slim young woman with dark hair and a narrow face whose work attire was presently masked by the uniform of a United Varig flight attendant. United Varig, of course, paid for the privilege of having its corporate logo so prominently displayed in an institute of learning. The nins didn't seem to mind. They were too busy trying out recommended travel phrases on one another.

"Keep practicing those short conversational routines," Alicia Tavares ordered them. "There'll be an oral quiz tomorrow." Groans rose from the well-dressed junior citizens. This was not a poor school district, Cardenas reflected. In the urb where he grew up, schools had no money for such frivolities as clothing masks.

"Can I help you?" She caught the flash of his ident. "Oh dear, I hope no one's in trouble. That business with the ice cream truck—"

"Has nothing to do with my visit here today," he finished for her. When he smiled, the tips of his drooping mustache rose half a centimeter. The action invariably brought a grin to the lips of anyone near enough to note the phenomenon, and Tavares was no exception.

"I'm relieved to hear it. What can I do for you"—she eyed the ident one more time—"Inspector?"

"This month you're supervising a student named Katla Anderson."

Tavares nodded, and her expression changed to one of concern. "She's not in any trouble, is she?"

"We don't know yet. If she is, it's not of her doing." He looked past the teacher, to the busy class of well-fed children. "She's not here today."

"No."

"You don't seem surprised."

She eyed him inquisitively. "You're very perceptive, Inspector. Katla's quite a bright girl. In some respects, brilliant. But she has a real problem keeping up her attendance. It's not her parents' fault, as near as I can tell. But there are days when she just doesn't show up. Her parents protest, and claim to have spoken to her about the problem, but it persists. Really a shame. Such a clever girl."

"Her parents didn't call in to say she'd be held out today?"

Tavares shook her head. "As far as I know, there's been no communication. These unexcused absences are random, so I don't think Katla's skipping to partake of some scheduled outside activity."

Cardenas nodded. "How does she get along with her fellow nins?"

"Well enough." Having replied reflexively, the teacher proceeded to qualify her response. "Although when not engaged in programmed activities, I have noticed that she does tend to keep to herself. Why don't you ask some of her sochemates?" Turning, she addressed two girls who were exploring trays of simulated food. "Malaga, Rose—could you come here a minute, please?"

Cardenas found himself looking down at two twelve-year-olds, one the color of coffee, the other of sand. He smiled, and his mustache danced. Eyeing him curiously, the lighter-colored of the pair glanced up at her teacher. "This isn't something that's going to be on the quiz, is it?"

"No," Cardenas assured her. "I just want to ask you about a friend of yours—Katla Anderson."

The other girl replied first. "You mean the goofac?" She giggled. "That's what we call her. Because she sucks up everything around her, but when you ask her a question, half the time all you get back is this weird smile, like she knows the answer but isn't sure how to tell it to you."

"That's right," added the first girl quickly, her words threatening to stumble over one another in the style of speaking common to twelve-year-olds. "Katla, *sí*, she's *muy* cerebro, but she's still a weird. *Cabeza* vareza, you *verdad*?"

Tavares made a face. "Malaga, mind your manners."

The girl looked up petulantly. "Hoy, the fedoco *asked*!"

"I don't care." The sandy-skinned girl was nearly as tall as he. "Katla's not here today."

"Noho," her friend agreed indifferently. "Shunted, you *sabe*?"

"You know where she might be?" Cardenas asked easily.

The girls glanced at one another before the taller one responded. "Nobody knows where the west wind goes. That's Katla."

He smiled softly, his words gentle. "You're lying to me, Malaga."

She looked at him sharply. "No I'm not. Some days, Katla just doesn't image-in."

"That's not what I asked." He leaned a little closer, his eyes boring into hers. "You know what I asked. And you know that I know that you're lying. *Por favor,* don't lie to me again, Malaga."

The girl looked to her friend for help. They were silent for a long minute. Then the one called Rose spoke up, though with obvious reluctance. She did not meet the visitor's gaze. "Katla's hard to talk to, sometimes. It's not like she's rude: just quiet. But sometimes—sometimes she'll tell us where she's been when she's not here." The not-quite-woman's voice had fallen to a whisper, as if she was afraid someone not present might somehow overhear the conversation.

"She likes to focus with the crazyboys."

Cardenas exhaled softly. "Katla Anderson is twelve. That's too young to be focusing with the ninlocos. They would laugh her off. She'd slow their pulse."

Malaga was shaking her head. "Not the subgrubs. They'll take you if you're eleven." Aware that she might have divulged too much forbidden knowledge, she added hastily, "That's what I induct, anyway."

The Inspector straightened. Subgrubs were loose, casual groupings of antisocs not yet old enough to be initiated into a real gang. Despite what the girl had told him, he had never encountered or heard of one as young as eleven being admitted to the clique. But twelve—at twelve you would be tolerated. Thirteen to fourteen was the average age of a subgrub, after which you moved on up to a real ninloco gang, went cleanie—or ended up solo on the Strip. Or dead.

Subgrubings were fluid bands of mature children and immature teens with no real structure or organization. Unlike the ninloco gangs, members owed allegiance only to one another. Bonds were formed through friendship and dissolved as casually as they were begun. Serious crimes were rarely perpetrated by the kids involved. Most turned to antisoc activities out of boredom, not conviction. They were delinquents rather than felons.

It was a good time to catch them out, before their lives started spiraling down the toilet. Especially a bright, apparently promising kid like the Anderson girl.

Drawing his spinner, Cardenas requested the names of all the known subgrub factions reported to swirl within a ten-kim radius of the school. Beyond that, a twelve-year-old would start to find herself in alien territory. "Gobreski," he recited aloud as the names appeared on the screen. "Narulas. Pinks, Habañeros, Terravillas. The Lost Perros. Vetevenga. Socratease. Convirgil."

"Vetevenga," murmured Rose. "That's the one. I don't know where they focus."

"There's something else." Cardenas shifted his attention to the taller girl.

"She—Katla mentioned the name of one antisoc a lot. A boy." Rose shot her friend a warning look that was ignored. "Como's himself 'Wild Whoh.' I—we—met him once or twice. He was never enrolled here, but they let him audit a few classes. Whenever he was here, he and Katla would hub." Raising one hand above her head, she held it out, palm facing down. "About this tall, kind of skinny. Short green hair, usually. Crossoed querymark shaved into the right side. One time I remember him saying he was fifteen—but I think he was boasting. Afranglo skin and features." She touched her left ear. "Always wearing a muse when he wasn't in session. Passing out nodes like some bigtime Noburu-san."

"They were a good match," a still-hesitant Rose added. "He was even weirder than Katla."

The Inspector recorded the info. "You've both been very helpful. Thank you." He turned to go.

A hand clutched tentatively at his sleeve. It was Malaga, for the first time looking very childlike. "Katla—she's okay, isn't she?"

"I hope so. I like to think so. If she should happen to focus anywhere around here, would you let me know? My name is Inspector Cardenas." He did not have to provide a number. How to deal with and make use of the authorities was one of the first things children learned in soche.

It was clouding up when he left the school. More monsoon weather, he reflected. More rain. It would untidy his day, but he didn't mind. Only a mental objected to rain in the desert, irrespective of how much purified desal they extracted and pumped north from the shallows of the Golfo.

Antisocs tended to lead largely nocturnal lives. Subgrubs were no exception. Calling in his intentions via vorec, he headed not for the office but for home. If he was going to chase grubs all night, it would behoove him to take a nap.

FOUR

ZAP-ATA AVENUE NEVER SLEPT. IT WAS WHERE the resident seeds of this particular pie-slice of the Strip came to play when they were in the mood to get a little spizzed and spazzed. Cleanies and antisocs, citizens and ninlocos, admins and techies and eeLancers mixed freely, their social differences temporarily set aside, bound together by a mutual desire to saturate themselves in a scintillating sea of tempormorality.

In search of a little illicit entertainment? Try a Texmexsexhex. Stimulating, but safe. UL-approved (though maybe not by Good Housekeeping). Feel the need for speed? Pilot a Disony mickeyed personal induction capsule around a 100% safe obstacle course at velocities designed to slap your lip flaps right back over your cheeks. In the mood to vitalize a little agro? Don a Karash stimsuit and take a run through any of hundreds of artificial environments, obliterating bad aliens, bad lifeforms, bad carnivores, and for a quick under-the-table, over-the-card supplemental fee, your spouse (scan-suitable 4X6 required; holos preferred) along the way.

Sample the cuisine of all seven continents, from Triobriand trochus tortellini to St. George krilliabase, Mamiraua cupuruçu ice cream sundaes to a Blue Hyacinth mochanocha shake (twice the plateau caffeine, three times the lowlands sugar, and you can't taste the guaraná until you start to come down). Choose your Samerican rodent barbecue: cui to capybara. Food, food, food, some of it crude, some of it lewd, a little of it even brewed.

Speaking of drink, the irritatingly persistent motile advert whispered knowingly in the Inspector's ear as he wandered down an open off the main boulevard, *half-liter blended brews are only a triplet apiece during happy* hora *at Robusto's Café, third court on your right, you can't miss it.* Flailing one arm, he waved the hovering electronic hawker away. Had he chosen to do so, he could have grammed his bracelet to broadcast a frequency that would have warned such nuisances away by identifying him as an on-duty officer of the NFP. Doing so, however, would allow certain elements of the population to pick up the specified carrier wave and thereby take note of his presence. Federales like himself who preferred to operate beneath the cloak of comparative anonymity were thus compelled to suffer the same glut of omnipresent advertising as any ordinary citizen.

Like any popular nighttime lair, Open No. 64 was saturated with adverts. Music filled the still-superheated air, not all of it commercial jangles. He found himself humming along with a popular contemporary enchanto. Emerging from a notably sediddy bistro that boasted proudly of its favorably reviewed Burmese-Cajun cuisine, a laughing young couple nearly ran into him, drunk on the wine of young love. He smiled tolerantly and stepped out of their way. Giggling, they tried not to stare too long at the bright-eyed older man with the imposing whiskers as they continued on past him, staggering up the street arm in arm. He hoped their happy condition would not leave them with a hangover.

As he had always done, as he did better than nearly anyone else in the department, he melted into the crowd, one more unremarkable presence among many that cried out for attention. With his bracelet hidden beneath the cuff of his shirt and in the absence of blue cap or blazer, he was one of the last nightcrawlers on the street that any of his fellow pedestrians would have identified as a federale—much less a senior Inspector. Blending in had always been one of his abilities. It was not one readily measured on the Department aptitude or skill tests. Superiors and colleagues alike valued it highly nonetheless. A great deal of what Cardenas could do was not quantifiable. This sometimes bothered the bean-counters, but not his fellow cops.

Four kids were loitering outside a Wanrow parlor, hoping to see someone thrown out so they could help him up and, in the process of rendering assistance, maybe pick the disoriented Wan's pockets. To anyone else on the street they appeared to be doing nothing more than standing and chatting. "Anyone else" did not see them as Cardenas did. Their attitudes, their posture, even their body odor told him they were intent on doing some moderate mayhem.

The oldest of the group was a boy of fourteen. A black pigtail curled down each side of his head, and the skullcap he wore was decorated with ancient symbols that ripped defiance in Hebrew. Likewise the tattooed Aramaic obscenities that covered most of his exposed right arm. It wasn't much of an arm—not at fourteen. But the promise of burgeoning nastiness was there. A Yesvit, Cardenas decided. A wannabe aiming to join one of the two or three organized orthodox ninloco gangs that roamed the western half of the Strip.

His companions were less flashy in both dress and appearance. The girls tracked the Inspector's approach uneasily. The smaller boy tried to make up for his lack of subgrub size and stature with inflated bravado.

"Whatch you wereing, homber?" the kid piped up brazenly.

"Yia, it suits you," added one of the girls. Her companion giggled. Both of them were still salvageable, Cardenas decided. But preado recovery was not his job.

"Nice night," he offered conversationally.

"Was," growled the bigger boy, the evident leader of the loitering quartet. "Until you arribed." His was not a very intimidating growl. The subgrub's voice had not yet changed yet.

"Still is." Hands in the pockets of his lightweight windbreaker, Cardenas smiled back. "I wouldn't portage a chopwire like that in my back pocket. Somebody waves the wrong sine wave and you're likely to lose a piece of your ass, *egoísta*."

The kid's boldness drained away like hygen gas from the belly of a long-range Gemmer as one hand whipped reflexively to the single wide pocket sewn into the rear center of his pants. "Chingaringa!" one of the girls exclaimed. "The homber's a bomber!"

"I don't want what you got," Cardenas continued reassuringly. "I want what you don't got."

"*Habla* me," the boy muttered warily. "What you need, fedoco?"

Ignoring the ebb and flow of laughing, chattering, squealing nightlife that flowed around them, Cardenas concentrated on the leader. So thoroughly deflated by now was the subgrub that he did not even glance up as a befuddled blancblanc, or anglo-saxon male, came stumbling out of the

Wanrow parlor. The two girls and the other boy fought hard to avoid staring in the dazed cleanie's direction. The citizen staggered off into the brightly lit Sonoran night, unaware that he had just avoided a likely spizzing.

"I'm looking for a Vetevenga subgrub about your age goes by the name of Wild Whoh. Skinny Afranglo, green brush hair with a querymark, venerates the Muse. Also a twelve girl, nonzafado, who likes to vete with him. Katla Anderson."

By turns sullen and fearful, the boy's voice had shrunk to a whisper. "Don't *sabe* the grub. Same for the girl-child."

Cardenas could lower his voice as well. "Don't try to fak yakk me. You get hauled downtown with a chopwire, you'll end up spending a couple of *noches* in the blender. You know what happens in there."

This time when the boy looked up there was real fear in his expression. One of the girls plucked at his hand, but he shook her off. "Wild Whoh thinks he's chingaroon, but he's not real nin. He just likes to play at it so the Vetevengas will let him ambulate with them. I don't know the girl. That's *verdad,* homber."

Cardenas knew it was so, just as he had known that the boy had been lying earlier. "Where can I find him?"

Clearly tired of the federale's inhibiting presence, the other boy finally spoke up. "Whoh's a major Noburu guru. He's got a completed belt and maybe half a dozen nodes to go with it. When he's not floating with the nins, he likes to drift around the Melarium. You know the Melarium?"

The Inspector nodded. It was a popular meeting place offering a thousand different kinds of libations, many legal; loud music, occasionally legal; and magsuit dancing for those who wanted to float rather than cling, legal depending on the degree of mutual consent.

He straightened. "Thanks. You've all earned a couple of bene points. Might come in handy someday." He turned to go, but not before favoring the deflated leader with a final, unflinching stare. "Go owling if you must, but I'd ditch the chopwire. That's so so *serioso*."

The Melarium was one of the most popular nightspots in Greater Nogales, as well-known to the police as to the public. It was another place where cleanies and toilers could mix, where engineers and mask artists and humble assemblers could mingle and converse without laboring beneath the burden of class preconceptions. In the glow of alcohol and stims, all citizens were equal.

He stood for a while watching the parade of people that flowed into the building and oftentimes came wobbling out. Hygen-powered private vehicles pulled up outside the entrance, emptied their excited, chattering passengers, and whisked themselves off to the nearest available parking spot. Assemblers and other commuters too poor to afford private transport arrived on foot from the nearest induction station, as well-dressed or better so than their more affluent fellow citizens.

Cardenas amused himself by observing and cataloging the amazing range of body language on display. When he'd had enough, he headed for the main building. Not for the main entrance but the side, away from the crowd. He was looking for wannabes, for those too poor or too young or too agro to be granted admission to the Melarium. He was looking for nins, and it didn't take long to find them.

With their tattooed skulls or elaborately braided hair, their sometimes wispy and often in-your-face-insulting attire, their threatening accoutrements, the ninlocos intimidated ordinary citizens without speaking a word. They knew it, and so when a lone middle-ager sauntered casually in among them, the assumption on their part was that he was either insane, drunk, stim-stymied, or something else. This outsider didn't act insane, did not totter as if drunk, did not babble incoherently like one stim-stymied. That left Something Else. They were instantly suspicious.

No one was surprised to learn that the man who had boldly come among them was a federale. But federales were too smart to plunge solo into a ninloco congregation. That suggested a fedoco who packed Something More on his Something Else. Along with their hate, there was hesitation. Cardenas used the time to ask questions.

Directed from the side to the rear of the Melarium, whose very structure seemed to pulse with the music and energy pounding within, the Inspector fixed Wild Whoh in his stare the instant he set eyes on him. The crossoed querymark was a dead giveaway. That, and the finished Noburu belt the kid wore proud and prominent around his waist. An integrated caster would link it to the muse glasses that covered much of the boy's face. His lightweight Striker slack strips rainbowed from deep purple to transparent according to how the light from the street struck the phototropic material. He wore no underwear. A plain filtered vest glowed with a series of querymarks that matched the one shaved into his head. While several girls were clustered around the prominent subgrub, none was Katla Anderson.

Placating muse motes or no, Whoh didn't like what he could see of the heavily mustachioed man who was striding toward him. With his prepube Rare Birds clustered protectively around him, he waited to see what words would bring.

"Hoyo, homber," he essayed from behind his glasses. "This is a free street, and we're not bothering anyone."

"You Security?" The girl who spoke indicated the throbbing mass of the Melarium, whose minimum age limit she and her companions did not meet.

Cardenas shook his head and ignored her to focus on the boy. "You Wild Whoh?"

"Who asks?" the boy responded warily.

By way of reply, the Inspector lifted his left arm. The sleeve slipped down to reveal his ident bracelet, flashing with a much wider than usual sequence of LEDs. Cardenas had adjusted them to pulse to the opto. Though he tried not to show it, the boy was impressed.

"Like I said-so, it's a free street." Stepping to one side, he made a show of making room for the adult to pass. "Don't step in any fedoco." A couple of the girls giggled.

Cardenas ignored the predictable juvenile rudeness. "I understand you like to vete with a prepube named Katla Ander—"

The mention of the girl's name produced an instant and extraordinary change in the hitherto confident nin. He shoved the nearest girl at Cardenas, who caught her reflexively to keep her from falling. At the same time, the subgrub's vest blew up as its owner pulled a tab that deliberately destabilized the composite magnesium fibers woven within. Momentarily blinded by the light, the equivalent of several dozen prehistoric camera flashes going off at once, Cardenas flinched. The girls screamed and rubbed frantically at their eyes as Wild Whoh spun and made a mad dash for the looming architectural mass of the Melarium.

As he fought to clear the fading purple and yellow spots from his eyes, Cardenas followed on the run. How the kid expected to get inside the building, the Inspector wondered as he gave chase, he did not know. But the subgrub would not have fled in that direction without having a specific rata hole in mind. Anyone else would have remained dazed by the disorienting flash, wondering which way the boy had fled. Cardenas knew where the kid was going because he had been looking and leaning in the direction of the Melarium just before imploding his shirt.

Certainly the subgrub was startled to see the police Inspector bearing down on him as he struggled with the old-style latch that secured the rear service door. Before he could slide the illegal desense patch over the lock, Cardenas had him by the shoulder. Expecting a struggle, or at least some form of defiance, the Inspector was surprised when the kid broke out crying. Tears spilled from behind the muse lenses. He was not scared of Cardenas—something else had him utterly terrified. Embedded miragoos rippled on his slim chest.

"Leemee 'lone! I didn't do *nada* . . . I don' *know nada! Por favor, madre,* please . . . !"

"Easy, *niño,* everything's *vacán.* Calm down." Gradually, the tears subsided. Breathing hard, his sallow, elaborately decorated chest heaving, Wild Whoh flipped up the muse lenses to blink uncertainly at the surprisingly strong homber who held him tightly by one arm. Without letting go of his quarry, Cardenas stepped back slightly, trying to give the still-apprehensive kid as much personal space as possible.

"You . . . you really are a federale, aren't you? *Verdad*?"

Nodding slowly, Cardenas ventured his most professional paternal smile.

"You're not gonna hurt me because . . . because I *sabe* Katla?"

Gently, deliberately, the Inspector let go of the kid's arm. Rubbing it, Wild Whoh gazed back at him. For an instant, Cardenas thought the subgrub was going to bolt again. But having already fired his flashirt to disorient his captor, his chances of getting away were now much reduced, and he knew it.

"Why would I, or for that matter anybody, want to hurt you just because you know Katla Anderson?"

"Chingame," the boy muttered. "Maybe because Katla talks to me, tells me stuff, and somebody's maybe afraid I'm a snaffler, a *horicón*."

"A jaw-jacker?" Cardenas smiled. "Why? *Do* you talk too much?"

Whoh shook his head rapidly. "No way. But there's people don' believe nothing an homber says, *sabe*? I know how to keep my mouth shut. But there's always those who want to shut it for you." His fear finally beginning to fade, he regarded Cardenas much as had Anderson's erstwhile friends at soche. "She all right, Katla?"

"We don't know. She didn't show up at soche today."

Whoh nodded slowly, as if this revelation was half anticipated. "I was afraid—I've always been afraid for her. Such a quiet one, Katla-key. Sweet sugar Katla." The Inspector was afraid the kid, uncharacteristically, was going to start crying again. "She used to—tell me things."

The throbbing din from within the depths of the Melarium was starting to give Cardenas a headache. He did not much care for contemporary music. As far as he was concerned, adding electronics, echoverb, and heavy bass to marimba was a *puta*-tive corruption of a fine tradition. In this he knew he was an exception. Most of his colleagues reveled in the thunderous amplified throbbing.

"What kinds of 'things'?" he encouraged the subgrub as considerately as he could.

A little of the boy's previous defiance resurfaced. "Why should I tell you anything, fedoco? If you're *verdad,* you ain't gonna do nothin' to me. Everything I got on me is legale." He tapped his skinny miragooed chest. "I'm not hiding anything."

Cardenas indicated the flamboyant belt that still encircled the boy's waist. "That's an impressive accumulation."

Slightly taken aback by the change of subject, Wild Whoh recovered quickly. With the muse lenses still flipped up, the Inspector noted that the boy had one blue eye and one black one. "No *mierde,* homber. Took most of a year to put together."

"But you're missing something." Cardenas pointed to a gap on the belt's right-hand side. "I can get you the Seventh Node."

Avarice replaced the last vestiges of real fear in the boy's eyes. "You're chinging with me, fedoco. Nobody can get a Seven Node. They're gone, *muerto*ed, finished, expiated. Noburu only shipped a few before the safety boardos made 'em cease an' defist."

Cardenas looked away, as if utterly indifferent to anything Whoh might think. "That's what I heard. You know, in the course of our work, we find ourselves confiscating all kinds of illegal materials that people try to sneak through places like Sanjuana and Peñasco."

"You can really get your hands on a Seventh Node?" When Cardenas maintained his silence, Wild Whoh rubbed a recently embedded miragoo with the palm of his left hand and muttered, "What you want to know, homber?"

"You're afraid for Katla because she knows certain 'things.' You're afraid for yourself because she told those things to you." Cardenas locked eyes with the subgrub and would not let go. "Now you can pass them on to me. Don't worry. I'll keep your name out of anything that follows."

Wild Whoh nodded slowly. "You better, fedoco, or you're liable to find me at the end of a *calle* someday with all seven nodes shoved down my voice-hole. Katla, she was always talking about her family."

"She had family problems?"

"Not Katla, homber, not Katla!" The kid made shushing motions and Cardenas resumed listening. "She was fine. Real fine. But *tranquilo,* like I said. Not a kid anymore, not a woman yet either. But here"—he tapped the side of his head, just above where the muse strap encircled it and below the hedge of green hirsuteness—"she was metal, homber. Metal an' Muse and wetbox, you *sabe?*"

"So she was smart."

"Not just smart, fedoco. Me, maybe I'm antisoc, but I got good crunch, you know? Tightlike. But compared to Katla, me and my *compadres,* we're krill. She wasn't the one with the *problemas.* It was the rest of her family." Leaning forward, he lowered his voice to a whisper, as if some vast, ominous presence might be lurking close, watching and listening. "You ever hear of an homber named Cleator Mockerkin?"

Cardenas thought a moment before shaking his head no.

"Katla's papa. A real *carácter feo,* a bad homber, *sabe?* A *verdad* chingaringa. That's what Katla used to tell me, anyway. He—"

"Wait a minute." Cardenas's tone was compassionate as always, but it still stopped the subgrub in mid-sentence. "Are you sure? 'Cleator Mockerkin'?"

The kid did not hesitate. "Hey, fedoco, you think I could mess up a name like that?"

The Inspector persisted. "Did she ever mention a George Anderson?"

The boy's expression contorted. "Anderson? He's the homber Katla said lives with her mother. What do you know about him?"

It was a question that had been much on Cardenas's mind. One to which the details, it seemed, were not to be forthcoming from this defiant yet fearful youth. "Never mind. So Katla didn't like her papa, told you he was a *malo*. What about him? What did she tell you?"

From the start, Wild Whoh had not seemed particularly wild. Now he just looked worried. "Stuff I promised not to tell anybody else. Hoy, I know you can get a warrant for a truth pump." Manchild eyes implored the watchful interrogator. "I'm asking you not to do it, man. Don't make me ratatattle on her."

"Take it easy." Cardenas did his best to reassure the kid: as much as any federale could reassure a ninloco. "I'm asking you back, not pressing."

Whoh gazed past the Inspector, past the looming, booming mass of the Melarium, into the night. "He's rich, her papa. Dines on *dinero*. Keeps to himself. Katla, she didn' know a whole lot about his business. Sometimes, she would hear him yelling into a vorec. Bad words, homber. Sewer brew. An' not just bad nasty, but bad threatening, *sabe*? She told me he would say horrific things, make terrible threats, if he thought he wasn't getting his way. Once, she was up late and she passed by his office, and she told me she thought she heard screams from inside. Screams, and loud noises."

"What kinds of noises?" Cardenas asked patiently.

Wild Whoh thought a moment. "Like this." Bringing his right hand down, he slapped the smooth pavement hard. "Loud but muffled, like something soft and heavy hitting the ground. She ran the rest of the way to her room. This Mockerkin, he fought with her mother, too. Surtsey?" The Inspector nodded. "Used to hit her with his hands as well as with words. Katla, she said her mother told her that the words were worse than the hands. I met her mama a couple times." The kid made an automatic, perhaps unconscious, gesture that signified mildly obscene approval. "What a mira-kel, man!" He hastened to qualify the compliment. "For an old lady, I mean."

"So Mockerkin used to beat up Katla's mother. And maybe other people. Anything else? What about Katla herself?"

Whoh looked away. "I promised I wouldn't tell, man."

Cardenas could be very persuasive. He leaned forward. "Just me, homber. I promise it won't go beyond here-and-now."

Still, Whoh hesitated. Finally, he pushed his mouth closer to Cardenas's ear. What he whispered made the skin crawl on the back of the Inspector's neck. He said nothing, just listened, and when the jittery subgrub was finished, stood back and regarded the boy solemnly.

"Did she say how often it happened?"

The kid looked away. "Too often. Once a week. Sometimes more. 'Playing friendly,' she said he called it. Said being touched like that made her sick, sometimes she'd go into her bathroom and throw up. But she never told. Never.

"So you see, man," the kid continued, "why she ain't real fond of her papa. That is what it was, that made her mama decide to waft, first chance she got. Even though Katla says her mama knew this Mockerkin would explode when he found out."

"So they've been running." The ghost of a gist of an explanation for at least a few previously impenetrable imponderables began to agglutinate among the eddies of the Inspector's thoughts. "From her husband and Katla's father, this Mockerkin character."

Whoh nodded energetically. "Katla told me that her

mama worked on their leaving for over a year. She was ready to die trying rather than live with the homber one more day." He smiled knowingly, the better to impart still one more secret. " 'Course, they needed something to live on. So Katla says her mom rotoed some of Mr. Mockerkin's money."

"How much?" Cardenas prompted.

The boy shrugged. "Nonada me. I ain't sure Katla knows, either. More than a million, less than a billion. That's *todo* total she'd tell me, anyway. Just that it was a *lot*. Enough to make papa Mockerkin even madder than he was gonna be anyway, when he found out his woman and kid had wafted. The way I *miro* it, this Surtsey *chica* respirate his home life, his money, an' his respectedness. Hoy, something like that happen to me all at once, I might get a little excessive myself, *sabe*? One more thing: they didn' do the do alone. Katla says her mama had a friend who helped them. One of her papa's tightest business associates— whatever that business is, man." He shook his head. "If this chingaroon Mockerkin wasn't mad already, bein' horned by a partner with his own woman ought to be enough to push him over the ridge, don' you think?"

"So Surtsey ran off with one of Mockerkin's partners, and his daughter, *and* his money. Katla tell you who the partner was? I'm going to bet his name was George Anderson."

Wild Whoh adopted a momentary but nonetheless welcome air of superiority. "Wrong *ese*, fedoco! Me, I never met the homber. But Katla, she mentioned him once. Said he was a good friend to her and her mama before they wired in with this Anderson homber. Bummer—no, Brummel. Hoy, that was it. Wayne, I think. Wayne Brummel."

Amazing, Cardenas mused, how hour upon hour of contemplation of a jumbled gram could lead to naught but brain-strain, when all that was necessary to lucidify everything was a word or two from a jumpy subgrub. Thanks to this edgy kid, the Inspector now knew for certain who Wayne Brummel was, as well as George Anderson. They were the same man, two identities, both deceased.

It explained why Surtsey Anderson-Mockerkin had been so nervous on the vor with Cardenas. It lucidified why she had never shown up at the morgue. It told him why her seemingly ordinary, unremarkable inurban home had been converted into an elaborate, robotized, highly adaptable bomb. She didn't fear the police. She didn't fear burglars, or wandering perverts. She feared, indeed was terrified of, the husband she had left behind.

Of course, it could be that George Anderson-Brummel had simply taken a wrong turn on a damp night, only to be vaped by a gang of roving ninlocos out in search of an easy target. His death might be coincidental, nothing more than another sorry-sad statistic on the evening's police tally. Obviously, Surtsey did not think that was the case. Daughter in tow, she'd wafted, ambulated, made herself indisposed.

Which, if George Anderson-Brummel had been confronted by the kind of humanoids someone like this Cleator Mockerkin could put on long-term lease, was probably a most sensible thing to do. It was not Angel Cardenas's job to find out which was the one true truth—but he had entered too far into the circumstancia now to back out with his conscience, far less his sense of professionalism, intact.

He dug deep inside one of his coat's interior pockets. Fishing out a wafer, he passed it through his spinner, performing a single perfunctory operation. Then he handed it to the subgrub.

"Take this down to Nogales Central. Or if you, um, have

reasons not to want to go there yourself, have someone else take it for you. Get it to Contraband Operations, third level. Tell them I gave this to you—it's ident stamped—and hand it to the officer on duty. They'll fetch you your Seventh Node from Property." When the staring, uncomprehending kid failed to respond, Cardenas added helpfully, "For your belt. I keep my promises." With that, he turned to go.

"Hoy!" Looking back, the Inspector saw the still-dazed subgrub staring after him. "You sure you a fedoco, homber?"

Cardenas smiled pleasantly. "We don't all of us look down on your kind as trash-wash, Wild. Me, I'm stuck with this conviction that there's a salvageable human being inside every corpus." His smile widened slightly. "No matter how many miragoos they think they have to wear to look *vacán*." He resumed his stride.

FIVE

OF MORE SIGNIFICANCE EVEN THAN THE
information he had gleaned from the street nin was that Fredoso Hyaki was awake, alert, and had been shunted out of
IC. Cardenas found him floating in a gel bath, looking for
all the world like a paralyzed gerbil trapped in the middle
of a giant pudding. While the medicated gel would slowly
permeate his flesh and help his entire body to heal, its real
job was to accelerate the regrowth of his normal epidermis
beneath the filmy protective coating of artificial skin. It was
cool, and soothing to the point where the injured sergeant
looked almost comfortable.

Almost.

An attached web of tubes still cycled food and its after-
products, though one positioned near his head provided ice
water and fruit juice he could actually take by mouth. As
Cardenas entered, Hyaki murmured a command and one of
the feeders entered his mouth. The Inspector waited until
his friend and partner had finished sipping before moving
into the sergeant's field of vision.

"Always room for Jell-O, I see."

Prevented by subtle, flexible supports from slowly sink-
ing to the bottom of the burn tank, Hyaki was still able to

turn his head far enough to focus on the speaker. "I like it better with some fruit, though I guess if you're swimming in it instead of eating it, you're better off with the pure stuff." He smiled, though not as readily as usual. "I'll never look at the La Brea Tar Pits again with quite the same detachment." The smile faded. "What happened?"

"The Anderson residence was jig-timed. You ended up wearing a lot of it."

"Let me guess." The wide body stirred ever so slightly within the gelatin bath. "You intuited what was going to happen, and that's why you're still walking around flashing that hangdog grin of yours while I'm stuck in this bowl of antiseptic-flavored flan with the mother of all sunburns."

"Yeah, that's it," Cardenas shot back. "I like getting blown up so much I thought I'd wait until the last minute so I could get a good whiff of cordite." His expression turned serious. "You doing all right?"

Hyaki's expression reflected his distaste. "Two thousand three hundred and sixty-two channels, and not a damn thing worth watching. You find mother and daughter Anderson yet?"

"No, but I found out some other things." He proceeded to enlighten the sergeant on the results of his investigating. When he had finished, the big man started to nod, winced, and lay still.

"Sounds like the motivation was something more than your standard-issue case of domestic abuse."

"No *mierde*," the Inspector agreed. "If this mama Surtsey is as experienced at hiding from her husband as it would appear, she's not going to be easy to find. It's not hard to lose oneself in the Strip. Especially if you've got enough cred—and are frightened enough."

"She won't put the girl back in a soche. Not for a while,

anyway. After the business with the house, they'll go even further underground than they were before." Hyaki went quiet for a moment. "I hope you find 'em before her ex-husband does."

Cardenas nodded gravely. He felt very strongly that if they did not, the discovery-recovery might prove even more disconcerting than it had been for a certain George Anderson-Brummel.

"I wish they'd let me out of here. I'd really like to help on this one." Hyaki flashed the wonderful faux Buddha smile that enchanted children and reassured women. "I don't hold anything against the mother and daughter. It was the house that did this to me—not them."

The Inspector leaned over the tank. "You're not going anywhere until you get your back back. I'll keep you posted." He turned to go.

"Hoy, Angel!" Cardenas looked back. "You know the worst thing about being stuck here like this?" The Inspector shook his head, and his partner explained mournfully, "I hate Jell-O."

It did not take a lot of crunch nor require the services of a box tunneler to access information on Cleator Mockerkin. There was more in the restricted macrolice file than Cardenas cared to know.

The man's present whereabouts were uncertain, although he was known to frequent residences in Greater Miami, Lala, Nawlins, and Harlingen. That was hardly surprising. A man like Mockerkin would have many enemies and friends beyond those bought and paid for. By all accounts he was a thoroughly unpleasant character: his rap sheet comprised a copious and detailed catalog of antisoc activities ranging from petty theft as a subgrub to embezzlement, arson-for-hire, assault with and without a deadly weapon, extortion, sexual abuse, up to and including no less than three arrests for murder—one direct and two for hire. Although he had done three separate stints in stir, none had been for any of the significant felonies with which he had been charged.

Interestingly, he was also charged with illegal weapons procurement. This indictment stemmed from his involvement in the Paraguayan Rebellions of '69 and '71. Principally through numerous contacts in Central and South America, he had grown wealthy enough to buy off or dispose of his most serious rivals. Worse still, he was able to afford that bane of all hard-working, honest cops: lawyers whose courtroom skills were inversely proportional to their moral sense. If his sheet was to be believed, he should be in jail right now.

In addition to the long stat list, there were some vit clips. In the privacy of his office cubicle, Cardenas played them back over and over. In surveillance and courtroom recordings, they showed a tall, well-tanned individual slightly younger than the Inspector, with very blond hair cut short, a muscular upper torso, and a small, tight mouth that opened only to talk, never to smile or to frown or show expression of any kind. The courtroom vits were especially interesting. Mockerkin had one of those voices that was traditionally referred to as an "acid tongue." Even his casual asides to his lawyers or supporters were tinged with venom. Surprisingly literate, his performance on the stand was characterized by a highly developed sense of sarcasm that would have done justice to a right-wing political pundit. The source of his sobriquet, among law enforcement and underworld representatives alike, was instantly apparent.

In the course of his career Cardenas had personally made

the acquaintance of more than one skew-level antisoc.
There was Little Napoleon, and Tipo Repo. There was Fre-
gado Freddy and Azina the Legs, Marianne Molto and Johnni
Half-Face, The Zipper and Gordo Carlos. To this long litany
of antisocs could now be added Cleator Mockerkin—alias
The Mocker. The Mock, for convenience. It suited the man,
the Inspector decided as he reran the vit file. An antisoc as
personally unpleasant as he was successful, and dangerously smart. Not the sort of individual you would want to
cross. In running off with his woman, his daughter, and his
money, his former associate Wayne Brummel had shown
considerable *huevos*.

Or exceptional stupidity.

How much of it had been Brummel-Anderson's idea,
Cardenas wondered, and how much Surtsey Anderson-
Mockerkin's? Successfully eluding the attention of someone like Mockerkin would take time and planning. By all
accounts, Mockerkin's ex-wife was sufficiently attractive,
and clever, to have carried off the flight without help. Had
she wanted a little extra protection around, for herself and
her daughter, or had she really been in love with the unfortunate Brummel? There were only two people who could
answer that question. One of them was dead, vacced and
drac'd, and the other was on a *serioso* waft.

Avoiding The Mock's skills and reach would likely en-
tail a good deal of moving around. Cardenas suspected that
if he checked the Assessor's records, he would find that the
Anderson family had not occupied their recently annihi-
lated habitation for very long. How long, exactly, the three
of them had been on the run he did not yet know. But he
would find out. Doubtless their change of residence coin-
cided with a corresponding alteration of identity.

One thing he was able to infer, if not technically intuit,

from the available information was the nature of the deceased Anderson-Brummel's occupation. He was a promoter, all right. He had promoted himself into Surtsey Mockerkin's confidence, promoted himself into The Mock's missing money, and promoted himself into at least half a dozen illicit meat banks in this segment of the Strip, where his assorted hastily appropriated body parts would fetch a good price. His death would not be enough to satisfy someone like Mockerkin, Cardenas knew. The Mock would not be content until the absent components of his runaway family were returned to him. In that event, Katla Mockerkin would probably survive unharmed. Physically, anyway.

The Inspector did not dwell on what such a resolution might mean for Surtsey Mockerkin. He had dealt with too many men like Cleator Mockerkin to hold any illusions about how they treated women who betrayed them. The Namerican Federal Police needed to find her, and her daughter, fast, before they were run down by The Mock's minions. It was too bad, he reflected, that those as yet unknown and unidentified individuals had not entered the abandoned Anderson house ahead of himself and Hyaki.

Now mother and daughter were on the run again. Presumably by themselves this time. He doubted someone as adroit as Surtsey Mockerkin would let more than one outsider into her confidence. With their male buffer gone, she would have to do everything by herself. As for Katla, in addition to those talents Cardenas had already learned she possessed, he now added the quality of resilience.

As he was pondering the shimmering depths of the box tunnel hovering over the far side of his desk, a note popped up in the lower right-hand corner. The Captain wanted to see him. Cardenas smiled inwardly. Very little got past

Pangborn. The higher-profile the case, the more the Inspector's superior's ass itched. If he was following this one, Cardenas knew he must be scratching like mad.

He saved the augmented macrolice, shut down the vit, and headed upstairs.

Shaun Pangborn had an office. Not a cubicle, not a subdiv sec of multiuse floor: a real office. From its location on the next-to-the-top floor of the Federal Police Headquarters, Nogales Division (the top floor being armored and reserved for ballistics and rapid-reaction deployment via chopter and vertiprop), a visitor could see halfway across the Strip, past office towers and green-garbed codos, past humming maquiladoras and malls, and dream of the distant cool waters of the Golfo California.

The Inspector settled into a chair opposite. He liked Pangborn, and the Captain liked him. They had a lot in common besides age and experience. For one thing, neither was wholly original. Both men sported replacement parts: Cardenas his eyes, Pangborn part of an ear—and other more sensitive areas everyone knew about but were careful not to allude to in his presence. They were senior federales, with a shared sense of right, wrong, and what maybe perhaps possibly sometimes could be done about it.

Neither, however, was an innocent. They knew they could not eliminate evil, only mitigate it. In the Strip, sometimes that was enough.

"Got a traba-job for you, Angel." Pangborn was studying a heads-up suspended to his right. From where he was sitting, Cardenas could not make out the details. "Over in Sanjuana. Branch of Macrovendi EU, Milan—you know that outfit?—is screaming because somebody's spazzing half their new mollyspheres before they can be inserted in their new senseware. Since their organic burrowers have come up with nothing, they've come hat in hand begging the help of the lowly federales." He waved a hand through the heads-up, temporarily distorting the carefully collated aura. "I thought maybe you'd like a few days at the beach. Do a little burrowing for Macrovendi, locus their compromise, issue a couple of warrants. The Department can always use some good PR."

Cardenas smiled diffidently. "If it's all the same to you, Shaun, I'd just as soon stay here and follow through on what I'm working on right now."

Frowning, Pangborn ablaed the heads-up away. In response to his verbal command, the informational wraith vanished from above the desk. "Chinga, Angel. Half the people in the Department know about the Macrovendi assignment, and for the last couple of days it seems like every one of them has been kissing my *nacha* trying to get it." He gestured expansively. "I offer it to you on a plate, and you come back at me with a no-thanks."

Cardenas shrugged. He could be as parsimonious with words as with his salary.

"That's neither answer nor explanation." Irritated, Pangborn summoned forth the heads-up on the other side of the desk. Commanding it, he examined the results intently, squinting at the display. After a couple of minutes, with the call-up still occupying virtual space on the side of his desk, he turned back to his visitor.

"Tell me, Angel: what's so special about this affair? I grant you there are some interesting characters involved, but the details suggest that the explanations are rote. Wife runs off with a big chunk of the husband's money, one of his partners, and their kid." He glanced briefly back at the heads-up. "Sure, given his record, it'd be a nice little coup to pin some pintatime on this Mockerkin culo. But this is scut work and track, follow-up and simple addition. Any junior officer can handle it."

"There's a homicide involved," Cardenas pointed out.

Pangborn rolled his eyes. "Ordinary revenge killing. Nothing out of the ordinary. From the particulars on the deceased Anderson-Brummel, I doubt that soche-at-*grande* has suffered any great loss. Let somebody else handle it. Go to Sanjuana, take a week burrowing for Macrovendi, spend some time on the beach miraing the *chicas*." He lowered his voice conspiratorially. "There's room in Accounting for a little drift. I think we can get you into the Coronado. As for this standard-issue sorryness"—he indicated the read-only that gleamed within the heads-up—"I'll put Gonzalez or Rutland on it."

Cardenas did not like to argue with Pangborn. The Captain was one of the very few in the Department who could almost understand what it was like to be an intuit. Almost.

"I really want to see this case through to conclusion, Shaun. As Senior Inspector, I can cogit some fluence."

Pangborn looked sad. "I guess it's true what happens when people start to get old. They suffer these attacks of dementia; mild at first, slowly evolving into episodes of insanity that eventually start to opaque their thinking." He sat back in his chair, which sighed appreciatively. "Either that, or you're being more than typically pig-headed. But then, you know that I'm just slagging you, and that I'm going to let you swim in your chosen slime. Don't you?"

Cardenas grinned. "Of course I do." And he was not lying.

When Pangborn rose, the Inspector stood with him. The two senior officers walked to the door of the Captain's office. "After thirty years on the force there are two things I've learned." Pangborn fingered his artificial ear, the one

whose prosthetic did not properly match the original carti-
lage. "Don't try to talk sense to someone who's spizzing on
sparkle, and never play poker with an intuit." He rested a
hand on the Inspector's shoulder. "Do me a favor, will you?
Wind this up as fast as you can and try not to get vaped in
the process."

Cardenas advanced far enough for the door to respond to
his presence, identify him, and open. "I'll try. Dying always
complicates an investigation."

"Not to mention the added paperwork." Pangborn dismissed him with a wave of mock annoyance. "I'll send
Gonzalez to Sanjuana. He can sneak his new bride along.
Put them up at the Coronado for a few days, and he'll raise
an icon to me." His tone grew more somber. "Watch yourself, Angel. I'm not concerned about the usual rent-a-
cutioner. But my read on this Mockerkin is—cautionary."

"Same here. Thanks, Shaun."

Cardenas felt no sense of triumph as he departed the division Captain's office. Only quiet satisfaction that he was
going to be allowed to continue with the assignment he had
set for himself. He felt he owed it to Hyaki. He felt he
needed it for himself. And for some reason as yet undeter-
mined, he felt he owed it to someone he had yet to meet.

A twelve-year-old girl named Katla Mockerkin.

The more he learned about The Mock, the less he liked
the man. What available information there was had to be
scrounged from the depths of the central Namerican macrolice box. There was next to nothing in the popular media.
Clearly, Cleator Mockerkin was one of those insidiously intelligent antisocs who neither needed nor wanted his picture
flashed on the evening cast, prizing anonymity alongside
power.

And power he had. Over the course of the next couple of days, Cardenas tied fiscal links to The Mock that crossed half a hundred boxlines girdling the globe. In addition to dealing in illegal weaponry on an impressive scale, Mockerkin drew revenue from trade in banned designer pharmaceuticals, siphoned crunch, endangered species (foodstuffs as well as the illegal pet business), and prohibited wafers and mollys. This income was supplemented with money from more mundane activities like extortion and kidnapping. None of it was kosh, all of it was stylishly laundered, and there was enough of it floating around to tempt even a knowledgeable subordinate who should have known better like the late Wayne Brummel.

A meticulously diversified feleon was The Mock. A real *verdad* nasty-ass chingaroon. If his disciples caught up with the fleeing Surtsey and Katla before the authorities did, Cardenas knew the upshot would not be acrimonious debate followed by a succession of mutually agreed-upon visits to a marriage counselor. About the daughter he could not surmise, but he seriously doubted that Surtsey Mockerkin was getting much sleep these days.

Following long hours spent staring at info, he relaxed by striding the streets of the Strip at night, his dark eyes flicking from side to side and taking everything in as he walked off the energy that built up during the day. He paid little attention to the gaudy displays, the glittering municipal art works, or the persistent adverts. People were what interested him; the bustling inhabitants of the Strip in all their manifold musky ethnicity, a potpourri of colors, sizes, and shapes. In this, the commercial center of the western hemisphere, a casual listener could snak yakk of several dozen languages and dialects, from Azeri to Zulu, in addition to the predominating Spanish and English. Underlying it all, like a set of conversational box springs, was the provincial patois of the Strip—the jumpy, jerky hybrid argot known as Spang, for English-Spanish slang.

Cardenas could volubate with the best of them. His fluency was a frequent surprise to the ninlocos and algaeaters he often had to deal with. What he could not inflect, he inferred—one of the benefits of being an intuit.

Why hadn't he taken Pangborn up on his offer? He was as fond of Sanjuana's beaches as the next indigene. The Captain had been perfectly correct that the business of the puzzling Anderson-Brummel-Mockerkin axis could be dealt with by junior inspectors. Was Cardenas, after all, the secret masochist that some of his younger colleagues suspected? It wasn't as if he was angling for a promotion. In the last five years he'd turned down half a dozen higher-paying (and far less risky) admin posts.

Seguro sure, he loved the Strip, with its noise and flair and surprises and the constant, never-ending action that was missing from his own life. But that was not explanation enough. Nor was his lack of a stable home life, although his recent relationship with the GenDyne designer Hypatia Spango had lasted longer than most. Maybe it was because he lavished the love he carried around like carefully guarded baggage on kids like Wormy G and Bac-a-ran and, most recently, Wild Whoh. *They* were his family. Where most federales gave out only citations, Angel Cardenas also dispensed hope. There were subgrubs and nins and orphanos out there he hadn't even met yet, and all of them doubtless deserving of salvation.

It was not only possible, but highly probable, that Katla Mockerkin was one of them, and he knew full well that any junior inspectors assigned to the case were unlikely to dispense their actions in light of that distinct possibility. Cardenas did not have to intuit the girl to know that she was worth protecting. He needed only to know that she was a seemingly normal twelve-year-old who had the misfortune to find herself caught between a duplicitous if protective mother and a corrupt, intimidating father.

Beyond The Mock's inner circle and the Namerican Federal Police, he did not expect anyone to be much interested in, far less know of, the circumstances surrounding Surtsey and Katla Mockerkin's frantic flight from the peaceful surrounds of Olmec inurb. So he was more than a little surprised when, finishing his dinner on the patio of the Tchere-cheri Restaurant down the street from his codo, he was approached by a tottering masque in human form from which issued the whispery phrase, "Follow me, *sí* see, fedoco, if you'd still like to dock The Mock." The gaunt figure did not stop, but continued to lurch down the pedestrian street like some psychotic scarecrow fled in secret from its farm of birth.

The fluid outlines of the morphmasque rippled with every step the camouflaged figure took. Hastily settling his bill, Cardenas followed in its wake. Without a clear view of the masque's owner, he could not even be certain if it was a man or woman who shambled along beneath the ever-shifting veil. When it turned down an alley lit only by the diffuse glow from the remaining phototropic paint that covered the surrounding walls, the Inspector hesitated. It was difficult enough to try and intuit the intentions of someone cloaked by a masque without the added burden of trying to do so in the dark.

But whoever was stumbling along beneath the fabric facade knew of his interest in Cleator Mockerkin. As that interest was something less than common knowledge, Cardenas was quietly burning to learn how his unseen guide had become aware of it. Also, it had, or claimed to have, information. Trailing the figure deeper into the alley, the Inspector let one hand cradle the frac he always carried in his right-hand pants pocket. It was capable of stunning a small mob; he did not doubt its ability to incapacitate one wandering masque, no matter how spizzed its owner might happen to be.

Near the end of the passage, the figure turned. Its appearance was now that of a tall, handsome young man. The scene was so quiet you could hear the condensation drip from the arterial network of conduits that served the buildings' air-conditioning systems. No water actually reached the ground, of course. Within the Strip, casual evaporation of recyclable water resources was a crime punishable, if not by law, then by the severe opprobrium of one's neighbors.

The morphmasque suddenly flared, and the image of a young man turned into that of a slender middle-aged woman. The Inspector's fingers tightened around the frac. But the display was a prelude to dialogue, not a threat. For a moment, Cardenas was afraid he had been lured sideways simply to view some adverts. If so, he had to admire the masquer's gall.

No, that couldn't be right, he told himself. The unseen wanderer knew of his interest in The Mock.

"You going to talk, *compadre,* or just flash me?"

The owner of the masque shuddered slightly, though whether from the effects of sparkle, degeneration, or laughter, Cardenas could not intuit. Young man became middle-aged woman became teenage ninloco became white-robed saint as multiple identities morphed rapidly before the Inspector's eyes. Having watched morphmasquing in action before, he had only a cursory interest in the process of shell-shifting. "You want to dock The Mock. The Turtle heard."

At least now it had a name, the Inspector reflected. "How do you know that?"

Continuously reinventing themselves, lights and land-scapes undulated across the masque; the inverse of camou-flage. The unseen owner became a street light, a postbox, a charging station and an altar, and, perhaps most tellingly, a garbage bin. "When you turn *tortuga,* you learn how to lis-ten. I hear things on the backStrip, I do." The quavering voice grew louder. "Things they say, 'That intuit who's straight, he wants to know about The Mock's woman.' " Cardenas tensed slightly. "Your rep precedes you, fedoco."

The Inspector ignored the compliment. "What do you know about Surtsey and Katla Mockerkin? Are they all right? Are they still in the Strip?"

The masque became a flickering bipedal pillar of crack-ling lights and spinning optos. "It's caramba time, fedoco. *Tiempo* tempo. Time for all turtles to find a hole to crawl into and be very still." The trembling intensified. That re-action Cardenas could interpret: this would-be informer was scared. Scared bad, right down to the bottom of his masque's swaddling skirt.

"I won't involve you. What do you want?"

"For the sequence? *Nada,* homber. But The Turtle has suffered too much *tampo tiempo.* Too much time in jail." The figure morphed into a quite detailed image of a narrow, barred cell. "Next time I'm in dock, maybe I call on my good *compadre* Cardenas the intuit, and they cut me a crease, you know so?" Again the serious shudder. "In Rehab they take away your shell!"

Trying to envision what lay beneath the morphmasque, Cardenas realized he still could not tell if the speaker was male or female. "You can always find me through the NFP box. I never forget a friend." He moved a little closer until the masque, now presenting the likeness of a small horse standing on its hind legs, flailed warningly with its front feet and flared a nervous red. "What about The Mock's family?"

"There's yakk on the backStrip." Beneath the masque, something shrugged. It might have been a shoulder. "You need to visit a certain infomaniac." The voice fell slightly. "You *sabe* Mocceca's Mall?"

Cardenas nodded. "I know where it is."

"In the back back past the bake rack. Talk to the Indian[2]. He'll know." Turning, the ungainly figure abruptly bolted from the alley.

"Wait!" The Inspector hurried after him. "One more question!"

He slowed when he reached the street. A few curious pedestrians glanced in his direction. Their stares did not linger. Cardenas was not in uniform. In the absence of NFP turquoise blue, he was not readily identifiable as an officer of the law. That meant he could be an officer of something else, so citizens did not stare. At night, even in well-traveled parts of the Strip, a lingering gaze was not a prudent accoutrement.

Of The Turtle, there was no sign. It might already have crossed the street, or entered a nearby building. Or he/she could be standing a foot or two away from Cardenas. The morphmasque would allow its denizen to blend in indistinguishably with its surroundings. A morph was not as sophisticated as an al-Levi military chameleon suit, but in an urban environment, it was effective enough.

He checked his ident. It was still early, although the time mattered only to him. Playplaces like Mocceca's stayed open 24/7, and no time off for good behavior. As he headed north, in the direction of the nearest public induction tube, he found himself pondering the identity of the individual who had been identified to him by The Turtle. Cardenas knew plenty of Indians. But an Indian "squared"? That was an ethnic description that was new to him. Did the designation refer to the indicated individual's shape, or his mindset?

Damn morphmasque, he muttered to himself as he lengthened his stride. You couldn't intuit through the damn thing, any more than you could see through a turtle's shell. Which, of course, was the intent of both kinds of animals.

SIX

MOCCECA'S MALL WAS BUT ONE OF TWO DOZEN interconnected commercial sites that occupied a peninsula jutting out into the shallow body of water that had been euphemistically named by its developers Lake Fox. That there had never been a lake in the sandy depression until its developers had contracted for it to be filled with recycled effluent did not trouble the owners. Such was the name-game of enthusiastic property mavens. The two artificial islands in the center of the lake had been given over to recreational ends, and were inhabited by robot foxes that energetically hunted robot mice. The real rats that had arrived to join them ignored their scentless mechanical counterparts as they patrolled the shore for tadpoles, frogs, fish, and the detritus of human fast food that eventually washed up on the islands' shores. It was an irony of contemporary life that the wrappers of hamburger and tostada, noodle and pizza, biodegraded faster than the scraps of food that adhered to them, for which the real rodents, as opposed to the automatonic ones, were ever grateful.

Like its companion malls, Mocceca's was a garish, brassy architectural album of small shops designed to appeal to visitors and residents alike. Within the one- and two-story faux

Mexican village and Indian pueblo buildings could be found quaint regional eateries, fast food restaurants, clothing boutiques, stim dispensers, demo outlets for the major box distributors, and, if one knew how and where to look, less savory entertainments and goods that bordered on antisoc.

A few casual inquiries were sufficient to guide Cardenas to the *comercio* of the proprietor known colloquially as Indian^2. The reason for the unusual designation became clear as soon as the Inspector entered the souvenir shop and introduced himself to the owner. Behind the counter, Mashupo Mingas displayed pictures of his Hindu mother and Zuni father. He was not twice-Indian, boasting lineage from two tribes, but Indian squared, with parents from opposite sides of the world. As an ethnic background it was distinctive, but not exceptional. Not in these days of massive migrations of human beings from every corner of every continent. It was, however, a combination the Inspector had not previously encountered in person.

Mingas remained cordial even after Cardenas revealed himself as a representative of the NFP. Slight but sinewy of build, he smiled readily as he pointed out the attractions of his *comercio,* which ranged from attractive canvases of southwestern scenes that glowed with the light of their quantum bead paint, to cheap, hoary traditional tourist take-homes like scorpions and tarantulas embedded in Lucite paperweights. As the taking of live desert arachnids was proscribed, the highly detailed creatures were sterile clones raised exclusively for the souvenir trade. There were also vits for sale, and map wafers, and an impressive range of regional foodstuffs, many boasting highly imaginative and often humorous packaging. A small porch out back was set with a pair of tables and chairs, where patrons could sit and sip drinks while gazing out at the distant islands and their robot foxes. A well-dressed Amerind couple was there now, their attention focused on the lake.

As he chatted with his visitor, Mingas was working his way through a Pilly sandwich. The Strip delicacy was a Philly cheesesteak served with red and yellow chilies instead of the usual onions, and jalapeño cheese in place of Swiss. Grease stained the self-heating wrapping. A brown droplet clung stubbornly to the shopkeeper's lower lip.

"So what can I sell you, Inspector-sir? A nice picture of the Golfo?" Moving out from behind the counter, he indicated a row of imitation Zuni fetish necklaces. Instead of small animals strung on silver and carved from turquoise and jasper and other semiprecious stones, these were garlanded with glowing plastic reproductions. Each fingernail-sized creature boasted a tiny, glowing LED eye or two. "See," Mingas pitched, "when you touch it, each fetish makes the cry of the particular animal being portrayed." He demonstrated by gently squeezing a miniature bear between thumb and finger. Through the necklace's integrated playback unit, it promptly emitted a terse, muted growl.

"Very clever. I'll take this one." The Inspector's response brought a look of satisfaction to Mingas's face. Hypatia would get a kick out of it, Cardenas decided. Sure, it was touristy, but it was cleverly designed and reasonably well-made. Probably factured right here in the Strip, in one of the giant souvenir workshops that tended to congregate in the Palenque industrial subdivision.

As Mingas ran the box containing the necklace through the gift wrapper, cocooning it in prismatic plastic, Cardenas amused himself by examining a rotating display wheel stocked with holos. "There's something else I'd like to buy."

Eagerness suffused the shopkeeper's voice. "If I don't have it, I can get it in on twenty-four-hour notice, sir."

Cardenas did not look away from the holos. "An acquaintance told me a busybody infomaniac like yourself might know something of the present whereabouts of a woman and her daughter named Surtsey and Katla Mockerkin."

Mingas finished wrapping the necklace, handed it over. "Here you are, Inspector-sir. No charge." His tone had become stilted, his smile forced. "I am a most firm believer in supporting my local police."

Now Cardenas did turn away from the holo rack. His eyes bored into those of the proprietor and his words grew clipped. "If you know anything about me, then you know that I'm in-to-it. That means I can tell when someone is holding back on me. I don't have time to backandforth with you. The two women are in real danger, and I have to find them before her ex-husband does. One person has already died. George Anderson, also known as Wayne Brummel. The man she was living with. That's one too many."

Mingas looked away. "I don't know anything about what you are talking about, Inspector-sir."

"You're lying."

"That is not a crime." Mingas remained defiant. "If you believe that one person dead is one too many, consider that my own death would make you feel twice as bad."

Cardenas cast a perfunctory glance over his shoulder. "There's nobody here but tourists and local cleanies. The girl is twelve and hasn't harmed a soul. I'd like to see her, at least, safe and *seguro*."

"I know my rights. You cannot arrest me for pleading ignorance." Mingas stared back at him.

"No, I can't. But I can for something else." Cardenas started to draw his spinner. "Give me a couple of minutes."

It was a contest of wills the shopkeeper was preordained to lose. Mingas slumped. "I like to listen to things. People, adverts, vit clips, waftwire. All kinds of things." He was apologizing for a legal but socially disreputable addiction. "A place like the Mocceca is perfect for that."

Cardenas paid for the necklace. "What have you heard? Do you have any idea where they might be now?"

The proprietor glanced out his rear window. The young Amerind couple sitting at one of the porch tables were intent on their drinks, their snakesnacks, the view across the lake, and each other. Not once had they looked away from one another to peer into the shop. Mingas lowered his voice anyway.

"The lady and her daughter could be anywhere. I have no idea where, or if, they are. There's vapor about them, that's all. Gazehaze. But this woman's toyman Anderson, the dead one?" Cardenas nodded encouragingly. "He had a rep for throwing lots of credit around, and not always with his lady. Vapor is that he was a habitual at half a dozen sextels from Agua Pri to Sonoyta." Mingas leaned closer. "Vapor says he had one special *seguro* in his stable. Hooker named Coy Joy, who pines her bliss regular at a registered copulation citadel called the Cocktale."

"I can find it," Cardenas murmured dispassionately.

"Find it by yourself, sir." Mingas moved back behind the counter, as if it could somehow shield him from the Inspector's penetrating gaze, and from a category of perception people knew about but did not understand. "But however you do, please do not mention me or my business."

"What establishment?" Cardenas picked up the packaged necklace and left as quietly as he had come.

The fact that the Cocktale was registered made it easy to find. It was one of a dozen similar establishments scattered among bars, love shops, and restaurants that featured private booths with accessories far more sophisticated than salt and pepper shakers. There were also a couple of sanctioned gloomers. The latter did not advertise their presence, but those in need of their special services knew how and where to find them. Designed to accommodate heavy hitters, they provided a safe place for users to indulge their addictions without fear of hurting themselves or any innocent citizens. A client could bring his own paraphernalia, or rent. Same went for the hit of choice. Designer straitjackets were available in all sizes, or custom-fitted.

Compared to the wary atmosphere that hung over the gloomers, the sextels were positively sedate. Within the individual or group rooms that honeycombed the larger establishments, Cardenas knew, the ambiance would be another matter. There, colors and sounds and scents would fill the air, suffusing the senses with an aura of unhindered and unrestrained desire. Or one could liberate oneself in surroundings that reeked of quiet tradition. Whatever a customer wanted, the sextels were ready to supply. There were still some things, Cardenas reflected, that could never be simulated no matter what grams or how much crunch your home box had at its disposal.

The induction tube had deposited him just outside the Sexxone. On one side of the station stretched a row of maquiladoras, within whose regimented bowels the evening shift was still laboring away. Exiting, the workers could go home, have something to eat, or indulge in more lubricious pursuits according to individual tastes. Cardenas headed in the opposite direction from the station. According to his spinner, the Cocktale was located at the far end of the xone.

It was busy, though the real crush would come when there was a shift change at one of the nearby assembly plants. Better to find the woman he sought before her schedule was booked. That was assuming, he knew, that she was onsite now. Just like the maquiladora plants, the amative establishments that served their employees operated on a twenty-four-hour work schedule.

A detour heads-up appeared in front of him. Following its instructions, he turned down a side walkway. He had gone less than twenty meters before it struck him that something was not as it should be with his fellow pedestrians. Probably no one else would have noticed it. But an intuit's schooling involved the sharpening of all the senses, not just those commonly employed by a fellow human.

The people moving around him, enjoying the warm evening air, looked normal, acted normal, sounded normal. Only one component of normalcy, in fact, was missing.

None of them smelled.

Stopping, he reached out to grab the arm of a solitary, well-dressed oldster who was heading in the opposite direction. His fingers closed around a fistful of air. At the same time, the old man smiled wickedly at him—and vanished. So did the couple approaching from behind. So did the walls, and street, and the glowing signs advertising the delights of the amatory establishments he was passing.

Except—he was not passing well-lit public businesses. He was not on a designated detour, but in an alley. Not proceeding according to a route prescribed by the department of public works, but heading down an increasingly narrow and isolated serviceway that was little more than a crack between buildings. The detour was an illusion. A very adroit one at that, he reflected as he turned to retrace his steps. Nothing more than an expensive miragoo.

The woman holding the projector that she had just switched off slipped it into the small pack that rode on her back. Silver-and-niobium earrings jangled softly as she brushed long black hair away from her face. Standing next to her was a second Amerind, a tall male. The headband encircling his forehead and holding back his dark hair flashed a steady stream of readily recognizable, three-dimensional southwestern symbols. Reaching up, he idly brushed the tips of his fingers across one side of the band.

Harmless, virtually touristic symbols for rain, for the four sacred plants (corn, beans, squash, and tobacco), for lightning and for thunder, for Mother Earth and Father Sky, abruptly gave way to an ominous mélange of glowing lines of lightning crossed with knives, spears, lasers—all dripping ethereally luminous blood. Cardenas recognized the symbols immediately. The man and woman were Inzini—the Southwest Amerindian equivalent of the Japanese Yakuza or the Italian Mafia.

Begun as a pseudo-religious organization back around the turn of the century, they had spread their influence throughout the Four Corners area and beyond, riding a wave of prosperity and illegal income born of the explosive development of the Strip. Disdaining Yakuza-style tattoos in favor of far more modern and flexible projectible symbology, they were deeply involved in illegal immigration, credit laundering, trade in endangered species, and half a dozen other antisoc activities. Essentially leaderless and free-wafting, they had proven exceptionally difficult for the NFP to suppress. Known in Navajo as the *hooghan haz'ánígíí nít'chi bee tíníziinii*, or "family of evil spirits," friends and enemies alike called them simply the Inzini.

The pistol in the man's hand was not as versatile as the one Cardenas wore in his shoulder holster. It could not dissemble, mask, or drug a target. Packing explosive shells, it could only kill. The assassin was ready to use it, the Inspector knew. He did not have to wonder. Intent and capability were amply evident in every facet of the man's posture, in his respiration, in his eyes.

"That's an expensive little toy," he began conversationally, referring to the portable projector the woman had just put away. "Usually they don't fool me, but I was preoccupied."

"Don't move," the man ordered him. "Raise your hands and put them on top of your head. Don't lock the fingers. If you reach inside your jacket or your pants, I'll kill you. If you move to touch your jacket or your pants, I'll kill you. Keep your movements slow and steady. Don't touch one leg with the other."

As he spoke, the woman had drawn a weapon of her own. Approaching Cardenas, she gave him a thorough pat-down, removing first his own gun and then his spinner. She proceeded to check the latter.

"It's open, but only sending location. He didn't have a chance to get anything off," she told her companion. As Cardenas looked on, she slapped a para-site over the unit and used it to finger in instructions. When she had finished her work, she slipped the device back into Cardenas's pocket. She did not smile. "The override gram I entered will tell your station monitor that everything's fine and normal for the next hour. Things will stay that way in actuality as long as you cooperate."

"What do you want?"

"You're NFP."

He nodded. "Inspector Angel Cardenas. I wish I could say it was a pleasure to meet you, Mr. and Ms. . . . ?"

The man gestured in the direction of the real street. "You spent some time talking with a shop owner in Mocceca's Mall. We have just come from there, where we had a short— chat—with him." Mention of the recently visited shopkeeper jogged Cardenas's memory. He recognized them now: they were the same couple who had been sitting on the porch behind Mashupo Mingas's shop.

While he had been interviewing the shopkeeper, they had been watching him.

"We know that you are in charge of the search for a woman named Surtsey Mockerkin, who is wafting with her daughter. Please tell us what the proprietor of the shop told you. If you will do that for us, we will just lie you down for half a day. Straight narcolep, nothing serious or addictive." He indicated the building to their left. "This is a comfortable place. We'll rent you a day room and inform the establishment's administrator that you are sleeping off a good time. No one will bother you. When you wake up, you'll feel more rested than you have been in weeks, and no harm done. By then we will have completed our follow-up on the information you provide and gone on our way."

The muzzle of the compact pistol shifted slightly. "If you do not tell us what we want to know, I will have to begin shooting your various appendages. Eventually, you will tell us. Why not spare yourself the pain and physical damage and save my ammunition?"

It was a nice speech, Cardenas thought. Intended to be reassuring. Except that it was a serene, efficiently delivered lie. As soon as they had the information they sought, they would kill him. Having made no effort to conceal their faces, they could not let him live to report their actions and presence. He would be shot and left in the alley to be scavenged, just as Wayne Brummel-Anderson had been. All this he could tell from the look in the couple's eyes, from the way they held themselves, and from the subtlest of inflections in the man's voice.

If he had half a minute he could expel the override gram

from his spinner and call for assistance. Since the device knew his location at all times, help would be forthcoming within minutes. The narrow serviceway offered no place to hide, and the walls were too high and too slick to scale. The alley was a dead end in more ways than one.

Hands atop his head, he tried to stall for time. If he could somehow distract them long enough to get a finger on the spinner, or speak to its vorec—but the woman was as attentive to his movements as was her companion. If he so much as twitched wrong, they could easily shoot him in the arm that was moving. That would prevent him from reporting his position, but not from talking. He didn't think feigning a faint would fool them. They would simply keep on hurting him until he responded to their demands.

The pistol shifted again. "Talk." The man glanced back in the direction of the main street. "And don't lie. If I think you're lying, I'll shoot something. Nothing essential—to begin with. You strike me as a reasonably fit fedoco. I would imagine you can handle six or seven carefully placed shots before passing out. They will not kill you, but you will become progressively more uncomfortable."

"I wish I had something useful to tell you, but the owner of the shop in question didn't know much of anything."

This time it was the woman who replied. "So you got bored, and just decided to visit the Poremas Sexxone to relax. A long way to come, so to say. And while on duty, too." Her expression remained unchanged. "Why travel all this way, to this particular Sexxone?" She indicated the street behind her. "What makes this xone so special? You don't look the type, anyway."

"No more delays." Lowering the muzzle of his pistol, her companion aimed it at the Inspector's left foot. "Limping is good for getting sympathy, but not for living the rest of a man's life. Talk to me, fedoco. And this time, give me the real *verdad*."

Out of options, Cardenas nudged an upper molar with the tip of his tongue. He was about to adjust its opposite number when a dull thumping sound filled part of the air. A look of mild surprise washed over the Inzini's face as he toppled forward. His face shattered as it struck the paving. The back of his skull, the Inspector noted with interest, had been caved in as if it had been struck by a bowling ball shot from a cannon. Blood and compressed brains splattered in all directions. With an effort, he held his tongue.

Whirling, the dead Inzini's companion raised her own weapon. As she brought the pistol up and around, something pushed her face in. The sight was unsettling enough to make even a federal Inspector with thirty years' experience wince noticeably. The faceless body stumbled backward and collapsed onto the unyielding pavement of the alley. Stuffed in her shirt pocket was Cardenas's own gun, ineffective until it could again be brought within range of the biochip key that was implanted beneath the skin of his right hand. He made no move to recover the weapon. He made no move at all.

Shapes began to emerge from the shadows. Two of them carried pistols while the remaining pair held long, serpentine lengths of what appeared to be tree branches. As the four men drew nearer, Cardenas saw that what he had initially suspected to be made of wood was in fact plastic designed to mimic. The tubes were decorated with colorful designs of animals and plants. Each of the men was clad in a jumpsuit boasting a distinctively different pattern of brightly colored specks and circles. The illuminated dots flashed in pointillist patterns sufficiently bold to give pause to a French impressionist.

Two of the newcomers were white and blond, while their

companions were blacker than any men the Inspector had previously encountered. One of the latter boasted a kinked white beard that made him look like a dusky version of the Ancient Mariner. He carried one of the strange, ornamented tubes, a much younger blond companion the other.

The older blond holstered his pistol as he stepped over the ruined body of the female Inzini. In so doing, he avoided looking at her romped face. Despite the threat she had posed to him, Cardenas could not.

"Nasty business, this." The blond smiled encouragingly at Cardenas. "You can put your hands down, mate." As the Inspector lowered his arms, the newcomer nodded in the direction of the other lifeless Inzini. "Those two wankers won't bother you anymore."

"Thanks for your help," Cardenas replied guardedly. "I was in a bad spot." His tongue moved over the second molar, but did not push. Not yet.

"Strewth." The blond mustered a ready laugh. "Lucky thing for you me and the boys happened to be around."

"Interesting coincidence," the Inspector observed noncommittally.

"Too right, mate. 'Course, you're probably thinkin' right now that it weren't much of a coincidence."

"The notion had occurred to me," Cardenas said. He indicated the artfully embellished tube the eldest among them carried. "What is that thing? And who are you people?"

"Us?" The blond embraced his companions with a sweep of one hand. "Why, we're the Ooze from Oz, mate. Visitin' your great Namerican Southwest, we are, and couldn't hardly leave without seein' that eminent engine of world commerce, the Montezuma Strip."

"You've been following me," Cardenas said accusingly.

"Not at all, mate, not at all." The blond pointed to the two dead bodies lying motionless on the alley paving. "Dinkum, we've been following those drongos. Won't have to do that any longer." His gaze returned to search the Inspector's face. "Won't have to follow anyone much longer, I hope. Want to get back home, we do. But first we're charged with finding and having a chat with a certain sheila and her kid. You wouldn't know anything about how we might go about doin' that, now would you?"

"No, I wouldn't." Nothing to lose by trying lying, Cardenas determined.

It didn't work. Gesturing with one hand, the blond beckoned his younger counterpart forward. The skinny foreigner held the painted tube firmly in both hands. "Now this here is what we call a didgeridoo, mate. Back where I come from, it's a traditional Aboriginal musical instrument. Not what you'd call real hitech-complex, like. You blow in one end, music comes out the other. These two beauties here, however, they're amplified. When they're charged up, you blow in one end, and a ball of sound shoots out the other. More like a shaped sonic wave, actually." He indicated the back wall of the nearby building.

"Bloke who knows what he's doing with it can blow a hole through concrete. Just depends on the level of amplification you specify. When it's boosted enough, the mechanism sort of becomes more of a, well—a didgeri*die*." A glance singled out the dead Inzini. "Bone doesn't stand up to it real well."

He nodded slightly and the younger man raised the tube. Putting the smaller end to his lips, he aimed the other at the Inspector's forehead.

"There's this traditional roo-tune we'd like to play for you, policeman. It's up to you whether we play it on the sidewalk—or on your head. You know something about where the Mockerkin sheilas are fled, or these two yobbos wouldn't have been tracking you. Tell us and we'll call it a fair go." When Cardenas continued to hesitate, the blond favored him with a smile anyone else would have believed genuine. "C'mon, mate. We don't mean to hurt the ladies. It's just business. And unlike these two wankers lyin' here, we really will let you go. Got no interest in vaping a Namerican cop. We'll never see you again, and you'll never see us. Once we've had our high tea with the sheilas, it's back to the Never-Never for us."

Cardenas, however, was not fooled. The blond was good, but not good enough to fool an intuit. The Inspector knew that once they had the information they sought, they would kill him as unhesitatingly as any Inzini.

"Okay then, I'll tell you." He indicated the younger man. The leader nodded, and his companion lowered the ominously gaping end of the didgeridoo. As he did so, Cardenas's tongue pressed against the other upper molar. Like its orthodontic counterpart, the tooth responded by bending slightly outward, in the direction of the Inspector's inner cheek. When both teeth were internally aligned, a circuit closed.

Imperceptibly woven into the substance of Cardenas's windbreaker were hundreds of highly conductive metal threads. These in turn were linked to a battery composed of similar material. Adjusting the two complementing composite teeth in his upper jaw allowed Cardenas to release the full charge stored in the flexible, woven storage cell.

The result was the invisible flaring of an electromagnetic pulse powerful enough to fry any unprotected electrical circuit within ten meters. Since every modern weapon relied on an electrical trigger coded to its owner's biochip, whether the latter was implanted or worn externally, this silent blast of energy rendered not only the pistols held by the men confronting Cardenas ineffectual, but also their musical instruments-cum-sonic thumpers. It also wrecked any communications devices they had on their person, right down to wrist chronometers, muse lenses, and even simpe watches. In addition, the lights on the buildings that weakly illuminated the service alley promptly crackled, sparked, and went dark. Only Cardenas's pistol and spinner, equipped with integrated police shielding, were spared the wave of electronic destruction. After the now-demised female Inzini had inserted her illusion gram in his spinner, she had slipped the neutralized device back in his inner jacket pocket. Unfortunately, his service pistol remained out of reach on her body.

The sudden onset of darkness within the alleyway, coupled with the actinic stink arising from their wave-fried weapons and other gear, distracted and disoriented the four Oozers just long enough for Cardenas to dash past them. He had to kick the last one standing between himself and the street hard on one patella in order to dash past. The man let out a groan and collapsed, clutching at his injured knee.

"Get 'im! Get the bloody cop!" Screaming imprecations, the blond raced in pursuit of the fleeing Inspector.

A glance back showed something in the foreigner's hand catching the light. It was a very large, folding blade. Despite the desperation of the moment, the irony of it did not escape Cardenas. Here he was, an officer of the law operating in the midst of contemporary late-twenty-first-century surroundings, being chased by a man wielding a knife. Though he could not yet see for sure, he suspected that the blond man's companions were equipped with similar primitive supplements.

If he slowed even a moment to activate his spinner, he risked losing ground to his pursuers. What he really needed was a couple of minutes' respite. Otherwise they were likely to fall on him and cut him to pieces even as he was shouting into the vorec for backup. He had to lose them for at least a little while.

Now all the recreational jogging he indulged in along the artificial green belt that flanked his codo complex began to pay off. Despite his age, he was in excellent shape. If he could just stay out of reach for the duration of the sprint, he was reasonably confident he could outrun his pursuers over the long haul. If they had been somewhere like Olmec, strolling cleanies might call help for him. But this was a pleasure xone, stacked with gloomers and congals. Those citizens observing the chase moved to the other side of the street and concentrated on minding their own business.

Though he was breathing hard, he still felt good. A second look back showed that he was slowly but perceptibly increasing the distance between himself and the pursuing Ooze. Another three blocks would bring him in sight of the induction tube station. If he could reach it, a shout should be enough to alert transport security. The arrival of an armed guard or two might not be enough to discourage the dedicated professionals from abroad, but it should give them pause. At least Cardenas would have a uniformed ally. Realizing that the alarm had been raised with local authority might induce his pursuers to back off.

Two blocks to go. A masked couple shouted in surprise as he barreled between them, then ducked into a doorway to avoid the men coming up from behind. Ahead, he could see the soft, welcoming overhead lights of the tube station. As luck would have it, a taxi was unloading passengers destined for the pleasure xone and boarding those already surfeited. If he could make it to the autocab before it closed its doors, his escape would be assured. He would not even have to alert se-

curity. The public transportation would whisk him to safety
before the Oozers arrived. Once the vehicle was sealed, he
could safely make faces at his pursuers as it boosted down
the street. With their weapons rendered inoperational, they
would not be able to touch him.

One more block. He was home free. And then he was
falling, bouncing, banging against the hard ground as he instinctively tucked and rolled to absorb the force of the kick.
Uncoiling into a sitting position, he saw the younger of the
two Aborigines standing over him. The upraised blade in the
dark man's fist caught the light from the tube station as it
began to descend.

SEVEN

CARDENAS THREW UP AN ARM TO SHIELD HIS chest, but his was not the one that blocked the thrust. That limb was larger, thicker, and composed of more than a dozen elements, none of which were flesh. Shards of welded metal gleamed in the ambient light that poured down from stolid street lights and flamboyant signs. Plastic flashed rainbow hues, fragments of salvaged machinery clanked and rattled, reinforced ceramic tinkled, and bits of metallic glass sparkled like clusters of ambulatory diamonds.

What looked like a giant crab fashioned from street scrap and industrial throwaway had clambered out of the nearby storm drain. While one arm blocked the Oozer's potentially lethal blow, a second tossed the heavy plastic drain grate aside. Blinking, Cardenas rolled to his right, onto the sidewalk and away from the street. His startled assailant bent to recover the blade that had been jarred from his fingers. A third metal leg struck him across the back of his head, knocking him senseless to the ground.

Catching sight of the fantastic mechanical apparition that had emerged from beneath the street, the downed Oozer's three murderous companions slowed to a halt.

Though the clanking contrivance did not have the slick, professionally finished exterior of a law enforcement device, they were strangers in Namerica and could be sure of nothing. What they did know was that it had intervened to rescue the downed federale. Taking it on in the absence of their own advanced weapons would be tantamount to trying to break into a tank with a can opener.

Leaving their unconscious associate to his fate, they backed off, whirled, and fled, flinging only impenetrable strine obscenities in their wake. Cardenas watched them go. Keeping an eye on the downed compatriot they had abandoned, he climbed slowly to his feet and began brushing himself off. As he did, the mechanism approached, whirring and clicking.

Though three times his size, its six folding legs allowed it to snug into a portal with a diameter even smaller than the storm drain from which it had emerged. LEDs flashed within its motorized depths, eclectic raspings and moans issued forth as cobbled-together parts scraped noisily against one another. Hanging in the center of the snarl of mechanical limbs was a basket of wishwire that wrapped several times around the singular figure ensconced at its core. With his scraggly long hair, deep-sunk red-rimmed eyes, dark stubble, and scarred arms, the half-naked man resembled a drunk who had just been swept up by the late-night patrol. Except he did not act drunk, and clearly he was in control of the embracing machine, not the other way around.

Responding to a twitch of the man's right arm, a powerful limb rose on hissing servos to dexterously flick grime from the Inspector's windbreaker.

"You okay, Officer?" It took Cardenas a moment to make certain the voice had come from the man and not the machine he was riding—or that was riding him. Gazing at

the fantastic plethora of parts and pieces, rubble and sal-
vage, it was difficult to tell.

"I'm fine, thanks. And how do you know I'm with the
police?"

"My friends and me been listening, I says." One eye suffered from a persistent twitch that was unnerving to look
upon. Cardenas was equipped to handle the spectacle better
than most. "Decided to jump in when you came free."

"Why not earlier?" Cardenas checked his spinner. It was
still operating under the deading influence of the para-site
gram that had been installed by the female Inzini. But if she
had been telling the truth, the gram would expire in—he
checked the chrono on his bracelet—forty minutes or so.

"Wasn't interested, I declares." The wishwire-cloaked
recluse was marvelously indifferent to the Inspector's possible reaction. "It was only after you broke free. That I decided to help. *Andale,* hey, me *hablas.* Reconned you done
did your part. 'Sides, four against one ain't fair odds." Behind and beneath the wire, he grinned, exposing teeth that
were yellow, blackened, or absent. "Feral Dick's the name,
avoiding taxes me game." The grin, unfortunately, widened.
"You can call me Feral, suggests I."

"You said you and your friends had been listening." Cardenas cast a meaningful glance behind the crab mount. "I
don't see anyone else."

"Tacka-tack—who said a thing about anyone? What's in
a name, but a thing to be named?"

They came swarming out of the open storm drain. Ten,
twenty, thirty—a bona fide multitude. Only once before had
Cardenas ever seen as many, and the panic they had in-
duced in the surprised soccer players and their fans who
had been the recipients of the manifestation had been real
enough, if ultimately unjustified.

Wugs.

Offspring of what had ultimately been designated, for lack of a better definition and in the throes of official bewilderment, wireless underground gofer systems, the wugs were tiny, exquisitely engineered, self-reproducing robotic lifeforms whose actions suggested but did not confirm that they were components of a communal mechanized lifeform directed by some kind of rogue artificial intelligence gram. Expecting the first true AI to arise from a confluence of mammoth research projects and profound university conferences, humans had been startled to see AI, when it finally manifested itself, take the form of mechanicals that were fist-sized and smaller. Initial fear and panic at the appearance of the wugs soon gave way to concern, then uncertainty, and finally to annoyance when the thousands of tiny devices exhibited nothing in the way of purpose, much less hostility.

Most of the time the wugs avoided people, hiding themselves in the enormous circulatory system of the Strip: airconditioning vents, water and sewer pipes, transport tunnels, fiber optic conduits, and induction tubes. Like mechanical cockroaches, they shunned the daylight. Unlike their arthropodic counterparts, they were clean and did not carry disease. Nor did they often enter private residences or disturb human food. They simply reproduced. As the engineers who struggled for several years to devise a means of exterminating them finally conceded, people might as well get used to them. Short of dismantling and shutting down every mechanism and machine in the Strip, the wugs were here to stay.

After a while citizens grew used to, if not entirely familiar with, their presence. As one wag put it early on in the course of the "invasion," irregardless of what anyone wanted, the wugs *was*. While no wug had ever injured a human being, humans were constantly squashing, smashing, dismembering, and otherwise demolishing the elegant little automatons. Even children soon lost their fear of them. The assaults by humans engendered no retribution, provoked no retaliation. Those paranoicos convinced the wugs were out to take over the world quickly found themselves shorn of their followings, especially when it became clear that the wugs were nothing more than an irritation.

Virtually the only thing about the wugs that continued to bother people was that nobody could manage to figure out where the heck they were coming from.

They certainly appeared to thrive in the congenial presence of Feral Dick, Cardenas observed. He held his ground while a couple dozen of the miniscule machines swarmed up his legs. They poked and prodded him for a few minutes, gently and with what could only be termed respect for his nonmetallic person. Sensors and wires caressed and tickled, taking measurements for what purposes the Inspector could not imagine. Then, as if in response to a signal unseen and unheard, they scampered as one back down to the pavement to disappear into the open storm drain. No two of the diminutive wonders had been alike.

Feral Dick gazed fondly at the cavity in the street. "I likes the wugs, and the wugs likes me."

Cardenas was genuinely intrigued. "Is that why you decided to intervene and save me? Because the wugs wanted to examine me?"

Within the sessile whorl of wishwire, Feral guffawed. "A funny cop, laughs I! I don't know what the wugs want. Nobody does. How many wiggles will a wishing wug want?" He giggled as he recited the common children's rhyme. "But they seem to enjoy veteing around with me, and I kind of like the company. You live beneath the street instead of above it, you take any company you can get, sombers I. At least they don't nag." He spat something off to one side. Cardenas was mildly surprised it didn't clang when it hit the pavement.

"That still doesn't explain why you decided to help me."

The mechanical crab-shape began to scuttle sideways, in the direction of the gaping storm drain. "There's times now and then, observes me, when a feral might have needs of a little federale goodwill. Believes in banking official amity, shrewds I. Besides, I wasn't doing anything else at the time." A metal-plastic-glass claw rose in casual salute. "Fondly remember me to your files, Officer." The wish-wire made it difficult to see those sunken, but not haunted, eyes.

Then, as swiftly as they had appeared, mechanical and riding master were gone, disappeared down the aperture. Walking to the edge, Cardenas could hear the tinny clattering of the cobbled-together vehicle's metal feet as the homemade transport ensemble skittered away under the street. Not a true antisoc, was Feral Dick. By choice he stood, or rather scuttled along, outside both belief systems.

The Inspector checked his spinner. It was still comatose, but not dead. A few minutes more or less and he would be back on line opto, with full access to the NFP box. If, he reminded himself, the dead Inzini had not been lying. There was no real reason for her to have done so, since she and her equally demised partner had intended for the spinner's owner to be far deader than his apparatus prior to its return to service.

A glance down the street disclosed only wandering citizens. There was no sign of the routed Ooze from Oz. He knew he ought to use a public comm to report in, to at least relate what had happened to him. But without the spinner he could not impart a true picture of his assailants. And if he waited too long, the woman he sought might go off shift—or worse, be visited by Inzini, Ooze, or some hypothetical other who shared in this sudden and unexpectedly irresistible interest in the whereabouts of Surtsey Mockerkin and her daughter.

Who were the Amerind assassins working for? The Mock, or themselves, or some other as yet unidentified group with an intense interest in Surtsey Mockerkin and her daughter? The same speculation applied to the Ooze. The more antisoc outfits that expressed a lethal interest in the pair, the more anxious Cardenas was to find them— first.

If he had to wait for a chance to talk with Coy Joy, he could do so just as effectively while simultaneously checking out her visitors. Turning, he headed back down the street in the direction of the Cocktale. This time he stayed close to groups of slumming cleanies. He also made a point of taking the measure of his surroundings every few steps, to ensure their reality. He had no intention of wandering mindlessly into another deceptive, misleading miragoo.

The Cocktale was easy to find. Located on the main street, right where Mashupo Mingas had indicated, it was squeezed in between the Featherdome and California Nights. Unlike some of the personnel hard at work within, all three establishments boasted fronts that were models of restraint. Their external lighting was subdued, signage was static rather than animated, and no lascivious adverts came barreling out of Madison ejectors to carny casual passersby. Though it had been a long time since he had worked a pleasure xone, Cardenas knew that not all sextels were alike. Based on what he remembered, these three neighboring businesses occupied a niche designed to appeal to upper-middle-class, or possibly lower-upper-class, clients.

Across the street, the enormous Rara Aves took up the better part of several city blocks. A joint Asakusa-Chubasco N.A. operation, it flaunted its wares as brazenly as it did its staff. Cheaper, less discreet, and downright Vegasian in its appeal, it boasted a steady stream of customers anxious to partake of its offerings, both hard and wet. In addition to satisfying one's lust of the moment, a patron of the Rara Aves could also spend the night alone, gamble, and consume in-house subsidized food and nonsexual entertainment. A one-stop international chain discount entertainment center for the employees of the maquiladoras, it enjoyed a solid reputation and was especially favored by blue-collar workers. There were franchised Rara Aves throughout the Strip, each virtually indistinguishable from the next. The merchandise on the shelves in Agua Pri was the same as that on offer in Elpaso Juarez, or Sanjuana, or Brownsville.

Although the sex trade had been legal in the Strip for more than half a century, there remained those citizens who for a great variety of reasons favored anonymity, not to mention a more personal style of service. This was to be found in confidential enterprises such as the Cocktale and its neighbors, as well as in those exclusive establishments that catered to the very rich. What was advertised on the outside was frequently supplanted by what a prospective consumer was offered within.

Furnished in period antiques from the late twentieth century, the outer waiting room was occupied by perhaps a dozen men and women. Some were waiting to penetrate, as it were, the inner recesses of the institution, while others were relaxing and having a rest subsequent to concluding their activities. One did not have to be an Intuit to tell which were which. Sauntering in, Cardenas drew an occasional fleeting glance from would-be and ex-customers. He was particularly taken with a middle-aged couple who sat on a couch, thoroughly engrossed in a vit program from a hundred years ago. It had no color, and was playing back on a vit the size of a small vehicle.

The unobtrusive lighting was tinted a soft pink, as if some deviant physicist had found a way to rouge photons. Landscapes on the walls showed scenes from Europe and South America. A picture of some French castle appeared lifted from a standard tourist brochure, until one noticed the orgy taking place in the courtyard. A southern Chilean forest scene conjured up memories of a visit to the Rockies, until you looked closer and saw what was taking place among the trees. Not to mention with the trees. Cardenas examined them with interest. They were very cleverly manufactured and, within the bounds of the subject matter they presented, surprisingly tasteful. Staring at them, he was not in the least embarrassed. This was not a place in which anyone should be embarrassed.

Off to his left, a well-stocked shop beckoned, proffering offerings unavailable even through a private box. The desk he approached was no different from what one might find in a well-appointed, mid-price hotel—provided one discounted the subtly writhing figures that comprised the expertly wrought sculpture clinging to the back wall. Attesting to the vitality of the Cocktale's business, there were three clerks: two women and one man, all clad in formal phototropic clothing that peekabooed strategically whenever they moved.

The woman who greeted him was in her late twenties. Though she was attractive, he knew from experience that she had been hired for her ability to process vertically integrated services; otherwise she would not have been stationed up front. Off to one side stood a silent, pale monolith with folded arms. The bouncer was as big as Hyaki. Cardenas suspected he was present more for show than action. If the management frequently required the services of someone that size, then they had already failed in their responsibility. Obstreperous clients were more easily dealt with by simply flooding a room or hallway with narcoleptic gas.

"Welcome to the Cocktale, sir. How may I help you?" Her welcoming smile was practiced and professional.

He smiled back. In a place like the Cocktale, if you did not smile, no one would take you seriously. "I think I'm in the mood for something a little out of the ordinary."

The girl nodded. Without missing a beat, she leaned forward and whispered (a nice, if wholly unnecessary touch, Cardenas thought). "Someone's told you about us, then. They put you straight. The Cocktale didn't get its reputation by slamming solely straight." Her lips were close, her perfume weeping synthesized pheromones. "Did you have anything specific in mind, sir? Whatever you wish, if we can't provide it on the spot, we'll send out for take-in. You can rely on our guaranteed rapidio delivery of whatever you wish within the hour, drawn from the full resources of the Strip. Just tell me what you want, sir." He tried to, but she was full steam into her spiel, so he decided just to let her run down.

"You want it, you need it? The Cocktale has it, or can get it. Are you interested in sex with tactiles? We offer the latest military technology adapted to our exclusive specifications. You can stipulate tints, ambiance, fragrances, and sound, from music to purring. Or if you prefer something a little louder, rest assured all our apartmentos are rigorously soundproofed. If you'd prefer to solo in comfort, we have instant unrestricted world box access. Just online are some new designs from Chengdu based on ancient Han scriptures. Originally fantasy, of course, but with our omniphonic projectors all things are possible."

She continued to smile at him, waiting for a response, trying to size him up. Cardenas offered no assistance, waiting for her to run out of suggestions. She seemed nice enough, for a procurer, and if he interrupted her well-rehearsed sales pitch it might cost her merit with her employers. The deliberately cozy feel of the salon notwithstanding, he did not doubt for a minute that the entire conversation was being remotely monitored.

"We also offer a full range of standard morphs," the girl continued, undaunted by his continued silence. "Male, female, animal. We have two registered eeLancers on staff ready to build a custom morph dedicated to serving your personal needs." Her whispery come-on sank even lower. "For a price, I might be willing to provide the template for mastering a child morph. Semi-licit, guaranteed not actionable, bond posted by our own legal department."

The Inspector's distaste must have shown in his face, because she backtracked hurriedly. "Or are you a traditionalist? If that's the case, in spite of what you've told me, maybe you would find one of our sister establishments more to your taste." Straightening and glancing down, she drew forth a floating list that was outlined in glowing pink and red sparkles. A nice decorative touch, Cardenas decided.

On a whim, he inquired candidly, "How about you?"

List forgotten, she looked up uncertainly. "I'm afraid I am strictly front-office, sir." Clearly, she hoped he would not press the issue, lest her supervisor order her to comply with a client's wishes. "I'm flattered, but I should warn you that I'm more than half bionic."

Cardenas parroted the expression he had seen all too many times on the faces of sex offenders who had been brought into the station for booking. "Which half?"

While not personally reassuring, his response convinced her that the sturdy visitor with the profound mustache had come to the right place after all. "If you find my physical type appealing, sir, perhaps you might allow me to suggest—?"

Having established his pervert's credentials, he saw no reason to prolong the discussion. "I know what I want. I also know who I want. I just wanted to watch you yakk for a while. I want two hours with Coy Joy."

He had a bad moment when she failed to reply. Had Mashupo Mingas fed him faulty information from the beginning? If so, Cardenas was in for some wearisome backtracking.

He was worrying needlessly. The delay was only due to the need for the girl to check on the current status of his query.

"You're in luck, sir. Ms. Joy is even as we speak returning from break. She will be available to you in"—she checked a concealed readout—"five minutes. Two hours, you say?"

Cardenas mimed what he hoped was a wicked smile. "I like to take my time."

The woman shrugged. "We are each of us different."

They negotiated a price, which Cardenas paid with the special card the Department issued to Inspectors to pay for extraneous investigative expenses. He wished he could be present to see the face of the Department auditor who would eventually process the expenditure. Several minutes later, he was escorted by a very tall, very beautiful, and very well-armed woman down a corridor and into an empty apartmento. Since he had not specified a setting, he was supplied with what was clean and available.

The spacious chamber had a double cotton hammock, soft undulating sand for a floor, live dwarf palms and other succulents, a triwalled holovista of a Pacific beach and sky, and automatonic fauna: crabs, gulls, a phlegmatic pelican, a couple of small lizards. The artificial "sun" overhead was less hot than its projected intensity suggested, and the imported salt water that lapped the sand pleasantly tepid. Killing time, he checked the contents of a nearby cooler. It was well-stocked with icy refreshments, toys, and an assortment of both pull-on and spray-on prophylactics, all no doubt hideously overpriced. As he absently took inventory, like any good customer, the pelican favored him with a lascivious, conspiratorial wink.

Apparently no one worried about the incongruity of a bathroom opening directly onto a beach, because that was where Coy Joy emerged from, in the midst of primping her pale, straw-yellow hair. She wore nothing beneath a clinging blue-and-gold ersatz chiffon dress. She was slimmer than he expected, slightly taller than he, and not as tired-looking as many sylphs he had encountered. Though utterly devoid of any suggestion of naiveté, her face was surprisingly unspoiled. The air of innocence, whether sincere or sham, was doubtless appreciated by many customers. He wondered how many she had facilitated prior to his arrival.

"I'm Coy," she began without preamble. "Do you want me to start? Since you asked for me, you know what I do."

Though his investigation did not demand that he know what she did, he was more than a little curious. Besides, it might acquaint him with something useful, however seemingly insignificant, about Wayne Brummel-Anderson.

"Sure." Taking a seat on the sand, which was pleasantly warm and electrostatically treated so it would cling neither to flesh nor fabric, he helped himself to a cold cerveza from the cooler and, to sustain the charade, loosened his shirt. "Let's get started."

Smiling sexily, she raised both hands high over her head. As well as pulling taut her upper torso, the gesture activated a small embedded gram that caused her clothes to disintegrate. The aerogel textile tinkled musically as it transformed into pixie dust and drifted to the sand. Music, low, languorous, and unashamedly erotic, began to emanate from hidden speakers. His eyes widened slightly, not as a consequence of viewing the dancing or hearing the music, but due to what was happening to Coy Joy's body. He now knew what her "specialty" was.

She was a color shifter.

Noting the change in his expression, she pursed her lips with satisfaction. "Like it?" she inquired softly. "Like me? You must, or you wouldn't have asked for me." Glissading to the slow, unsubtle throbbing from the unseen speakers, she ran one hand up her other arm, then alternated the self-caress. "Cost me a bundle, it did, but good gengineering is expensive. And every girl needs a specialty. This one was a lot of work, but in the end it's safer than some. And there's an added benefit. I like myself this way."

Entranced in spite of himself, Cardenas followed the performance with something more than just professional detachment. Color shiftering was only one of a thousand come-ons available in the sextels of the Strip. Though milder than many, as she had pointed out, it required a permanent commitment on the part of the catalyzer. He found himself wondering what had prodded her to undergo the extensive and complicated, though not particularly dangerous, course of treatment.

Coy Joy was the recipient of gengineered chromatophores. Derived from the epidermis of members of the order Cephalopodia, they had been implanted in her skin to give her the ability not only to change color, but to create a plethora of exotic patterns simply by visualizing them. As she pranced and pirouetted before him in time to the slowly swelling, throbbing music, her slender naked form changed from pale beige to dark brown, then to black, and back to beige again. All familiar human skin tones. But royal blue was not, nor burnt umber, nor teal or chartreuse or a flickering maroon. It was a performance any of her genetic antecedents, be they octopus or squid, cuttlefish or chambered nautilus, would have admired.

Fascinated, he watched as she began to move faster. Responding to a corollaried gram, the lights in the room dimmed. As she slipped deeper and deeper into the performance, her emotions were reflected in her appearance. Rapid color changes were enhanced by the patterns that flowed like light across her skin, except that they came from within her own body. Scale patterns replaced smooth flesh, to be banished in turn first by images of flower petals and then black leather. Red stripes appeared, giving the appearance of light whip strokes, to be replaced by three circles of light that burst outward from her main erogenous zones like spreading ripples in a pond. Her nipples flared pink, then burgundy, and finally a deep, pulsing scarlet. Faster and faster the emerging circles blinked, not lights but actual color changes, enticing him and drawing him toward her as she extended her hands in his direction. Her parted lips pulsed with a soft inner, unnatural pink no lipstick could realize.

She was changing color so fast and so frequently now that her flesh had become one continuous erotic blur—teasing, tempting, a veritable living maelstrom of panchromatic curves and searing light. And all of it was very close now, inclining toward him, half blinding his dazed vision. As he felt the heat of her body, so close to his own, he found himself concentrating on her eyes—virtually the only visible part of her that did not change color. Arching forward, she leaned her face toward his. The waves of crimson that swept outward from the center of her deepened to purple as they neared her extremities. All her extremities. Mesmerized by the sight, he swallowed hard as she reached for . . .

Taking a deliberate, deep breath, he drew himself reluctantly back from the abyss into which, on another day, on another occasion, he might gratefully have allowed himself to be drawn. Raising his left arm, he activated and flashed his ident bracelet. Her expression fell alarmingly. As if an internal switch had been thrown, the erotic panoply of pattern and color vanished from her exposed flesh. Once again she stood before him slim, naked, and brutally unadorned.

"This is a legal sextel, and I'm fully licensed," she snarled angrily. "What do you want? My health certificate was revalidated only last month, and I'm up on all my taxes. Has someone complained? If someone's complained, you've got the wrong—"

"Take it easy. I need some information. Nothing compromising, I promise you. And I've paid for two hours, so your commission is secure no matter what you do—or don't do. Look on it as time off."

"Fuck you. Or I guess not. I'm not telling you a thing, fedoco."

Cardenas sighed and took another drag of his self-chilling beer. It was starting to fill him up. Sometimes, being nice, being polite, could be counterproductive. That would do neither him nor the sylph any good.

"We can do this here or at the station. You know it'll go better for you here. If you end up coming with me—or I guess not—your employers won't be happy no matter what story you feed them."

She slumped, her breasts bouncing, and took a seat on the sand in front of him. She made a point of staying out of arm's reach. "Two hours. I hope to hell you haven't got two whole hours' worth of stupid questions."

"So do I." He shifted his own position on the sand and, after a moment's thought, helped himself to another cerveza from the cooler. The automatonic pelican was studiously ignoring him. "I'm interested in anything you can tell me about one of your regulars. Might have called himself George Anderson, but more likely went by the name of Wayne Brummel."

Her head jerked up and around. "If you know he's one of my regulars, then you probably know more about him than I do. I don't have anything to say. You want to skip me to the station, I'll dig out some stable clothes and we'll go, and to hell with Administration. If you want to know about Wayne, why come to me? Why not *habla* him yourself?"

As ever, Cardenas's tone remained unchanged. "Because a few days ago, somebody had him extirpated."

As her eyes widened and her lower jaw took a notable

drop, her entire nude body straight away turned a blindingly pure ivory-white. Here, Cardenas realized as he looked away, was a witness he would not have to intuit. She could no more conceal her emotions from him than she could fly to the moon.

Although, he saw compassionately, she could no doubt imitate the flight.

EIGHT

IN CARDENAS'S EXPERIENCE IT WAS A GEN-
eral rule that whores did not cry. But there was no mistaking the anguish in Coy Joy's eyes: more than one would
have expected a sylph to shed for a dead client, even one
who might have been gentle, straight, and tipped lavishly.

"This Brummel was more to you than just a steady
mark?"

She nodded, her face contorted as if she was trying to
weep but had forgotten how. Continuing to reflect the emotions boiling within her, the blinding pallor of her skin had
given way to a light brown flecked with intermittent blobs
of uncontrolled blueness that expanded and contracted in
time to her sobs. Through the ambiguous miracle of gengineering, Coy Joy had moved far, far beyond wearing her
emotions on her sleeve. She wore them everywhere.
Though it was all but impossible to avoid looking at her attractive, naked, color-saturated body, Cardenas struggled
hard to maintain a professional detachment. If he did not,
he sensed he would get nothing out of her, no matter what
threats he might propound.

"I understand your concern, and I'm sorry for your loss.

Your reaction answers my question, but I promise that you'll feel better by tomorrow morning."

Her face streaked with tears and softly pulsating indigo splotches, she looked up at him over her cupped hands. "How—how do you know?" she sniffed.

Without elaborating, he simply smiled and told her, "I can tell. Brummel was good to you?"

She nodded despairingly. "He never hurt me, always overpaid, even waited for me those times when I thought he was done with me. Never asked for anything spazzed."

Contemplating the bright blue whorls that spattered her lower body and turned both supple legs into kaleidoscopic echoes of ancient barber poles, only in color, Cardenas wondered what someone like Coy Joy would consider abnormal.

"He was— He said that as soon as this big project he was working on gealed, he would leave the woman he was living with and we would get married. He talked a lot about us moving, about getting away from the Strip."

What a charming homber the dead Brummel had been, the Inspector mused. Surtsey Mockerkin had chosen to run off with a man who had promptly begun their new life by cheating on her. Suggestions of domestic abuse from the subgrub Wild Whoh notwithstanding, it was looking more and more like Ms. Mockerkin and the late Brummel-Anderson probably deserved one another. Cardenas did not need to draw his spinner to record the conversation. Anything relevant he committed to his own, as opposed to an artificial, memory.

"Move where?"

"I don't know—some place he called Friendship."

Cardenas shook his head. "Never heard of it."

"Neither had I. And he wouldn't ever tell me any more

than the name." As she struggled to smile, her upper body, from shoulders to forehead, pulsed a pale rose hue. "Wanted it to be a surprise, he said."

The tears and tints began to flow again. Cardenas let them come, admiring the startling play of colors within her skin, before putting an end to the weepery with another question.

"What about this business of his, his big project? Did he ever talk about it, ever mention the names of partners or existing concerns?"

Reaching down, she picked up a beach towel and used it to wipe her eyes and nose. Behind her, the simulated sea washed the synthetic shore, suffusing the apartmento with the artificial scent of marooned kelp and crystallizing sea salt.

"Wayne never said anything about partners. I guess maybe he didn't need any, because he had access to the money of this other woman, the woman he was living with. Apparently she had plenty. I didn't worry about him, about us, taking it for our own use, because he told me she had stolen it from her husband."

Cardenas was watching her closely. "Did Wayne ever mention the husband?"

Coy shook her head. "No, never. Just a daughter, the girl he and the woman were living with. Wayne talked about her a lot. I guess he thought she was kind of special, even though she wasn't his."

"He didn't talk about the woman?" Cardenas was puzzled.

"No, not the woman. He never talked about her, unless it had to do with the money he was going to take. Just about the girl. Katey—no, Katla, that was her name. The special project? He was never real clear on that. Said something, once, about wanting to keep me under a shield of ignorance. It all centered around the girl." She shook her head. "Don't ask me why."

Cardenas was now as intrigued as he was confused. "Brummel's big business deal revolved around *Katla*? Katla, the twelve-year-old, and not Surtsey?" He saw neither need nor reason for now to bring up the name Mockerkin.

She shrugged. "That's what Wayne told me. Hey, I didn't press him for details. It was enough that he said we were going to get married and go to this place of friendship. Or Friendship place. He'd get real dreamy-eyed talking about it. Said it was warm, and beautiful, and private. Just wouldn't tell me where it was."

"What kind of unusual business could someone like Wayne be working with a twelve-year-old girl?"

Rising, Coy Joy apathetically began to slip into a new dress. Her body was a symphony of sinuous movement and subdued, internally generated color. Cardenas's blood pressure had finally diminished to something approaching normal.

"I dunno." She raised one leg engagingly, using both hands to smooth the diaphanous material against her skin. The mood music that had been playing continuously in the background had, mercifully, finally stopped. "He said she was a tecant, but he didn't go into details. Said she had done a lot of work for her father."

So shy little Katla Mockerkin was a technology savant, Cardenas mused. One who had been working with her father, The Mock. While the nature of that labor remained a mystery, Cardenas began to understand why Cleator Mockerkin might be anxious to regain custody of his hijacked offspring. Irregardless of the nature of that work, it was manifestly one that had caught the interest of Wayne Brummel. The abilities of a natural tecant could be extremely valuable to someone involved in complex business dealings. With tecants, as for example with intuits, age was not necessarily a limiting factor where natural ability was concerned.

"He didn't discuss the character of the business at all?"

"I told you." Reflecting her annoyance as she fastened the dress, angry red stars appeared as blotches on the still-exposed portions of her body. "He didn't go into detail with me about anything except the two of us, our relationship, and this Friendship place. He never talked business beyond what I've already told you." She rested her face in her hands. "I didn't *want* him to talk about anything except us." Taking a deep breath, she composed herself as best she was able. Except for occasional flare-ups of blue and gold, her skin color had returned to normal.

"That's gone, now. All gone. Him and us, Friendship; everything." She glanced in the direction of an artfully concealed chrono. "You've still got time left that you paid for. You sure you don't want to . . . ?"

Her words as she spoke them to him now were as hard, as cold and drained of emotion, as any Cardenas had ever encountered. Even if he were inclined to pursue some non-police activity with her, her tone would have killed any interest he might have had.

"No." His reply was full of empathy as he rose from the sand. "You've done everything I've asked of you."

Beneath the form-fitting material of the dress, her lethargic shrug was barely perceptible. "I've told you everything I can remember. There isn't anything more. Now there never will be." Lower lip quivering, she tried very hard to smile. "If you really don't want me for anything else, I could really use the next hour to myself."

"Why don't you just quit for the night?"

Her response was more of a twitch than a laugh. "Yeah, right," she replied tartly. "I'll just go up to whoever's running the front desk now and turn in my timer for the rest of the evening."

"I can get you off." The Inspector uttered the claim with quiet confidence.

"Why bother?" Her tone was brittle as she headed for the door that led to the bathroom. "I'm already coged." Whether from indifference, numbness, or house rules, she did not bother to close the door behind her.

On his way out, Cardenas made sure to strew compliments in his wake. It was all he could do to help her, since she would not let him arrange for her to take the rest of the night off. No one accosted him as he stepped outside the entry to the Cocktale and started up the street in the direction of the tube station. It would be light out soon. As he left the sextel behind, he was more mystified than ever. Clearly, it was more than the chance to live on pilfered funds that had drawn Wayne Brummel to Surtsey Mockerkin. It was her daughter. Knowing that, it followed naturally that it was twelve-year-old Katla who The Mock really wanted back.

What business was she involved in, this quiet girl whom her former sochemates had spoken so well of? What work had she been doing for her father? A versatile, talented tecant could do many things.

In this instance, enough to get other people killed.

In spite of all his street and spinner work Cardenas was unable to come up with a single reliable, pursuable lead as to the whereabouts of Surtsey Mockerkin and her daughter.

If they were hiding somewhere in the Strip, their identities were not registering on any of the usual trackers. Official inquiries through customary channels had turned up nothing. Mother and daughter had vanished utterly from public ken.

Which meant they were hiding out somewhere. Unless The Mock's minions had already caught up with them. Or some other interested cartel like the Inzini, or the Ooze. The extraordinary and unexpected interest in Katla Mockerkin made the Inspector only that much more anxious to find her. What kind of business would someone like The Mock entrust to the care of a twelve-year-old, even if she *was* his own daughter and an acknowledged tecant?

Running and hiding from someone like The Mock would require intelligence, street smarts, and plenty of money. It was now evident that Surtsey Mockerkin possessed all three. Having eluded the attentions of her dangerous and no doubt enraged husband for this long, she was clearly determined to continue doing so. The fact that she was not specifically hiding from the police would not make the job of finding her any easier.

At least he now had some idea of why she was running. Knowing that allowed him to adjust his search parameters accordingly. But it was rapidly becoming plain that if he was going to find them before The Mock, he was going to have to seek help outside official channels.

It was one reason why he repeatedly turned down the array of desk jobs he was offered at regular intervals. Nice, safe assignments in climate-controlled cubicles that would allow him to spend the remainder of his years until retirement in comparative comfort and safety. Nice, dull, boring assignments that were suited neither to his soul nor his temperament. It was not so much that he loved the street as that he could not seem to do without it. The Strip was in his blood. That was only appropriate, he knew, since he had left so much of his blood in the Strip.

Which was why, not to mention how, he found himself striding imperturbably down an unmarked, unnamed street in a corner of the Strip as far removed from the comforting lights of downtown Nogales or Sanjuana as Mocceca's Mall was from the dark side of the moon. The pose and posture he adopted were deliberate. Look too purposeful in such a setting and you risked making yourself a target. Appear lost, and you became a target by default. But affect an air of nonchalance, and the brains behind the eyes that invariably tracked your progress from corners and crannies, windows and zipwalls, would pause to reflect.

Here, they would conclude, was someone who flashed confidence like a gun, and loaded it with attitude. So while some might covet his clean clothes and hidden assets, the furtive inhabitants of the Bonezone hugged their hiding places and let him pass unmolested.

The Bonezone was a low-priority area for patrols, "low priority" being bureaucrat-speak for "a place taxpayers don't give a damn about." Certainly Cardenas encountered no fellow federales as he wended his way deeper and deeper into the 'zone. Piles of ergonomic trash overflowed recycling bins and filled alleyways, uncollected but not unsifted. Stray cats devoid of implanted ident chips prowled and yowled among the organic garbage excreted daily by dozens of small food shops and cheap apartment buildings. Qwilk shops hawked the latest in electronic fills and gadgets, much legal, some less so, and usually but not always out of sight, unpleasant but sought-after paraphernalia that did not belong in private hands.

It was a testament to Cardenas's guise that he was not immediately spotted and identified as a federale. The shop-keepers and restaurant owners and beggars and contemplative but wary scaves and skim artists took him for a veteran visitor, one knowledgeable and experienced in the ways of the 'zone. They harangued him openly, soliciting business or charity according to their station, but otherwise left him alone to pursue his agenda. Bareheaded and hunched forward, he advanced with hands in pockets, unsmiling and apparently lost in a world of his own. None were ready to run the risk of interrupting his fixation, whatever it might be.

Had they known his intended destination, he would likely have drawn even less attention. In the bowels of the Bonezone, there were many cults, not all of them benign. It was the experience of professional thieves that fanatics usually made chancy victims, and in any case, carried little worth stealing.

One of the few blessings to be found in the 'zone was the absence of the pestiferous motile adverts. There was no point in squandering good advertising money on barely-citizens who possessed little in the way of disposable income. On the distaff side there was the noise: an omnipresent drone of cut-rate electronics, buzzing sensoria, mindless street chatter, and loud, sometimes lethally loud, vit and music. Blocking out the 'zone drone as best he was able, he concentrated on finding his way through a maze of small streets and passageways long since neglected by the district public works department. Assuming the place hadn't moved, his spinner could have led him to his intended destination straight away. But pulling a police spinner would be a bad way of maintaining the kind of anonymity that kept one integral this deep in the Bonezone.

A pair of dogs crossed his path, snarled, and continued on their way out of sight behind a darkened apartmento off to his right. The schnauzer had two artificial front legs, while its companion cocker flaunted a pair of miniature reception dishes in place of ears. Both wore broadcast collars, indicating that they were not strays. Someone had taken pity on them and, instead of having them put down, had repaired them enough to survive on the streets. Biosurge talent was plentiful in the 'zone, even if most of it was focused on procedures that would get a legitimate practitioner locked up and his license revoked.

As Cardenas walked, he found himself brooding on the meaning of "friendship" as it had been related to him by Coy Joy. Had her paramour Brummel been speaking metaphorically of it, or had he been referring to an actual place? A check of Strip place names as well as a more exhaustive search run farther afield had found no urb, no street, no development named Friendship within a couple of hundred kims. There was a Friendship, Pennsylvania, and a Friendship, Iowa. Even a Friendship, Manitoba. Contacting the local registries in each community had identified no recent relocations who could conceivably be taken for Surtsey and Katla Mockerkin. If Brummel had been speaking of another actual place, it lay outside the boundaries of the Namerican States.

Was that the right passage, there, off to his left? Or was it the next one down? He struggled to remember the nexus sheet the spinner had spun. Resolutely, he turned down the first narrow lane that presented itself. If he was remembering incorrectly, the worst that was likely to happen was that no one would respond to his presence. Unless someone made him for a federale, in which case he might find himself staring down the quadruple barrel of an Ithaca spitter, or something equally unpleasant.

The passageway terminated in a door that appeared to

have been cobbled together from scraps of wood and scrap metal, but in actuality was a single sheet of cold-effused alloy sufficiently impervious to do any old-time bank vault proud. There were no handles, no windows or ports, no visible hinges. Equally invisible was the speaker that barked hesitantly at him.

"What is the word, byte?"

"There is no word," Cardenas replied evenly. "There are only numbers masquerading as words."

The hidden interrogator did not reply. Cardenas envisioned acolytes on the other side of the door conversing animatedly with one another. It would take a moment for word of his presence to be passed onward.

Finally, "What do you seek?"

"Aurilac the Wise—if he's at home and not indisposed," Cardenas added solicitously.

"You're a fedoco." The tone was slightly accusing. The Inspector did not search for the concealed vits through which he was being observed, nor the weapons that were doubtless trained on him and could easily prevent any flight to freedom down the narrow, constricting lane.

"I'm a searcher after truth, like yourself."

"Is that what you seek from the Wise? Truth?" the voice wanted to know.

"None of us have access to true truth. Not even the Wise. We can only search for it. I'm a fellow searcher." He smiled at the unseen speaker. "The Wise seeks the peace that lies in studying the places between man and machine. My work is ensuring the peace of the first. On behalf of that, we've exchanged communications previously. Sometimes information arrives in my personal box that I know comes from him. Sometimes I have the opportunity to help his Order." He leaned forward slightly. "There are those who don't like what you believe and what you do. Who consider you all borderline antisocs. I'm not one of them. I'm a friend."

"And a voluble one, at that." The door opened to admit him, not by moving inward, but by scrolling up and disappearing into the top of the lintel. "Enter, seeker."

"I'm armed," he warned them before stepping through.

"We know." The door closed behind him.

Standing in a very small hallway, he found himself bathed in a pale blue light. When it shut off, an unexpectedly voluptuous young woman clad in a single garment comprised of melted-down, thin-rolled, and recast discarded electronic components greeted him with a contented half-smile. Lights winked and flashed from her uncomfortable-looking costume, but she did not seem to mind how it bunched up and bound. Seeing his eyes wander, her smile widened.

"It keeps those of us who strive to learn the Way alert," she explained.

"What Way is that?" he asked as she turned and he followed her.

"Why, the Right Way, of course. But if you are truly a seeker, as you claim, and not just another dumb, Neanderthalic fedoco, you already know that."

"The blue light?" he inquired as they turned a sharp corner in the featureless corridor.

"We don't fear ordinary weapons such as you bear on your person. We have ways of dealing with those. Our concern was that you might have carried, willingly or otherwise, a disruptor on your person. That would concern us." Glancing back at him, she smiled beatifically. "We can't have intruders spizzing our crunch."

"I feel exactly the same way," he replied truthfully.

The corridor opened with unexpected abruptness into a

large, darkened room. The ceiling above had been removed, allowing the ranks of coil chairs to move freely between two floors. Screens glowed and heads-up projections filled much of the available space. More than two dozen acolytes of the Wise sat or slumped before the astonishing plethora of displays. Some of the attentive operators were directly wired in via contact caps, while others murmured to sensitive vorecs or fingered keyboards. The soft rise and fall of their voices as they whispered verbal commands to their consoles reminded Cardenas of muffled Gregorian chant, though the language they were speaking had as much to do with Latin as Finnish did with Fijian.

In the center of it all, at the far end of the chamber, Aurilac the Wise reposed contentedly in a reclining lounge that pivoted in response to his murmured commands. Gray of hair and sardonic of aspect, alert of eye and swollen of body, he waved off the woman who had just finished filling his half-meter-long glycol pipe and languidly blew a cloud of aromatic smoke in Cardenas's direction. Sampling the puff with a sniff, the Inspector identified at least three different soporifics in addition to the masking fragrance.

"Why don't you just ingest?" He halted before the lounge. If intended to give the appearance of a throne, it was decidedly cavalier in design. The young woman who had escorted him folded her hands and remained by his side. What surprises besides her undeniably attractive self lay concealed beneath the nictitating electronic garb that covered her from head to toe he did not know, but he suspected they would be potentially lethal.

Aurilac the Wise waved the pipe like a conductor halfway through a Ravel largo and grinned. "Could. Be more efficient. But there's no aesthetic appeal in popping a pill. This is more fun, and I really think it enhances the potency." His gaze narrowed. "You're an intuit."

For the first time since he had entered the outside alley, Cardenas was surprised. "How do you know that?"

"I didn't. But I'm a good guesser. You have to be, when you're forced to live with my physical problems." Wincing, he shifted his mass on the lounge.

"Is that a truth you've learned?"

"Better believe it, brother. There's no truth like incurable back pain. It's all bound up with reality. But then, reality is all about being bound to something. You're bound to your work, Camille there is bound to her preferences." He made a sweeping gesture, taking in the room of active acolytes. "We're all of us bound to something. It's those few who understand the nature of those bindings who have reached something of an understanding with their inner selves, and with life." He took another puff of the pipe. Smoke curled upward like translucent snakes preparing to strike. "Being an intuit, you already know that."

"I know a few things," Cardenas replied sincerely.

"But not enough." Coughing, Aurilac set the pipe aside. "Or you wouldn't be here."

The Inspector nodded imperceptibly. "I need your help. Yours, and that of your fellow believers."

The woman attending the reclining ecclesiastic spoke up sharply. "Why should we help you? Why should we tell you anything? The NFP has never done anything for us."

"I beg to differ, señora. We have left you alone."

Aurilac chuckled. "Ah, the wondrous benefits of official oversight! A fedoco with a sense of humor. Humor is a wedge for opening reluctant truths." Sitting up, he winked at his visitor. "Part of being a successful cleric is knowing how to dispense pithy aphorisms."

"You're good at it," Cardenas told him truthfully.

"Something else that binds us together. I suppose you're bound to ask me some questions. Doesn't mean I'll answer them."

"You don't have to. This isn't about you, or your sect. I'm trying to find a woman."

Beside him, Camille laughed softly. When she did so, the lights adorning her raiment flickered more brightly. "You need to look in a sextel, not the Bonezone."

Cardenas eyed her tolerantly. "A woman and her daughter."

Camille returned his gaze. "I rest my case."

With a sigh, the Inspector turned his full attention to the mildly curious Aurilac. "Others are looking for them as well. Some want to question them, some to kill them."

Aurilac grunted. "And which is it you intend?"

Cardenas took a deep breath. "I just want to find out what the hell is going on."

Exhibiting unexpected energy, the ecclesiastic sat up sharply, so quickly that he startled his doting attendant. Closing his eyes, he brought both hands down in front of him and genuflected in his visitor's direction. A look of satisfaction creased his features.

"Wonder of wonders! All praise to the Universal Box. A fedoco who not only has a sense of humor, but hints at wisdom. Who would have thought to see such a thing." Leaning back, he recovered his pipe. "That, my friend, is as close to a universal truth as any I have heard expounded. At least in the past week. I'm not saying we can help you, but what is it you want to know about these two females. Why do others want to question them, or wish them dead?"

"When I find them, I'll ask them," Cardenas replied. The Wise was coming around. The Inspector could tell.

Aurilac sighed. "Bound or unbound, they're all the same, and they don't even realize it." Setting the pipe aside, he picked up a vorec in his thick fingers. "What are their names?" By way of reply, Cardenas fingered his spinner and passed the cleric a wafer containing much of what had been learned about Surtsey and Katla Mockerkin.

Speaking directly into the vorec, Aurilac communicated with his flock. Immediately, new screens winked to life and freshly charged heads-ups glowed to one side and overhead. Less than a minute passed before the Wise rubbed the tiny receiver clipped to his right ear. His expression was not encouraging.

"No record of their current whereabouts. They are not bound to the community. You're sure of the names and likenesses?"

Cardenas's lips tightened. "Positive. I thought your people had access to closed boxes."

Aurilac shrugged slightly, and the soft flesh overlying his shoulder blades rippled. "Ay, it doesn't matter what you search if there's nothing inside. If the two you seek are within Namerica, there is no record of their presence. They must be well and truly hidden. Perhaps even by surgery."

An impatient and disappointed Cardenas shook his head. "They've had time enough to run or undergo alteration, but not both."

Aurilac was apologetic. "I'm sorry. If they were extant, we would know." Again he took in his flickering, luminous surroundings. "People can hide, but not numbers. You know that 'numerology' used to mean something entirely different?"

Cardenas had no more time for philosophical chit-chat. "Can you look for them one more time? In a place called Friendship?"

Aurilac passed the information along. Word came back almost instantly that no woman and girl of the indicated description had recently been reported in Pennsylvania, Iowa, or Manitoba.

Cardenas refused to admit defeat. Surtsey and Katla Mockerkin had to be *somewhere*. Confident of the some, he needed only to pinpoint the where. "Try linguistic analogs," he finally suggested.

"Which ones?" asked his host.

"All of them. The nearest physically and linguistically together."

So much crunch was employed for the search that the room dimmed noticeably. Somewhere, Cardenas knew, crunch and power were being drawn down from legitimate enterprises, no doubt illegally.

While the search was in progress, Aurilac the Wise had gone mute, chin slumped on his chest, eyes shut. Now he lifted his head, and a relieved Cardenas knew the gist of what the other man was going to say before he opened his mouth.

"Got 'em." For a cleric, Cardenas thought, Aurilac the Wise was not given to interminable pontificating. A heads-up materialized between host and visitor. It displayed a flickering recording of a line of travelers passing through an unpretentious customs queue. As two walked through, Cardenas recognized mother and daughter. They had changed their hair color and styles and wore clothing designed to disguise their physical features, but based on soche records, he was unquestionably looking at Surtsey and Katla Mockerkin.

"When and where?" he asked briskly. Everything he was seeing and hearing was being taken down by his open spinner.

In response to a command from Aurilac, the heads-up moved in, and around, to focus on the form the customs officer was perusing. In the course of the recording, the view lasted only a second. Freezing it locked the information in place. All but stepping into the red-tinged heads-up, Cardenas read.

"Costa Rica," he murmured. "No wonder they didn't turn up in the NFP search. They've gone outside our jurisdiction."

"*Your* jurisdiction," the female attendant pointed out with undisguised relish.

"La Amistad." Cardenas worked his spinner. "In English, *Friendship* National Park, spanning the border with Panama. Biggest untouched tract of rainforest left in Central America." Glancing up from the spinner, he met Aurilac's gaze. "Yes, that would be a good place to hide from determined pursuers." He slipped the spinner back into its jacket repository. "My name is Inspector Angel Cardenas, and I am in your debt."

Aurilac waved aloofly. "Seekers after truths are bound together by greater ties than debt, my friend. Next time you're deep in a box, spare a thought for those of us who have dedicated our lives to searching it out. Leave us in peace to continue our questing."

"I'll do that." Cardenas turned to depart. "Just try," he asked with a parting smile, "not to steal too much crunch in the process."

"What, us?" Aurilac the Wise indicated the busy chamber. "Everything you see around you, we pay for."

"*Verdad,*" the Inspector replied, "but in what kind of currency?"

"Binding currency, of course," his host assured him by way of parting. More solemnly, he added, "I hope you find this half-family before those others you spoke of do so. Gratuitous killing disturbs me."

"As opposed to explicit killing?"

"We are a peaceful order." Aurilac raised one hand. It was both a blessing and a dismissal. Cardenas chose not to point out the nature of the lethal apparatus concealed beneath the charming Camille's decorous and well-lit gown. It would not have been polite.

NINE

OF SUCH HUNCHES WERE INVESTIGATIVE CA-
reers made. Cardenas had made many such in his long years
with the Department. It was not, after all, unreasonable to
assume that the garrulous Wayne Brummel had discussed
his potential refuge with the woman he was living with as
well as with the one he had been cogering on the side. What
left the Inspector shaking his head was the ironic realization
that having grown up speaking English and Spang, he had
managed to overlook the possibility that an anglo like
Brummel might make use of the language of Cardenas's
grandparents.

According to the records, The Mock had been brought
up on charges more times than Cardenas cared to count.
Most times he had been let go, sometimes on a technicality,
usually for lack of hard evidence. According to the law, a
wife could not be made to testify against her husband in
court. The relevant statutes were less clear where a child
was concerned.

Besides which, given their apparent current state of
mind, Cardenas was convinced neither Surtsey nor Katla
Mockerkin would have to be compelled to give testimony.

Finally learning the whereabouts of the Mockerkin

women was no guarantee he would be able to extradite them safely, or even get to see them. As Aurilac the Wise's surly attendant had so succinctly pointed out, Costa Rica was well outside the NFP's jurisdiction. While the USN had dozens of treaties with the Central American Federation, they did not extend to formally allowing law officers of either territory to operate openly within the borders of their neighbor.

Informal incursions, he reflected as he stepped out of the induction tube station beside the hospital, were (as was so often the case when matters of law enforcement were involved) something else entirely.

Hyaki was waiting for him, squeezed uncomfortably into a wheelchair next to the discharge desk, looking less like a contented Buddha and more like a dyspeptic gorilla who had been confined in a small packing case for far too long. He gazed mournfully at the Inspector as the older man approached.

"They won't release me officially until somebody from the Department signs for me," he grumbled. "Times like this I wish I wasn't a bachelor. I feel like a damn registered package sitting off all by its lonesome at the post office, waiting for someone to come and claim me."

"Does that mean I can have you stamped 'Refused, Return to Sender'?" Cardenas quipped. Hyaki's response was an uncharacteristic vulgarity. The sergeant continued to mumble with annoyance as Cardenas signed off on the necessary forms.

He did kick the wheelchair when he was finally, formally, allowed to vacate it in the drivethrough facing Reception. It was a mild kick, or the chair would not have survived.

"How's the back?" Cardenas inquired sympathetically.

He did not have to ask, of course. He knew. But after long, boring days spent in rehab, his friend would need to talk.

Not that Hyaki was an especially voluble individual. The sergeant discoursed only briefly on the numbing delights of hospital downtime before taking up again his interest in the case that had resulted in his enforced vacation. As he yakked, and listened to Cardenas's replies, he frequently shrugged his shoulders or twisted his torso, as if his newly regrown skin was a too-small suit that did not quite fit properly.

"Costa Rica," the big man muttered as the Inspector pulled the cruiser away from the curb. "La Amistad. A funny place for someone with money to run to. You'd think maybe Prague or Petersburg. Not the jungle."

Cardenas swung into mild traffic, leaving quiescent the flashing warning beamers that striped the top of the official vehicle. They were in no hurry. "Evidently, hiding is more important to them than comfort. If you get vaped, it doesn't matter whether it happens while you're lying in a five-star hotel or a parking lot."

Hyaki rubbed one cheek, gently massaging new epidermis. His skin did not crawl, but it did itch. The hospital had provided a spray to minimize the effect. "Amistad, Amistad— seems to me I've run across the name before."

His partner flipped on the cruiser's scanner and ordered it to tune to a soft classics station broadcasting out of London's East End. The soaring melodies of an early symphony by Braga-Santos backgrounded the interior of the vehicle.

"It's the biggest piece of virgin upland rainforest left in the CAF. And of course, Reserva Amistad just means Friendship Reserve. I can't believe I missed on that."

The sergeant smiled. "Too many new words to learn. When you live in a place like Nogales, where the dictionary gets updated daily, it's easy for your cerebro to lose track of the obvious." For emphasis, he tapped the side of his head. The absence of hair, blown off in the explosion that had destroyed the Anderson residence, made him look more than ever like an Asian version of the Enlightened One.

"If they're hiding in the middle of the CAF," he commented, "that takes us out of it."

Cardenas's fingers stroked the steering wheel. "Not necessarily."

His partner looked over in surprise. "You intuiting that, Angel?"

A hint of a smile crossed the Inspector's face, raising slightly the points of his drooping mustache. "You've got some sick leave coming. I have vacation time accumulated. I've discussed it with Pangborn. Seems there are official duties and unofficial duties. And then there's semi-official duties." He looked across at his friend. "You and me, we're going to take a little semi-official trip. I've already stocked up on mosquito antipherms."

Hyaki crossed his arms over his chest and slumped lower in his seat. It left him with his knees blocking his view out the forward glass. "So much for a little post-op rest and relaxation," he griped.

Cardenas ignored the complaint. "You'll like Costa Rica. I understand the beaches are beautiful."

The sergeant looked back at him. His partner was concentrating on dealing with the traffic.

"You said the absent Ms. Mockerkin and her kid were heading for high rainforest. No beaches in the high rainforest."

"I said the beaches are beautiful," Cardenas replied dryly. "I didn't say we were going there."

*   *   *

San José's Intel International Airport nestled nervously between green-clad hillsides and active volcanoes, surrounded by industrial fabrication and assembly plants that in many aspects not only mimicked those of the Strip, but supplied components for it. As early as the late twentieth century, the energetic Ticos of Costa Rica had recognized that the future lay not in banana or copra farming, but in hitech and ecotourism, and had structured their country accordingly. Now Costa Rica was the richest member of the CAF, the envy of its neighbors, and a model for successful burgeoning economies in Panama and Belize.

They were passed formally but politely through Customs and Immigration before being asked to step inside an office with heavily opaqued windows. Initial uncertainty gave way to reassurance when they were greeted by Lieutenant Corazón of the CAF police. A short, stocky, hard-bodied blonde in her early forties, she sat them down in front of her desk, proffered cold drinks from an office cooler, and spoke while studying a heads-up whose contents were not visible to her visitors.

"Semi-official visit, is it?" she commented in perfect English, meeting Cardenas's gaze with an unwavering, unblinking stare. Her small stature notwithstanding, he knew he would not want to cross this woman in a fight. "We don't get many of those. I see here that you are trying to find a Namerican woman and her daughter."

Cardenas nodded. "They're running from her husband, as well as from other interested antisoc parties. A lot of money is involved, plus some confidential information that may be in the daughter's possession. We'd very much like to find them and take them home so they can be placed in a secure protection program. Right now we believe that they are panicoed."

"And you're convinced they've panicked their way here?"

"To La Amistad." Cardenas crossed his legs. The interview might be routine, but Lieutenant Corazón definitely was not.

"For a mother and child believed to be panicking, they seem to have done rather well." She smiled challengingly. "They've managed to elude your people, for example."

Cardenas would not be baited. "We didn't know where they were going until long after they had left."

The lieutenant nodded, studied the screen afresh. Then she exhaled softly and instructed it to shut down. Her attention darted between the two visiting federales. "You know what is in La Amistad rainforest? Besides quetzals and sloths and jaguars and *ormegas soldados*?"

"Lots of rain?" Hyaki speculated offhandedly.

She favored him with a look of disapproval. "La Ciudad Simiano is there. It contains the only authorized habitations. Everything else has been left wild, as decreed by the government, the WWF, the OTS, and all the other vested scientific organizations that have responsibility for preserving the health and biodiversity of the park. If your two ladies are in La Amistad, they are there with the permission of the Simiano administrators." Her tone hardened. "They may not look favorably on a visit from a pair of Namerican federales."

"We'll have a talk with them." Hyaki indicated his friend. "My partner can be very persuasive. He has a way with people."

The engaging smile Corazón bestowed on an unequivocally intrigued Cardenas was belied by her tone. "I can tell that he does," she murmured enticingly. "Unfortunately, once you enter Ciudad Simiano, you will no longer be dealing with people."

Cardenas smiled. "I know."

Hyaki looked confused. "Well, I don't. I've been laid up, and we flew down here in kind of a rush. I'm not a research guru like Angel here. What's this 'Ciudad Simiano,' and why do I have the feeling you think it might present problems for us?"

"It all depends on how the residents perceive you. All I can do is inform the Reserva Director's office that you are on your way. If you are lucky, you will be accorded admittance with no trouble. If not"—she sat back and shrugged—"then even I or my superiors cannot get you in." She proceeded to explain.

The short commuter jump to Ciudad Neily, the nearest town with an airport to the greater Amistad Reserva, was accomplished in quick time and with only a few bumps through the tropical air. Beyond securing the best available vehicle for entering the mountains—a quad fuel cellpowered 4X4 with sleeping and cooking facilities for two—the amiable if dubious Lieutenant Corazón was unable to help them. They were, after all, traveling semi-officially. This meant that while the local police would not interfere with their activities, neither could they step in to render official assistance. This did not bother the two federales. They had come in search of acquiescence rather than help.

The road out of Neily was excellent, but beyond the mountain town of San Vito it changed character rapidly. Past Sabalito it quickly degenerated into a mountain track. At over a million hectares, the expanded Reserva de Biosfera La Amistad was the largest intact expanse of undisturbed rainforest north of South America. Clearly, those responsible for its integrity intended to keep it that way.

Banging eastward, steadily gaining altitude, they found themselves surrounded by green-clad mountains on all sides. To the north, Fabrega, at 3336 meters, overtopped the entire region. Though they could not see it, they did not feel cheated. The terrain that closed in around them did not lack for unsettlingly steep slopes or dramatic cloud-piercing peaks.

They topped off the heavy-duty 4X4's cells at Progresso, the last town before entering the wilderness of the Las Tablas Zone. The Reserva continued over into nearby Panama, but the border was not marked. Despite the altitude, both men were sweating liters. They were used to the dry heat of the Strip, not the sweltering humidity of the jungle.

"Going to see the Simianos?" the attendant at the one-stop inquired in his halting English.

"If we want to enter the Las Tablas Zone, we don't have any choice." Hyaki had marked well the words of the helpful Lieutenant Corazón.

The old man nodded as he shut off the hygen filler and resealed the vehicle's tank. "Loco folk, those Simianos. Keep to themselves. Don't see them much outside the Reserva. Things are better that way, *sí*?"

Cardenas smiled tolerantly. The old man was not afraid of the Simianos; his indifference glowed like a dim bulb. "What do we owe you?"

"Namericanos!" The attendant muttered to himself as he processed the Inspector's card. "Always testing limits. Always pushing their luck."

He wished them good fortune anyway. After all, they were tourists, and as such, their presence in his small community was to be appreciated. The Ticos had learned the lessons of the late twentieth century well.

Outside Progresso, the road soon degenerated into a damp, gooey mush in which gravel occasionally put in an appearance like candy chips in a pudding. Repeated tropical downpours had sawn gullies in the track like parallel slices in a cake. Behind the wheel of the rented vehicle, Hyaki suffered more than his companion from the continual jolts and bumps, since his fuzz-covered skull barely cleared the roof. As if the way was not difficult enough, it began to rain.

As the road grew steadily more slippery, they soon found themselves measuring progress in terms of one meter slid sideways for every two gained forward. The rain stopped as suddenly as it had begun, giving way to feathery gray-white clouds that swept down from the emerald mountaintops like gathering ghosts. Once, an enormous bird, all white and black feathers, talons and beak, soared directly past the front of the car, screeling sharply as it wheeled out of the oncoming 4X4's path. Even a brief glimpse was enough to show that its wingspan was greater than two meters. A startled Hyaki slammed on the brakes, forcing Cardenas to grab the dash with both hands to keep from being thrown forward. Fortunately, none of the six protective foambags surrounding him inflated.

"Sorry," the sergeant apologized. "It surprised me. I was watching the road and didn't see it coming. What the hell was it, anyway? The damn thing looked like a hang glider."

"Harpy eagle." An attentive Cardenas heard the high-pitched screel again. It was far away now, and fading. "You're not supposed to see it coming."

His partner eyed him uncertainly. "How do you know that's what it was?"

"I watch a lot of nature vits." He nodded at the tattered track that continued to unspool in front of them. "Take it low and slow when it shifts back in gear. We don't want to put too much pressure on the sensors, and we definitely don't want to get stuck here. It's a long, wet walk back to Progresso."

"I know that." Grumbling, Hyaki reached for the shifter to put the vehicle back in drive. There was only one forward gear, of course. The car's onboard box would sense whenever anything lower was required, and allocate power accordingly.

A figure materialized from among the trees off to their left, stumbling downslope. He wore a simple plastic rainshawl striped in local colors. Except for the rainshawl and the hitech walking stick he carried, he might have stepped straight out of a Mayan stela. He was followed by a young woman carrying a babe in arms and two more men who were visibly younger than their predecessor. While these three waited by the side of the road, which under the effects of the intermittent pounding rain had become virtually indistinguishable from its center, the patriarch of the group hobbled toward the idling 4X4, using his walking stick for support. Hyaki lowered his window.

"Your pardon, *señores*," he said in passable English, "but my family and I were caught out in the weather today." Turning slightly, he gestured up the graded quagmire of a thoroughfare. "Our truck, full of produce from our farm, broke down on the way back from the Reserva. We are very tired, and my daughter-in-law's child is cold and hungry. Could you perhaps give us a ride into the Ciudad? From there we can arrange for the parts necessary to fix our truck."

Cardenas scrutinized the speaker and the waiting supplicants. "Sure, we'll be happy to help." He reached into an inside pocket. "Here's a little something for the *niño*."

As he drew his gun and pointed it directly at the petitioner's face, Hyaki pressed himself backward as far as the driver's seat would allow and used his left hand to recline it even farther. The eyes of the rainshawl-bedecked local widened as he stared down the barrel of the tiny but lethal pistol.

"Step back." Most of the time, Cardenas's voice was calm, even soothing. But when he wanted to, he could chill it deep enough to neutralize habañero sauce. "Keep your hands out and up where I can see them. No sudden moves. Fredoso, get us moving."

"Oh yeah," murmured the sergeant tensely. Staying back, he maneuvered his bulk until he could reach the shift controller. The 4X4 started forward, sensors in the wheels and the undercarriage combining their readings to determine that full low gear was in order. The transmission responded accordingly.

As they inched forward and began to roll past the tiny family group, the young woman brought both arms up and to one side and threw the cloth-swaddled babe she was holding straight at the windshield. With a shout, Cardenas shoved open the door on his side and threw himself out. Hyaki did the same on the driver's side, landing hard in the gravel-flecked mud. Detecting the absence of an operating driver, the vehicle immediately shut down its engine and started to slide into park. It never made it.

The bundle that struck the windshield bounced once off the non-conductive transparency before landing on the hood. Containing nothing organic, it promptly delivered itself of a violent electric discharge. The smell of ozone flashed through the damp air as sparks erupted from the hood, roof, sides, back, and underbody of the 4X4. Designed to instantly electrocute any occupants of the car, the packet ended up frying only the electrical system of the vehicle, which promptly caught on fire.

Rolling madly, the Inspector brought his weapon up and around as something hot and superfast sliced a groove in the ground precisely where he had been lying a moment earlier. The young woman who had hurled the packet had flung her rainshawl aside and was in the process of aiming the multibarreled burster in Hyaki's direction just as Cardenas's second shot tore through her right shoulder. Her face contorting, she dropped the burster and grabbed at her upper arm. On the other side of the road, Hyaki had rolled into a ditch and was now firing steadily.

While the senior member of the phony farming quartet provided very unpeasantlike covering fire, the two younger men grabbed their wounded associate and half dragged, half carried her off down the road. One of the sergeant's shots caught the retreating elder in the ribs and forcefully evacuated his chest cavity. As he slammed facedown into the mud, his three retreating colleagues increased their pace. In less than a minute, they had disappeared around the first bend in the road.

A heavy mist began to fall as the two federales warily approached the unmoving body of the man who had asked them for a lift. There was no sign of his three companions. Blood and drizzle swirled together and collected in puddles, to be soaked up by the ever-porous tropical soil.

Hyaki holstered his weapon as he peered back the way they had come. "I don't think the others will be back. What was that all about?"

Kneeling beside the dead man, Cardenas pushed back a sleeve to expose a tattoo lavish with coiling serpents, feathers, and Mayan glyphs. "Sensemayá. Primarily a CAF gang, but they've been known to reconnoiter as far north as Four Corners."

The sergeant ran a big hand from his forehead across his reviving scalp and down the back of his neck. "I've read about them. How'd you know, Angel?"

"That they were Sensemayá?" He straightened, brushing clinging mud from his pants. "I didn't, until just now. What I did know was that they weren't simple farmers, and that they wanted more than a ride." Hyaki nodded perceptively. Better than anyone else, he knew his partner's capabilities.

Cardenas considered the body. "Their postures were all wrong. Stiff instead of submissive. Taut instead of tired from walking. The woman held her 'baby' the wrong way. The two agros with her were tense and apprehensive instead of hopeful." Bending, he picked up the fallen walking stick and turned it over in his hands, studying it with interest.

"Grandpa here had the best teeth and the smoothest hands of any farmer I've ever seen. As for his cane, it's a fine piece of facading, but the dissimulation isn't quite perfect."

Turning, he pointed the upper segment of the walking stick toward the rainforest and ran a finger along a depression embedded in one side. There was a flash of flame, and a good-sized tree, blown in half, toppled noisily into the surrounding jungle. Hyaki contemplated the weapon respectfully.

"What do you think, Angel? Mataros sent out by The Mock to intercept us? Maybe people working with the Inzini, or some other faction?"

Cardenas sounded dubious. "They may not be farmers, but they looked and acted local. According to what I read before we got here, this is still pretty wild country. All kinds of banditos and scaves hide in the mountains and pop out to ambush unwary travelers." He indicated their vehicle, from which smoke continued to pour. The flames had already been dampened by the vehicle's integrated fire-suppressant system. "Probably thought we were tourists, or maybe researchers bound for the Ciudad. Easy marks, little likelihood of any resistance, much less a fight, and loaded down with credit and valuable gear." He shook his head regretfully. "Didn't even have time to flash an ident at them. Not that it would necessarily have changed their minds."

They discussed the veiled features of the lethal walking stick as they cautiously approached their 4X4. Its internal systems had finally succeeded in putting out the fire. In lieu of the preceding flames, black smoke now rose from beneath the vehicle's hood as well as from the interior dash. The bundle that had been thrown by the young woman lay melted and motionless on the hood. Fully discharged, it was now perfectly harmless.

They didn't have to open the hood to surmise what they would encounter beneath, but they did anyway. The scorched wires, slagged chips, and smoldering components that greeted their gaze confirmed what the rising smoke had already told them: that this vehicle would never travel under its own power again. Letting the hood slam shut on its ruined lifters, they moved to inspect the interior. From the fire-blackened center storage console and still-hot glove compartment they extracted respectively, among other items of newly-made rubbish, two lumps of blackened and seared equipment: their respective police spinners. As Cardenas let the now useless lumps fall to the wet ground, Hyaki leaned one massive hand on the composite frame of the ruined vehicle and gazed glumly at the surrounding greenery.

"Now what?"

Slogging around to the back of the 4X4, Cardenas manually dropped the tailgate. "Can't talk, so we walk. We're a lot closer to the entrance to the Reserva and the Ciudad Simiano than we are to Progresso. Besides, I didn't come all this way to go back."

"I didn't come all this way to get filthy dirty and soaked to my new skin, either, but at least it's not cold." Bending over alongside his friend, Hyaki began gathering those meager supplies that had survived the vehicle's brief but intense internal conflagration. Their luggage, containing most of their clothing, gear, and their reserve spinners, resided unharmed back in the room they had rented at the Posada Progresso.

Making a face, Cardenas contemplated the cloud-filled sky. "Wait until tonight. At this altitude, even the jungle gets cold."

"Thanks for apprising me of that fact," Hyaki responded mordantly. "Frankly, I would have been happier dwelling in ignorance."

TEN

THEY HAD MANAGED TO COVER LESS THAN A couple of kims when the rain resumed. Munching on the whole grain and fruit snack bar that constituted half his surviving rations, Hyaki glumly planted one foot in front of the other, his bare arms crossed over his chest. A small bottle of water bobbed in one pants pocket. Anticipating an afternoon arrival at the Reserva, they had brought little with them in the way of provisions.

At least they did not have to worry about conserving water. Though it added notably to their discomfort, the cool rain sufficed to slake their thirst. Save for their cupped palms, they had nothing to collect it in except their clothing, which was soon soaked through. Like almost everything else they had brought with them, their rain-repelling slickers had perished in the blaze that had consumed the doomed 4X4. In this dejected fashion they plodded grimly forward, wet and unhappy, waiting to hitch a ride that never materialized.

"Not many tourists up this way." Cardenas tried to identify a small, bright red bird that was pecking at some fruit on the lower branches of a nearby tree. "La Amistad isn't Monteverde or Corcovado."

"It isn't Nogales, either." The shoes Hyaki had chosen were comfortable for walking—when they were dry. He glanced back the way they had come. "Surely a supply truck or ranger cruiser has to make regular runs along here?"

"I'm sure they do." The Inspector leaped carefully over a deep, water-filled pothole. "Those feleons would avoid them. I guess we don't look like rangers." He looked over at his partner. "Some good comes out of everything. Maybe next time the survivors will think twice before trying to jump the first 4X4 that comes along."

"I wish they'd thought about it this time." The big man grimaced. "I need a steak."

"Pretend you're a twentieth-century urban beat cop." Bending, Cardenas scooped up an arm-long length of fallen wood and tossed it toward his friend. "Here, have a nightstick."

Hyaki swatted it aside, sending bark and droplets flying. "I'd rather have a beefstick. On a couple of fresh tortillas." He glanced up at the lowering sky. "It's getting dark."

Cardenas squinted skyward. "Maybe the rain will go down with the sun."

"You really think that?" So hopeful was the sergeant's tone that Cardenas did not have the heart to tell him otherwise.

Surprisingly, the rain did let up as the light faded from the world. It did not come to an end completely, but instead was transformed into a clinging, all-pervasive mist. At the same time, the temperature actually rose as night descended. The result was an increase in cloying humidity that canceled out any benefit they might have enjoyed from the cessation of the rain.

Enough light lingered to show the track ahead of them

branching off in three directions. Installed at the tripartite junction was a first-rate weatherproofed road sign, newly stamped and finished, that had been knocked sufficiently askew to render the directions imprinted thereon as useless as tits on a boar hog. Tired and discouraged, both men looked for a place to camp.

"Can't go on in the dark," Hyaki pointed out unnecessarily. The past couple of hours of heavy slogging had convinced him that the mud beneath their feet was imbued with a life of its own, and was deliberately crawling over his ankles and up his legs. "Wish I smoked."

"Why is that?" Cardenas was hunting for a tree with enough of a leafy overhang to provide some added protection from the weather.

"Because then I'd have a lighter, and we could make a fire."

"Don't be too hard on yourself. Look around." The Inspector indicated the sodden rainforest. "Where would you find anything to burn?"

The big man considered their rapidly darkening surroundings. "This isn't my style, Angel. I'm used to chasing nins and baggerags through the back streets of Agua Pri and Sonoyta. Wilderness survival is way down on my résumé."

"Mine also," confessed Cardenas as he began to gather fallen leaves to construct a makeshift mattress. "Maybe like you said, somebody will come by. If not, we'll resume hiking tomorrow."

Pulling his second and last snack bar from a pocket, Hyaki flashed it at his friend and made a face. "At least there's no need to worry about breakfast. It's already cooked. Not that I wouldn't prefer a couple of breakfast burritos, with cheese and chorizo and sour cream and maybe a side of—"

"Shut up," Cardenas snapped at him. "I don't have to intuit the rest."

Thankfully, the rain did not resume as they sat down next to one another beneath the ample bole of a big cecropia to wait for morning. With exhaustion compensating for the lack of a bed, they slept surprisingly well in spite of their saturated clothing.

Nor did they have to worry about oversleeping.

Cardenas awoke to a crawling sensation the likes of which he had experienced only once before, twenty years earlier while engaged in a stakeout in a rattrap of a motel in the worst part of Tucson. Those legs had been larger, but the sensation was the same.

Leaping to his feet, ignoring the stiffness in his bones, he began slapping and swatting at himself. His awakeners fought back with stings and bites. Fortunately, few had slipped beneath his outer clothing. With hands and face most at risk, he concentrated on those first.

Hyaki blinked sleepily, then gaped at his afflicted friend. "Tell me the tune you're dancing to, Angel. I could use a—" The sudden realization that he had also become unwilling host to a sample of the uninvited sent him rocketing to his feet.

Together, they hopped and flailed at the ants that had invaded their clothing. Cardenas knew all about stimstick abusers, and crunch masters, about life on, above, and under the Strip. Living in the vastness of the Sonoran Desert had not prepared him to deal with the tropics. Had he been more versed in local ecology, he would have known that trees of the genus *Cecropia* are usually home to a varied assortment of tropical ants who live on and within them, and who do not take kindly to uninvited visitors.

It took twenty minutes of slapping, flicking, and inspecting before both men were reasonably confident they had rid themselves of their tiny but ferocious guests. They were now wide awake—and tired again.

Resignedly, Cardenas started forward down what he hoped was the right road, given the unhelpful angle of the single road sign. Wisps of damp fog clung to the treetops. Hidden birds hollered haunting cries. Within the canopy, unseen residents had commenced their morning commute. If their spinners had not been fried in their barbecue of a 4X4, the two federales could have called for a ride.

"How far do you think it is to the park boundary?" Hyaki found himself wondering if the anticipated ranger station was located on the edge of the Reserva, or deeper within.

Cardenas shuffled along beside his mountainous companion. "I don't remember from the map. Didn't pay much attention to it. Left it to the car's navigation system."

"*My* navigation system is sputtering." The sergeant gazed longingly into the rainforest, envisioning bananas hanging ripe and heavy from beckoning branches.

The image notwithstanding, he was as startled as his partner when the three uakaris landed in front of them. Both men halted in shock. With their bright, pinkish-red, hairless faces and long white fur, the dog-sized simians resembled nothing so much as a trio of downsized yetis. Adding to the visitors' astonishment was the realization that each of the newcomers carried a simple but undeniably efficient-looking knife and a small backpack.

Men and monkeys regarded one another silently. Then the smallest uakari scampered up into the tree nearest the road, pulled a small communicator from his backpack, and began fingering the front of the device.

"They're from the Reserva." Hyaki kept his voice to a whisper.

It was hardly necessary to point that out, Cardenas knew. The Ciudad Simiano located within the Reserva La Amistad had been created back in the '50s to provide a home for those simians who had been the subject or the offspring of now-banned research in genetic manipulation designed to enhance their intelligence. The focus of more than forty years of fighting between scientific and wildlife organizations, such experiments had also been carried out on dolphins. But while intelligence-enhanced dolphins had oceans in which to roam, no such preserves were available, in a world ever more overrun by humanity, for the altered apes and their relatives. Hence the creation within La Amistad of Ciudad Simiano—the City of Simians.

Knowing this, however, had not really prepared Hyaki and Cardenas for a face-to-face encounter with the inhabitants.

"I read that they moved about freely," the Inspector murmured to his friend, "but I didn't know they were allowed outside the boundaries of the Reserva."

"Did you know they were allowed to carry weapons?" Hyaki was paying attention to the knives. They were made of metal and composite, not hewn from wood or bone. Sensibly, he kept his hands out where they could be seen, and away from his service pistol.

"No, I did not." Cardenas was concentrating on the two uakaris still on the ground, trying to read their eyes and their movements. In the course of his long career he had seen and experienced a great deal, but this was the first time he had ever tried to intuit a monkey.

With a muted crash of branches and leaves, the energetic broadcaster descended from the treetops to rejoin his taciturn, pallid companions. Cardenas smiled and crouched, bringing his line of sight more in line with theirs.

"Look here, hombers. My friend and I are with the Namerican Federal Police. You know—policia? Federales? We are expected."

Two of the uakaris exchanged a glance and palavered softly among themselves. What was their intelligence level? the Inspector found himself wondering. Were they capable of understanding human speech? Or did they communicate only via their traditional chatter? Chimps in the wild had been observed using simple tools like rocks and sticks as long ago as the mid-twentieth century. From carrying a stick to wielding a knife did not require much in the way of a cerebral jump. As for the compact communicator, it might have been preprogrammed to send out one of several compacted signals, a procedure that could easily be taught, and reinforced, with rewards of food.

"Maybe," Hyaki ventured thoughtfully as he listened to the uakaris converse, "the Reserva's rangers have come out to meet us."

"Or maybe it's sheer coincidence." Movement in the trees off to one side drew his attention away from the muttering, energetic monkeys.

Half a dozen veldt baboons came ambling out of the brush. Larger than the uakaris, they carried bigger knives. In the forefront was a single slim, remarkably human-looking chimp. Leather straps crisscrossed his chest, while the ubiquitous pack rode on his back. Unlike his simian companions, he approached on two legs and carried no weapons.

"That's a bonobo," a fascinated Cardenas murmured to his colleague. "They're considered to be the most intelligent and humanlike of all the apes."

"How do you *know* all this stuff?" Hyaki's attention kept shifting from the bonobo to the far more suspicious baboons.

"I told you." Cardenas waited as the confident chimp drew near. "You need to watch more vit."

Standing, the bonobo was nearly as tall as Cardenas. Its expression was impossible to read. Slowly, it extended one powerful hand toward the Inspector's face. Cardenas tensed but held his ground. Dexterous fingers grasped one side of the human's drooping mustache and tugged gently. Letting go, the bonobo stepped back, scratched pointedly at his own whiskery visage—and grinned hugely. At this, the baboons and uakaris set up a howl of delight.

"Don't," Cardenas whispered tersely to his companion, "say *anything*."

"Who, me?" Hyaki studiously avoided his friend's stern gaze.

When the general laughter had died down, the bonobo slapped his chest and grunted. "Joe!"

Cardenas and Hyaki duplicated the gesture, following which Cardenas removed his ident bracelet from an inside pocket of his still-damp Willis and Geiger. With the loss of their spinners in the burned-out 4X4, it was all the official identification that remained to him. As a visitor to the CAF, he could carry but not wear it. Would the ape recognize it, and what it stood for?

The bonobo's response was as insightful as it was unexpected. Reaching around into his backpack, he removed a bracelet that was nearly identical to the Inspector's own. The colors and patterns were different, but there was no mistaking the significance.

"I'll be damned," a dumbfounded Hyaki muttered. "A fellow cop!"

"*Sí*—yes," declared the bonobo proudly. Turning, he made an unmistakable gesture for the two men to follow. They did so without hesitation, pleased to see that their intimidating bodyguard of baboons had sheathed their weapons. Having swung effortlessly up into the trees, the uakaris were watching everything from above.

After walking for less than ten minutes, they came upon a small convertible truck. The top was down, exposing both the forward seats and the open bed. An elegant circular emblem on the passenger-side door featured rainforest trees, a floating sun, and an upreaching and distinctively hairy arm and hand. Hyaki kept thoughts of crossed bananas with coconuts rampant to himself. Pointing to the vehicle, the bonobo smiled again and indicated they should climb in.

"*Sobres*—all right!" Unable to fit in the front, Hyaki piled in back. "No more hiking in this humidity!" He plucked dejectedly at the front of his sodden shirt. "Not that we could get much wetter than we already are."

Cardenas slipped into the passenger seat up front. "Wonder where the driver is?"

His question was answered when Joe hopped into the seat behind the wheel. Activated by the broadcast unit that ringed his left middle finger, the engine hummed to life immediately. The truck bounced down the track, and soon picked up surprising speed. In the back, Hyaki found himself surrounded by half a dozen curious baboons whose front canines were longer than knives the sergeant had taken off street-skimming subgrubs. He smiled wanly while hanging on to keep from being jounced out of the vehicle.

Concentrating on his driving, Joe spoke without looking at his guest. "Angel police—Joe police!"

"Yes," Cardenas assented. "So is my companion. You are a policeman in the Reserva?"

"Ranger in Reserva," the bonobo replied proudly. "Policeperson in Ciudad Simiano. Protect and serve." Now he glanced over. "You and big friend have visitor permit?"

"In my pocket," Cardenas assured the driver, greatly relieved to have in his possession actual hardcopy documents. Had the permission to enter the Reserva they had obtained in San José been forwarded in purely electronic form, it would have been lost along with everything else on his spinner. Only by good fortune had he absently kept the relevant credentials in the back pocket of his pants.

The bonobo nodded vigorously. "Good! Not many human visit La Amistad. Only scientist, mostly. Even less come to visit Ciudad. We like it that way."

"We'll try to be good guests," Cardenas assured him, "and to leave as soon as possible."

His host shrugged. "You stay is okay with Joe. I like humans." He gestured back toward the bed of the rattling, bouncing truck. "Harder for lower types to make friend. You know history of experiments? Only few of the great apes smart enough to make real use of brain boost. Chimpanzees, mostly. Also orangutans and few more. These guys"—he indicated the baboons and then the uakaris who were following along in the trees—"not real bright, you savvy? Tamarins, squirrel monkeys, colobus—they all pretty simple folk." Changing tack, he asked animatedly, "You like Hundel?"

"You mean Handel? There are a few pieces that—"

Joe interrupted before Cardenas could finish. "Great human composer. Good stuff. We got small choir in Ciudad. Maybe you get to hear howler monkeys do 'Hallelujah, Amen, Amen' from *Judas Maccabeus*." He chuckled appreciatively. "Pretty special."

The road continued its gentle climb up into old-growth, primary rainforest, Cardenas listening to the spirited patter of their hirsute driver, Hyaki smiling uncomfortably at the sharp-toothed simian sextet with whom he was compelled to share the bed of the truck. Along the way they passed a number of signs. Cardenas remarked on one illuminated floater that dominated a fork leading off to the left.

"Storage facilities." Joe deftly avoided a pothole the size of a small fishpond. "Reserva headquarters ahead. We go to Ciudad." He looked over tentatively. "Unless you no want go now."

"No." Ride this out and see where it took them, Cardenas had long since decided. "The Ciudad is fine."

The bonobo's enormous grin reappeared. "Ciudad is best. Not many human visitors. You talk Sorong."

"Sorry," Cardenas replied. "I don't mean to bore you."

"No, no!" Joe slapped his chest in amusement. "Sorong head of Ciudad. Very bright guy, you see. Genius, some human research folk say. Nice fella, too—even if no bonobo."

It was disconcerting to see a guarded gate in the midst of so much magnificent, undisturbed jungle, but Cardenas supposed it could not be avoided. He remarked on the absence of fencing.

"Reserva," Joe explained as the truck began to slow. "Animals need freedom to move around."

Cardenas nodded. "The local Ticos don't kill them if they wander outside the Reserva boundaries?"

Joe shook his head. "Tourists come to see wildlife. No wildlife, no tourists. No tourists, no money. People know. Even humans understand."

As they approached the gate, the Inspector remembered his history. "They didn't always. Tell me, Joe: are you happy that some human scientists manipulated"—he almost said "monkeyed with"—"the intelligence of your ancestors?"

The bonobo shrugged. "Sure. As means for communication, speaking words beats screaming and throwing your excrement every time. Joe can still ouk-ouk with the best of them, but language better. Feel sorry for the little guys, though." With a jerk of a thumb, he indicated the baboons in back. "They just no get it." He tapped his throat with the back of his free hand. "Anyway, no room in here to lower their larynxes. Larynx stays up, no possible to have real speech. Just like in human babies in first three months."

Cardenas was not sure what to expect as they neared the Simiano compound. An absurdist vision of crenellated battlements manned by armored chimpanzees clutching crossbows and slings harked back to novels of fantasy he had read as a boy. The reality was far simpler and more prosaic. They passed a succession of signs warning travelers that they were approaching a restricted area that could not be entered without prior authorization, then an automatic gate that recognized the truck and rose to let them through, before finally crossing a narrow, well-maintained bridge. The modest river it crossed was no moat, but effectively served the same purpose.

The headquarters compound was no different from what the two visitors might have expected to find in a comparable human zone: small prefab buildings designed to withstand the elements scattered about a trio of slightly larger, more solid, two-story structures. Several were evidently dedicated to ongoing scientific research, though whether these studies focused on the rainforest or the residents of the Ciudad the Inspector did not know. Primates of various species swung above the compound on a network of synthetic fiber ropes. Beneath these aerial pathways, larger apes ambled about.

"Have our own laws and regulations here." Disdaining the door, the bonobo vaulted effortlessly over the side of

THE MOCKING PROGRAM   171

the truck. Baboons spilled from the rear bed, while Hyaki disembarked more slowly. The rough ride had been hard on his still-healing skin. "Take care of ourselves."

They drew curious stares as they walked toward the main building. Cardenas indicated the nearest research facility. "Who works in there?"

Their host drew his upper lip back to expose teeth in a huge smile. "You mean, humans or us? Mostly humans. No ape got university degree—yet. Have enough trouble trying to get CAF allow us to vote." He spread gray-black arms wide. "You tell me, man. What am I—citizen, or exhibit? Is this town, or zoo?"

"I'm just a guest," Cardenas replied tactfully. "I don't have enough knowledge to even begin to discuss the subject."

Joe executed a perfect backflip, out of which he jabbed a long finger in the Inspector's direction. "Someday humans got to take a stand." He started up the steps. A wide covered porch ran around the building. There were no chairs on the plastic flooring, only lounges, hanging baskets, and a couple of swings made from old truck tires.

There was no receptionist. With its rooms largely devoid of furniture, glassless windows, and open doorways, the entire structure had the air of a jungle hostel. Reaching the rear of the building, they found that they had passed through the entire structure. A second covered porch in back overlooked a steep slope, allowing a view into the rainforest canopy.

"Leave you here now." The bonobo gave them each a hearty slap on the back that jolted Cardenas slightly forward and made even Hyaki wince. "Joe got work to do. You talk to director a while. Get your answers." He winked broadly. "Maybe Joe see you later."

"Wait a minute," Hyaki began—but the chimp had already turned and scrambled off on all fours back into the building. "That's just fine," the sergeant muttered. "What now? Where's this 'director'?"

A gray mountain that Cardenas had assumed to be a decorative stone sculpture uncoiled from the far end of the porch and started toward them on all fours.

Both men held their ground. Maybe it was the two hundred kilos of muscle that made him hesitate, or the knowledge that those long silvery arms could pull off his legs as easily as he would remove drumsticks from a Christmas turkey, or the jaws that could crush bone like popcorn, but Cardenas felt that flight was not an option.

The huge silverback gorilla halted less than a meter away. Then it sat down before them, crossed both legs, placed massive hands against one another palm to palm, and inclined its head forward in a terse nod of acknowledgment.

"Welcome to Ciudad Simiano, gentlemen." One hand gestured at a nearby couch, the only article of human furniture in sight. "Please, sit down. I am Sorong, the Director of the simian compound." The other hand extended in the Inspector's direction. Instinctively, Cardenas reached out, and felt his fingers completely enveloped. The grip was firm but controlled, and he withdrew his digits intact.

Sensing their unease, the Director dug into a satchel slung at his side and removed the largest pair of spectacles Cardenas had ever seen. Balancing them on his blunt nostrils and tucking the gripping arms against the sides of his head, the great ape smiled reassuringly.

"One of Joe's askari uakaris informed me via comm of your coming. I understand that you had some trouble with a vehicle? No one walks into the Reserva. He also told me

that you are police from Namerica. Doubtless the pair that
San José informed us several days ago we were to expect.
How can we help you?"

The eyeglasses gave the enormous primate the appearance of a squat, furry, and very nude professor of literature.
It was a sight to make one smile. Neither federale did so,
fearing such a reaction might be taken the wrong way.

But for the first time since the encounter with the Sensemayá on the road, Cardenas felt he could relax.

ELEVEN

"WE'VE COME IN SEARCH OF TWO NAMERI-
cans, a mother and daughter, who we have reason to believe
may have fled into La Amistad. We know they arrived in
San José not long ago. We were told by the authorities that
the Ciudad Simiano administers and monitors all entry to
the Reserva. It would be a great help to us if you could
check your records, to see if anyone matching descriptions
we will provide has entered at any time in the past several
weeks, and if so, where they might be located now."

"I see." The gorilla nodded. "You used the word 'fled.'
That is a very strong word, Mr. Cardenas."

"It may not be strong enough. We believe the mother and
daughter have come this way seeking refuge from those
who intend them harm. If you could just check your entry
records, we may be able to single them out even without
available visuals. They may be periodically changing their
appearance as well as their names."

Leaning forward slightly, the Director rested his prominent chin on one fist. "These bad individuals you speak of:
you really think they might try to follow these females all
the way into the CAF?"

Hyaki nodded vigorously. "Sooner or later, they'll track

them down. Even to a place as remote as Amistad. The NFP doesn't know all the details yet, but there seems to be something of considerable importance at stake. Whatever is involved is big enough that people are willing to die to control whatever it is. My partner and I, representing and on behalf of the NFP, would dearly like to know its nature. We'd also like to help these women survive. We have a highly evolved witness protection program that could be of great benefit to them."

Sorong sat back and placed an enormous hand on each knee. "If they have tried to enter here, Amistad is a big place. Lots of room to hide, plenty of trails into the mountains. If they have acquired assistance from someone in Progresso or another of the human communities, they could be impossible to track."

"These days, no one is impossible to track," Cardenas responded tersely. "The people who are after them are sophisticated, and they have resources. They're not your average street loco. My partner and I have had the opportunity to become personally acquainted with their capabilities. This woman, Surtsey Mockerkin, and her daughter Katla, *will* be found. It may take those hunting them some time, but when money is no object, results are invariably forthcoming. I've looked at and smelled too many spizzed bodies to think this state of affairs will turn out any differently—unless we can take them into protective custody first."

"That's assuming," Hyaki put in, "that they haven't been tracked down and taken away from here already."

Heaving a ponderous sigh, the gorilla adjusted his spectacles. "They haven't."

Though he had failed to intuit the Director's reaction, Cardenas was not slow in responding to it. "You've seen

them? Then they *are* in the Reserva." He worked to keep
his voice steady. "Do you happen to know where they are
now?"

"I do."

"Well then," Hyaki blurted out before Cardenas could
restrain him, "tell us!"

"Perhaps." Unperturbed by the sergeant's agitation, the
Director turned to contemplate the rolling, untouched jungle beyond the porch. "What if I were to assure you that
both females are in no danger of being forcibly removed
from the Reserva?"

"There's no way you can do that," Cardenas replied
bluntly. "There's no way you can prove that to my satisfaction."

Sorong half closed his eyes, as if pondering weightier
matters, before looking back to his guests. "Let's take a
walk." Rising, he led them back through the building and
down the front steps into the central courtyard. Although
plenty of primates were present, garrulous Joe was not
among them. Hyaki was in an agony of impatience, but
Cardenas saw that there was nothing to be gained by insisting. Attempting to pressure an entity like Sorong could
prove counterproductive. Their host would help them in his
own time—or not at all.

"We didn't ask for the raise in intelligence we were
given," Sorong explained as they crossed the neat, well-
kept grounds, "but now that it has been given to us, we have
no intention of handing it back. The relevant genes appear
to be dominant, and are being passed along to descendants
at a rate of four to one. Those who are not so gifted at birth
are loved and cared for here as affectionately and appropri-
ately as are any comparably impaired human infants. Those
primates who are only capable of lower forms of intelli-

gence, from macaques to vervets, are looked after by the rest of us. There is less intelligence prejudice here than in your typical human community." Rising up from all fours, he gestured at the buildings of the compound and the intact rainforest that swept up to cover the surrounding mountainsides in varying shades of pristine green.

"For those of us who now live here, Amistad is a primate paradise. As per the articles that established the Ciudad Simiano, no humans are allowed in the Reserva without our permission. Not even scientists wishing to do research. We run our own affairs. In return for being allowed to do this, we are better guardians of the park than any human rangers could be. Since the advent of our stewardship, not a single species of plant or animal has gone extinct within the Reserva. No other park in the Americas can make such a claim." Deep-set, heavily browed eyes regarded Cardenas unblinkingly.

"Chimps and gorillas who have undergone training here are working as park rangers in Africa, in South America, and in Asia, guarding preserves difficult for humans to watch, scanning for poachers, taking readings for scientists. It is a relationship that has benefited all who are involved. Meanwhile, as I said, the more intelligent apes look after the lesser ones. As a system, it functions quite well. The only humans allowed in are those who have been preaccredited and accepted by us. No one else."

Hyaki watched a quartet of sifakas lope across the path in front of them. "But you told us that there are many ways for people to slip into the Reserva."

Sorong nodded. "It is difficult but not impossible to make an illegal entry. But to remain within the Reserva boundaries unobserved for any extended length of time is very difficult. Few try. One reason is that because of our presence here the park has acquired ... a reputation. Largely undeserved, but we do not make an active effort to discourage it. Anyone found inside the Reserva boundaries without authorization is arrested by Joe's people. The sight of a dozen or more of us, irregardless of size, aggressively wielding knives and other weapons is usually enough to humble the boldest intruder."

"Meaning," Cardenas observed sagely, "that if the Mockerkin women *are* within the Reserva, as you claim, and you know their current whereabouts, then they most likely are here with your permission."

A large, free-standing statue dominated the far side of the courtyard. Wreaths of flowers had been placed at its base. The eyes of the beautifully sculpted figure appeared to be gazing off into the distance, beyond the compound, beyond the rainforest. Both hands were upraised, the thick fingers spread in a complex gesture. The figure was that of an aged, wizened mountain gorilla. Set in the base was a single bronze plate on which were inscribed multiple dates, and a single name.

KOKO

Hyaki gazed up at the solemn, yearning countenance that had been memorialized in bronze. "Friend of yours?"

Their host was gazing respectfully, if not reverently, at the statue. "No, not a friend. A long-deceased relation, I am afraid. A most remarkable individual in the annals of primate development. A predecessor, you might say. Koko was a project. One who learned a great deal of universal human sign language, and in so doing helped to pave the way for the present intellectual circumstances of the inhabitants of this compound. Among us, Koko is venerated the way your kind revere an Einstein or da Vinci."

Cardenas did not wish to appear impolite, but much as

he was personally enjoying the tour, professionally he was no less keen to pursue their lead than was his partner. He said as much to Sorong.

The gorilla sighed and dug at the fur under one arm. "I was afraid it might come to something like this when we signed on to the original arrangement."

His visitors exchanged a glance. "What arrangement?" Cardenas inquired without hesitation.

"Between ourselves and the females you seek. They did not use the name you mentioned earlier, but given their circumstances, one would expect them to employ many different names."

"Just so you should know," Cardenas informed him, "Mockerkin is their real name. Surtsey and Katla Mockerkin. Have they told you who they are running from?"

"Just that they are in danger, and needed a refuge."

The Inspector nodded understandingly. "They're fleeing the woman's husband and the girl's father, who is from all records and accounts a particularly nasty sort of felon. There are others after them as well, some for reasons we can determine, others for purposes we're still not sure of. This matter has already resulted in the deaths of several people, among whom my partner and I were nearly included." Leaning forward, he tried to bring all his considerable powers of persuasion to bear. "Based on what we do know, and have already undergone in the course of pursuing this case, the presence of these women constitutes a danger to anyone and everyone who happens to be in their vicinity."

Sorong looked distinctly unhappy. "If that is so, then those who agreed to the present arrangement, myself included, were not told the true extent of the risk. Understand," he explained calmly as he adjusted his glasses, "we of the Simiano are not afraid of anyone who might be tracking the two females. The jungle is not the city, and those who arrive here planning to make trouble usually find it. We know how to take care of ourselves."

Eyeing the two-hundred-kilo silverback, Cardenas saw no reason to doubt the Director's claim. Jumping someone walking the streets of the Strip was one thing; trying to root them out of a jungle hideaway defended by intelligent, weapons-bearing apes was something else entirely. The Inzini, the Ooze from Oz, and their fellow antisocs would likely as not find themselves as out of their depth in these green canyons as did Cardenas and his partner. On the Strip, they could blend in easily. In La Amistad, they would stick out like tofu in a steakhouse. Surtsey Mockerkin and Wayne Brummel had chosen well their refuge of last resort.

The Inspector prodded their host. "You spoke of a 'present arrangement.' "

"We do not provide sanctuary for nonsimians out of the goodness of our hearts. Our resources here are limited, and perforce must be allocated on behalf of those who need them most. Charitable donations, stipends for maintaining the integrity of the Reserva, and volunteers who aid in medical research cover the majority of our expenses. And there is the substantial annual royalty that accrues to the Ciudad from our assistance in ongoing research to develop a final AIDS vaccine. Still, there are always needs." He eyed Cardenas evenly.

"We have a financial arrangement with these females, to see to their safety and security. The thought of breaching that agreement, even on behalf of the law outside the Reserva, troubles me."

"It would be to their benefit. They can't run and hide forever. Not even here." It took Cardenas a moment to realize that Sorong was waiting to hear something else. "The NFP maintains a fund for compensating those who assist in police work. If you're concerned about losing a source of income, I'm sure we can work something out so that all concerned parties are satisfied."

The great ape nodded slowly. "You know, federale, Ciudad Simiano is still a controversial project among many humans. They feel threatened." Like the rest of him, Sorong's smile was something to behold. "As if revenge were a trans-species sentiment! As if those here brooded over justice for all of our relations who have been tormented in primitive medical labs, or cooped up in tiny cages in what feebly passed for zoos, or slaughtered for bush meat, or stolen as infants for the pet trade."

"I'm glad to hear," Cardenas replied softly, "that you're not vindictive."

Huge arms spread wide in a gesture of helplessness. "What would be the point? Both the victims and their perpetrators are long dead. Meanwhile, humans kill other humans far more frequently and with greater gusto than they kill us. Here at Ciudad Simiano, we hope to move beyond that. But there are humans who are terrified of genetically enhanced grasses. I can hardly begin to describe to you how such Luddites react to the existence of my friends and I." He leaned forward slightly. "Have you ever reviewed an ancient vit series with the cluster title *Planet of the Apes*?"

"No, I don't believe I have," Cardenas told him.

The Director sat back. "Scare tactics. Nothing but scare tactics. However, the ignorant are always with us, and are ready to swallow any sort of codswallop the many extant myopic organizations care to dish out. It therefore behooves those of us who live here to avoid trouble and unfavorable publicity. We just want to be left alone, to be ourselves, so that we can work out the ultimate ramifications of this enhanced intelligence as best we can."

Hyaki had been quiet for some time. Now he chose to rejoin the discussion. "A local war between yourselves and antisocs from all over the northern hemisphere might not be the best way to accomplish that."

"I see that we are of one mind in this." Grunting profoundly, Sorong thumped himself on the chest with one closed fist. The action generated a dull booming sound. "If the financial details can be worked out—and I see no reason why they cannot—then in the interests of preserving the peace and ensuring the safety of the two females, we might agree to release them into your custody. After all, they are human. It is not as if they are bonobos." His expression narrowed. "But we will do this only if they consent to go with you of their own free will. The Ciudad Simiano does have a reputation to maintain."

Cardenas turned away from the imposing icon of Koko. "So does the NFP. I wouldn't want to see either damaged."

"I suppose you would like to meet with the two females and make certain they are indeed the pair that you seek."

Hyaki contained his excitement. It was starting to look as if the long trip south was going to turn out to be productive after all. "That would be a good next step, yeah."

Cardenas nodded agreement. "How long before you can locate them and bring them back here, or take us to them?"

Sorong grinned like an overgrown kid. "About five minutes." Raising a massive gray arm, he pointed to one of the many tracks that led back into the surrounding jungle. "They're staying in guest house number three. It is clearly marked, you cannot miss it. I would go with you, but I have much work to do. After you have introduced yourselves, we can proceed from there. Be sure to announce your arrival before entering the building."

Thanking him, they parted ways, the two federales heading in the direction of the indicated path. Dense verdure quickly closed in around them. The proximity to exotic rainforest vegetation and the plethora of insects and arachnids it accommodated probably did not bother the primates. Used to cityscapes and open spaces, the two urbanized visitors from the north were considerably less at ease in the thick jungle. Cardenas was glad it was only a short walk to their indicated destination, and said so.

"It's not so bad." Bending low, Hyaki ducked beneath an overhanging branch heavy with leaves and small nesting epiphytes. "All you have to do is pretend that you're walking through the botanical gardens in North Tucson. The smell's the same."

Glancing back at his partner, Cardenas's eyes widened slightly. For once, it was left to the sergeant to do the intuiting. "Something wrong?"

"Depends." The Inspector continued to stare. "On whether you can pretend that the spider that's riding on your shoulder is like the ones you're likely to find in the botanical gardens in North Tucson."

Looking to his left, Hyaki found himself eye to eye with a typically enormous representative of the group of arachnids known as the orb weavers. With legs longer than the federale's fingers and a black-and-yellow abdomen the size of his fist, the giant orb spider made for an imposing presence on the sergeant's shoulder. Spurning his visitor's sartorial elegance, Hyaki began yelling and thrashing wildly with both hands, until the huge arachnid had been knocked off into the brush. That it was not particularly poisonous mattered not an iota to the unhappy sergeant. Even had he

been aware of the fact, it was doubtful he would have reacted any more calmly.

Cardenas could not blame him. In his experience, few
folk liked spiders, and he was not ashamed to admit that he
could count himself among them. Righting itself among the
leaves and other forest detritus where it had landed, the orb
weaver scuttled rapidly out of sight.

Hyaki continued to twitch nervously and brush repeatedly at himself for several minutes following the encounter.
"Brrrr! I'd rather face a squat of ninlocos." He held up
thumb and forefinger. "The damn thing was this close to my
face!"

"I'm told it's not what you can see that gets to you in
places like this." Cardenas warily pushed aside a sapling
that was sprouting from the center of the trail. "It's the
things you can't. Leeches, for example. Ticks and fleas.
Flies carrying leishmaniasis. Bugs that—"

His partner cut him off. "I get the point. Me, I was ready
for the streets of Nogales as soon as our shuttle landed in
San José. Give me thick walls and high pavement anyday."

"And the coffee and beignets at Rosa's Café." Cardenas's voice dripped with longing. "Crêpes with prickly pear
jam and whipped cream. Lingonberry sopapillas."

"I *told* you," Hyaki groused at his friend. "I get the
point."

"That must be it." As they emerged from the narrow trail
into a small clearing, Cardenas increased his stride, grateful
to be out from beneath the undergrowth.

In front of them, backing up against the imposing fo-
liage, was a building unlike any they had encountered in the
Ciudad compound. Constructed largely of local materials, it
appeared to be an architectural throwback to an earlier
time. Set on pilings driven into the ground, the single-story

structure was spacious enough to contain three or four good-sized rooms beneath the thatched palm roof. Twenty steps fashioned of split logs comprised the wide stairway that led up to the covered front deck, from which any inhabitants would have a fine view of the surrounding jungle. There was no sign of the usual wiring that defined modern construction.

Cardenas led the way up the stairs. No glass was in evidence; windows and doors alike featuring only mesh screening. The periodic *hiss-sst* of an unseen electronic insect repeller indicated that the edifice was equipped with at least one piece of modern technology. Evidently, an inclination on the part of the building's residents to return to the wild did not necessarily include an urge to feed it.

Cardenas was a little surprised to find the screen door unlocked. Exchanging a look with his partner, he entered. It was surprisingly cool and dry within, clearly due to the silent exertions of artfully concealed air-conditioning and dehumidifying appliances. Moving slowly down the hallway and looking to his right, he found himself gazing into a comfortable sitting room. Couches and chairs fashioned of rattan and other local materials cradling cushions imported from the outside world clustered around the ubiquitous vit. Floor mats of woven coconut fiber alternated with decorative pads fashioned from palm fronds. As for the inventive paintings and bas-reliefs and colorcrawls that decorated the walls and rested on small wooden tables, he found himself wondering if they had been fashioned by human hands—or by those belonging to close cousins.

"Who is it?" a strong feminine voice inquired from the far side of the hallway. "I hope you were able to find some—"

Turning, Cardenas found himself confronting a slightly

stocky and undeniably attractive woman in her early thirties. Shoulder-length blonde hair was drawn back in a single ponytail, an eminently sensible do for the high tropics. Her face was devoid of makeup and cosmetics of any kind. The single wraparound pale yellow garment she wore was dominated by a bold bougainvillea print, more South Pacific than Central America. Her feet were small and bare, the nails unembellished. A sole concession to contemporary convention was the small audio-only muse player that fit neatly into her right ear.

"Surtsey Mockerkin?" Cardenas started to reach into the inside pocket of his short-sleeved shirt to show her his ident bracelet. "I'm—"

The blood seemed to drain from her face. Her expression grew stricken. *"Roger!"* she screamed.

Before either man could explain himself further, a bulbous streak of muscular red-orange came tearing into the room, brushing past the frightened woman as it flew at the pair of visitors. A heavy, tree sap–stained machete gripped tightly in one hand struck first at Hyaki, descending with enough force to cleave an arm from a shoulder. Remarkably agile for such a big man, and used to dealing with assailants, the sergeant lunged to one side and struck at his attacker as he rushed past. Powerful enough to bring most men to their knees, the blow didn't even slow the figure wielding the big bush knife.

But then, it wasn't a man.

Whirling, the furious orangutan took a second swipe at the sergeant, who darted behind the rattan couch and picked up a chair to defend himself. With one hand the orang, kilo for kilo far stronger than any human, lifted the couch and flung it out of the way. While the reddish-orange ape stalked Hyaki, Cardenas was able to rush to the woman's side. Since her whole posture was reflective of profound inner fear, he hastened to reassure her. Reaching into his shirt, he pulled out his ident.

"Surtsey Mockerkin? Inspector Angel Cardenas and Sergeant Fredoso Hyaki, Namerican Federal Police. I spoke to you in Nogales. We're here to help you." He gestured in the direction of the two grim-visaged combatants. "Call off your dog."

Some of the tension eased out of her, but her expression remained wary. Keeping her eyes on Cardenas, she spoke without turning. "Roger! It's all right—they're police, not mataros."

Holding the machete over his head with both hands, the orang slowly lowered his long, powerful arms. Only when the blade neared the floor did Hyaki begin to put down the chair he was holding defensively in front of him. The ape blinked large, deceptively child-like eyes.

"Surtsey sure?"

"For now," she told him. "Wait outside, on the porch." The tone in her voice carried an implied threat as she continued to address her words to the man standing next to her. "I'll call you if I need you. And before you go, fix the couch."

Obediently, again using only one hand, the orang flipped the casually cast-aside piece of furniture back onto its feet, repositioned it on the floor, and tossed the loose cushions back where they belonged. Favoring both Hyaki and Cardenas with a warning glare, it ambled out of the room, still clutching the ominous long blade.

"Your friend?" Cardenas gestured in the direction of the departed simian.

"My bodyguard. He was assigned to me by the Simiano association. I pay them to protect and shelter me here." Her expression softened slightly. "They rotate bodyguards. None of them is especially fond of human company. But they know how to do their job."

Having set the wicker-and-rattan chair back on the floor, Hyaki promptly slumped into it. In the high humidity, the brief burst of physical exertion had started cascades of perspiration from his face and upper body.

"I wouldn't dispute that."

She hesitated a moment longer before finally gesturing toward the furniture. "Well, you're here. I can't do anything about that. So you might as well sit down."

Taking the chair next to the couch, Cardenas folded his hands and leaned forward earnestly. "You said that you pay the, um, people here to shelter you. Where's Katla?"

Surtsey Mockerkin seemed to sink in on herself. Another time, another place, this would be an exceptionally attractive and probably vivacious woman, Cardenas thought. The tropics reduced everyone to the same low, sweaty, common denominator of appearance.

"Since you found me, you obviously know about her." She looked out a screened window. "When she's not sitting in front of a box teasing mollyspheres, she likes to take walks in the forest. Says she's inspired by what she sees." Mockerkin shook her head. "I'm glad for her. This was the safest place I could think of to run to, and I had contacts here."

"You did," Hyaki pressed her, "or Wayne Brummel did?"

She looked over at the big man, but not in surprise. "So you know about Wayne, too?"

Cardenas nodded sympathetically. "That's what started us on this case. You didn't keep your appointment to meet me at the Nogales morgue."

Turning to her left, she passed a hand over a large mock-wood sculpture of a tapir. Its back slid aside to expose the interior. Reaching within, she removed a bottle of local beer and flipped the cap, activating the integral refrigerator. As she waited for it to chill she did not offer one to her visitors.

"Poor Wayne. He truly loved me, you know. As much as he hated Cleats, he loved me." Reduced to watching her take a slug of the ice-cold brew, actual pain shot through Hyaki. "Wayne's problem was a common one among men: they always think they're smarter than they actually are. I miss him, but not as much as I thought I would." She indicated their surroundings. "He was the one who did the scut work looking for a safe haven, in case we might need one. Too bad he'll never get to enjoy it." Taking a more decorous sip of the golden liquid, she eyed Cardenas appraisingly. "I'm telling you the truth."

"I know." The Inspector responded comfortingly, without bothering to explain how he really did.

She crossed very alluring legs, most of which were visible below the hem of her tropical shorts. "My first thought when I saw you two standing here was that it was all over, that you were mataros sent by my husband." Her face screwed up in an expression of visible distaste. " 'Nobody mocks The Mock,' he always used to say. *Pinche cabrón,* that bastard!" Her tone turned pleading. "He fascinated me, at first. I was very young. Eventually, things got to the point where I couldn't take it anymore. I ran away half a dozen times. Each time, his people found me and brought me back." She looked away from her visitors. "Each time I was brought back things got—worse.

"Then Katla happened. I stopped running away. To raise her, and also to get him to ease off. When I felt she was old enough, strong enough, I started looking for a way out.

Having failed so many times on my own, I'd finally figured out that I'd need help. I was just flailing around, going nowhere, until I met Wayne." She drained more of the beer. "It wasn't so much that Wayne was a good guy. After all, he worked for Cleats. He was just less bad than most of the other men I'd met. And he loved me, and tolerated Katla.

"That was enough for me. I told him what I wanted to do, and he did it. Together, we made the break, tried to lose ourselves in the Strip." She shook her head. "Four new identities in two years, and it still wasn't enough. All the time, Wayne kept searching for a safe place, in case we had to leave Namerica. I don't know how he stumbled on the idea of coming here, but he did. He reasoned that it was one place even The Mock's mins couldn't get in." She offered up a wan smile. "We didn't talk about the federales."

"Your house almost got us," Hyaki felt compelled to tell her.

She glanced sideways at him. "That was Wayne's work, too. It wasn't intended for you. It was designed as a greeting for The Mock's hombers in case they ever showed up. How'd you get away, anyhow?"

Hyaki indicated the quietly attentive Cardenas. "My partner is real good at sensing anomalies in a situation." He added accusingly, "Your house nearly blew off my ass."

She shrugged. "I'd apologize, if I thought it would make a difference. Nothing matters now. Nothing matters anymore." There was a genuine yearning for closure in her eyes as she gazed up at Cardenas. "If you could find me here, then it means that Cleats can do so also."

"Not necessarily," the Inspector corrected her. "Not every official channel of information is compromised, you know. The facts of your case are known only to a very few."

He indicated Hyaki. "Technically, Fredoso and I are here on leave, and not here on official business."

She looked as if it made no difference. "Doesn't matter. I can't leave here. The Ciudad Simiano is my last, and best, hope. Katla's, too."

"The NFP has a highly successful witness protection program."

Her laughter was sharp and brittle, though not entirely unexpected. She gaped at him in disbelief. "You must be kidding! Leave this place, where nobody gets in without permission, to go back to the Strip and give testimony against The Mock? I may not be as smart as Katla, but we do share some of the same genes. I'm staying here—even if Cleats's mins *can* find me." She threw a hand in the direction of the hallway. "Let 'em come. Let's see how they like dealing with Roger and his kind! But go back? Not a chance, fedoco. Not if you could convince me you could sell shaved ice in Spitzbergen."

"All right," Cardenas responded. "If that's the way you feel about it. But if you'll tell us what this is all about, maybe the NFP can extend you some additional help. You wouldn't be against that, would you? If you know something that we can use against Cleator Mockerkin that doesn't involve an actual courthouse appearance on your part, there's always a chance we can move against him while you remain out of sight here. That would remove the threat to you and your daughter without you having to return to the Strip. Wouldn't you like to see that happen?"

For the second time, she hesitated. "You're not going to force us to go back with you?"

The Inspector shook his head. "Can't. This is the Central American Federation, not Namerica. You're not accused of any crime, so extradition law doesn't apply. You can speak freely." He met her gaze without blinking. "I wouldn't try to take you and your daughter against your will, anyway."

She mulled his offer. Suddenly she looked younger than her years, more like a frightened teenager than a hardened survivor of the Strip. "It's the money. The Mock's money. Cleats's cash. Wayne and I, we appropriated quite a bit of mutable credit. Nobody does that to The Mock and gets away with it. The fact that I was involved made it that much worse. Makes him look the goat as well as the goof. He wants his money back. He wants *me* back."

The Inspector nodded comprehendingly, leaned toward her without smiling, and replied softly but firmly, "If you're going to lie to me, Ms. Mockerkin, I'm not going to be able to do anything to help you. The money you and Wayne Brummel–George Anderson stole is only a very small part of this."

Her face flushed with outrage and she half rose from the couch. "I'm not lying, you damn fedoco! Why else do you think someone like The Mock would want me back?"

Not in the least perturbed by her outburst, Cardenas tried to remain as sensitive and sympathetic as possible. "I'm not so sure that he does want you back, Ms. Mockerkin. But we do know that he wants your daughter."

TWELVE

SHE STARED AT HIM. SAVE FOR THE RAIN-forest sounds that drifted in through the screened windows, it was dead silent in the room. "I don't know what you're talking about, Inspector. Katla is a bright, perfectly normal, ordinary twelve-year-old, who suffers only from the problems that are common to girls her age. Beyond the fact that she's his daughter, I can't imagine what special interest my husband would have in seeking her return."

Hyaki sighed resignedly. "Give us some credit for doing our jobs, Ms. Mockerkin. We found you, didn't we? Besides, we can tell when you're lying." He nodded in the Inspector's direction. "My partner is an intuit."

Their host looked sharply at Cardenas. Most of the time he preferred to keep his particular ability in the background. This was not one of those times. She saw the truth in his eyes, and slumped.

"We've talked to your daughter's friends, Ms. Mockerkin. Both inside and outside the soche you had her enrolled in. We know that Katla is rather more than 'bright.' We know that she is a tecant, and that she was working on some important project for your husband when you both disappeared."

Fingers twisting and pulling against one another, Surtsey Mockerkin gave ground only grudgingly. "Katla's my daughter, gentlemen, and I love her." Raising her head, she gazed imploringly at the attentive Cardenas. "But I don't pretend to understand her. Where she got her kind of smarts I'm sure I don't know." She laughed sardonically. "Not from me, I can tell you! Me, I've got street smarts, and plenty of them. But book smarts—maybe it comes from Cleats's side of the family. I'm not so sure that's such a good thing.

"She's real shy, Katla is, but sometimes, when she was sure we were alone and unmonitored, she would try to talk to me about things. Cleats's project was one of them. He—he told her that if she didn't work with him, with his people, then something might happen. Not to her, but to someone else."

"He threatened you to get her to work with him?" Hyaki remarked.

"Not by name." Her attention shifted to the big man. "He didn't have to. It was enough to suggest that something might happen to someone close to her. He might have been talking about a sochemate, or a casual friend. You've never been around him, Sergeant. There's a quality to his voice. It's unforced, natural, but The Mock can order take-out Chinese and make it sound like he's going to commit serial murder. When he actually *is* making a threat . . ." There being no need to finish the sentence, her voice died away.

Cardenas pulled the conversation back to an earlier thread. "This project of his, the one that he had Katla working on: can you tell us anything about it? We don't know any details, only that it's of some significance. Apparently, others besides your husband are very interested in it."

She spread her hands wide and shrugged. "I told you.

Katla tried to explain it to me, several times. I only remember a little about it, and I don't pretend to understand even the parts that I remember. It has something to do with a procedure she called 'quantum theft.' "

The two federales exchanged a glance. "That's all?" Cardenas prodded her.

"Oh no, there's lots more. I just don't understand any of it."

Brow wrinkling, Surtsey Mockerkin struggled to remember terminology and designations, definitions and descriptions, that were clearly beyond her. As she rambled on, it became increasingly evident to Cardenas that much of it was equally beyond him and his partner. What was worse was that, in the absence of their charred spinners, they had only their own inadequate minds with which to try and record any of the details.

"It all centers on the remote controlling of the optical switches that drive the commercial ganglions of the Box. I'm talking about the global Box, not some local offshoot dendrites." Seeing the expression on their faces, she added wryly, "I *told* you I didn't understand it. I just remember some of it."

"Go on," Cardenas urged her, desperately wishing he had his spinner. Or the knowledgeable presence beside him of Aurilac the Wise.

The remembering seemed to help her relax. In between declamations, she drained the remainder of the beer. "Apparently the trick—that's what Katla kept calling it—is to tune the relevant multiple amplifiers so that the lasers being controlled at the opportune moment exactly match a certain wavelength. If correctly pumped, this is supposed to create an onsite duplicate of whatever information is being scanned at that time. The instant this exact duplicate is created at the remote site, the original is destroyed." She shifted her backside on the couch.

"It's supposed to duplicate bank numbers, or stock details, or whatever information is being pumped, on someone else's molly."

"And at the same time," Cardenas added, straining to make sense of what she was telling them, "the original information is rendered useless?"

"Not just rendered useless," she corrected him. "It's obliterated, as if it never existed. But it does, in the form of the perfect duplicate that's been created elsewhere."

Both men were quiet for a moment, trying to digest it all. As he so often did, Hyaki neatly summed up what they had just been told.

"The banks are gonna *love* this."

"Very nifty," Cardenas observed. "Not only do you steal information, you simultaneously eliminate the original record of its existence. Like running away from someone while brushing out the tracks you leave behind you." His brows drew together slightly as he regarded Surtsey Mockerkin. "*If* it works."

Setting the bottle aside, she extracted another from storage and flicked on the chill. Once again, she did not offer any to her guests. Cardenas supposed he couldn't blame her.

"I couldn't tell you that. I wouldn't know if something like that was working right even if I saw it in action."

"So you don't know if this wild concept is anything more than a theory? You don't know how far along any practical application actually is, or if your husband's people have gone beyond just theorizing?"

"No," she muttered, "I don't. But I do know one thing. I

got tired of watching my daughter be used, much less drawn into that bastard's line of work."

Hyaki nodded contemplatively. "The couple of million you and Brummel took off with had nothing to do with it, of course."

Her voice rose. "What the hell was I supposed to do, fedoco? Get a job washing floors, or making beds in cheap hotels? If you're going to run from The Mock, you'd better run far, and fast. That takes money." She subsided a little. "Wayne wasn't such a bad guy, considering."

"So you miss him a lot," Cardenas ventured sympathetically.

The gaze that met his was so steeled that for an instant, he thought she was intuiting *him*. "I didn't say that. I said he was okay, and he was. My first concern, my only concern, was to protect Katla. To get her away from her *pinche* father."

"Not to look out for yourself." Hyaki was no longer smiling.

The steel faded from their host's gaze and she looked away. "Think what you want. A dead mother isn't a very useful mother." Another long swallow of cerveza, and when she again considered her visitors, some of her resolve had returned.

"I'm not going anywhere with you, *gentlemen*. You can keep your goddamned protection program. You've got no jurisdiction in the CAF, and less than none in the Ciudad Simiano. I know. Wayne's research was real specific on that point. Sure-o, this isn't the Strip, or Nueva York, or even Agua Pri, but Katla and I can manage. We've managed this far. If I go back, if I set foot inside Namerica, I'm cold meat." Her speech was beginning to take on a slight slur, a consequence of the second beer. "That *pinche cabrón* can shoot his lasers and his programming up his ass. He's not getting Katla back."

"All right." Cardenas rose. "We won't bother you anymore, Ms. Mockerkin."

Hyaki gaped at his partner. "Hoh, Angel, are you . . . ?"

The Inspector spoke firmly to his partner. "She doesn't want to leave, we can't make her. She's content to stay here, I'm happy for her." Returning his attention to their hostess, he added, "Assuming Sorong grants permission and we can arrange a place to sleep, my partner and I will be here for another couple of days. Think about the offer, Ms. Mockerkin. Think about everything I've said. After a while, living on the run, even in a place as congenial as you might find the CAF tropics, starts to wear a person down. I know: I've seen it happen. It ages you fast and vapes you quick. There are more insidious killers than a bullet. Anticipation is slower, but can be just as deadly." On a hunch, he nodded in the direction of the sitting area's rear window. "One thing for certain: it's no place to try and raise a child."

Holding tight to the beer, she muttered a dismissal. "Wish I could say it's been fun, Inspector. But it hasn't."

He started past her, keeping one eye on the shadowed hallway ahead lest they run afoul of a certain easily aggravated orangutan. "Couple of days. Think about it."

They left her sitting on the couch, drinking but not necessarily enjoying the cold cerveza, lost in thoughts Cardenas could only hope would ferment within her mind.

Once outside, Hyaki finally felt free to give vent to his frustration. "What was that all about, Angel? I thought you had her leaning toward coming with us, and you let her slip away."

Remembering the spider that had tried to hitch a ride on his friend, Cardenas studied the entrance to the trail that led back to the central compound with something less than unreserved enthusiasm. "She isn't going anywhere, Fredoso. She's too scared. She needs time to think about her future, not just about tomorrow. Time to ponder her daughter's future." He gestured at their verdant surroundings. A pair of scarlet macaws flew by overhead, skimming the treetops and filling the air with their raucous cries.

"This is a beautiful place—for a few months, maybe a year at most. It's not a permanent refuge for someone used to living in the Strip. I don't care how quiet and reserved and introverted this Katla may be, or how many walks she takes in the jungle—she's still a twelve-year-old girl. The CAF isn't Namerica. For a career biologist, a life in the Reserva *might* be tolerable. But even then, only barely."

This time, Hyaki led the way back along the trail, forcing Cardenas to duck the branches and leaves that occasionally came snapping back in his direction. "Okay— but can we wait a year for Ms. Mockerkin to make up her mind?"

"Of course not. And I don't think we'll have to. She's already said she realizes that if we were able to find her, so can The Mock's people. It comes down to whether she thinks she's safer here, and can stand the isolation, or whether she and her daughter would be better off turning responsibility for their safety over to the NFP." Carefully, he stepped over an effervescent column of army ants that were crossing the trail.

"Maybe we can't wait a year—but we do have a couple of days to spare." A small smile creased his face. "After that, Pangborn is going to get antsy for some feedback. Not to mention that we'll just about be out of 'vacation' time."

They emerged from the forest into the open courtyard of the Ciudad compound. Across the way, a cluster of young primates was being marched back to class by a matronly and very dignified chimpanzee.

"So the plan is that we leave her alone to stew over the proposal, and don't apply any more pressure?"

"*Exactamention,*" Cardenas agreed.

"She might not tell her daughter anything about this, about our visit. The girl might have an opinion of her own."

"Probably would." The Inspector started across the courtyard. "But the girl is not of age, not even in the CAF. The last thing we want to do is give the mother another reason to dislike us. Better to leave her alone and let her sort things out for herself."

"Think she'll come to the right decision?"

Cardenas paused to watch a troop of mixed macaques and smaller tamarins performing acrobatics on an enormously elaborate gymnastic sculpture that had been constructed adjacent to the jungle. When combined with their innate athleticism, the precision of their routines was dizzying to contemplate.

"I hope so. For her daughter's sake if not for her own." Resuming his stride, he angled toward the Administration building. "If they have facilities here for sanctioned researchers, they can probably put us up for a couple of days."

The managers of the Ciudad Simiano could—for a fee, of course. The visitors' quarters were a pleasant surprise: neat and clean, they were equipped with lightweight tropical linen, mosquito nets, and insect repellers. There was even a vit player—but no comm units and no box access. If they wanted to talk to the outside world, they had to use a monitored unit in the Administration building. A way of ensuring guests' privacy? Cardenas wondered—or of screening all contact between the Ciudad and human civilization?

A way of protecting visitors—or of isolating residents? No matter. Neither he nor his partner had any secrets to reveal.

The food served to guests was another surprise. Anticipating a wholly vegetarian diet, both men were delighted to see everything from fish to venison on the menu, though there was no domesticated meat. The inhabitants of the Ciudad did not raise other animals for food, though they were perfectly content to kill and consume those they could catch in the wild. Chimpanzees in particular were traditionally fond of animal protein. Over the course of the federales' brief stay, Hyaki developed a taste for tropical locusts fried in sesame oil. Besides the inherent crunchiness, the battered bugs contained twice as much protein as beef. Demurring on the unusual dish, Cardenas found himself reveling in the local fruits, many of which he had never encountered before.

On the second day, a bored Hyaki stumbled across a tennis court set in the rainforest. There he made the acquaintance of a young orangutan named Pahek. Although physically smaller, the orang's reach exceeded the sergeant's own, and they engaged in several energetic matches.

Envying his partner's ability to unwind, an increasingly pessimistic Cardenas extended their stay into a third day, still without any word from Surtsey Mockerkin. It was beginning to look like the only testimony they were going to be able to obtain from her concerning the death of Wayne Brummel and his likely extirpaters would have to be inferred. They could not force her to testify, either via recording or by returning to Namerica. For that matter, they still had no incontrovertible proof that could tie her felonious husband directly to the vaping. As for any disreputable exploitation of her daughter by the girl's father, no one had suggested that a prosecutable crime had been committed.

Where a court of law was concerned, without testimony given or recorded in the presence of counsel, any information provided by Katla's mother would remain nothing more than hearsay.

All in all, it had not been a very successful trip. They had obtained information regarding The Mock's intention to develop a means for engaging in something called quantum theft, which might prove to be anything from a genuine threat to nothing more than a harebrained hypothesis. Surtsey Mockerkin had confirmed that her husband was searching for her, and that he had reason to be furious, perhaps lethally furious, with the man she had run off with. And that was all. There was no hard evidence of murder for hire, crunch theft, or child abuse. It was suggestive that others were willing to kill to learn what Katla Mockerkin presumably knew, but it did not implicate anyone directly in the murder of Wayne Brummel.

Which was, after all, the case he and his partner were supposed to be pursuing.

The good food and congenial, if isolated, surroundings, did little to lift the Inspector out of the funk of frustration into which he had fallen. If they could secure hard testimony from Surtsey Mockerkin to the effect that her husband had ordered Brummel's killing, or even that he was in all likelihood the one who had ordered it, then they could at least pick up The Mock on suspicion, and subject him to questioning. But if she refused to do even that much, they could do nothing but catch the next shuttle home. And as afraid as she was of her husband, Cardenas was not sanguine about convincing her even to admit that she knew where he was living.

They could not afford to linger a fourth day. Not without results. All they could do was pay Surtsey Mockerkin one last visit, repeat both their plea for assistance and the offer of asylum, and hope that time and contemplation had worked on her mind sufficiently to persuade her to change her position. Neither man was hopeful.

Having resigned himself to disappointment, Cardenas had already booked them out on the following day's shuttle from San José to Nogales via Mexico City. Still, he reflected as he led Hyaki up the steps of the guest house, there had been times in the past when logic and reason had failed him but sheer stubbornness had paid off.

Despite the outward simplicity of the structure, their prior visit had confirmed that it employed its share of concealed servotronics, including one that must have notified her of their arrival. Surtsey Mockerkin met them in the main hallway. Her manner was guarded but confident.

"Come in. I'm in the middle of putting up some things in the kitchen."

They followed her to a part of the house they had not previously seen. The kitchen occupied the opposite side of the building from the sitting area where they had conversed three days earlier. Outfitted to handle the needs of two or three people, it held dehumidifier-equipped, insect-proof cabinets; a small oven and stove; sink, chiller, sonic scrubber, and a floor-to-ceiling pantry. As the two federales looked on, their hostess removed dishes and tumblers from the scrubber and stacked them in an open cabinet.

"I understand that you gentlemen are getting ready to leave."

"So we are," Cardenas admitted. "How did you find out?"

She set a pair of brightly colored self-chilling plastic tumblers on a half-full shelf. "I have been here long enough to make some friends, you know." Eyes that had seen too much met his. "If you've come to say good-bye, it was nice meeting you. If you've come to make a last stab at talking me into leaving, forget it."

Trying to defuse the tension between them, he ventured conversationally, "It's a shame we won't get to meet your daughter. As you said before, she must be very fond of her forest walks."

Mockerkin's smile was humorless. "She prefers machines and nature to people. Can't say that I blame her."

"How about you, Surtsey? You don't miss people, urban excitement, having things to do and places to go?"

Looking away from him, she returned resolutely to her stacking. "What I want doesn't matter. All I want anymore is what's best for Katla."

She was lying, Cardenas knew. Maybe better than she knew herself. She wore boredom like an ill-fitting brassiere. Another month, maybe two, isolated in this place, and a vivacious, highly sociable woman like herself would really begin to feel the effects. Could they wait another two months for her to begin to break down?

Such decisions were simplified by the fact that they had no choice. "If you should change your mind," he told her, "you can contact me directly." He nodded in the direction of the compound. "The address is on the Administration's molly. Use a secure connect."

She avoided his gaze. "Have a nice flight, gentlemen." A skeletal smirk crossed her lips. "Watch out for wandering farmers on your way out."

Cardenas smiled, nodded, and turned to go. Together, he and Hyaki exited the kitchen.

"Well, that's that," the sergeant submitted. "We tried our best, Angel."

The Inspector nodded as he turned toward the hallway.

"If she won't testify, much less come back, then we can't pursue the case. It's *muerto*ed for sure." He glanced behind him. "I would have liked to have met the daughter, though."

Hyaki's brows rose slightly. "Think she could have changed the mother's mind?"

Cardenas shook his head. "Not if what Surtsey was telling us about her daughter is true, and I think it is."

"That's it, then." Hyaki turned into the hall, heading for the front doorway. "He thinks, therefore it is." Whereupon the big man halted so abruptly that Cardenas nearly ran into him.

Coming up the front steps was a mass of mandrills. The big, florid-faced baboons were advancing in silence. Each carried a knife that was only slightly longer than their imposing upper canines. Cardenas started moving backward faster than he had been leaving.

"Kitchen," he growled tightly.

Looking up sharply at their sudden and unexpected reappearance, a startled Surtsey Mockerkin reached into a drawer and pulled out a pistol that, while small, was in no wise especially feminine. Peering down the barrel, Cardenas nodded curtly.

"Good. I have a feeling you're going to need that. Got any more?"

Her expression twisted in confusion. "What are you talking about? What are you doing back here? What's going—?"

"Here they come!" shouted Hyaki as he ripped the portable oven off the wall and heaved it at the first mandrill. It struck the ape square in its chromatically colored snout, prompting a shriek of anger and surprise.

That was the signal for the remaining primates to rush

the kitchen. The narrowness of the room worked against the attackers. Unable to flank their quarry, they were forced to try and overwhelm the three humans with a frontal attack. It was immediately apparent that the two federales were not the target of the invading apes. They were simply in the way.

Knife gripped between powerful teeth, one mandrill tried to leap over Cardenas as the Inspector attempted to draw a bead on it with his pistol. He did not get the chance to fire. Surtsey blew its face off, at the same time nearly amputating one of Hyaki's ears. Two more rushed the sergeant in an attempt to get around him. With a smaller man, the ploy might have worked. Unfortunately for the ferocious, frenzied primates, Hyaki was so big that his mere presence blocked their access to their intended victim. His own weapon flared, reducing one of the two swift-moving attackers to ground chuck.

A knife caught the sergeant's left arm, ripping the exposed skin revealed below the short sleeve of his shirt. Hyaki brought the edge of his thick right hand around in a downward arc, slamming it against the mandrill's rib cage. The beast screamed with fury, bounced off the wall, shook its head, and leaped at him again. Meanwhile, another had darted past Hyaki's legs, not even bothering to take a swipe at them in passing. Teeth and blade were intended only for the woman cowering near the rear of the kitchen.

Cardenas jammed the muzzle of his pistol against the back of the baboon's neck, indenting the fur and pressing into the flesh beneath. Screaming with uncontrolled rage, eyes blazing, it reached backward as he pulled the trigger. Fragments of baboon splattered the Inspector's face. The mortally injured primate fumbled wildly at the wound, bouncing off cabinets and floor and screeching hysterically.

As the Inspector hunted for another target, Surtsey Mockerkin put one, two, three explosive pellets into the jerking, twitching body, until there was little left of the invader except hunks of bloody meat and fur.

Having seen its companions eliminated one after another, the lone remaining simian assassin drew back its hand and flung the knife it held. The whistling blade just missed its target, whizzing past Surtsey Mockerkin's head to bury itself in the rear wall of the kitchen. Raging in frustration, the surviving mandrill whirled, sprayed the kitchen with urine as it turned, and fled on all fours back the way it had come. They could hear it banging down the steps outside as it retreated.

Breathing hard, Cardenas helped his partner gingerly slip his wounded arm underneath the single arching spigot in the sink. Cold water immediately began to flow over the gash, mixing with the sergeant's blood to spiral down the drain. Behind them, their hostess was still clutching her weapon in both hands, gazing wide-eyed at the carnage that had bloodied her kitchen.

"Sprayskin," Cardenas requested tersely. When she failed to respond, he raised his voice to a shout. "*Surtsey!*" The edge in his voice drew her attention away from the dripping butchery. He moderated his tone. "Sprayskin: do you have any? Also disinfectant aerosol, and bandages."

"I—I'll go and check. I think so. Maybe." She started for the doorway.

Hyaki spoke through clenched teeth. "What a faz assignment this has been. First a house tries to kill me, then monkeys."

"Tries to kill *us*," Cardenas reminded him as he kept pressure on his friend's arm. "Don't feel singled out. You didn't have to deal with the Inzini or the Ooze."

"Wouldn't want to keep all the fun for myself," the sergeant shot back. A moment later, Surtsey Mockerkin's scream and the sound of her gun going off reached them from the hallway.

"Mierde!" Cardenas rushed from the kitchen. Wrapping a towel around his injured arm, Hyaki followed.

The primate sitting on her shoulders was not very big. Certainly it was a lot smaller than the invading mandrills. But the howler was big enough, and strong enough, to wield the machete that hung from one powerful, hirsute hand. As they entered, it dropped the blade, and in a single prodigious leap reached the front doorway, caught hold of the lintel, and swung to freedom. Seconds later there was a screech, followed by a squeal. Though he was admittedly ignorant of the meaning of ape sounds, to Cardenas it did not sound like a cry of triumph.

Staggering, Surtsey Mockerkin turned to face them. Her expression was blank, her eyes vacant of comprehension. As the two federales looked on in horror, she slowly sank to her knees, then toppled forward face-first onto the floor. Both men raced to her side. A single glance told them more than they wanted to know. Nothing could be done for her. She had been half decapitated.

An enormous figure appeared, completely blocking the doorway. Hanging limp in one hand was the body of the big howler. Absently, Sorong tossed it aside. It rolled a couple of times on the varnished parquet floor before tumbling to a still, soundless stop. Its back had been broken.

Supporting his weight on his knuckles, the silverback slowly approached the body of Surtsey Mockerkin. With one huge hand he lifted her head, let it fall loosely back to the floor. Looking up at Cardenas, he observed quietly, "This is not going to do our reputation any good."

The Inspector hardly knew how to reply. Awareness of his partner's presence finally presented him with a response. "My friend's been hurt."

Sorong glanced at the cut that ran the length of Hyaki's upper arm. "I'll take you to the infirmary myself." His gaze returned to the pitiable female corpse. Blood had spread across half the floor. "Roger is outside—dead. What happened?"

Cardenas did his best to reconstruct the attack. "The howler must have been waiting in the rafters, and dropped down on her from above." He indicated the sitting room's exposed beams. "I think one of the mandrills that attacked us might have gotten away."

"It will not get far. The female activated a warning device. Alarms travel quickly, but those of us who are not machines must still travel on foot. I deeply regret my tardiness. Tell me"—he looked at Cardenas—"had she agreed to return with you?"

"No." The Inspector tried to avoid looking at the body. "She was going to stay here. She felt safe here."

Slow thunder rumbled deep in Sorong's broad chest. "I know that she sought sanctuary here from those who intended her harm. I know you spoke of them. But who would do such a thing?"

"People hired by her husband. Perhaps others. When she left the States, she left enemies behind."

The silverback bowed his head. "I cannot believe that simians would do this. And for what? Money?" He spat the word. "Is this what elevated intelligence leads to? Greed? A craving for things that we never used to need? A willingness to mimic all the moral faults and ethical imperfections of *Homo sapiens*?"

Hyaki murmured low under his breath. "Monkey see,

monkey do." While he intended it as a serious observation, the sergeant was careful to keep it to himself. Even though it was entirely devoid of intentional humor, he realized that someone like Sorong might not look kindly on the reference.

"I have one favor to ask," Cardenas told the gorilla. "When your people run down the one who escaped, see if they can find out who paid for them to do this. There are pathways I'd very much like to backtrack."

The huge, heavy-browed head nodded slowly. "I promise I will do that. And in return, I would beg a favor of you."

Cardenas hesitated. "If it's something I can manage, it's yours."

"I think you are not only the kind of human who can do this thing, but are one who is not unfamiliar with what is required, as you may have had occasion to do it before." Reaching out, he picked up the lifeless form of Surtsey Mockerkin, holding it as easily as if it weighed nothing at all. Her head flopped at a crazy angle. Cardenas was glad her blonde hair hid her face.

Deep-set, painfully intelligent eyes met those of the waiting human. "Would you be the one to tell the daughter?"

"Mierde!" Cardenas's gaze shot toward the doorway. "The ones who did this may try to kill her, too. We've got to find her, and fast."

Sorong looked thoughtful. "If she is not here, then she is probably out on one of her rainforest hikes. She likes to get away from talk. She always goes with someone to guide and watch over her, and for a short walk they will not have taken communicating gear with them. We will go and find out when she is due back. Do not worry, friend Cardenas. I am sure she will make it back safely."

It was the first time in his life Cardenas found himself relying on the word of an ape.

THIRTEEN

THE SILVERBACK WAS CORRECT IN HIS ASsumption about his visitor. In the course of his long career, Cardenas had all too often been obliged to deliver terrible news to the grief-stricken. However, ever since his elevation to the rank of Inspector, that particularly onerous duty had not been required of him in many years. But with Sorong having made the request, and no one else available to carry it out except Hyaki, Cardenas felt himself left with no alternative.

As they waited for the girl to return from her rainforest hike, he tried not to worry about her safety while systematizing what little they knew of the daughter. Because of his singular talent, he was better equipped than most to handle the forthcoming confrontation anyway. That meant it might go easier for her—but not necessarily easier for him. While he would be able to read her emotions and anticipate certain reactions in ways only another intuit could replicate or understand, it also meant that he would feel her pain that much more deeply. Still, he knew he had no choice. There was no one else to do it.

It would help that, by all accounts, the girl was unusually mature. Or maybe it was just easier to *think* of her as unusu-

ally mature, as a uniquely gifted tecant, than as a lonely, isolated twelve-year-old on the run whose mother had just been
brutally murdered. How much did she know about the reasons
behind their flight? How much had Surtsey told her? Was she
aware of the circumstances that had guided their time on the
street, living with a stranger named Wayne Brummel who was
not her father? Or had she endured it in comparative isolation,
allowed to lose herself in studies of technology and nature?

They would find out very soon. According to the chimpanzee he and Sorong spoke with in Administration, she was
due back from a morning walk with her bonobo guide in time
for lunch. Care would be taken to protect her when she returned to the camp and then to channel her, not to her now-
unsafe house in the trees, but to a quiet room within the main
compound research building. As the solicitous silverback
solemnly and sensibly pointed out, that structure lay alongside the Reserva infirmary. If her reaction proved health-
threatening, she could be rushed next door for immediate
treatment.

Offered lunch, the two federales refused it. They preferred
to wait in the designated room, surrounded by the silence and
efficient air-conditioning that made it possible for visiting
human researchers to carry on their work in the otherwise op-
pressive environment of the jungle. Hyaki toyed absently
with the sealtight that had been placed atop the sprayskin. At
the rate he was sacrificing personal integument on this case, it
wouldn't take long before he replaced his entire outer layer.

While his partner retired to the restroom to fix his bandages, Cardenas relaxed by admiring the paintings hanging on
the wall. All of them, he had been informed, had been done
by residents of the Ciudad. Some boasted bright colors but
amateurish technique. A notable few reflected a sophistication
of skill and acuity of observation that would have been the

envy of any human photorealist. At least four of the local artists represented, the two guests had been told, contributed nicely to the Ciudad's income thanks to gallery sales of their work in Nueva York, London, and Zurich.

His ongoing appreciation of simian aesthetics was interrupted as the door opened and Hyaki poked his head into the room. "She's here, Angel."

Cardenas nodded resignedly. "Has anybody told her anything?"

The sergeant shook his head. "She knows that something bad happened to her mother this morning. She knows that some visitors from outside the Reserva would like to talk to her. That's all. Sorong escorted her over himself. I'll send her in." Withdrawing, he left his partner to contemplate the forthcoming encounter.

Having only seen a picture of Katla Mockerkin, Cardenas had no idea what to expect. The twelve-year-old who joined him in the sitting room of the research facility was tall and slim but in no wise gangly. On the contrary, she carried herself with a poise and maturity that suggested she was no longer on the cusp of womanhood, but had in fact already slipped over to the sweet side. Clad in tropical shorts, blouse, and hiking shoes, already almost as tall as her mother, she had straight black hair and green eyes, a startling combination in a tapered face that was attractive but solemn. The Inspector studied it intently, seeking clues to behavior, secrets of personality, subtle references to the young person he was about to confront. Hers was a beautiful mask, a chador projected from within.

But she was only twelve, and no matter how practiced and perfected the veil she chose to draw across herself, it would not prevent someone like Angel Cardenas from seeing inside.

"Olla-lo, Katla. My name is Angel Cardenas. I am an In-

spector with the Namerican Federal Police." When she remained standing, he indicated the small couch opposite his.
"Won't you sit down?"

"Sorong told me there were people from up north who
wanted to talk to me. He was being very mysterious." Accepting Cardenas's suggestion, she took a seat, knees pressed
tightly together, ankles touching, elbows at her sides and
hands clasped together. A bound box, he resolved, as tightly
closed physically as she was mentally.

Having done this all too many times before, he knew that
postponement only led to the kind of rising anxiety that made
everything worse in the end. "We've come to take you back
to the States, Katla. It's the only way we can protect you from
what happened to your mother this morning. I'm truly sorry.
There was nothing we could do to prevent it." He waited expectantly. There was no way to predict how she would react,
but he knew she was smart enough to make the requisite in-
ferences. It was kinder than saying it out loud.

She didn't move. Just sat there across from him, eyes
downcast, thinking. When she finally replied, her preadolescent frame, like her voice, seemed to have grown visibly
smaller. "That's why she wasn't there to greet me. That's what
LooJoo and Tip and Ripeness were doing at the house with all
the . . . cleaning materials. I wondered why they were looking
at me so funny." She swallowed hard, fighting her youth, trying to be very adult. "Can I see her?"

It was so very tricky, Cardenas knew, to be simultaneously
firm and compassionate. "It's probably better if you don't.
Sorong's people can deal with it. Another time might be
better."

A grim, humorless smile appeared. "Another kind of
cleaning crew, huh? Mom always said this might happen. But
she didn't think it would happen here. Not here."

"I'm sorry," he repeated consolingly. "She must have been happy here."

"Happy?" Katla Mockerkin looked up sharply. Sensing what was coming, announced by the subtle movement of her muscles and the slight change in her skin color, he was not as surprised by her reaction as someone else might have been. "Mom was never happy here. I don't know that she was ever happy anyplace. She wasn't happy with Daddy, and she wasn't happy with Mr. Brummel, and she wasn't happy by herself." Black hair rippled. "I *think* she was happy when she was with me, but I was never really sure about that, either."

"Well then," Cardenas opined in an attempt to get the subject off her dead mother, "at least you were happy here."

Katla did not laugh. Scrutinizing that wax-smooth visage, Cardenas suspected it had not been jostled by genuine laughter in quite some time. "What, *me*? There's nothing to do here but walk in the jungle and look at birds and swat bugs all day long. Some of the monkeys are nice, but they're still monkeys. There's no real dancing, no music, no club, no tech leks. Nobody to swap ideas with except Sorong, and he's always too busy to spend time with somebody who's just twelve. Even if they happen to be human. 'Happy'? I was bored to death from the day we got here. I used to take long hikes in the rainforest and dream of being back in the Strip." She made a face. "I told Mom they inspired me. And they did. They inspired me to think about leaving here." Her speech dropped to a mumble. "But Mom—Mom thought we would be safe here."

"From your father?"

Her entwined fingers were clenched so tight they were turning white. "My father, yeah. My father, 'The Mock.' " She looked up. "He wants me back. I know that. But I don't want him back. I didn't want him back before, and I especially don't want him back now."

Keeping his tone as gentle as possible, Cardenas tried to meet the eyes that were avoiding his. "Because he makes you do things, right? Work on things for him?" She looked off to her right and nodded tersely. Anything, he noted, to avoid meeting his gaze. "He wants you back to work on this quantum theft machine."

Her head snapped around in obvious surprise, and her eyes finally did meet his. Dark and unflinching, she peered into his own—and laughed sharply.

"Is that it? Is that what you think?" Tilting back her head, she rolled her eyes at the smooth, sound-absorbing ceiling. "*That* old thing!"

For the first time since she had joined him in the room, Cardenas was confused. "You mean, his organization isn't making an attempt, with your aid, to build such a device?"

"Oh, there's a plan, all right!" He saw that she was unaware of the true source of the hysteria that was beginning to seep into her voice. "*Seguro*, there's a plan. But that's all it is. You'd need the kind of facilities they have at Livermore or Sandia or Elpaso Juarez just to build the models. It's lots of yakk, and hangle, and *gordo lordo* from engineers and techs my father keeps on retainer." She all but hissed. "I don't get a retainer, because I'm his 'daughter,' and I'm just supposed to help. Out of the goodness of my heart, and respect for my father. Respect! Dirty old men, most of them. And one dirty old woman. I hate them all!"

"Calm down," Cardenas told her. "You never have to see them again. Ever. I promise you."

"You?" She looked him deliberately up and down, sizing him up, and was clearly unimpressed. "You're just a spizzed old fedoco. You'll take me back and turn me over to Child

Protection Services or something, and move on to the next job. The Mock will have me back in less than a month."

Cardenas shook his head slowly. "No he will not. We're going to put you in Witness Protection. You won't go anywhere near the usual CPS people. You'll get a new life. We can do that for you, I guarantee it. Not even your father will be able to find you, not with all the crunch he can hire. I wish it didn't have to be that way. You don't deserve to have your life turned inside out when it's hardly begun."

"How do you know what I deserve?" She challenged him openly. "Maybe I'm a bad girl, my daddy's girl. Maybe I do deserve this." She slumped back against the cushions. "Maybe I should just go back to him and do what he wants me to do."

Cardenas leaned forward so suddenly it startled her. "Don't say that! Don't *think* that. You're an individual human being, with a life of her own that's just beginning. And it can be a good life. You're not a feleon. You're not a 'bad girl.' I know. I can tell."

"Can you?" The sarcasm that dripped from her tongue was disconcertingly adult.

He smiled knowingly. "I'm an intuit, Katla. You know what that is?"

Her eyes widened a little and she looked at him in a different light, as so many people did when they learned that singular and significant truth. "Really? You are?" He nodded. "I've never met an intuit. Sure, I know what it is. Can you really read people's minds?"

"No." He sighed wearily. "That's just a street myth. What I *can* do is look at an individual, study that individual, talk to them, and tell a little more about them than almost anybody else. Doing that here, now, with you, I can tell that you're not a bad person. You deserve the kind of life that's been denied to you up to now, and you certainly don't deserve to be forced to go back to your father."

She clutched at his words like someone trapped underwater who'd just been handed another cylinder of air. "You really think you can hide me from him?"

He nodded briskly. "The NFP has resources even those who work for it aren't aware of. But to make use of them, you have to come back with my partner and me. Back to the Strip."

She nodded understandingly. "At least I'll be able to catch up on the vits I've missed. And dig into a real box. And maybe see some of my friends."

Cardenas would not lie to her. If she caught him in just one, he sensed, she would cease forever to trust him. "I don't know about that. We'll have to see. So you'll come back with us?"

She shrugged. "What else can I do? I can't stay here. Not without—without . . ."

It had been building ever since she had sat down on the couch. Now the tears came, fast and copious, in concert with deep, heaving sobs. He let her fall forward into his arms, and he held her as close and tight and secure as he would have one of his own, had he had any. The young girl's hands and arms that clung desperately to him were surprisingly strong.

What could he say to help her to stop? he wondered after several interminable minutes of uncontrolled weeping. Something to shift her thoughts, to make her focus her attention elsewhere.

Gently, he disengaged himself from her clinging grasp, though he remained within reach. "Tell me something, Katla. If the quantum theft mechanism is nothing more than talk and theory, then why is your father so anxious to have you back?"

Wiping at her eyes with the backs of both hands, she

sniffed repeatedly and tried to focus on the unexpectedly compassionate older man. All at once, she smiled. "I'm s-sorry. I got . . ." She pointed, and it almost seemed as if she might laugh. Almost. "I got your mustache all wet."

Reaching up, Cardenas felt of his drooping mustachio. It was soaked with her tears and—other fluids. The expression of distaste that wrinkled his face was partially truthful, partially calculated. To his satisfaction, it provoked the desired response. Her smile widened as she continued to rub and wipe at her eyes.

"You really don't know, do you? My mother didn't tell you?"

"I really don't know," he confessed as he pulled up the hem of his shirt, exposing his slightly hirsute belly, and used the cloth to try and wring out his facial hair.

"I'm not just a tecant. I'm also a mnemonic. My father, The Mock, he doesn't trust anybody else. Never lets anybody get close to him. Not even my mother. But me . . ." Her voice threatened to trail away, broken by reminiscences of a submissive, unhappy childhood.

Speaking in little more than a calming whisper, Cardenas gently urged her to continue. "It doesn't matter what it is, Katla. I'll understand." Reaching out, he used a forefinger to tenderly elevate her chin. "Look at me." Once more her dark, grown-up-too-soon eyes met his. "You know that I'll understand, don't you?" There was no nod of acquiescence, but she did find her voice again.

"Daddy—The Mock wants me back because . . ." She stared off in one direction after another. "He calls me his 'little curly-haired mollysphere.' "

Cardenas blinked. "I'm not sure I understand. You memorized some things for him?"

Now she did nod, her black hair bobbing with the vigorous

up-and-down motion of her head. "Not just some things. *Every*thing."

The Inspector was taken aback. "By 'everything,' you mean . . . ?"

Solemn-faced, the girl touched her forehead with a finger. "His whole business is right here. I don't know that I understand it all. Maybe it's better that I don't. But everything I was told, or shown, I retain. Names, places, people, transactions, times, dates—numbers. Lots and lots of numbers. Mostly about money, but also about—other things."

"Transactions," Cardenas murmured. "What kind of transactions?"

She shook her head. "I can't tell you. Daddy said that if I tell anybody, it makes me an accomplice to whatever I talk about."

In as earnest a voice as he could muster, Cardenas murmured intently to her. "You're a twelve-year-old girl, Katla. Your mother has just been killed. You haven't done anything bad, and you're not guilty of anything except having the wrong man for a father. I swear to you, nothing you tell me will make you an accomplice to anything. All you've done is memorize things. Facts and figures. Like from a book, or a molly. Can a book be an accomplice?"

She hesitated. "I guess not. I suppose not." Her face took on a slightly dreamy, distant expression as she proceeded to relate, at random, a handful of the kind of "transactions" she had been compelled to commit to memory.

The small hairs on the back of the Inspector's neck stiffened as he heard her recollections. Keeping his expression carefully neutral, he listened to a sampling of horrors and transgressions that would have left the typical twelve-year-old trembling with fear. Katla did not appear fazed in the slightest, leaving him to wonder, in spite of what she had said, how much of what she was reciting she really did understand.

Eventually, she returned from wherever it was she had gone, apparently none the worse for the self-induced trance. "Was that enough? Should I tell you more?" For all that it had affected her, she might as well have been describing the contents of last week's favorite vit shows.

"No, Katla. That's fine. Tell me: do you know what 'meroin' is?" She shook her head. "How about 'seventy caliberon'?"

She wrinkled her nose. "I think the first one is some kind of medicine. Isn't the other some kind of machine?"

"It has to do with a certain type of gun," he told her, holding nothing back. "The first one is— It doesn't matter." Since she did not question him as to the meaning of evisceration, he chose not to return to it for discussion.

No wonder The Mock was so desperate to recover custody of his daughter. Better than any spinner, or vorec controller, or para, she was a walking, talking, breathing gram. One he could call upon at any time to confirm the details of a business deal, or recite statistics relating to a previous transaction, or itemize the history and personal characteristics of a friend, an enemy, or a casual commercial contact. Within her innocent, preadolescent self she bore the details of his entire illicit business. What a boon that memorized information would be to a competitor! the Inspector realized. He now had an explanation for the sudden, avid interest shown in the girl by others, such as the Inzini and the Ooze.

Unlike a box or a molly, there was no way she could be hacked, no means of electronically or remotely accessing the information she retained. The Mock's twelve-year-old "curly-haired mollysphere" could not be corrupted by a virus or copied by a scanner. She could not, as a member of immediate family, even be compelled to testify against him in court.

That did not mean she wouldn't, he realized. Any lingering friendly feelings she might have held regarding her father had probably perished with her mother's violent death.

"I didn't want to do it," she was saying. "At first it was kind of fun. Like showing off, just to prove that I could. Then I got tired of it. But Daddy kept insisting. So I kept doing it. It was easy for me. When I got older and started to understand some of the things he was telling me to remember—not like the words you just asked me, but other things—I realized that they involved bad stuff, *muy malo*. But Daddy, he . . ." She paused, gathering herself. "Never mind that. I don't like thinking about that.

"He made me keep on doing it. He made me! I didn't tell Mom. I thought if she didn't know about it, Daddy wouldn't do anything to her. When she asked me what I was doing all that time with him and his friends, I lied and told her it had to do with the quantum theft project. Then she came to me one night, real late, when I was asleep, and told me to wake up and get dressed. I didn't understand what was happening until we got in the car and I saw Mr. Brummel. We drove away. We ran." She looked down at her clenched hands.

"But you can't run away from The Mock. That's what Daddy always told me. 'Nobody runs away from The Mock.' And he was right, he was right, and now Mom's gone, and I'm alone, and what am I gonna do?" As she buried her face in her hands, the tears began anew. "Where am I going to go? I don't have anybody."

"No aunts or uncles, no cousins?"

"If I do," she told him between sobs, "I don't know their names, or where they are. Mom never mentioned any to me.

Maybe she didn't want me to talk to them because it might get them in trouble. With The Mock."

Rising from his couch, Cardenas moved to sit down next to her. When one strong arm went around her shoulders, she let herself lean over against him. She did not look like someone who carried within her mind the entire history and records of a worldwide criminal syndicate.

He waited until she was finished, letting her weep into his side. Then he sat back, gripped both her shoulders firmly, and looked into her eyes. "You'll be safe, Katla. Safe and well taken care of. I'll see to that myself. You'll be able to start a new life, with new friends, in a different place. And eventually you'll grow up, have a normal life, and be able to forget much of this."

Chest heaving, she shrugged indifferently. "Maybe what you say is true. Maybe it will happen like that. I don't know. It doesn't matter. Mom's gone, so it doesn't matter. I—I'd like to believe you, Mr. Cardenas."

He grinned and sat back a little farther. "I told you: call me Angel. Use the English pronunciation if it makes you feel better."

She had to smile at that. "No matter what happens, I won't be able to forget. See, I *can't* forget anything. I've never been able to. I don't know how."

A voice came from behind them. "Hey, you two. How's everything going in there?"

Cardenas glanced back at the concerned sergeant. "We're managing, Fredoso. Be done here soon, I think." The big man nodded and closed the door.

"Who's that?" Katla was looking past the Inspector. "Friend of yours?"

"My partner. Sergeant Fredoso Hyaki. He's a good man. When we get back to the Strip I'm going to let him take you around to meet some people who will help you to begin your new life." He eyed her questioningly. "If that's all right with you, that is."

"Why can't you do it, Mr.—Angel? You said you'd look after me yourself. I think, maybe, that I could like you."

It was enough. A weight lifted from Cardenas's chest. "I'll be there, to be with you, every moment I can, Katla. But as an NFP Inspector, there are other things only I can do. I'll visit you and take you around myself as often as I possibly can. When I can't, Mr. Hyaki will look after you." He smiled encouragingly. "You'll like Fredoso. Everybody does. He's just a big teddy bear."

For the first time, her mood seemed to lighten ever so slightly. "He reminds me of Sorong."

Cardenas repressed a laugh. "Now that you mention it, he does, doesn't he? You be sure and tell him that, every chance you get. Just think of him as your protector. Anything you need, you can ask him." He rose from the couch. "Will you come with us, Katla? Will you let us help you?"

"Why not?" Standing, she was almost as tall as he was. "Like I told you before, there's nothing for me here. Not anymore. So I might as well go with you." Her tone, her expression, even her posture radiated hatred and loathing. "*Anything's* better than going back to Daddy and his lepero friends."

Putting a comforting arm around her shoulders, Cardenas guided her toward the doorway. "Is there anything you'd like to bring with you? From here?"

She shook her head sharply. "I don't want anything from here. I don't want to remember this place at all."

"No clothes, personal items, nothing?" he reiterated.

She looked up at him. "If the NFP has the money to give me a new beginning, then maybe it could buy me some new clothes?" She showed signs of coming back to life. "I remember some shoes I saw in Olmec. Black, with flutterheels. Of course, I don't guess I can go back to Olmec, but . . ."

He patted her shoulder. "The Strip is full of stores. Even *I* know that a girl can't buy shoes off a box; you have to be able to try them on."

She nodded. Color was returning to her face. "You can do a virt fitting if you have the right kind of scanner, but that doesn't tell you how it feels to walk in them. They don't have a sim for that, yet."

"You're a tecant. Maybe you can design one."

"It'd be fun to work with shoes. See, if you just had a little activatable sensing platform that could link to the virt, and could figure out an algorithm that would let you compensate for the differences in customer mass, you could . . ."

As he listened to her rambling, disjointed soliloquy about women's shoes and pressure-sensitive coils and body fat analyzers, he grew more and more aware of what a remarkable young-woman-to-be they were about to accompany back to Nogales. Given some time to grow up, a little peace and quiet, and a suitable education, a bountiful future stretched out before her. A new identity would protect her from such as the Inzini and the Ooze. All they had to do was ensure that she did not revert to being a molly for The Mock. The best way to accomplish that would be to remove from the equation the one individual who most desperately wanted her back.

As soon as they were safely home in the Strip a determined Angel Cardenas, just as he had promised Katla Mockerkin, intended to take care of that little matter personally.

FOURTEEN

IT MEANT CALLING IN A LOT OF FAVORS. IT
meant long hours of manipulating private as well as departmental crunch, of staring at a vit screen until his eyes
seemed to be floating loose in his head. When he could
make the time, he visited with Katla Mockerkin as often as
possible. For reasons he could not entirely fathom, she
found his presence reassuring in a way that Hyaki and the
NFP Child Protection Services representatives were not.
Not that he minded. Spending time with the precocious,
thoughtful girl was a mutual pleasure.

As it took time even for the specialists at the NFP to construct an entirely new identity for Katla that would survive
the most comprehensive search, she was placed in a secure
Nogales-area residence under twenty-four-hour watch.
Since she had agreed to help them against her father, the
need to ensure her safety and security was greater than ever.
While still keeping that in mind, every effort was made to
render her surroundings as commonplace as possible. Considering her background and what she had already gone
through, everyone from the federales to the psychys agreed
that the more run-of-the-mill and unpressured her immediate environment, the better it would be for her health and

well-being. So when she went out on her occasional approved excursions, usually to an entertainment center or mall deeper within the Strip, she was accompanied by only one case worker. While Hyaki trailed the meandering pair from nearby, two to four other incog federales shadowed them all, alert for the unexpected, the unusual, and the potentially dangerous.

There were no incidents. Katla had been delighted to oblige her concerned hosts by dyeing her hair and changing its styling, by utilizing more mature cosmetics to make her appear older and wearing special shoes to make her taller. But she adamantly refused to don the prosthetic stomach weight, even just to go out. Cardenas had smiled at that. You could change a girl's appearance as long as she felt it would make her more attractive. Layering on artificial fat was not an option.

Like anyone else in his position, The Mock tended not to stay in any one place for very long. Owner of a number of elaborate residences both within and beyond the borders of Namerica, he moved around frequently, both to attend to his various enterprises and to prevent rivals and law enforcement from having time to focus on his activities.

Nearly three weeks had passed since the two federales had returned from the rainforest depths of the CAF with Katla Mockerkin safely in their care when the call came down to Cardenas, seated in his cubicle, that Research had finally pinpointed what they believed to be the heart of The Mock's illicit domain. Eagerly studying the information that hovered in the box tunnel above his desk, he was only moderately surprised to see that the hub centered not on one of the Mock's isolated outposts in the Turks and Caicos, or Cuba, or Hispaniola or Nueva York, but in the Strip itself.

Once more, the old saw about hiding in plain sight held true.

While The Mock *vamos*ed around, his operations center had been built in the center of his operations. Although no one could tell for certain whether Cleator Mockerkin himself was presently staying at his nerve center, analysis of the man's movements indicated that, historically, he was likely to be in residence at the site for a particular two months out of the year.

Cardenas hastily checked his calendar. He had ten days left.

"I don't think it's a good idea."

Pangborn stood with one hand on the door of his cruiser. Around them, the Nogales Central garage surged with activity: the whine of cruisers coming and going, specialized service vehicles shuttling back and forth, the yammering of officers and support personnel echoing off the underground walls, with the occasional curse or spark of excitement rising above and then falling below the general din. The noise within, like that of the Strip itself, was unrelenting around the clock.

Missing the Captain in his office, Cardenas had tracked him to the subterranean facility. Confronting him when he was on his way home was probably not the best way to secure permission for what the Inspector had in mind, but he was loath to waste even a minute's time.

"I've thought it through very carefully."

Pangborn rolled his eyes. "You always do, Angel. But that's not what concerns me here. Not even *you* can just walk into a place like that and ask to see the boss."

"I don't want to see him. I want to arrest him and bring him back."

"Oh, well," Pangborn responded with blunt sarcasm, "that makes it easy, then! That eliminates all my concerns." He eyed his friend and subordinate closely. "I don't want to lose you, Angel. You're the best intuit I've ever seen. You're also a great poker partner."

"I'm retiring in a few years, so you're going to lose me anyway, *verdad*?" He smiled winningly, the tips of his profound mustache elevating in tandem with his cheeks.

"I'd rather not retire you on permanent disability. Or worse." Pangborn could have escaped the conversation simply by slipping into the driver's seat of the cruiser and closing the door behind him. That he did not was a sign of the respect he had for the Inspector—and also because he was wavering. Cardenas sensed it—of course.

"Until this *cabrón* is put away somewhere, his daughter will never be entirely safe. No matter what Witness Protection says or does. Besides," he argued, "even if no one else was involved, even if the future of an innocent twelve-year-old wasn't at stake, this homber should be removed from circulation."

Pangborn was obviously torn. Locking up someone like The Mock wouldn't hurt his record one bit. "At least take Hyaki with you."

Cardenas shook his head. "This one has to be done solo. If I go in with a squad, even if they're opto incog people, there's too much risk of them being recognized. Individuals like Mockerkin are always alert to unusual arrivals in their neighborhood. That's why the smart ones don't live in busy, crowded areas. Too much folk-flux. As for Fredoso, he's as big as a whole squad himself, and draws even more attention. Me, I can blend in. I've always been able to do that. Besides, I can usually tell—"

"How people around you are going to react; yeah, yeah,

I know." Pangborn chewed his lower lip. "You might miss him. Research might be wrong and he could be off fishing in the Bahamas or cogering his current pos somewhere."

Cardenas gave an eloquent shrug. "Then I miss him. I know there's a chance of that. But I'd like to try. For the girl's sake."

The other man gave up and gave in. "I know it's no use arguing with you. You're always going to be able to anticipate my arguments. That doesn't mean," he added sternly (and largely for appearance's sake), "that I can't order you not to go."

"Then I can requisition transportation?"

"I suppose. If not, I know I'm going to have to listen to you for the next ten days, and it's hectic enough around here as it is. Go on, go on. Get out of here." He waved diffidently and finally did take a seat in his cruiser. "Take another trip, spend the Department's money. I only see you when you need something, anyway." One hand on the door handle, he looked up at the satisfied senior officer gazing down at him. "Where is this criminal command center that Research found, anyway? You said it was in the Strip."

Cardenas nodded. "Masmatamoros."

The Captain grunted. "Just barely in our jurisdiction. Too far for the tube. Take a flight. It's right in Masmata'?"

"Not exactly. According to the specs who traced it down, it's all the way at the east end, out on the water. On the artificial archipelago they built landside of South Padre back in the thirties."

Pangborn nodded thoughtfully. "It makes sense. Easy to spot trespassers, a couple dozen ways to escape an assault. I read about it once. Never been there myself."

"That's why I have to go in alone," Cardenas told him.

"I wish I could say that I think you're crazy, except I

know that you're not. Your personnel file says so. Watch yourself, Angel. I want to tell all the best jokes at your retirement myself. Unless I end up quitting before you."

Cardenas stepped back as Pangborn closed the door of the cruiser. The powerful hydroelectric engine whined to life and the vehicle slid smoothly out of its charging cradle. The Inspector watched until it turned and disappeared, swallowed up by the vehicular maelstrom of the garage. Then he spun on his heel and headed for the nearest elevator.

For the second time in as many months, he had a shuttle ticket to book.

Coming in low over Masmatamoros, he was barely able to distinguish through the pervading haze the extensive industrial-commercial development that covered this gentle coastal curve of Namerica like brown algae on a stale tortilla. Strict environmental controls prevented the release into the atmosphere of the worst contaminants and toxins, but industrial discharges could not be eliminated entirely. Only mitigated.

They sure as hell mitigated the view, he reflected disappointedly. It didn't matter. He was not here on vacation.

Masmata' was the end of the Strip, the terminus, the last stop on the induction tube line that ran all the way across the continent to distant Sanjuana. Beyond lay the powder blue-green of the Gulf of Mexico. In between there was only the enormous harbor complex of Port Isabel, its deep-dredged and artificially maintained waterfront uniting this easternmost end of the Strip with the rest of Namerica and the world.

Cisneros International Airport had been constructed well inland, north of the main commercial belt and away from

any threat of hurricane storm surge. A rapid-phase induction car carried him from the terminal direct to downtown
Masmata', from where he took a local out to Port Isabel. So
far, he had not worried about being noticed and had been
able to blend in effortlessly with the crowds. Beyond Port
Isabel, outside the commercial center of the Strip, he would
have to be more careful.

The narrow spit of sand that ran for dozens of miles up
the Texas and down the Tamaulipas coast consisted, on a
map, of North and South Padre Islands as well as those that
bordered the great Laguna Madre to the south. In reality,
these attenuated strips of Gulf sea bottom were a cease-
lessly shifting maze of unstable sand and soil. As a barrier
to hurricane storm surges, they were an invaluable natural
resource. Protected for more than a hundred years as recre-
ation and wildlife refuges, they boasted little commercial
development except at their very northern and southern extremities.

But the explosive expansion of the Montezuma Strip from
Sanjuana on the Pacific coast eastward along the old U.S.-
Mexican border and then on down the Rio Grande had its
oceanic terminus at Masmatamoros and, finally, Port Isabel. Having exhausted some decades earlier the available
developable coastal land in the vicinity of the Port, numerous powerful and impatient mercantile interests had banded
together, lobbied for, and eventually secured permission to
build not on protected South Padre Island, but behind it.

Thousands of noncorrosive composite pilings were sunk
and computer-stabilized floats put in place. One after another, floating or fixed structures rose behind the sand spit.
Directly behind the island itself, moderate to very expensive homes and codos went in, allowing their inhabitants
access to the waterways of the South Bay, the Bahia

Grande, and the Gulf of Mexico. Behind the booming residential area, commercial and low-impact industrial development was allowed to blossom. At its back and still closer to the mainland was the intracoastal waterway, busier than ever shipping products north from the maquiladoras of the Strip. It was an arrangement that suited everyone but the greenies. Having long since given up trying to save anything but isolated fragments of the Strip's original ecology, they had shifted their fight to more receptive climes.

Both bays, the mouth of the Rio Grande, and the heavy development in the region known loosely as West Padre were served by a motley, colorful assortment of large ferries and small water taxis. Sleek, high-speed personal hydrofoils crossed paths with slower but more flexible amphibious hovercraft and ancient powerboats. In the midst of this inspired marine chaos, seemingly suicidal pleasure sailboaters cruised back and forth with improbable aplomb. Looming over them all were the huge bulk carriers and transports flying flags of convenience from dozens of nations.

In the midst of this salty South Texas brew, Cardenas chatted amiably with the operator of his hovercraft and tried to ignore the marine bedlam through which they were presently weaving. He had never been much of a swimmer. The sooner his hired vehicle touched down on West Padre #4, the better he would like it. He made an effort to hide his feelings from the boat's pilot, lest the man become curious about a lone middle-aged traveler who, despite harboring a fear of the water, was nonetheless going to spend his vacation in a floating hotel.

Similarly, he did his best to mute his relief when the craft slid up a landing ramp and turned down a floating street. Jockeying for position with cars from the island, the

driver pulled into the drive-up of his passenger's chosen
lodge. Cardenas had picked it from a box brochure for its
blatantly ordinary yet comfortable amenities—and for its
proximity to what Research claimed was the location of
The Mock's hub within the Strip.

His room overlooked a neat but nondescript line of
codos that occupied the next strip of artificial terrain to the
west. Beyond that, and separated from the tourist/residen-
tial belt by an open waterway, lay the first commercial and
industrial structures. From his third-floor balcony, the Inspector could not see the building where with any luck
Cleator Mockerkin presently toiled. No doubt The Mock
had learned of his double-crossing wife's assassination
soon after it had been carried out. The intervening days
must have seen him in a paroxysm of frustration over the
lack of information as to the subsequent whereabouts of his
daughter—of his "little curly-haired mollysphere," Cardenas corrected himself. The same smug confidence that had
led The Mock to consign the history and records of every
one of his illegitimate enterprises to the remarkable mind of
his extraordinary daughter must now be causing him un-
bearable discomfort.

Good, Cardenas thought. He remembered the near-
decapitated cadaver of Surtsey Mockerkin. Let the lepero
suffer, until Cardenas could take him into custody on suspicion of contracting murder for hire. The Inspector was relying on his knowledge of The Mock's type to allow him to
get close enough to execute the warrant. Men and women
like Mockerkin were ever on the alert for an assault by
competitors, or heavily armed law enforcement agents.
Mockerkin ought not to be expecting one man, and a physically unprepossessing one at that. Under normal circumstances, a reputation for ruthlessness in dealing with

interlopers probably was enough to keep lone operatives at bay.

A brand-new spinner containing nearly all the information that had been stored in its predecessor rested in its service pouch, snug against Cardenas's chest. It had taken less than five minutes to download the relevant files from NFP central storage, and half a day to customize it to its owner's personal requirements. A matching vorec rode in his pants pocket. Strapped to his ankle, beneath the right leg of his pants, was a transparent flicker. Loaded with potent, fast-acting narcoleptic ampoules, it could bring down any individual with one shot and keep them harmlessly immobilized for up to six hours. It and its clip of four hypos were manufactured entirely of tough, neutral plastics and composites that rendered them invisible to metal detectors. The size of a pack of stimsticks, perfectly square in shape, and disguise-molded, it would also not arouse suspicions if imaged by a sonic, x-ray, or magnetic resonance scanner.

In the other inside pocket of his rippling maroon windbreaker reposed a more serious device. Made of tough nonmetallic and nonconducting ceramic, the shocker fired tiny charged pellets to a distance of twenty meters. On making contact, a pellet would instantly flood its target with the full force of its stored electric charge. This was strong enough to knock even someone as big as Hyaki flat on their back, and keep them there for up to an hour. Neither weapon was of much use at a range longer than that, but he was not going in as a snapper. He was anticipating that any unavoidable confrontations would take place indoors.

Other equipment rested in his remaining pants and windbreaker pockets. Around his waist beneath the hem of his trousers he wore a tactical medibelt that kept half a dozen tiny, cool sensors pressed against his skin. Derived from its only slightly more powerful military counterpart, the belt was his most reassuring backup: a buckled-on infirmary.

Anxious as he was to meet the man about whom he had heard and read so much during the past weeks, and to place him under arrest, Cardenas forced himself to be patient. It had been a hectic, if not particularly long, travel day. He needed food and a good night's sleep. Tomorrow he would execute the warrant cached on his spinner. Patience, he knew from long experience, had saved more cops' lives than any amount of firepower.

High-speed delivery vehicles and mass-capacity tourist barges shot or sailed past as the pilot of the second water taxi he had employed in as many days greeted him at the cab slip behind the hotel. A quick glance showed that the one other taxi driver in attendance was paying no attention to the traveler or to his more fortunate competitor. Instead, she had her face buried in a reader. Faint strains of masalsa drifted out over the water.

Neither hydrofoil nor hovercraft, the little boat was an engaging antique, as was its operator.

"Good morning, siryore. Where can I take you?" The slim, deeply tanned pilot cast a speculative glance skyward. "Nice day for the beach. Or would you prefer See-tacea Park? I understand that there's a migrating pod of pilot whales in attendance."

Using the available hand rail, Cardenas stepped carefully down into the boat. "No thanks. I'm here on business." He nodded astern. "Just around the corner, thanks."

Muttering disappointment under his breath at the picayune fare, the driver nevertheless hopped down and took a seat behind his console. It being a fine morning, he had retracted the craft's acrylic dome. With a soft belch of air and stir of wake, the boat backed out of the slip, paused, and then moved out into the narrow waterway.

Traffic was noticeably busier on the far side of the industrial zone, facing the intracoastal waterway and the subsidiary port of Laguna Vista some fifteen kims across the bay, than it had been in the tourist belt. Large passenger 'foils plying the busy Gulf coast route roared northward in the direction of Port Aransas, Corpus Christi, and Galveston, southward to La Pesca and Tampico. Huge cushionbarges filled with agricultural and chemical products plied the center of the waterway. Pleasure craft and local transport hugged the inner and outer shorelines, struggling to avoid the chop kicked up by the larger commercial craft. The waterway was not crowded, Cardenas reflected, but it was active, like an afternoon in Agua Pri, when the day staff was in the middle of their shift.

Night and fog would have formed a more atmospheric backdrop for his incursion. Instead, the South Texas day was bright and harsh, a sallow white haze smeared across the otherwise deep sapphire sky like dietetic mayonnaise on blue corn bread.

As they neared the address he had given the pilot of the little boat, Cardenas checked his gear one more time. This was not Nogales or Naco. He was here undercover. Fearful of possible leaks, neither he nor his department had even informed the Masmata' or Port Isabel authorities of his arrival. A cry for help shouted into his vorec would not bring a chopter-borne tactical team on the run. He was on his own.

It was not the first time, and he rather liked it that way.

That did nothing to suppress the iron butterflies who were presently whacking away at his gut. Outwardly, he looked like a traveling businessman preparing to pay a visit to a fellow entrepreneur. Certainly the operator of the water taxi sensed nothing amiss. Dropping off his fare at an unprepossessing passenger landing, he ran Cardenas's card for the amount of the fare and tip, and departed grumbling, in the manner of cab drivers everywhere.

Alone on the floating landing, the Inspector turned his attention to the buildings that rose behind him. Too massive to sit on floats, they rested on hurricane pylons driven deep into the bottom of the waterway, the footings themselves cast in a complex system of interwoven reinforced concrete and nonferrous cables. Beyond emblazoned logos and physical addresses, there was little to differentiate one undistinguished commercial edifice from another.

His own objective certainly looked innocent enough: a modest jumble of interconnected prefab metal buildings that taken either individually or together were in no way remarkable. The eggshell-white dome that crowned the tallest structure was designed to protect the sensitive antennas within from the ravages of coastal weather, but by itself was hardly enough to arouse suspicion. Every other commercial development on the waterway brandished similar instrument blisters. A number flaunted several, like ivory warts on the hides of slumbering tortoises.

There were no battlements, no turrets, no weapons ports designed to allow alerted security personnel to sweep the waterway and walkways with ravening gunfire. It looked like an ordinary warehouse, painted green to blend in with both its natural and artificial surroundings. On its side, in tall white letters of industrial plastic, was the name TAIEESH IMPORT AND EXPORT. At first glance, it was a building no different from the dozens with which it shared the waterway.

Standing on the landing for twenty minutes, Cardenas had yet to see anyone go in or out. That did not mean it was

abandoned. Those who worked inside might very well be
busy at their assigned tasks. Or there could be a submerged
entrance, out of view of passing traffic as well as any pa-
trolling authorities. Given the nature of much of The
Mock's business, Cardenas all but expected it.

Fortuna favet fortibus, the philosopher Barks had oft declared. Readying himself, the Inspector headed for the nearest visible doorway. Pausing before the inset metal door
that was as nondescript as the rest of the structure, he
buzzed for admittance. Aware that he was certainly being
scanned, he strove to appear as innocuous as possible.

There was no response. He tried again, several times,
each time to no effect. Either no one was presently monitoring this particular entrance, or they were neglecting their
job. Stepping back, he examined the fluted green wall that
rose before him. The trio of seagulls reposing on the edge
of the rooftop studiously ignored his presence. The few
windows that interrupted the building's smooth side were
long, narrow, and inset high up on the wall. Far too high to
reach.

Endeavoring to give the impression of a man lost, alone,
and harmless, he started to walk around the building. The
rear was identical to the front, except that instead of the
open water of the intracoastal waterway, it faced another,
much larger industrial structure from within which arose
the sounds of thrumming machinery. A narrow strip of
water, canal as alleyway, divided West Padre #4 from West
Padre #3.

There was a large roll-up access door whose dimensions
were designed to accommodate sizable deliveries. Using a
suction crane, a quartet of workers was in the process of unloading a pair of large packing crates from a shuttle barge
moored in the service canal. The gruff, impatient barge op-

erator was offering loud, helpful, and not always serious suggestions to the men working on the quay.

Taking a deep breath, Cardenas adopted his most businesslike mien and approached the workers. They ignored the casually dressed stranger, intent on the task at hand. The Inspector watched for a moment, like any interested sightseer, before confronting the man he took to be the supervisor.

"I'm looking for your boss. Got a special delivery all the way from Nogales."

Neither question nor statement aroused the slightest suggestion of suspicion on the part of the foreman. Attention focused on the heavy crates, he jerked a thumb over his shoulder. "Inside. Tall guy with the blue hardcap."

"Thanks." Turning, Cardenas entered the main structure. No one moved to stop him.

He found himself in a large warehouse lit by reflectors suspended from the peaked ceiling. Crates and cylinders were neatly stacked on clearly marked pads or stored in oversized shipping bins. Loading machinery idled where it had been left, awaiting direction.

Other workers of both sexes were busy shunting goods or instructing robotics at various tasks. An air of quiet efficiency permeated the area. More than half the staff in evidence wore custom-molded hardcaps to protect their heads from falling objects.

Cardenas worked his way toward the center of the operation, occasionally pausing to ask for further directions—until at last the individual he sought strode into view. The man was as tall as Hyaki, but not nearly as massive. Disdaining a depilatory, he flaunted heavy stubble on dark, almost Middle Eastern skin. His eyes were as black as his hair, and his nose prominent. In one hand he held a slender commercial spin-ner, gesturing with it as he spoke to two other workers.

Turning away, Cardenas made a show of scrutinizing a nearby cylinder labeled "Perishable—Flash Dried Fruits" in both English and Portuguese. When the conversation tak-ing place behind him ended and the two workers wandered away, he turned and moved quickly toward the tall man in the blue hardcap. One hand slipped over the shocker riding in his pocket, his index finger easing onto the trigger.

Dark eyes turned to look down at him. Curiosity but not suspicion showed openly on the man's face.

"Yes, can I help you?"

"Got a special delivery from Nogales." His hand tight-ened on the shocker. "For The Mock."

Honest puzzlement further contorted the man's features. "For *what*?"

"Not what—who. For The Mock." Something was wrong, Cardenas saw. "For Cleator Mockerkin."

Plainly bemused, the tall overseer shook his head slowly. "Never heard of him. I'm Yogesh Chanay, day shift super-visor. You *sure* this guy works here?"

The man's confusion was open and forthright, Cardenas saw. No competent intuit could fail to see that, and the In-spector was far more than competent. "Then I need to speak to your boss, or whoever you take orders from."

"There's nobody like that here," Chanay informed him without resentment. "During the day, I'm in charge of the whole facility." Pushing back the brim of his hardcap, he scratched his forehead as he pondered his visitor's request. "I can get you some corporate addresses in Nueva York. Would that help?"

"No, that's not necessary." Momentarily adrift, Cardenas

mulled over his next step. "I really need to make the delivery to this particular guy. I was told he worked here."

"Well," responded the cheerful Chanay, "it looks like somebody steered you wrong." He started to turn away, paused. "Say, maybe he works in the annex."

Cardenas tried not to show more than casual interest. "What annex?"

"Downstairs. Company maintains a data-processing annex. For compiling and research, that sort of thing. You know, crunch-munch? Not real exciting stuff." He grinned. "I'm not big on thick compilations of statistics, myself. Never been down there. Hardly ever see anybody go in or out. I imagine most of the operation is automated. As it should be. Got nothing to do with me and my crew up here."

The Inspector nodded gratefully. "I suppose I could check and ask."

"You can try." Chanay was less than encouraging. "If there's nobody down there today you won't be able to get in."

"I guess I'll give it a shot, anyway."

The supervisor pointed. "Through that storm door over there. There's an elevator, but you won't be able to operate it without a passkey. Fire stairs to the left. It's only two floors down. The intracoastal here isn't that deep."

Cardenas nodded. "Thanks." Heading for the doorway in question, he cast more than one surreptitious glance over his shoulder. There was no sign of alarm or unease in the supervisor's face, nothing suggestive about his body posture. He appeared wholly oblivious to the visitor's movements.

Chanay's remarks were as accurate as his directions: the elevator Cardenas encountered beyond the storm door did not respond to his requests. Neither did the opaque poly-carbonate barrier marked FIRE ESCAPE. The electronic lock did, however, finally yield to one of the compact devices he carried. Descending the stairwell, he went through a second storm door and down plastic steps, treading as quietly as possible. At the bottom, a final door opened to reveal a dark hallway. Overhead lighting responded to his presence by fluttering to life, illuminating a hard-floored passageway that ran off to the east, toward the rocky underpinnings of South Padre. Unseen fans kept the air fresh and cool.

Advancing cautiously, he walked perhaps thirty meters down the unadorned, bare-walled corridor, uncomfortably aware that there was nothing beyond the ceiling over his head and the floor beneath his feet but tepid Gulf salt water. The corridor terminated in a cul-de-sac boasting three doors. His hand hovering in the vicinity of the shocker, he tried the one on his left first. It opened at a touch to reveal a multistall bathroom. The second door accessed a store-room that was a jumble of office supplies and equipment. The third—he hesitated outside the third. Licking his lips, he finally pushed on the access switch. Like its predeces-sors, the barrier folded inward without complaint.

Half a dozen old-fashioned desks flanked by ancillary cabinets greeted his entrance. There were communicators, desk processors, and nondescript pictures hanging from the walls. One wall boasted a passable holovit of what looked like a snow-fed lake high in the Rocky Mountains. Synthe-sized sunlight dappled the clear blue water while virtual trout swam in the pellucid shallows. At the far end of the room a trio of expensive, but stock, commercial parallel compilers hummed softly as they efficiently and without human supervision processed data. As with the bathroom and storeroom, the workplace was devoid of human presence.

He tried to access one of the compilers. Its security was minimal, and he slipped in almost effortlessly. Too easy. Nor did it appear to contain anything more than the most banal lists and records of information pertaining to the business operating above his head.

Backing out, he stood in the hallway and speculated. The annex made no sense—unless Taieesh Import and Export was a legitimate business in which The Mock had no interest, and all the effort that had been expended by himself and the Research people at the National NFP database had produced nothing better than a false lead.

There was much to be said for hiding in plain sight, except that nothing and no one appeared to be hiding here. Fuming silently, Cardenas resolved to conduct the same kind of thorough inspection of his surroundings that any federale would carry out. Retracing his steps, he began near the front of the office. Finding nothing insinuative, he moved on to the storeroom. How much time he had, he didn't know. It largely depended on whether or not the amiable Yogesh Chanay would remember his visitor and think to have someone check to see if he had taken his leave of the building.

So he worked as rapidly as possible, his depression increasing as each successive room proved to be nothing more than what it appeared to be. In the bathroom, he paused to make use of the facilities before concluding his inspection.

A small service door at the back of the room, beyond the last stall, did not even have an electronic handle. The undemanding latch yielded to a moderate tug. On the other side was a closet with shelves to left and right piled high with paper, disinfectant, soap, and other lavatory supplies. A couple of ancient mops leaned up against one set of shelves. He started to close the door, hesitated. There were no shelves on the back wall.

Silly, he mused, but he felt he still had a little time, and he was almost finished here anyway. He fumbled at the service belt concealed beneath the waistband of his pants until he found the pouch holding the tool he wanted. Without much enthusiasm, he proceeded to run the Schlage sesame over the back wall. Nothing. Reaching the bottom, he was about to slip the device back onto his belt when a pair of telltales abruptly and utterly unexpectedly changed from red to green. Crouching, eyes narrowing, he began to slowly pan the tool over the floor near the base of the rear wall. The green lights brightened. A muted beeping began.

Gently setting the device on the floor, he flicked a couple of switches on the front plate and stepped back. Thirty seconds passed, following which there sounded a virtuous click. This was followed by a deep-throated mechanical whirring sound.

As he took a another step back, the floor fell away and the back wall swung up to reveal a brightly lit, downward-sloping ramp. Placing his right hand over the shocker again, he started down and in.

FIFTEEN

THE WELL-LIT CHAMBER AT THE BOTTOM OF the ramp was spacious and carefully laid out, the ceiling low but not uncomfortably so. Planar walls of taupe-tinted Hitach firecoat were devoid of the animated pictures and holovit that had decorated the office on the level above. Individual Suva-Shiva box stations were alive with lights, and the floor underfoot was pebbled and cool to the touch. At the far end of the room was a plain door flanked by a two-meter-wide slash of mirrored glass.

Movement. Off to his left. Drawing the shocker, he whirled and crouched—only to relax and drag the back of his other hand across his forehead, as if that could somehow erase the tension there.

A pair of identical half-meter-high robot cleaners trundled into view. Ignoring him, they proceeded to sweep and vacuum the composite tile floor. Designed to operate in office environments while work was in progress, they went about their business in eerie silence, as soundless as a pair of mechanical undertakers.

Relieved, he started to rise, when something else made him turn. Whether it was intuition, or a sound that did not quite belong, or a hint of shadow, he was not sure. He didn't have time to analyze it. Whirling, he saw a large, winged shape diving straight for his face. At the last possible instant he threw himself to one side. Only his extraordinary reflexes, honed by decades on the force and coupled with his unique training, saved him.

A seagull, one of the phlegmatic, roof-sitting trio that had observed his disembarkation at the passenger dock, smashed into the floor next to his feet, skidded several meters, and slammed into the wall. Rolling over just in time to witness the impact, Cardenas expected to hear bones snap and see feathers flying. Instead, bits and pieces of plastic and metal and teased glass flew in all directions as the synthetic Laridae shattered into a hundred or more pieces.

On hands and knees, keeping a wary eye out for any other unexpected arrivals, he crawled over to inspect the ruined apparatus. It was wonderfully, even imaginatively, made. Though twisted sharply to one side, the head was still largely intact, the tiny tracking cameras located behind the eye shields still locked in scanning position. The beak was cracked open, so he could see inside the mouth.

A sharp pinging emerged from the debris and he yanked his hand back. The extendable pressure dermic that occupied the place where a bird's tongue would be just missed making contact with his exploring fingers.

Rising, he brought his right foot down hard on the quivering head, and applied his weight. Struts and supports molded from finely wrought composite cracked noisily. Like the stinger of a dying wasp, the dermic stabbed wildly, seeking flesh to penetrate. Only when Cardenas was certain the device was utterly defunct did he draw back his foot, and only then did the dermic, nearly as long as his hand when fully extended, cease trying to impale him.

Breathing hard, he looked around warily, his gaze flicking from walls to ceiling, from the open doorway behind him that led to the facade of a bathroom to the darkened glass at the opposite end of the workplace. The attack had caught him almost completely off guard. Who needed human sentries? They were conspicuous, likely to draw suspicion to themselves, potentially corruptible, and expensive. The seemingly deserted annex was not so deserted after all.

Overhead, Taieesh Import and Export provided perfect camouflage. What better cover for a center of illicit operations than a legitimate business whose employees were utterly and honestly ignorant of the unlawful activities that were going on beneath their very feet? It was akin to running a counterfeiting operation from inside a bank vault.

His eyes continued to scrutinize the far corners of the chamber. There had been three of the birds. How the devil had they gotten in? It occurred to him that ventilators that brought in clean air could also admit other things. Things that had been programmed to navigate their way through tubes and conduits. To navigate—and to kill.

Lights glowing dimly behind the swath of dark glass hinted at the existence of still another room, accessible through the single rear door. There was no sign of movement save for the cleaning robots. Did The Mock and his underlings do their work only at night? That would go a long way toward explaining the emptiness in which he found himself. It did *not* mean that Mockerkin left his principal place of business unattended, relying for defense only on the sham reality of the import-export enterprise above. The shattered remains of the wrecked aerial assassin that lay in a still crackling and popping pile at his feet attested to that.

Standing in the middle of the room, he was too exposed.

There was too much room for flying killers to maneuver. He wanted more cover.

Something told him not to try for the passageway that led to the surface. The short ramp that led to the storage closet and the bathroom beyond would be a perfect place to stage an ambush. Anyway, he wasn't ready to leave.

Keeping an eye on the temptingly vacant exit, he turned from where he was standing and strode briskly toward the rear door. Almost as soon as he turned his back on the exit, a second replicant gull came lunging in through the rear passage, having to turn sideways so that its wings would fit through the opening. A glance was sufficient to allow Cardenas to spot the fully extended dermic that was aimed right at him.

Pulling the shocker from his windbreaker pocket as he ran, he fired once, and missed. With only enough time for one more quick shot before the vacant-eyed assassin reached him, he stopped running, whirled, and dropped. Taking the best aim he could as he slid backward on the floor, he fired. The bird-thing erupted in a shower of sparks less than a meter from his face as he threw up his free hand and turned away from it. He felt the warmth of a secondary explosion as it banked sharply to the right and crashed into the floor behind him.

Panting, the shocker hanging from his fingers, he rose to his feet and assessed the damage. Thrashing and twitching like a live thing, the artificial gull spewed sparks and smoke for more than a minute before it finally stopped flailing its composite wings and lay still. He looked up.

No voices rang out challengingly. The cleaning robots continued to run their preprogrammed routines as though nothing had happened. One was already busy sweeping up the remains of the first gull. Otherwise, the chamber was as silent as the seabed on which it rested.

Where, he wondered as he cautiously resumed walking toward the back door, *was the third bird?*

Though it boasted only an ordinary plastic handle and no visible security, the door would not respond to his tug. Expression tight, keeping a cautious eye alert for mechanical sea birds, he pocketed the shocker and removed the compact instrument he had previously utilized to access the concealed doorway in the bathroom storage closet. Starting at the top of the door, just as he had done with the closet's rear wall, he began slowly and methodically running the device over the door. This time he would not neglect to check the floor.

"Hello there, son. Watcha doing?"

Swapping the sesame from his left hand to his right, Cardenas fumbled awkwardly for his pistol. At the sight of his questioner, he relaxed slightly. But he kept his hand near his chest, in the vicinity of the gun, as he pretended to scratch at the front of the windbreaker.

Framed in the entranceway at the bottom of the ramp that led to the bathroom storage closet was an old man. Too old, the Inspector knew instantly, to be The Mock. Although in an age of synthollagen injections and epidural neuron massage and skin replacement therapy it was difficult at a glance to tell anyone's age for certain, Cardenas was reasonably confident that the intruder who had surprised him was at least in his seventies, and quite possibly older.

The Inspector would also have been surprised if the man weighed much more than fifty kilos. He was considerably shorter than Cardenas. Amerind characteristics sharpened the highs and lows of his weather-worn face, the type of environmental facial sandblasting that began early in life in the kind of small villages that were scattered all through southern Namerica. Instead of weaponry or communications gear, the service belt encircling his waist contained janitorial supplies. Both hands clutched an electrostatic broom.

"Looking for someone," Cardenas finally thought to respond.

The old man flipped a switch on the broom and began to work it methodically back and forth in one corner, occasionally pausing to move a chair out of the way. The idling box terminals and busy floor robots ignored him, and he them. While adding an invigorating flow of ions to the air, the broom's charged fibers silently sucked from crevices, cracks, and other hiding places the dust and debris that the tunnel-visioned robot sweepers had missed.

"Ain't nobody here. Ain't been nobody here for a while. I reckon you belong, or you wouldn't have been able to find your way in."

Cardenas saw no reason to disabuse the elderly custodian of this useful assumption. He fell back on the same story he had recounted to the warehouse supervisor. "That's right. I have a special delivery from Agua Pri, for The Mock." Hesitating only briefly, he added, just to make certain, "You're not by any chance The Mock, are you? That's not a clever disguise?" Able to tell in most cases whether someone was lying or not, he waited expectantly for the custodian's reply.

It took the form of a quiet chuckle. "Me, The Mock? Why would you say something like that? C'mon, son; you're having fun with an old man." He flashed a smile replete with man-made teeth. "I'm Rodrigo. I do the cleaning."

Pointedly, Cardenas indicated the still-active floor robots. "What about them?"

"They need cleaning and maintenance, too. They are a big help to me, since the owners of this place seem to want as few people in here as possible. But they are not as good as a person. They miss some spots." He shook his head diffidently. "I don't know why. I could use some nonmechanical help, and it can get lonely down here." The smile returned. "But it pays well." And with that, he returned to his sweeping.

Still on the alert for murderous airborne mechanicals, Cardenas walked back to the ramp and peered upward. Nothing flew in at him, nor was there a downward charge of mataros, security guards, ninjacs, or anything else. Nor were representatives of the Inzini, the Ooze from Oz, or any other malevolent organization waiting in the bathroom to monitor and sponge off his progress. Except for the old man preoccupied with his cleaning and the meticulous floor robots, he was alone in the sanctum.

"Do you happen to know," he inquired carefully, "where I might find The Mock?"

Halting his sweeping, the grizzled senior leaned on his broom and regarded the visitor. "I guess you really do not know. Not if you are trying to make a personal delivery to him. Siryore Mockerkin died three months ago." His elderly expression wrinkled with remembrance. "I think it was three months." With a shrug, he resumed his sweeping. "It might have been three and a half."

Standing in the center of the underwater command center, surrounded by dynamic online consoles and multiple readouts burning bright, Cardenas gaped at the custodian. The old man's reply was, to say the least, not what he had expected to hear.

"What do you mean he's dead? He can't be dead."

Rodrigo kept working as he spoke. "We can all of us be dead, siryore. I was told about it by Ms. Larrimore, who worked in here. Mr. Mockerkin was coming out of the Brazos Mall in Harlingen after doing some shopping. He was with two other employees when they were hit by a bus that had gone out of control. Mr. Mockerkin and one of the other men were killed immediately. The other went to hospital." The maintenance man scratched at his thinning gray-brown hair. "I think he got out last month, but I am not sure."

Cardenas's thoughts were churning furiously. "Would Mr. Chanay, the supervisor of the warehouse upstairs, know about this?"

The custodian shrugged again. "I do not know. You would have to ask him. I never see the people who worked down here and the ones who work in the import-export place mix with each other. I believe they are different businesses. But I do not know. I am only a janitor." He smiled easily, Cardenas noted. "I do the cleaning."

"What about the other people who do work down here?" The Inspector indicated the empty chairs that faced the multiple consoles.

"I don't know, siryore. It's not my business. I don't concern myself with such things." He looked contemplative. "I suppose they are working when I am not here. Or maybe they were told to stay away for a while, after Mr. Mockerkin was killed. I really don't know."

Was killed, Cardenas found himself repeating. Months ago. This was crazy! It made no sense. If Cleator Mockerkin had really perished in an accident on the streets of Harlingen, then who the hell these past several months had been furiously, even ferociously, directing the ongoing effort to abduct Katla Mockerkin, and who had continued the hunt that had resulted in her mother's murder?

"Might someone besides yourself show up here today?"

Rodrigo was beginning to sound tired. "Please, siryore. I do not know. You would probably know better than I."

Cardenas nodded slowly. "All right. I won't bother you anymore. Go ahead and finish your work."

Rodrigo was patently grateful. Cardenas waited until the janitor had finished sweeping the floor and airdusting the softly humming electronics. As he was preparing to leave, the old man looked back at him from the bottom of the ramp.

"Are you going to wait here, siryore?"

"Yes," Cardenas told him. "Yes, I think I'll wait for a while longer, to see if anyone shows up. If you don't mind, that is." He smiled engagingly.

Rodrigo pushed out his lower lip. "Why should I mind? It's not my business. I'm a custodian, not a watchman." He started up the ramp.

"One more question," Cardenas called after him. The old man paused and looked back. "If what you're telling me is true, and your employer is dead, then why do you keep coming down here and cleaning this place?"

The old man eyed him tolerantly, as one would a child. "Because when I access my bank, the money is always there. I keep getting my pay."

Cardenas could not let it go. "Who pays you? One of the other employees, someone who's not here right now?"

The aged head swung slowly from side to side. Visibly tiring of the endless string of questions, Rodrigo injected a note of impatience into his reply. "Once again, siryore, I do not know. I just know that when I check my account, my pay is there. As long as that is so, I will keep doing my work. Until someone tells me to stop, or until the money stops being paid. I never thought much about it. I suppose it is a program of some kind, that pays me automatically." He shook his head again. "Often I think some things were better in the old days, when not so many things were automated." He winced slightly. "Do you have any more questions?"

"Just one." Turning, the Inspector indicated the single remaining door that stood next to the inset of mirror glass at the back of the room. "What's in here? Another storeroom?"

"I don't know. It is kept locked. I've never been asked to clean in there, if that's what you mean."

"Ever see anybody go in, or out?"

"No, siryore. I haven't."

That, Cardenas reflected, *was interesting.* In his mind, he had already dismissed the old man. "Thank you for your help."

The custodian nodded. "You are welcome, siryore. If you will excuse me, this is my last work of the day, and I want to go home now." Turning, he climbed slowly up the ramp. In his wake, the entryway remained open and clear.

If The Mock was dead, Cardenas reasoned restively, then someone else must have taken up his work. Some trusted lieutenant, or second-in-command. But who? He could understand an underling being intensely interested in the quantum theft project, however ephemeral its prospects, not to mention the complete records of The Mock's organization—either of which would explain the ongoing effort to abduct Katla. But why follow through with the obviously Mock-ordered revenge killing of Surtsey Mockerkin? The Montezuma Strip was not ancient Calabria, or Sicily, or even Moscow. Modern-day criminals were inter-

ested in vacuuming crunch and credit, not in pursuing another individual's personal vendettas. No matter how loyal
a second-in-command might be to his former master The
Mock, Cardenas could not see any reason for a subordinate
to pursue a contract murder that he or she had no personal
interest in seeing carried to fruition.

Unless, perhaps, Surtsey Mockerkin had covered her
bets by dallying with another of The Mock's minions besides the unfortunate Wayne Brummel, and had then left
them in the lurch along with her late husband.

It still didn't add up. Every time he pieced together a new
scenario based on the facts as he knew them, it immediately
fell victim to conspicuous flaws of internal logic. The obvious fix for the irritating conundrum lay in the acquisition of
additional facts. The room in which he presently found himself was clearly the place to start searching for them.

While he pondered how and where best to begin, he kept
a circumspect eye on the exit. Unless the old man was the
greatest actor Cardenas had yet encountered in his long
years on the force, the custodian was nothing more than the
simple maintenance worker he claimed to be. Nevertheless,
on the off chance the senior had patiently waited out the intruder's questions only to sound the alarm elsewhere, Cardenas periodically walked over to the bottom of the ramp to
check the approach through the storage closet.

When not occupied in making sure his escape route remained clear, he contemplated the multiple work stations
that lined the walls of the underwater chamber. Which
mollysphere was most likely to be susceptible to a probe?
What sort of booby-traps might he reasonably expect to encounter? He had done this sort of thing before, most recently when he had been assigned to probe the dangerously
compromised corporate box at GenDyne's main research

tank in Agua Pri. Invasive box sorties were inevitably fraught with treacherous surprises. The possibility that any of the mollys or the main box in a place like this would operate without some kind of integrated protection never once crossed his mind.

Eventually, as he had suspected they would, his thoughts returned once more to the door at the back of the room, and to what might lie behind it and the pane of thick mirror glass. If it was nothing more than a simple storeroom, why prohibit entry to the custodian already entrusted with the key code to this secluded chamber?

It would probably take only a few seconds of his time to check out. Alongside the door handle was a small vertical slot designed to accept a simple, straightforward coded key. From his belt he once more pulled out the sesame, slapped it over the slot, flicked it to life, and waited. In less than thirty seconds the device ascertained the combination and applied it. There was a click. Trying the handle a second time, he found that the door opened easily toward him.

Too easily.

He found himself looking into a small antechamber perhaps two meters square. There were a pair of storage cabinets, a small office-sized refrigerator, and on the wall a small holovit showing a pink tile-roofed house in a tropical setting. Within the holovit, the moon was slowly rising, casting golden glimmers on the stream that ran left to right in front of the house. To Cardenas's immediate right, another door beckoned, temptingly ajar. Twisting and bending while remaining outside the antechamber, he found he could not see very much of the room beyond through the limited gap thus presented.

Worms and artful lures were designed to attract fish. Open doors invariably drew curious people. He had no intention of ending up gaffed and gutted in the presence of an obvious hook.

There appeared to be nothing to hinder his entry, which was exactly why he held back. After studying the antechamber for several minutes, he turned and strode back through the larger outer workplace and up the ramp. Seizing on the pair of old-fashioned mops he had seen during his earlier sojourn in the bathroom storage closet, he returned with them to stand once more before the door he had just unlocked. It stood ajar, exactly as he had left it.

Setting one of the mops aside, he grasped the other with one hand at the top and the other near the bottom. Holding it vertically, he pitched it into the antechamber.

There was a sudden flash of light that left multiple afterimages dancing on his retinas. Instantly and effortlessly sliced into sections, four pieces of mop clattered metallically to the floor.

Had *he* stepped unthinkingly into the alcove, there would just as efficiently, but considerably more messily, have been four pieces of him.

SIXTEEN

THUS STARKLY ENLIGHTENED, CARDENAS proceeded to reinspect the seemingly innocuous alcove.

He found two of what he was looking for concealed in
the pair of cabinets, one hiding in the front door of the refrigerator, and the other artfully concealed behind the window of the house depicted in the holovit. Normally a
brilliant crimson, the industrial lasers that had rendered the
mop into instant scrap had been customized with canceling
optics that nullified their conventional color without affect-
ing their potency. Peering into the antechamber, a visitor saw
nothing but empty air; stepping in, he would find himself
sliced and diced without ever getting a chance to ascertain
the cause.

There was no visible controlling switch, either for the
harmless overhead lights or the rather less inoffensive optical sentinels that guarded the entrance to the room behind
the inner portal. Intended to liberate him from minor in-
conveniences and allow him to enter locked rooms and
boxes, his service belt offered nothing designed to cope
with a sentry system quite this elaborate—or lethal.

After contemplating the unoccupied but deadly alcove,
he turned and once more made his way back through the

outer room and up the ramp. This time he did not stop in the bathroom storage closet. Selecting one of the two large wall mirrors that were installed above the bathroom's double sinks and utilizing the tools on his belt, he soon had it pried loose from the industrial adhesive that kept it fastened to the wall. Retracing his steps, he carefully set the mirror aside and picked up the remaining mop. Following the first into the antechamber, it suffered the same fate as its sacrificial predecessor.

Turning the mirror on its end yielded a reflective shield that was nearly, but not quite, as tall as Cardenas. Sacrificing the second mop had allowed him to memorize, albeit hastily and imperfectly, the angles at which the beams of the colorless lasers crisscrossed the alcove. Hunching down to keep as much of himself as possible behind the mirror, he carefully and slowly edged forward into the antechamber.

There was a single bang, followed by a strong smell of burnt paneling. Advancing at a snail's pace, he worked his way through the alcove, past the softly humming refrigerator and beneath the deceptively soothing holovit. Feeling the freely swinging lure of the inner door against his back, he pushed it open, stumbling slightly as he duck-walked through the now-unobstructed portal.

When he was as confident as he could be that he was beyond range of the invisible sentinels, he stood up and set the providential mirror aside. Deflected and reflected by the glass, the lasers had burned a pair of thumbnail-sized holes in the far wall of the antechamber and another two in the ceiling. The tiny black cavities smoked slightly and stank mightily, but he saw no flames, and no fire-detection alarms were sounding. This was not unexpected. Any place as important as this underwater redoubt would have been fabricated of fireproof and fire-retardant construction materials.

It would take more than a little smoke to set off any integrated fire alarm system.

The room in which he found himself was dimly but adequately lit. To his left, a single holovit of open desert filled the entire wall. As he looked on, a three-dimensional Gila monster scuttled out from behind a woolly bear cactus to disappear behind a rock. Soaring from right to left, a Swainson's hawk cried out, its screech muted. Looking to his right, the Inspector saw the outer room, with its empty workstations and the bathroom closet ramp beyond, clearly through the high-quality one-way glass.

In front of him was a small work area dominated by a single comfortable chair and an idling box tunnel. On the otherwise empty desk, a vorec sat waiting in its holder. There was no keyboard for optional manual input. Below the subdued tunnel that appeared to run to a softly glowing infinity, the impassive glass eye of a scanner poked out of the wall. Hefting the bathroom mirror, Cardenas once more held it out in front of him as he approached the station and sat down in the chair. Nothing jumped out at him, and the chair did not blow up beneath his butt. Gratified but still vigilant, he examined the vorec carefully before removing it from its holder. It was a Pelurinho Amado 24. Expensive, multilingual rated, but with relatively straightforward controls, it was intended for a user who wanted the best available voice recognition technology but was not particularly technologically sophisticated. Flicking it active, he brought it to his lips.

"Open," he murmured softly into the discreetly padded pickup.

Words emerged from within the box tunnel as a dull inner light animated the scanner eye. "Access denied. Authorization required."

"Verbal?"

"Yes," the supple mechanical voice informed him.

Here was a simpler, and less lethal, problem to deal with than annulled lasers, Cardenas saw. Removing his service belt, he laid it out on the desk so he could more quickly and easily access its contents. While essential industrial mollys and boxes were usually defended by multiple layers of security, physically smaller and less significant ancillary devices—devices like vorecs—generally boasted less elaborate safeguards.

Removing his spinner from its pouch, he snapped his own vorec into the appropriate receptacle. From onboard storage, he punched up a vorec operations file. Delving into the National NFP tank in Washington in the course of doing research on The Mock, Cardenas had tracked down a voice file of a line tap that included a couple of innocuous sentences uttered by one Cleator Mockerkin in the course of his checking into the Four Seasons Havana some ten years ago. Using the tiny file as an aural template, police techs in Nogales had successfully generated a syntharym that perfectly mimicked the individual sonics.

As soon as the relevant file had been shunted, he placed the caster node of his own unit against that of the one he had removed from the holder on the desk. Some judicious juggling of the controls, and the syntharym was transferred to the resident vorec. Easing the spinner back into its pouch and returning his own vorec to its holder, he gripped the local and repeated his earlier command.

"Open," he reiterated. If the syntharym was sufficiently precise, and had made a full transfer, the vorec he was holding should now convince the molly behind the wall and the box it connected to that it was being addressed by, if not Cleator Mockerkin himself, then someone with sufficiently similar speech patterns to satisfy the security gram. Of course, Mockerkin might never have been in this little room, much less utilized its box. It might simply be a protected facility utilized by, say, his chief financial officer. But where this level of carefully thought-out physical artifice and internal security was employed, it seemed reasonable to suppose that the individual at the top of the command chain ought to at least be able to check on the work of underlings.

Or not, he realized pessimistically as the box voice replied, "Access denied. Authorization required."

He tried again, on the off chance that the syntharym had not been transmitted accurately the first time. The result was the same. Lips pursed, brow furrowed, he sought elucidation.

"Erroneous verbal command entered?"

The box responded without hesitation, the artificial voice emerging clearly from within the open tunnel. "Verbal command accepted. Visual authorization denied."

He had suspected from the moment he sat down in the chair that this would not be easy. Muttering under his breath, he set to work yet again removing necessary gear and material from the service belt's pouches. A quick glance showed that the entryway leading to the bathroom storage closet remained blessedly silent and deserted.

It had been a long time since he had been obliged to make use of a chameleon. Removing the flexible mask from its belt pocket, he unfolded it and spread it out flat on the desktop. When he thumbed the power switch woven into the back, the opaque epidermoid sprang to life. Carefully he slipped it into place over his face and snugged it tight. The familiar tickling sensation that ensued indicated the mask was working, busy molding itself to his features. Wearing the mask made breathing difficult but not impossible. When the chameleon felt it was set and ready, it so informed him by sounding a tiny beep.

Swiveling in the chair and turning back to face the scanner set in the wall, he addressed the vorec anew. "Open."

The box replied without hesitation. "Verbal command accepted. Visual authorization denied."

This time he was not disappointed. He had expected the response. Even the most efficacious chameleon needed time to work its morphing magic. After a moment's pause to allow it to process the information it had received, he repeated the request. Again it was denied. And again.

Each time he voiced his request, the wall scanner played over his face in an attempt to identify him. And each time it did so, the sensors implanted in the chameleon tracked the scan, refracting the light from the pickup as it progressively built up a topology of the scanner's own sought-after parameters. With each subsequent failed request, the epidermoid was able to build greater density into the constantly metamorphosing mask. Nanonic motors within the sensitive material carried out subtle adjustments to its shape, continuously folding and remolding features. The mutable lenses from behind which Cardenas regarded the obstinate wall flexed in response to information gleaned by the mask's built-in analytical instrumentation as it tried to feed the box what it wanted to know.

It took nine attempts before the box finally answered, "Verbal command accepted. Visual command accepted. Retina scan accepted. Authorization complete. Welcome, approved visitor."

He was in. The molly supporting the tunnel, and via it the box, was now amenable to access, though that did not mean everything within had suddenly become an open book. Tentatively, he called forth records and contents. As they appeared in the tunnel before him, shifting and steadying in response to his orders, he scanned them with a policeman's eye, wishing he had the time to make detailed recordings. Further analysis of The Mock's illicit little empire would have to await the attention of the NFP's forensic accountants. Right now, he was only interested in information relating to the death of Surtsey Mockerkin and the concurrent attempts to abduct her daughter.

Unable to isolate anything directly relevant, he was eventually compelled to resort to a more straightforward variety of oral interrogation.

"Surtsey Mockerkin is dead," he informed the box. "Were you aware of that fact?"

"I have already logged that information," the molly told him, speaking from the escher depths of the tunnel. Cold and emotionless as a stony plain in central Greenland, it added, "That particular gram has been terminated."

Cardenas found that he wanted to be rid of the chameleon and its claustrophobic, form-fitting, sensor-impregnated resilience as quickly as possible. It limited his vision and left him feeling edgy and uncomfortable. "What about the efforts to repossess Katla Mockerkin?"

"That operation is ongoing. As per relevant instructions, if the individual in question cannot be recovered, she is to be terminated, to prevent the possible dissemination of restricted internal data. The appropriate apposite instructions have been disseminated."

A chill ran down Cardenas's back. What a wonderful person was The Mock. The more he learned about the dead man, the more he came to understand how someone like Surtsey Mockerkin would risk death just to get away from him. Unfortunately for her, it had turned out to be a bad risk.

If the lepero couldn't get his daughter back, he was going to have her killed, to keep the information stored in her mind out of the hands of competitors and the authorities. Swell way for a man to treat his own daughter. Like a storage chip. A disposable storage chip. The Inspector pondered a response. "I wish to terminate that undertaking, effective immediately."

"The gram in question can only be canceled upon receipt of a specific command paradigm compiled by Mr. Cleator Mockerkin."

Dead end. He tried an oblique approach. "I will provide it in a moment. Meanwhile, please take the necessary preliminary steps to terminate the recovery effort."

The box was adamant—albeit in the polite, detached AI manner of its kind. "The gram in question can only be canceled upon receipt of a specific command paradigm compiled by Mr. Cleator Mockerkin."

He was stuck. If he used vorec and spinner to instigate a penetration probe, he was likely to trigger the hidden and probably armored mollysphere's built-in defensive mechanisms. He did not know what those might be, but given the character of the man in whose chair he was currently sitting, they were likely to be unpleasant. If he continued to press the demand verbally without providing the called-for paradigm, a hitech box like this one was likely to grow suspicious and either cut off his access cold or request some additional form of identification. When he failed to provide it, other alarms might be raised, other defense devices besides the alcove lasers activated.

He could vape the incog he had adopted, call in, and have the power to the box shut down, or for that matter, secure an order for shutdown or even demolition of the entire West Padre #3 industrial complex. That was what police insurance was for. But a suitably advanced box designed to juggle secure national, much less international, information and data would be in constant touch with several, perhaps dozens of backup mollys scattered all over the planet. If he had this one destroyed, the rest of the system might continue to function unobserved and undetected for an indeterminate length of time. That would include continuing to process the gram demanding Katla Mockerkin's capture or destruction.

On the other hand, any command accepted here would promulgate instantly throughout the entire network—including one to terminate that order. In addition to which, if he called in a demolition team, all the rest of the valuable information currently residing on the box, threads that could lead to the arrest and prosecution of dozens, maybe hundreds of wanted individuals and enterprises, would be lost. Now, more than ever, he had to proceed with discretion.

There was one more thing he could try. It might set off a flurry of unwelcome responses, but he was determined to chance it. If it worked, at worst it might shut down the entire system without providing a response to his request, but might do so without damaging any permanent files. Those were, and had to remain, secondary to securing the health and safety of a certain twelve-year-old girl waiting back in Nogales. Grim-faced behind the chameleon, he once again addressed the machine.

"Cleator Mockerkin is dead. Therefore all ongoing grams requiring his input should immediately be suspended."

He waited breathlessly, uncertain of what to expect. Depending on their level of AI sophistication, different mollys responded in different ways to directives that offered the prospect of internal conflict. He expected one this advanced to ignore him, or to reject the input as unprocessable, or possibly to demand elaboration.

He did not expect it to say, without wavering or hesitation, "I know. Mr. Cleator Mockerkin was struck and killed by an out-of-control bus going north on Houston Street, outside the Brazos Mall, in the inside lane, temperature thirty-eight degrees Celsius, relative humidity sixty-four percent, at three fifty-four P.M. on the afternoon of September seventeenth."

Cardenas swallowed. "If the gram relating to the recovery or . . . termination . . . of Katla Mockerkin can only be canceled by a command paradigm compiled by Cleator Mockerkin, and Cleator Mockerkin has been dead for going on more than three months, then how is the gram to be canceled?"

"Under the scenario you describe, it cannot be canceled." The box exuded a chilling assurance that was maddening. "However, the gram will lapse when its parameters have been fulfilled."

"But there's no one left who'd want it fulfilled!" *Easy,* Cardenas told himself. *Calm, collected, composed. Be like the box. Be a molly. Spin, but not off your axis.* "The individual who entered the original gram, Cleator Mockerkin, is deceased. Therefore there is no one left to see the gram fulfilled."

"There is," the box replied, with utmost seriousness.

Cardenas sat back in the chair as if he had been slapped, and gaped at the tunnel that glowed with restricted lists and stats and images. There was a face somewhere back there, and it was not the face of a person. Impartial, unsympathetic, unmoved, and efficient, it was interested in only one thing: carrying out its programming. Scattered among the already unfathomable labyrinth of information that bound the world together, it could not be effectively neutralized except from this central source, and then only by expert operatives with ample time to ferret out its secrets and avoid the traps that must lie buried within.

Cardenas would see to it that they were put on the job as soon as it was safe to do so. But first he had to secure Katla Mockerkin's safety. If specialists were set on The Mock's box, that might be enough to cause it to shut down this main terminal in alarm and automatically decentralize its operations. The effect would be the same as blowing the place up. Conversely, if it remained in operation despite the probing, there was no guarantee even the most skilled specialists would be able to get into the guts of the main molly in time to save Katla Mockerkin.

In the absence of Cleator Mockerkin, and the instructions only that one now-unreachable man could provide, The Mock's box was determined to carry to fruition every extant gram that had been written to its widely scattered but tightly interlinked mollys. Mockerkin had been dead for months. It was the box that continued to issue orders to underlings to recover or kill Katla Mockerkin. It was the box that continued to run The Mock's far-flung businesses and dealings, no doubt in the face of Mockerkin's less than sophisticated subordinates. After all, as the old custodian had pointed out, nobody cared who was doing the paying as long as they continued to get paid. And as he had suggested, the process was indeed automated. To a degree no one could have imagined.

Ruthless kidnappers and mataros with unimaginative one-track minds could be paid in exactly the same efficient, wordless, depersonalized fashion as a janitor, Cardenas realized.

It was the box, he saw with sudden clarity, that was responsible for the death of Surtsey Mockerkin. Gruesome postmortem revenge for her deceased husband. Even in death, he was a murdering feleon.

The local molly sitting somewhere behind the wall and generating the access tunnel could not be destroyed, or the connection to The Mock's wider box would be lost, along with any chance of getting the system to stand down the order to capture or kill Katla Mockerkin. When the amiable Yogesh Chanay had mused openly about imagining that the subsurface operation he had never visited must be largely automated, the innocent warehouse supervisor could have had no idea how appropriate his vision would turn out to be.

The only way to ensure Katla Mockerkin's safety in the future was to neutralize the gram containing the order for her abduction or murder. And the only person who could do that was dead. The only *person*.

Unless . . .

The box had not said that Cleator Mockerkin had to personally input the requisite command paradigm to terminate the relevant gram. What it *had* said was that "the gram in question can only be canceled upon receipt of a specific command paradigm compiled by Mr. Cleator Mockerkin." There was, just possibly, one other person who might be familiar with the requisite paradigm, and therefore able to input it.

"Close," Cardenas snapped brusquely. The tunnel obediently, and without comment, went dark. Reaching up and back, he gratefully peeled the chameleon off his head, ran a hand through his hair and fluffed it out as he breathed deeply of air he no longer had to sip through a permeable membrane. Shaking out the mask to dry it, he refolded it and slipped it back into the empty storage pocket on his belt. Rising, he wrapped the service belt around his waist and secured it.

For the second time that morning he hunched down behind the borrowed mirror as he inched his way back through the entry alcove. Once safely clear of the lethal antechamber and back in the outer office, he set the mirror aside and stretched. Not wishing to upset the kindly, helpful old custodian, he fully intended to affix the mirror back in place, using one of the industrial-strength adhesives that were included among the many odds and ends in his belt.

Unfortunately, one of the belt's alarms chose that moment to start beeping. Loudly. Either he had finally done something to arouse the suspicions of whatever automated security system monitored the room, or he had manually tripped some concealed defense mechanism.

He saw no indication of the gas, nor smelled it, but the sensors built into the belt did. Anyone caught in the room without such protection would doubtless crumple to the floor without ever knowing what had hit them, to awaken later. Or never. Leaving the mirror where he'd set it down and placing one palm over his mouth and nose, he ran for the exit as fast as he could. Only when he had scrambled back up the entryway ramp and out through the storage closet into the bathroom beyond did the beeping subside.

Ordinarily, he would have taken the time to return the camouflaged doorway to its original state. But with The Mock dead, he saw no reason to hide the fact that someone had accessed the hub. That much he could leave to the custodian. Right now his only interest lay in outpacing any trailing gas. Hurrying from the bathroom, he didn't slow down even though the sensor on his belt had gone silent.

The portals to the other two outer rooms he had explored when he had initially arrived remained closed, just as he had left them. There was no sign of the old janitor. As Cardenas exited the bathroom, that door slammed shut behind him. No matter. He'd seen all he had come to see, and learned all he could. All that remained was to get back to his hotel room, pack up the few personal items he had brought with him, and catch the next flight back to Nogales.

As before, the elevator at the end of the narrow hallway did not respond to his touch. Anticipating as much, he did not linger over it, and prepared to return to the surface the way he had come, via the nearby stairwell. He grabbed the handle and pulled. When it failed to give, he tried again. Repeated attempts to unlock the barrier using the sesame proved equally fruitless. Frowning, he returned the device to its holding pouch, stepped back, gripped the handle with both hands, put one foot up against the wall alongside the door, and pulled with all his strength. Nothing. Letting go of the handle and taking a step back, he began high-kicking in the vicinity of the lockseal. The sound of his foot slamming against the metal barrier echoed down the corridor. As for the door, it didn't budge. Exhausted, he splashed backward and wondered what he was doing wrong.

Splashed?

He had inadvertently triggered another defensive mechanism.

Looking down, he saw that water was rising rapidly around his shoes. It was over his ankles and climbing toward his knees by the time he reached the doors at the opposite end of the corridor. All three were, unsurprisingly, locked, sealed, and inviolable. The atypical slamming behind him of the bathroom door that led to the concealed workplace now assumed an ominous significance. The stink of the intracoastal waterway, a pungent mix of salt water, fuel oil from older vessels, and commercial runoff from West Padre #3 & 4, began to permeate the available air.

Sloshing back to the elevator and stairwell, he started to reach for the door handle one more time, but stopped. Removing the compact police cutter from its belt pouch, he made a hasty examination of the metal barrier. The handle was embedded in an armored lockplate. Struggling against the water as he moved to his left, he activated the cutter and started in on the middle of three hinges. The alloy was tough, and it took the cutter longer than Cardenas would have liked to slice all the way through.

By the time he began on the bottom hinge, the water was up to his chest and rising faster than ever. Even as he worked frantically, manipulating the cutter while wishing it was a more powerful commercial model, he found himself admiring the straightforwardness of the trap. Filling the access corridor with seawater was not only a way of creating a significant barrier against intruders from the surface, it was also a means of dealing very efficiently with anyone who had already gained unauthorized access and was subsequently trying to leave. While the flooding corridor did its work, staff could relax in their self-contained, watertight offices and continue their work unhindered.

Now only the topmost hinge remained in place, holding the door to the metal jamb. As he waited anxiously for the cutter to cleave the metal, he wondered how many guests who had offended The Mock had ultimately been floated out of his presence instead of walking away under their own power. Certainly when The Mock was in residence, visitors had been searched prior to being admitted. Any weapons, anything like a cutter that might enable them to make an escape, had surely been confiscated prior to admittance.

The water was up to his chin. Designed to function in any environment and manufactured to meet tough NFP specifications, the cutter continued to slice at the stubborn remaining hinge. Seawater swirled around him. He half expected to see smelt or sardines finning past. Three times, he had to fill his lungs and work underwater. The last time, there was barely enough of an air pocket between rising sea and impermeable ceiling in which to snatch a breath.

Ducking back down once more, he placed the cutter over the hinge, working from the light of its glow. When the beam finally severed the last of the implanted bolt, he switched it off, stuffed it in a pocket, and began kicking as hard as he could at the middle hinge where it was attached to the door. The surrounding water slowed and weakened his kicks. But with all three hinges cut through, the door began to give. Sensing weakness, and a potential outlet, the weight of the water surrounding him added its own pressure to the effort.

For a terrible moment, he thought the door was going to stay jammed in place despite his best efforts to free himself. A lifelong resident of the desert Southwest, he did not particularly like the ocean. Of all the possible deaths he had envisioned for himself in the course of nearly thirty years with the Department, of all the near misses he had experienced working the mean streets of the Strip, the last thing he would have imagined was drowning in the course of doing his duty.

The pressure of the rising water proved irresistible. With it supplementing a hard kick from his right foot, the barrier finally gave way. Handle and lock remained tightly fastened, but the door bent inward off its severed hinges far enough to admit a single human body. Almost out of air as he struggled through the gap, propelled by the escaping water, Cardenas found himself giving murky thanks for his modest stature. Hyaki could never have made it through.

He banged his head on a railing when the roaring water threw him hard against the stairs on the other side of the lower landing. Dazed by the impact, sucking in huge, re-invigorating lungfuls of fresh air, he paused to collect himself on the third step. With water gushing out of the corridor behind him, he struggled to his feet. He stumbled up the stairwell, using the railing for support and to pull himself upward.

Thankfully, the door at the top was not locked and he was able to leave the lifesaving cutter in the pocket where he had absently shoved it. A pair of hardcapped workers saw him stagger out of the stairwell entrance and immediately started in his direction. Still coughing up seawater and breathing with difficulty, Cardenas fumbled for the shocker holstered inside his sodden windbreaker.

Tall, bearded, and powerfully built, the bigger of the two reached for him—to put a steadying hand on his shoulder. "Facilit, homber. You okay? You look like you've been in a real frog strangler!" His equally concerned companion mustered a reassuring smile.

"Around here, *compadre,* we prefer to do our fishin' with poles." The other man's expression of honest baffle-ment as he peered past Cardenas reinforced his appearance of innocence. "What the hell happened down there, any-way?"

Cardenas let his hand fall away from the shocker. He'd been needlessly concerned. Like their supervisor Chanay, these men were blithely ignorant of the illegal activities that had been an ongoing concern beneath the warehouse.

Digging into a belt pouch, he pulled out some fragments of sea grass along with his ident bracelet and weakly flashed both at the two men. "Angel Cardenas, Inspector, NFP." He nodded back the way he had come. The sound of rushing water could be heard clearly now, rising from the rapidly filling stairwell. "You may have a leak in one of your subsurface chambers. I can't say for sure. I'm a little tired and not feeling too well. I wonder if one of you could—could . . . ?"

Reacting swiftly and simultaneously, both men reached out to grab him as he fell forward.

SEVENTEEN

HE CAME TO, DRY AND AT EASE, IN A HOSPI-
tal bed in Masmatamoros, with the faint but fading taste of
the Gulf still clinging tenaciously to the back corners of his
mouth. Recuperating in bed for the rest of the day, he had
time to reflect on how his hospital visit was considerably
less physically taxing than his partner's had been.

As soon as he could wrest an official discharge the following morning, he communicated all that had transpired to
Pangborn. The Captain would see to it that The Mock's apparently vacant command center was carefully monitored,
in case any of the deceased feleon's subordinates attempted
to make use of its facilities. As per the Inspector's specific
instructions, the authorities would not try to enter it or interfere with its latent functions until the safety of Katla
Mockerkin could be guaranteed.

Pangborn also informed him that the janitor Rodrigo's
story checked out: there had been a double fatal accident
outside the Brazos Mall in Harlingen in the time period the
custodian had specified. Interestingly, neither man had been
traveling with any documents, and conclusive identification
of both was still pending.

It was good to be back in Nogales, where the humidity

fluctuated between low and desiccated and the smell of salt filled the nostrils only when one's face drew near to the rim of a glass full of sloshing margarita. Hyaki was as glad to see him as the Inspector was to be home.

"How's the back?" Cardenas spoke as they checked out a cruiser from the NFP's subterranean garage.

Hyaki rolled massive shoulders. "Good as can be grown. I nearly get fried, you almost get drowned. That's enough medical for one case. I'm ready for a vacation."

Cardenas slipped into the passenger seat. "You just had one, remember? Beautiful Costa Rica of the Central American Federation. Didn't you have a nice, relaxing time in the scenic World Heritage rainforest?"

Hyaki guided the cruiser out of the garage and up into the brilliant Sonoran sunshine. "Oh *sí*, sure. Only problem is, I can't look at a banana quite the same way I used to."

Leaving the interminable, unbroken arcomplex of the Strip behind, the highway narrowed as it began to wind through canyon country, leading into the designated parkland that surrounded Boboquivari Peak. Stores and strip malls, cool codo developments, and finally expensive single-family residences gave way to flaming ocotillo and peridot-colored paloverde. Overhead, a trio of buzzards circled something distant and dead. Once, a roadrunner darted across the road, head down, tail outstretched, a dead snake dangling from its beak like scavenged spaghetti. The snake danced and jumped with the bird's movements like an out-sized rubber band.

Entering parkland, they left all commercial development behind. The bored guard at the access gate came to life slightly when Hyaki flashed his ident. A parkland employee, he was far out of the NFP loop, and had no idea what was going on within his own jurisdiction.

A converted ranger outpost, the safe house lay at the bottom of a winding canyon reachable only by air or a bumpy dirt road. Its inimitable modern air suspension notwithstanding, the cruiser still reacted to a few sharp bumps and jolts as Hyaki negotiated the awkward track. They found themselves wishing for the jungle-outfitted 4X4 they had rented in San José. Remembering the vehicle fondly, Cardenas regretted leaving it a burned-out hulk.

Both men were grateful when the rambling, single-story structure hove into view. Constructed of gray block, with a white peaked roof and triple-pane, thermotropic, bulletproof windows, it featured its own water and power supply. The communications dish mounted on the roof kept those inside in constant contact with the outside world, with the Strip, and with NFP headquarters in Nogales. A parklands helipad out back allowed for quick arrival or departure, as the occasion demanded. Cardenas had opted to take a cruiser rather than fly in because he wanted the flexibility of having his own transportation, and also because he knew he and his partner would be able to relax and enjoy the drive.

They were not the only ones. An unmarked cruiser stood parked between a pair of larger 4X4s beneath the shade of the carport. Hyaki slowed as they approached the compound gate. The lengths of wire fence it clasped together were not impressive to look at. Cardenas knew that the amount of voltage they carried was rather more so.

As soon as they were cleared, the gate was raised to grant entry. Hyaki steered the cruiser through and into an open space beneath the carport roof. Despite having been cleared at the gate, they were met by two officers wearing parklands uniform. Attire notwithstanding, both men were actually in the employ of the NFP, not the Park Service.

Handshakes and greetings preceded the newcomers' admittance to the building. A third officer, who met them just inside the door, turned out to be an old friend of Hyaki's. While the two of them headed for the kitchen in search of cold drinks and warm conversation, Cardenas sought out the Department case worker who had been assigned to watch over Katla Mockerkin until her safety had been assured and more permanent living arrangements could be made for the girl.

She found him first.

"You're Angel Cardenas, aren't you? I was told to expect you."

Turning, he found himself gazing into the eyes of an attractive, dark-haired woman in her late thirties. She was as tall as he (or as short, depending on your perspective), with hair cropped short on one side in the fashion currently favored by many civil servants. A single long silver-and-sugilite earring, probably Navajo, dangled from the shaved side of her head. Cosmetics had been applied decorously, to enhance her unusually large eyes and high cheekbones. Her grip was firm and assured, the handshake of an experienced professional.

"I'm Minerva Fourhorses."

Cardenas smiled engagingly. "Nice to meet you." His gaze rose to look past her. "Where's Katla?"

"Katla, is it?" His familiarity pleased her. "You two must have talked a lot, down in Costa Rica."

"Enough to where I feel as if I know her well enough to talk to her on an informal basis, without having to remind her that I'm federale." Side by side, they headed down the hallway. The floor, he noted, was reinforced and epoxied Saltillo tile. It clicked loudly beneath the case worker's shoes, as if she was wearing castanets in place of heels.

"That helps. She's a quiet girl, though she's willing enough to talk. Reserved, though. Guarded." Her tone revealed honest concern, the hallmark of any first-rate social worker. "Hardly surprising, considering her background and what she's been through. I've read the official reports."

Cardenas nodded knowingly. "Not what you'd call a normal childhood."

"Having her mother killed like that." Fourhorses's lips tightened. "If it wasn't for box access, I think she would just sit and stare at the walls. The box is her sanctuary. She looks on it as a place of refuge. It's accepting of her, and she doesn't have to justify or explain herself." Moon-pool eyes met his. "I've never seen anyone so proficient with a vorec. Not even the specs downtown."

"She's a tecant," Cardenas explained. "A natural."

The social worker nodded. "It's in the report. But it's one thing to read about it, another to watch that kind of ability in action."

They turned up another corridor. Seated halfway down the hall, another plainclothes officer looked up from the screen he was reading. Recognizing Fourhorses, he smiled and passed them onward.

"It's that ability that has caused so much trouble for her," Cardenas explained. "It may also be what guarantees her future."

Fourhorses's apprehension was palpable. "You're not going to ask her to do anything that will stress her further, I hope. Outwardly, she may look and sound like she's in good health. My own take these past few days is that she's actually quite fragile." Her voice took on a harder edge. "I couldn't give my approval to anything that would risk further damage to her mental well-being. What she needs now is stability, and reassurance. Most of all, she needs hope."

"That's what I want to give her." He smiled at the visibly concerned woman. "We both want the same things for her, Ms. Fourhorses."

"Minerva." The case worker spoke absently as she stopped outside a double set of wooden doors. "She'll be in the tunnel, working. She always is." Reaching up, she knocked three times.

For a long moment, Cardenas thought no response was going to be forthcoming. Then came a soft, girlish voice that he remembered well from his recent southerly sojourn. "Come in, Ms. Fourhorses."

Leading the way, the case worker opened one of the two doors. Cardenas listened as he followed her in. "Good morning, Katla. There's someone here to see you." Stepping aside, Fourhorses watched with obvious interest to see how her charge would react to the visitor.

Spinning in her chair, Katla Mockerkin recognized the swarthy, heavily mustachioed federale immediately. If not overtly welcoming, her smile was still somewhat more than just polite.

"Hello, Inspector Cardenas. I remember you."

"Hoh, Katla. It's nice to see you again." Entering farther into the room, he set himself down in an empty chair and wheeled it over to her side. "I'd like to chat for a little while—if that's okay with you?"

She shrugged and set down the vorec she was holding. Sensing the movement, the vit pickup of the box she was working darkened the tunnel she had been facing.

"You don't have to talk to Inspector Cardenas if you don't want to, Katla," the watching woman reminded her.

The girl smiled shyly. "That's all right, Ms. Fourhorses. I know Mr. Cardenas—Angel. He was nice to me when I was—when I had to leave the Reserva. He's a good man."

Her smile turned to a sly grin. "Even if he is a spizzing federale intuit."

In a way that no other officer could, Cardenas knew that it was not an insult. Fourhorses was watching him closely. "How are you doing, Katla?"

She glanced longingly back at the muted, softly glowing tunnel. "All right, I guess." A hint of the subtle slyness he had come to associate with her crept back into her voice. "But you'd know that anyway, wouldn't you? You're just making polite conversation."

He grinned. "When I was your age, the other kids used to tell me I was too smart for my own good." She looked back at him sharply. "So I know what it's like to feel different from everybody else. From all your friends. No more small talk, then." He leaned slightly toward her. "I have some news for you. Your father, The Mock, is dead."

Her expression did not change. But he observed the slight tensing of the muscles in her neck and forearms, detected a heightened rate of respiration. She did not show it—at least not to anyone else—but she *was* reacting.

"He was hit by a bus while crossing a street."

By way of acknowledgment, she nodded once, almost emotionless. "I'm glad to hear it." Then, somewhat to his surprise, as well as that of the watchfully observant Fourhorses, she snickered mockingly. "I heard him talk about dying, once. He said that the federales would never capture him. That if he didn't die of old age, he would go down in a storm of fire. He was hit by a bus?" Cardenas nodded. "That's great! Real ordinary. That's just what he deserved—to die like anybody else, unnoticed and overlooked, without having his nasty, mean, lepero face spread all over the vit. I'm glad it happened that way!" As her anger subsided, her exceptional intelligence took over. Cardenas waited patiently, knowing that it would.

"But," she began anew, stammering slightly, "if Daddy died months ago, then who ordered that my mom be killed only weeks ago?" Lowering her eyes, she sank into profound contemplation. "Mr. Brummel couldn't have done it, because he was already dead, too. Mr. Vanderberg doesn't like violence, and Ms. Beryl wouldn't know how to compile the necessary instructions." Her confusion and puzzlement was plain to see as she looked back up at Cardenas. "Do you know who ordered it?"

He nodded bleakly. "They come from the same source that is still trying to have you abducted or killed. A source you probably know better than anyone. Your father's company box, the one that's headquartered in Southeast Texas."

Her mouth opened in a little *O* of surprise. "It's that stupid molly at Padre! Daddy had it grammed so it would run everything when he wasn't there to supervise it personally. But I don't know anything about the kind of gram you're talking about. He must have entered it into the box after Mom and I ran away with Mr. Brummel."

Fourhorses couldn't take it any longer. The conversation between her charge and the federale was leaving her further and further behind. "I don't understand. Who is trying to kidnap or kill Katla?"

"A program." Cardenas looked back in her direction. "One implanted by her father. He was, by all accounts, an unforgiving, merciless son of a bitch." He nodded in the girl's direction. "The molly containing the gram stays in touch with every element of her father's illegitimate domain. It promulgated directives to subordinates ordering the killing of Wayne Brummel, who was Katla's mother's consort and partner in a pretty large-scale embezzlement of funds. It expanded that order to include the recent slaying of her mother. Now it's trying to capture or kill Katla because she's a tecant who, among other things, has much if not all of her father's business dealings committed to memory." Turning back to the girl, he favored her with renewed sympathy. "She's a walking mollysphere."

Fourhorses's tone showed that she still did not entirely understand. "But if her father is dead, why is this monstrous gram of his still interested in her?"

"Because it hasn't been formally canceled," he explained tersely. "Until it is, it will continue to issue what it deems to be applicable directives to elements of her father's domain that still respond to commands from the central hub. They will try their best to comply with these commands, because they believe them to be coming from her father, or from her father's second-in-command—whomever they assume that might be.

"Eventually, word will trickle down to the lowest ranks to ignore any and all such directives as coming only from a molly. That's fine. The only problem is, we can't wait for that to happen, for nature to take its course. Because by then it may be too late for Katla."

Fourhorses started toward him, arms spread imploringly. "Well then, expiate this damn molly that's spinning these orders! Shut it down, turn it off—blow it up!"

Cardenas shook his head slowly. "Can't. That is, we can, but if we destroy the molly, there's no guarantee that built-in backups won't kick in throughout the box. Without knowing where all the wishwire is located, we can't be certain of shutting down the gram completely. And we can't risk allowing it to spread to secondary hubs whose location we don't know, because then we'd never get the gram vaped. It's like a snake. You can cut off its head, but the body will keep on twitching for hours."

Her unhappy expression showed that she understood. "Then there's nobody who can order this gram to terminate itself?"

"I was there. I spoke to it. It insists that termination of the gram can only be accomplished by input of 'a command paradigm compiled by Cleator Mockerkin'—her father."

"But—her father's dead," Fourhorses exclaimed. The Inspector nodded. "Then, there's no one left to bring closure to the program."

"Maybe one." Cardenas turned back to face Katla Mockerkin. So did Minerva Fourhorses.

His spirits sank at her reply to his unasked question.

"I can't do it."

"Why not?" His heart went out to her; to this poor, abused, brilliant girl who had had no real childhood. She deserved better. Anyone her age deserved better.

"Because I don't know the paradigm. Just like the order to kill, my lepero of a father must have compiled and inputted it after Mom and I ran away with Mr. Brummel."

They were left with no choice, he saw. He would have to give the order to disable the molly still spinning away in the bowels of the underwater redoubt in Texas. If they were lucky, the gram would not propagate throughout The Mock's surviving box. If they were unlucky . . .

She was gesturing shyly at him, interrupted his sad reverie. "What is it, Katla?" he asked as gently as he could.

"I can't input the paradigm, because I don't know it. But there is something else I think I might be able to do."

"What's that, Katla?" Forgetting that she was supposed to keep to the background for the duration of Cardenas's visit, Fourhorses had come up to stand alongside the federale.

Young but far from innocent eyes stared back at them both. "I might be able to wipe the entire system. That's an entirely different paradigm. It's problematical—there's a lot of steps—but it's a doable thing. I think."

Cardenas's thoughts whirled. Wiping The Mock's box would surely eliminate the gram that persisted in ordering her abduction or assassination, but it would also result in the loss of information of incalculable value to the NFP's central office. Names, figures, statistics, locations, histories of crimes committed, plans for crimes expected: all would be lost. He said as much, and in so doing, drew a dirty look from Minerva Fourhorses.

Katla Mockerkin begged to disagree. "You won't lose any of that, Mr. Cardenas. The Federal Police can have it all. I'm only going to try and wipe the box." Meaningfully, she put the tips of her fingers to one side of her head. "The rest of it, all the other *muy malo* stuff—it's still up here."

In his immediate concern for her safety, he had forgotten about her capabilities, and why The Mock had valued her so highly in the first place. He vowed he would not do so again.

"Tell me what kind of facilities you need."

She gestured at the wall unit. "It can be done from here, I think. As long as I have uninterrupted access to a megaspeed connection and enough crunch. I just"—this time she didn't meet his gaze—"I just don't know . . . if *I* can do it."

Reaching out, he put a reassuring hand on her shoulder. "Why not, Katla?"

She continued to avoid his eyes. "My mom's dead. I don't have any brothers or sisters. If I have any cousins, I don't know who they are or where they are. Now my father's dead, too. I didn't like him very much. He did bad stuff to a lot of people. But—he was my dad. The stuff in the box is all that's left of him. Wiping it—it'd be kind of like killing him myself."

"The gram he compiled is responsible for the death of your mother."

"I *know*!" Suddenly, she was near tears. "Don't you think I remember that? Don't you realize that if I had been paying more attention to the box, I might have come across this rotten, terrible gram and been able to do something with it or to it *before* Mom was murdered? If I had been monitoring like I should have been, she might not have been killed. But I stayed away from Dad's system. I didn't want to go near it, or have anything to do with it. I thought—I thought if I probed too much, it might tricktrack me, and find out where we'd gone. But I should've done just the opposite. I should have stayed on it. It's my fault. She didn't have to die! She didn't have to die!"

Sobbing, she fell into his arms. He held her tight, held her close. Looking up, he saw that Fourhorses was eyeing them strangely.

I know there's a bond here, he called out to the woman even though he knew she could not sense his thoughts. *You see it, and I feel it. But, God help me, I've never had a kid of my own, and I'm not sure what to do. Thirty years of intuit training, and I'm not sure what to do.*

Fourhorses knew what to do. Gently, she disengaged the weeping twelve-year-old from Cardenas's compassionate but awkward grasp and slowly rocked the tearful girl back and forth, murmuring reassuringly to her all the while. His thin shirt stained dark by tears, Cardenas sat back and watched. When he felt enough time had passed, he addressed the girl as empathetically as he could.

"I realize how this could be difficult for you, Katla. But if you don't stop this program now, it's going to keep sending out orders telling people to catch you. That wouldn't be so bad. But the orders might also be for people to do something worse." He leaned forward imploringly. "You're the only one who can put an end to this, Katla. And I have to disagree with you about what you just said. It's not like you'd be killing anyone. The Mock's box is only a system compilation, a collection of soulless embedded grams. Just like any other box."

Fourhorses's tone reflected careful control. "You're asking a twelve-year-old girl who's been under tremendous emotional strain to dive right back into the middle of the source of her discomfort."

"It's—it's all right, Ms. Fourhorses." Katla pulled back and wiped at her eyes with the backs of both hands. "Mr. Cardenas is right. I'm the only one who can do this. It has to be done." She sniffed between sentences. "It should have been done a long time ago. Maybe if it had, my mom would still be here." Rising, she walked back to the little desk in the corner of the room. Picking up the vorec, she twirled it round and round in her hand, manipulating it with her fine, diminutive fingers the way a conductor would warm up a baton prior to leading a concert.

As Fourhorses and Cardenas looked on, the social worker leaned toward him and whispered apprehensively, "If the child suffers any adverse effects as a consequence of this, I'm going to have to hold you and the NFP responsible."

"I've been accepting responsibilities for serious happenings for a long time, Minerva." He nodded in the girl's direction. "The only one who can save her from this is herself." A paraphrase from an old read leaped into his mind. *The bad grams that men program live after them; the good ones are oft interred with their old mollys.* He moved a little closer to Katla.

"Can you really do it from here?" He indicated the vorec that was connected to the standard-issue commercial molly, which in turn was linked by the Nokarola dish on the roof to the Big Box beyond. "Do you need anything else? Any custom gear, or backup links, or technical assistance? Fresh wishwire or specialty wafers?"

Light glinted off the tears that were still drying on Katla's face as she shook her head briskly. Her reply was full of confidence. "Huh-uh. No problemo, federale." The small smile she managed to muster made her look much younger than her dozen years. Her expression was heartrendingly childlike.

Both were in striking contrast to her words and actions, which were those of an experienced prober and eeLancer. As Cardenas rejoined Fourhorses, the two adults lapsed into silence, marveling at the speed and skill with which the girl first accessed and then began to burrow deeply into the Big Box. Commands that were often as incomprehensible as they were complex spilled effortlessly from her lips. Images flowed and morphed so rapidly within the tunnel that Cardenas could not follow them. No mean box cutter himself, he followed the agile, effortless performance with awe.

Fingers dug into his shoulder. Forcing himself to look away from the girl's ongoing bravura performance with the vorec, he found himself staring into the startled eyes of Minerva Fourhorses. Her mouth was open, but no words were forthcoming. Instead, she was pointing with her other hand.

Half a dozen tiny machines had taken up positions at the foot of the double bed that dominated the other side of the room. The largest stood just over a centimeter high and sported three wiggling antennae. Next to it was a dull-surfaced, single-eyed creature that resembled a tank-tracked millipede. The other four devices were equally outlandish. One did not have to be an engineer or designer to recognize what they were doing.

Just like the human occupants of the room, they were observing Katla Mockerkin at work.

"Wugs," he observed succinctly.

"What do they want? How did they get in here?" Fourhorses's reaction to the utterly unexpected appearance of the miniscule mechanicals was no different from anyone else's. She was at once fascinated and chary. "Nothing's supposed to be able to get in here. This is a safe house."

"It's still safe." Cardenas could not guarantee the claim, but past experience had shown him that whatever it was the wugs wanted, it would not involve violence. Unless one counted human violence against the wugs, that is. "They won't bother her, or us. Just ignore them."

"That's what everybody says to do." Fourhorses's attention remained fixated on the oddly engaging little bitbots. "I'm more worried about Katla."

Cardenas nodded in the girl's direction. "Her body may be here, but her cerebro is racing around somewhere inside the Box. I doubt she's even aware of our presence anymore." Indeed, the vacant expression on the girl's face showed that she was working in as near to a self-induced trance as a twelve-year-old could be expected to manage.

So Fourhorses held her peace, and did not move in the direction of the tiny intruders, or shout out a warning to Katla. For their part, the wugs squatted, or sat, or stood, according to their construction, and looked on in near-total, inscrutable silence. Like Fourhorses, Cardenas found himself wondering what they wanted, what they were thinking. If they did think. What was known for certain about the life of wugs would not fill a chip off a molly the size of a ball bearing.

They forgot all about the wugs, wug origins, and wug intentions when something boomed softly in the distance and the room shook slightly but disarmingly. Fourhorses frowned.

"Sounds like somebody ran a truck into a wall. Or dropped something big."

Cardenas was already on his feet and heading for the room's only window. Flicking the switch that pulled down the glass pane covering the lower air vent, he squinted out through the charged bug mesh. His gaze skimmed gravel and decorative landscaping as well as the whitewashed concrete wall beyond to sweep up the rocky hillside that cupped the west end of the canyon. Movement was lacking, for which he was grateful. At the sound and feel of the unexpected rumble, Katla Mockerkin had looked up from her work, but only briefly. As she resumed her probe, an apprehensive Fourhorses bent down alongside Cardenas.

"What is it? Do you see something?" Her eyes widened as she saw the gun in his hand. It was a sizable department model. Unlike the ultra-compact weapons he had taken to Costa Rica and Masmatamoros, the big triclip pistol was anything but transparent. "What's that for?" she asked, almost immediately conscious of the sublime stupidity of the question.

"Get down." Gripping her shirt sleeve with one hand, he pulled her down next to him. "That wasn't a truck." As he spoke, a second rumble rippled through the bedroom, a miniature sonic boom that was far from sufficiently distant for the Inspector's taste. "Someone's shooting at the compound."

"But they can't!" The social worker was appalled—and, Cardenas saw, unashamedly frightened. "I was told that nobody can enter this canyon without clearing NFP security."

"We'll be sure and tell that to the people who are doing the shooting." Cardenas was in no mood to waste words on social niceties. If Fourhorses didn't care for his tone, she could go lock herself in the bathroom. Raising his voice, he called out, "How are you coming, Katla?"

The girl's response was a distant, muted murmur. "Okay, I guess." She did not offer to elaborate, and Cardenas wisely chose not to push her. Let her do her work. Meanwhile, he would do his. Looking one way, he saw a maelstrom of information seething within the box tunnel. Glancing the other, he saw six wugs sitting on the floor blissfully ignoring him as they raptly monitored Katla's efforts. They had not moved, nor had they reacted to the pair of explosions.

Something banged against the door. Inhaling sharply, Fourhorses tried to move toward Katla, but Cardenas held her back. At the same time, he sat down on the floor and shoved his back up against the unwavering mass of wall beneath the window. Hot, dry desert air poured in above his head, ruffling his hair as it collided with the room's air-conditioning. Raising the muzzle of the service pistol, he dialed through Narcolepsy and Paralysis before settling on the setting for Explosive. If he now so chose, he could blow away the door, a good chunk of hallway wall behind it, and anything organic unfortunate enough to find itself sandwiched in between.

As Inspector and social worker waited motionlessly, the

door was flung wide. A massive figure clutching an over-sized automatic weapon came charging into the girl's room. Fourhorses's eyes went wide as she sucked in a lungful of air, and Cardenas's finger tightened on the trigger of the pistol.

EIGHTEEN

LETTING OUT THE BREATH HE HAD NOT RE-
alized he had been holding, Cardenas lowered his weapon
and gestured for Hyaki to get down. Dropping to all fours,
the sergeant crawled over to join the wide-eyed social
worker and his partner. The booming that had first alerted
the Inspector to the fact that something was wrong was
louder now, closer and more frequent. Echoes indicated that
the defenders of the compound were starting to return fire.

"How many?"

Hyaki nodded politely at the cringing Fourhorses.
"Can't tell for sure yet. Ten, maybe more."

"How'd they gain access?"

"Don't know." Raising his head into the warm incoming
draft, Hyaki peered out the window. "Worry about that
later. Right now everyone's more concerned about how
many we *haven't* been able to count. A couple of them have
made it in as far as the vehicle port. Main structure integrity
is still intact. McCurdy is busy trying to establish a secure
perimeter." He looked in the direction of the raging tunnel.
"I take it she's not playing a game."

Cardenas's expression was all the explanation the sergeant required. "That's what I figured. What's she doing?"

Turning, the Inspector raised himself up slightly and rested the barrel of the pistol on the windowsill. There was movement on the far hillside. He pushed the gun forcefully forward until it was poking through the bug screen. Taking careful aim, he fired. Fourhorses jumped. Lost in a world of her own, Katla Mockerkin ignored the commotion behind her. Beyond the compound wall, a surprisingly large quantity of granite, cedar, and underbrush erupted in a shower of newly made gravel and flying splinters. The movement on the hillside was not repeated.

"Killing her father," Cardenas informed his partner. "Maybe exorcising would be a more appropriate description." As his gaze continued to sweep the hillside, he proceeded to explain.

"So you think whoever's out there is operating under orders from this rogue gram?" Hyaki had positioned himself alongside his partner, his own much larger weapon piercing the bug screen at the other end of the window. Fourhorses sat with her back to the wall, her arms drawing her knees up to her chest.

"Can't be sure." Cardenas had always been a good shot. Of course, the explosive shells his gun was now keyed to fire allowed for a considerable margin of error when taking aim. "Could very well be. I might have been followed here. Or someone could have cracked the location through the Department box." He nodded in the direction of the hillside. "Might be Inzini, or Ooze, or some other group that would dearly love to wring the girl's mind like an old washrag. That's not going to happen."

"No." Repositioning his weapon, Hyaki fired. For so impressive a killing device, its report was surprisingly muted. "It's not." Noticing something off to his right and slightly behind him, he nodded in the direction of the watching wugs.

"Where'd they come from?"

"Answer that," Cardenas replied succinctly, "and you can name your own price and buy your own police force."

Something struck the roof west of the room. Fragments of ceiling, insulation, and disturbed dust came showering down on those huddled within. As with everything else, Katla Mockerkin ignored the intrusion. Cardenas had never seen anyone, child or adult, so focused on the mechanics of a probe. Equally unperturbed, the wugs did not move.

"Easily frightened little *cucarachas,* aren't they?" Hyaki remarked irreverently.

"It's not hard to be fearless when you don't know the meaning of death." Cardenas's finger again started to tighten on the trigger of his pistol, but eventually eased back without firing. The sliver of movement he'd locked on was only a terrified jackrabbit, bolting from a burrow as speedily as the bundles of fast-twitch muscle fibers in its remarkable legs could carry it. The booming of gunfire was constant now, like the approaching thunder of an impending monsoon storm.

"At least," he finished, "I assume they don't know it. I've yet to encounter a machine that does, other than abstractly."

"Please, will you two shut up talking about that kind of stuff?" Reflecting professional concern, Fourhorses jerked her head sideways in the girl's direction. She needn't have worried, Cardenas noted. Katla was deep into playing the box, all but oblivious to the gunfire and commotion that threatened to engulf her.

No one came running to tell them to evacuate, or to move to another part of the compound. In that respect, Cardenas mused, no news was good news—Lincoln's comment to the contrary notwithstanding.

Someone did come running for another purpose, however. The woman was very slight, very agile, and exceedingly determined. But in the time it took her to throw open the door, quickly scan the room, and locate Katla, Cardenas and Hyaki had time of their own to turn their attention away from the window. As the intruder raised her gun and Fourhorses tried to scream a warning, both men fired simultaneously. When the dust cleared, there was very little left of the matara—or for that matter, the door.

"Probably going to dock our pay for that." Hyaki nodded in the direction of the still-smoking wreckage that had been the entrance to the room.

Cardenas replied impassively. "Police work is a messy business." He indicated a spot on the near wall where a tiny pressure hypo had embedded itself in the composite. The woman had managed to get off one shot before the two federales had blown her away. The ph would contain a miniscule dose of something unpleasant, and probably lethal. Drawing an invisible line between impact point and shooter, Cardenas estimated the shot had passed less than half a meter above Katla's head. Insofar as he could tell, she had never so much as looked up.

Strange images boiled within the tunnel as the girl played the box like an electrified violin. A number of three-dimensional apparitions that swiftly came and went were particularly disturbing. They did not seem to trouble the serene twelve-year-old, who continued to croon into the vorec. The way she rolled it between her fingers and let it hover above her lips verged on the perverse.

"Angel!"

At Hyaki's shout, Cardenas retrained his pistol on the ruined doorway. The eyes of the pistol-wielding man who had appeared in the opening bulged. His feet scrambled for purchase on the floor, slipping amid the debris and the remains of would-be assassin.

"Jesus, watch it, you guys!"

Both federales lowered their weapons. The new arrival was one of their own. Breathing hard, his gaze flicked from the girl working the box, to the frightened social worker, to his armed and trigger-itchy colleagues.

"We've got three points secured on the perimeter, with the fourth coming under control." Flush with adrenaline, he was young, and managed to look simultaneously scared, exhausted, and excited. Having someone shoot at you does that to people, Cardenas knew. "Lieutenant McCurdy says it's safe to relocate to the entry hall, if you want to."

Keeping clear of the window, Cardenas rose slowly to his feet. "We're okay here. Tell Mitch."

The young federale nodded energetically. "If there's any change, I'll let you know."

"How'd they get inside Security?" Hyaki was back on his feet. He also avoided standing in front of the window.

The herald shook his head. "They're working on that. Mitch says not to worry. They'll recon the breach, and plug it." He disappeared back down the hallway.

A crackling from the vicinity of the dimly roaring tunnel drew Cardenas's attention. As he looked on, the raging images faded, the tunnel going to black. Katla Mockerkin set the vorec down on the desk. Her final words might have reached the aural pickup—or maybe not. Off to the right, there was an echo of activity on the floor. Cardenas caught a fleeting glimpse of fleeing alien constructions of ceramic and metallic glass and composite. Putting his head to the floor and turning it sideways, he struggled to see under the bed. It was dark, and he could not see a hole. But the wugs were gone, as silently and furtively as they had come.

"Good-bye—Daddy," he heard Katla Mockerkin say. Limpid eyes looked over at him as he rose to his feet. "I'm tired, Mr. Cardenas."

"I know you are, Katla," he replied sympathetically. "I know." He indicated the now-subdued tunnel and, by inference, everything that had just wailed within. "It's done?"

She nodded and brushed hair away from her face. "Gone. All gone. I wiped the whole system, from South Texas to Sanjuana, right across the Strip. From Maine to Madagascar. It's all gone. Everything my father made. I cut all the strings."

"Good girl," was all Cardenas could think of to say.

Looming up beside him, Hyaki was not shy about venturing his own opinion. "Local branches will have backup."

"For local concerns. Any extended box, legit or illicit, is like a dragon. Cut off its head and the parts can still cause you trouble. But only if they can cooperate with each other. The main thing was to ensure Katla's safety. The gram that concerned itself with her was highly centralized. With the core wiped, that's no longer a concern. Something like that, something that intensely personal, wouldn't be backed up at the local level. Even a lepero like Mockerkin wouldn't have allowed it." He met Fourhorses's concerned gaze. "Now that the danger has been wiped, we can safely go after the surviving isolated segments of The Mock's nasty businesses. Katla will tell us how and where to find them."

Hyaki nodded meaningfully. "What about the others who've been after her? The non-Mock elements?" He gestured outside, beyond the window. "Elimination of the command to recapture or kill the girl won't affect them."

"No," Cardenas admitted, "but they've wanted to get

their hands on her so she could supply them with the inner workings of their competitor's business. When that business starts to fall apart, either from attrition, lack of direction from the center, or the fact that NFP will be busily arresting people, they're going to lose interest fast. Katla's detailed knowledge of a collapsing enterprise will quickly lose any value. As for imaginary quantum means of stealing fiscal and other kinds of valuable crunch, word will get around pretty fast that it was nothing more than a harebrained pipe dream." His head tilted back as he turned his gaze upward. A much deeper mechanical drone than that emitted by chopters invaded the room.

"Evac vertiprop coming," he remarked. "Took them long enough." Holstering his pistol, he looked back over at the girl. Fourhorses was standing next to her, murmuring maternal reassurances. Katla was nodding in response. The Inspector nudged his partner. Hyaki caught his friend's drift, and the two federales wordlessly exited the room, leaving the social worker to continue comforting the emotionally wrung-out twelve-year-old. As concerned as he was for the girl, Cardenas had been around long enough to know that there were times, personal involvement notwithstanding, when it was better to let someone other than himself do their job.

Besides, he was thirsty, and hungry, and irregardless of the status of the current situation outside, had to take a piss really, really bad.

He had just emerged from the shower when the pleasant feminine voice of his codo synapse informed him that he had visitors. Rubbing the back of his head with the bath towel he carried, he walked over to the alwayson tunnel that clung to one corner of the den and solicitared identification.

Amplified for full-room pickup, the vorec fed his request directly to his concealed molly.

An image materialized within the depths of the tunnel. Standing in the visitor's alcove on the ground floor awaiting admittance to the elevator was Minerva Fourhorses. In contrast to the last time he had seen her, she looked striking in casual weftfiber suit, matching purse, the latest slide shoes, and wide-brimmed thermotropic hat. As opposed to the last several times he had met with her, the appearance of the social worker's companion was even more arresting.

Clad in a flex dress of light blue and green blinker that swirled up her budding figure like a clinging python, Katla Mockerkin looked not only several years older than her actual age, but downright sophisticated. Matching lightweight rainbow headgear shielded the top of her head from the Sonoran morning and swept down the back of her neck to entwine itself in her hair. It twinkled and shimmered when she moved, even in the codo complex's confined entry alcove. A pair of muse lenses peeked out of the fortified safety purse that hung from her shoulder. The heels of her semi-dress shoes were powered down for walking, the integrated internal hydraulics quiescent.

"Minerva, Katla! What a pleasant surprise. Come on up," he told them via the tunnel, following the invitation with a spoken clearance code that would allow the two women to access the codo tower's elevator.

Rubbing the last of the moisture from his hair, he moved quickly to put on some clothes. Several weeks had gone by since he had seen either The Mock's daughter or her case worker. The press of work at the Department had caused him to sink naturally back into the ebb and flow of life in the Strip. He had not forgotten about the girl, but he had been fo   o push that particular concern to the back of his thoughts. One of the first things a rookie learned at Academy was that a preoccupied cop was a cop solicitaring an early death.

The change in Katla Mockerkin was pronounced, and went far deeper than her stylish attire. Her eyes looked out at the rest of the world instead of inward, and she stood straight instead of hunching over like a child expecting always to be hit. Even her stride was different, longer and more confident, as if she was seeking out the next place to go instead of fearfully avoiding it. The attractive, confident individual standing before him was now much more young woman than frightened child.

But the wariness was still there, in the way her gaze sought the far corners of the room and glanced quickly to the window that led to the outside. With time and tranquillity the fear and mistrust should fade, though Cardenas suspected it would never leave her entirely.

He started to give her a hug, but held himself back. Whatever relationship had developed between them was entirely artificial, a consequence of the tragic circumstances that had caused them to be thrown together. It would not stand the test of time. Attempts at reinforcement, however innocent or well-meaning on his part, would do nothing to augment the girl's growing independence. He settled for a cordial, thoroughly professional handshake and smile.

"It's good to see you both again." He turned his attention to the social worker. "To what do I owe the honor of this visit?"

"We have some news." When no one was shooting at her, Fourhorses glowed. "Good news. Don't we, Katla?"

The girl nodded, focusing half her attention on Cardenas while reserving the rest for the interior of his codo. Even in the home of a federale, it was plain she still did not feel entirely safe.

"I'm going away. Leaving the Strip. I'll miss some of my friends, but everyone says I can't go back to my soche. I understand why." Her smile was still shy, her manner withdrawn. "It'll be okay. I'm used to moving around."

Escorting them inside, Cardenas gestured for them to have a seat on his couch. Minerva gratefully accepted a cold guaraná, while the girl opted for a rola. Cardenas, as usual, brewed himself an iced coffee.

"You should be safe now, Katla," he told her. "Using the information you gave us, we've brought in nearly all of your father's most important associates along with a great many of the minor ones, and shut down their scattered operations. The other bad people who were after you have taken note of that. As best as we have been able to determine, it has caused them to rapidly lose interest in you. But the Department of Social Resources people and my friends at the NFP are right: just to make certain, you'd be safer and more comfortable living under a different name, in a different place."

"That's what we came to tell you." Fourhorses was clearly excited for the girl. "Genealogy managed to track down an aunt and uncle she didn't even know she had. In New England. Small town, nice environment. Everything's been checked out and rated secure. The couple has two children of their own; a boy, fifteen, and a girl, fourteen. They've agreed to welcome Katla into their family. After a year, formal adoption procedures will be initiated. I anticipate no problems. Katla will become Harmony Jean Francis."

The girl ducked her head shyly. "I always liked singing

harmony, but I never had much. Now I get to *be* Harmony. It's pretty *vacán*."

"I think so, too," he agreed. Color suffused Katla's cheeks—or maybe it was hope.

He pondered a moment. "How would you like to meet an old friend of mine? Someone you can talk with safely even in your new home in New England." At Fourhorses's look of alarm, he hastened to reassure the social worker. "Don't worry. This will not compromise her new identity in any way."

"Sure." The girl eyed him curiously. "I'm game."

Rising from the couch, he directed her to follow him to the far side of the den. Seating her in the chair that faced his desk, he stood next to her.

Picking up the vorec, he activated the tunnel and instructed the molly driver to accept open commands. Then he handed the verbal input device to her. She was looking at him expectantly, more at home inside a box than in someone's apartment. Leaning down and putting his mouth close to her ear, he murmured something too low for Fourhorses to overhear. The social worker looked on uncertainly, her expression reflective of her bemusement.

Katla listened intently, made a face, but finally nodded. Bringing the vorec to her lips, she repeated to the waiting molly the command he had whispered to her.

"Enter Charliebo: dog."

The holomage that built in the tunnel was so full of life and synthesized expression that a stranger walking into the room at that moment could have been forgiven for thinking it real. It could become more authentic still, Cardenas knew, but it would not do so without provocation of a specific, specialized kind that Katla soon-to-be-Harmony would hopefully never encounter. Leaning farther forward, he spoke into the vorec.

"Charliebo, the person next to me is Ms. Harmony Francis. She's a good friend of mine. I'd like you to be her friend, too."

The extraordinarily lifelike holomage of the big German shepherd gazed solemnly back at him. Then it turned its attention to the girl, glowing tongue lolling loosely from the left side of its mouth, tail of shimmering crunch wagging briskly, regarding her out of eyes composed of incalculable accumulations of intricately compiled ocular grams.

Katla was entranced. "What can he do?"

"You'd be surprised. *I* was surprised. I could tell you, but I'd rather let you experiment on your own. Charliebo's very versatile. He'll play with you, and keep you company, and even watch over you." He put a comforting, paternal hand on her shoulder. "And you can have him with you whenever you want, wherever you go. Wherever there's access to the Big Box, that's where you'll find Charliebo." He stepped back. "Why don't you two get acquainted?"

Thoroughly spellbound, she lost herself in making friends with the canine gram. Leaving her to the screen, Cardenas and Fourhorses quietly made their way back to the sitting area that faced the wide phototropic window.

The social worker was beyond impressed. "That's the most realistic animal program I've ever seen! Where did you buy it?"

"I didn't buy it. It's an outgrowth of some work I had to do a while ago, at GenDyne. Charliebo was a real dog. My dog. For a while, years ago, he was also my eyes. He died doing his job, but the essence of him got vacced and turned into an independent psychomorph. Don't ask me to explain the technology. Better box designers than I are still trying to figure it out. But organic or grammatic, he's still my dog. Now he's Katla's, too, even if he exists only as a morphological resonance haunting the deepest interstices of the Big Box."

Fourhorses struggled to understand. "You said he could be her friend. That much I understand. But what did you mean when you said he could watch over her?"

Cardenas's expression grew serious. "If the situation requires it, Charliebo can go fully tactile."

Her jaw dropped. "No private gram can go tactile! That kind of technology is restricted to the military." He said nothing; simply gazed back at her. She exhaled sharply and nodded slowly. "Okay, I'm impressed." She glanced toward the girl, seated before the tunnel at the far end of the room. "You're sure it can't hurt her?"

"Charliebo won't hurt anyone, or anything, that I've okayed. She'll be fine. And even if she never needs to call on him for help, she'll feel a lot safer knowing that he's there. It's like the imaginary gun your father put under your pillow when you were a kid for you to use against the night monsters."

"What?"

"Never mind. I've got two days off. What are you doing for dinner tonight?"

The look on her face revealed her surprise. Truth be told, he was a little stunned at the alacrity of the offer himself.

It was a month later, as he was sitting in front of the active tunnel in his office downtown, scrolling through the relevant background information on a case he and Hyaki had been assigned to investigate, when the declaration brazenly splashed itself across infovoid before him.

REVENGE FOR THE MOCK!

It startled him, and Angel Cardenas was not one to be easily startled. It sat there, glowing softly before his eyes, the letters floating in the darkness of the tunnel. His first reaction was that it was a joke, probably concocted by Hyaki or some of the boys in Records.

But a quick trace failed to identify the sender or the source, and a deeper probe quickly lost itself in the nether mists and mysteries of the Big Box. One thing he was able to determine: irregardless of who had sent it, it had not originated within the Department.

That did not preclude it being a gag perpetrated by a friend or colleague. Even so . . . He made a record of it and the relevant backtrail, as far as he was able to trace it. Could it have originated with one of The Mock's subordinates? Most of them were incarcerated, awaiting trial or already serving time. But there was no guarantee that the sweep that had been carried out based on the detailed information supplied by Katla Mockerkin had caught absolutely everyone.

There was the hostile gram, of course. The one that had sought the capture or elimination of The Mock's daughter. The one that had almost drowned him at The Mock's underwater command center in Southeast Texas. That mollysphere had been dismantled and dissected, providing a rich lode of infocrunch to law enforcement authorities in ten countries.

Had the central molly spit out a last, vengeful command prior to being severed from its box and extracted? Retribution was not a quality that was usually attributed to inert boot grams. Suppose some last-minute, apostate permutation of The Mock's main molly had escaped detection, and from its base in Belize or Barbados or Botswana was contemplating vengeance against the federale responsible for the termination of its core activities?

It was a thoroughly outrageous notion. Few would have granted it even a moment's credence. But Cardenas had spent more time probing the Big Box than most, and had seen the worst of what it could do. It was a strange land, the Box. A place where no one, even those who added to it and maintained it and used it on a daily basis, entirely understood the nature of what they were working with. A place that was continuously evolving. Usually in concert with humankind—but sometimes, according to whom you chose to believe, without it. Who could say what was and was not possible within the mysterious, half-magical mathematical milieu that was the Box?

It did not matter whether someone had a gun pointed at him or a gram: he took any and all threats seriously. He would treat this one no differently. If it was a gag, he would have words with the perpetrators. If it was a gram, he would have input.

Picking up the vorec, he began to fight back.

The leaves of brown came tumbling down. Harmony Francis sat in the window seat of her second-floor Vermont bedroom watching them pile up on the lawn outside the house. It was a quiet September Sunday morning. Her adopted siblings were still asleep. They slept longer than she did because they were used to quiet Sunday mornings. Since she had enjoyed very few in her life, they were still a novelty to Harmony. As such, she did not want to miss or waste a single one of them.

Her Uncle Jim walked into view, powerake in hand, and proceeded to embark on the eternal New England early-fall outing known as mustering the leaves. Downstairs, she knew, Aunt Loise would be synthing batter for blueberry waffles to go with the eggs and bacon and chocolate whale milk.

A sound drew her attention away from the window. Looking down, she saw a six-legged machine the size of her thumb standing on the carpet next to her left foot. Four tiny lenses peered back up at her as the miniscule head cocked curiously to one side. A soft, continuous, and not unpleasant mechanical purr emanated from the device.

"Well," she exclaimed in quiet surprise, "where did *you* come from? Out of that mouse hole in the attic?" A familiar child's ditty sprang unbidden into her head. *How many wugs would a wise wug whip if a wise wug would whip wugs?*

Wugs watched, but did not interact. That was the commonly accepted wisdom. Instead of simply staring, or withdrawing, this one approached. Aunt Loise would panic if she saw it, Harmony knew, and Uncle Jim would probably take a swing at it with the nearest shovel or shoe. After a moment's hesitation, she reached down. The wug immediately scuttled forward and into her palm. Lifting it up, she stared wonderingly into its quartet of miniature ruby-red lenses.

"What are you teeny guys, anyway? What do you want from us? What do you want from *me*?"

From beneath her bed, from the bathroom, from under the closet door, more wugs appeared. Dozens more. The range of shapes and sizes was breathtaking. No two were alike. It was almost as if they were experimenting with themselves, searching for an ideal structure, trying to find the best way to be whatever it was they were. She could understand that. In many ways, she had embarked on the same kind of journey. Whirring and buzzing and humming softly to themselves, they climbed up onto the window seat, and onto her.

Evolving together they might be, she reflected, but there was no disputing who was the more ticklish. Covered in curious wugs, she began to giggle, then to laugh.

She wondered what that nice federale Angel Cardenas would have thought of it.

El Fin

GLOSSARY OF SPANG

(Spanish-English slang)

Expressions

"Hoh"—Strip exclamation. Variant of "Whoa!"

"*Como se* happening?"—combination of Sp. "What is" & English

"To the opto"—to take something to the max(imum)

"What's skewed?"—what's wrong?

"*Verdad*"—truth; it's for sure. From Sp. for "truth"

"Faz"—fabulous, great, wonderful

"*Andale!*"—go! Get going! From the Sp.

Verbs

Note: In the slang of the Strip, many Spanish verbs are "spanged" by having their original suffixes anglicized. To wit, *solicitar* (to solicit or request) adds the Eng. -ed and -ing, instead of the usual Sp. endings. As in "he solicitared (something)" or "he was solicitaring."

abla—to talk or say something. From Sp. *hablar*, to talk

ambulate—to go, move

arribed—arrived; to arrive. From Sp. *arribar*, to arrive

boney—to scavenge someone's bones and marrow

bungo—used like "nez"

canyon—to cut deeply

carny—to assail a citizen with advertisements

coge—to fuck. From Mex. slang *coger*, to fuck

cogit—to create, make, invent. From Eng. *cogitate*

cojone—to make something tougher. From Sp. *cojones*, balls

coz—to make use of. As in "to cozy up to something"

dock—to get somebody (as in archaic "put them in the dock"—only worse)

drac—to scavenge someone's blood

expiate—to kill

eyedee—to identify someone, something

facilit—to take it easy, relax. From Eng. *facile* & Sp. *facíl*, easy

facture—to make or manufacture something

flash—to show advertisements

mess—to send a message; communicate

mickey—to customize something; esp. by the Disony entertainment multinat

nez—to screw up or mess up

pop—to open

portage—to carry

rainbow—to change color

respirate—to extort, usually money

romp—to ruin. From Eng. *to romp* & Sp. *romper*, to destroy

roto—to steal; to mug someone

sabe—to know. From the Sp.

shrewd—to speak or perceive shrewdly

shunt—synonym of ambulate

skip—to take or drag

skrag—to beat someone up bad

slag—to lead someone on; to tease. Also, to melt something

snak—to catch, intercept something

solicitar—to solicit, request. From the Sp.

somber—to say or speak somberly

vape—to kill

vete—to hang out with someone

vitalize—to make or create or bring something into existence

volubate—to talk, speak. From Eng. *voluble*

waft—to go away; tell someone to get lost

whirligig—to pass something along

Other

agro—aggression. An aggressive person. From N. Zealand slang

antisoc—an antisocial person, criminal element

baggerag—a low-class mugger

Big Box, the—contemporary equivalent of the old, historic Internet

biosurge—a surgeon with advanced mechanical handling skills

Bonezone—a dangerous, lawless area

boxes—linked computers. Intranets to infranets to the Big Box itself

buitrees—from Sp. *buitre,* vulture

burley—especially messy or nasty garbage; junk. From Aust. slang

cerebro—brains; brainy

chameleon—a highly sensitive, sensor-equipped device that fits over the face and is capable of mimicking another person's facial features.

chica—a chick, a girl. From Sp. slang

chieflado—the head of a ninloco gang. From Eng. *chief* & Sp. *chiflado,* crazy

chingaroon—a real tough fucker. From Sp. *chingarón* (a tough fucker) and the vinegaroon, an especially ugly desert arachnid

chopter—a modern helicopter

chopwire—a pocket-sized weapon for delivering a paralyzing electrical charge

cleanie—a solid, upstanding, middle-class citizen

codo—a condominium

comm—a telephone or other communications device

colorcrawl—a glowing, neonlike, kinetic wall décor

comercio—a shop or business. From the Sp.

crunch—computing power

culo—asshole. From Sp. slang

desal—desalinated seawater

dinkum—the truth; for real. From Aust. slang *fair dinkum*

Disony—the giant Disney-Sony entertainment multinat

disruptor—a device for discharging a powerful electromagnetic pulse

drool—a snitch

drongo—a bum, loser, bad guy. From Aust. slang

duroble—tough guy; from Eng. *durable* and Sp. *duro,* tough

eeLancer—a freelance technology expert

federale—from Sp. for cop, policeman

fedoco—a disparaging term for a federale

fejoada—a spicy Brazilian dish

feleon—a real nasty bad guy. From Eng. *felon* & Mex. slang *feón,* an ugly sucker

feral(a)—an unregistered resident of the nether regions of the Strip

flashman—a PR specialist. May be either sex

flicker—a gun that fires hypodermic shells; invisible to most weapons detectors

frac—an anti-personnel grenade

gazehaze—rumors

gengineering—genetic engineering, often for cosmetic reasons

giggilo—comb. of *giggle* and *gigolo*

gloomer—a sextel featuring hard sex

goofac—(juvie slang) a doofus

gordo—Sp. *fat*

gram—a computer program

hangle—a detailed discussion. From Eng. *haggle* and *hang*

hardzine—a printed newspaper, magazine, brochure, etc.

homber—from original Sp. *hombre*, but pronounced as Eng.
    A guy, a male

huevos—"balls." From Sp., literally "eggs"

husher—a device that enhances silence by canceling out
    other sounds

induction tube—a maglev mass transportation system com-
    mon through-out North America

infovoid—the usable three-dimensional area of an open, ac-
    tive box

integral—intact, whole, undamaged, unharmed

juice—any kind of drug

keiretsu—a huge industrial-commercial combine. From the
    Japanese

kims—kilometers

kosh—as in "kosher cash." Legitimate money

krilliabase—food made from krill

lepero—From Mex. slang *leperó,* leper; a foul-mouthed, ob-
    scene creep

Madison ejector—a device for foisting multiple, alterable
    ads on a helpless public

macrolice—a large police file

maquiladora—an old border (Strip) manufacturing plant

masalsa—country-style north Mexican music. From Mex.
    salsa, a type of music, and *masa,* a corn flour used in the
    making of tortillas

mataro(a)—assassin. From Sp. *matar,* to kill

medoggle—specialized hitech goggles for use by medical personnel

meroin—a synthetic opiate

mierde—shit. From the Sp.

miragoo—a mirage tattoo

molly—a mollysphere. A spherical hard drive suspended in a magnetic field that is read by a laser as it rotates. The integrated laser not only reads information stored on the surface, but can change focus, thus enabling it to read from many multiple layers within, as if reading information imprinted on the concentric layers of an onion.

monger—someone with a complaint; a talker

muerto—a dead person. From the Sp. Also used as a verb, to kill

multinats—giant multinational corporations, companies

muse lenses—wearable, eyeglasslike device for sensory playback

muy malo—very bad. From the Sp.

neg and pos—boy and girl. From Eng. *negative* and *positive*

nacha—ass. From Mex. slang

Namerica—North American Union, consisting of old USA, Canada, & Mexico

NFP—Namerican Federal Police; the federales

nins; ninlocos—literally, "crazyboys." From Sp. *niño* & *loco,* child & crazy

nodester—a dealer in muse wafers

nonzafado—not with it, not "in"

nypron—very strong but near-massless fiber based on aerogel technology

OTS—Organization for Tropical Studies

para-site—a Web site

pend—penis. From Mex. slang *pendejo*

pinche cabrón—a fucking asshole. From Mex. slang

psychys—psychologists and psychiatrists

qwilk shop—from "quick click." A store with high-tech componentry for sale

Rara Aves—Rare Birds. From the Latin

Sanjuana—the future arcomplex of greater San Diego and Tijuana

scave—a scavenger

seamyvits—porno

sextel—a licensed brothel

sheila—a woman. From Aust. slang

shocker—a small pistol-like device that fires electrically charged pellets

soche—a school-like environment for teaching children life skills

Schlage sesame—a device for decoding and unlocking an electronic lock

siryore—a male honorific; combination of Eng. *sir* and Sp. *señor.*

skim artist—a con man

slywire—a wire-thin knife blade

snaffler—someone who's too talkative. In Mex. slang, *horicón*

snapper—a police sniper. From archaic 20th-century American slang

soulpool—a poor part of a big city; not necessarily a slum area

spacebase—an illegal narcotic

sparkle—another illegal narcotic

spizzed; spazzed out—wiped out, overwhelmed

sponging—working the box (computer, Net, Web, etc.)

stimstick—a legal smokable narcotic

strewth—the truth, *verdad.* From Aust. slang

strine—Australian slang

subcue—a personal identification chip installed under the skin; subcutaneously

subgrub—a preteen

sylph—a high-class whore

tactile—a program that can be "felt." Uses enormous amounts of crunch

tambaqui—a very large, very tasty fish from the Amazon basin

tecant—a technological savant, i.e., a technical talent

Tico/Tica—a nickname for male/female residents of Costa Rica

todos—that's all

tortuga—turtle. From the Sp.

toyman—a kept man

traba-job—a job, work. From Sp. *trabajo,* to work, and Eng. *job.*

trochus—an edible mollusk from the South Pacific

vacán—something that's cool, with it. From Peruvian slang

vapor—talk, rumor

vapowraith—an image formed out of "solid" smoke. More aerogel technology

Verdes—ecological activists. From Sp. *verde,* green

vertiprop—an aircraft that can fly like a plane but take off and land vertically

vit—video pickup, camera, show . . . multiple usages referring to video

vorec—voice recognition device, handheld, for controlling electronics

wafers—small, flexible electronic storage media

wanker—a goof-off, a no-good. From Aust. slang

wishwire—electronic ganglia

Wugs—wireless underground gofer systems. The individual

components of a communal AI lifeform that haunts the Strip

WWF—World Wildlife Fund

yakk—talk, chatter; talking ability

yobbo—loser, bum. From Aust. slang

ABOUT THE AUTHOR

ALAN DEAN FOSTER is the bestselling author of more than one hundred novels, including *Kingdoms of Light*, the Journeys of the Catechist trilogy, and the Flinx series. A world traveler, Alan Dean Foster lives in Arizona.

VISIT WARNER ASPECT ON-LINE!

THE WARNER ASPECT HOMEPAGE
You'll find us at: www.twbookmark.com then by clicking on Science Fiction and Fantasy.

NEW AND UPCOMING TITLES
Each month we feature our new titles and reader favorites.

AUTHOR INFO
Author bios, bibliographies and links to personal Web sites.

CONTESTS AND OTHER FUN STUFF
Advance galley giveaways, autographed copies, and more.

THE ASPECT BUZZ
What's new, hot and upcoming from Warner Aspect: awards news, bestsellers, movie tie-in information . . .